Truck Off

A Grumpy Sunshine, Mistaken Identity Small Town Romance

The Mutter Brothers
Book 3

Aria Bliss

MISADVENTURE PRESS

Published in the United States by Misadventure Press, Gainesville, FL.
www.misadventurepress.com
info@misadventurepress.com

Book Layout, formatting, typesetting and cover design by
Angelique's Designs, a Misadventure Press Author Service
https://misadventurepress.com/author-services/

FIRST EDITION
ISBN (Original paperback): 978-1-948169-91-2
ISBN (Special Edition paperback): 978-1-948169-92-9
ISBN (eBook): 978-1-948169-90-5
Printed in the United States of America

Books by Aria Bliss

Trigger Warnings

This series deals with some heavy themes including abandonment, anger and rage, physical and mental abuse, fear and helplessness, growing up too young, guilt, loss of childhood, jealousy and hatred, substance abuse, emptiness and inadequacy, self-harm, neglect, self-loathing, self-doubt, low self-esteem, domestic violence, and poverty. While all themes are not presented in every book, there may be hints to them throughout the series. However, this is still a romance and a happily-ever-after will be delivered with a heavy dose of humor along with all the big feels you expect from an Aria Bliss novel.

Specifically, this book portrays the life of a drug addict and a recovering alcoholic (both are supporting characters, not main characters) and the impact that lifestyle can have on family members. This novel also includes a dive into a life of poverty. If either of these subject matters are triggers for you, then skipping this story might be best. The situations represented in this novel are based on the real-life experiences of the author and are not representative of anyone else's experiences.

To Gabriel and Bethany.

We lived through hell and saw so much we never should've seen at such a young age.
We weren't always strong, and sometimes the light was impossible to see, and yet we still managed to save each other.

Chapter 1

Cold showers

Lina

Dammit. He lied to me. I fucking hate liars.

I waited a good twenty minutes for the water to turn hot, and nothing. It's still cold as fucking ice water. Turning it off, I head down the narrow hallway of the rundown trailer I live in with Dad. It's not much—barely holding together—but it's a roof over our heads.

And until three weeks ago, a major bonus of our subpar living conditions was we still had hot water. Now, we don't even have that.

When I reach the utility closet, I swing the door open and sigh. There's no sign the water heater has been touched.

I fight back the tears that I refuse to let fall. I don't cry. *Ever.* But if I were to let these tears break free, having to take another cold shower is a damn good reason to shed them.

Back in my bedroom, I unplug my phone and dial my brother's number. He answers on the second ring.

"Hey, sis. What's up?"

"Don't hey sis me. You said you came down yesterday to change the heating element. Why did you lie to me?"

I can hear the dismissive shrug of his shoulders, and it pisses me off even more. "Couldn't fit it in. Got busy."

I close my eyes and fight the urge to scream. "Then why didn't you just say that when I texted you last night?"

"You texted me?"

"Jonas! Don't act like you don't remember. I messaged you around ten and asked if you got it fixed. You responded to me that you did."

"Huh." He pauses like he's thinking really hard. Or maybe he's reading over our text conversation to see if he can dispute my claim. "Well, look at that. I must have misunderstood what you were asking. I was at the bar when you messaged me."

I drop my head and rub my eyes.

"You promised." The words come out weak and hurt and I hate it. I never let anyone see my pain. Not even my piece of shit brother. "Going without hot water is torture."

"Hey, sorry," he says like we're talking about him eating the last piece of candy and not him lying to me about fixing the water heater. "I'll try to make it next weekend, but no promises. I'm really busy."

"You're always busy. You haven't visited us in months."

"Yeah, well, I've got a life. And now I'm late for work. I've gotta get going."

"It's Sunday. You never work on Sundays."

"I took a double-time shift. Money's too good to pass up. People pay a lot for emergency plumbing issues."

"Glad to see nothing's changed. What's the point in having a plumber for a brother if he refuses to help his family in need?"

"Hey, I gotta get paid. It's not cheap living in Columbus."

"Well, your sick father needs hot water. It's not healthy living like this."

"Lina, I said I'm sorry. But I gotta go. Work is calling."

"Fuck you, Jonas." But the line is silent before I even get the words out.

Typical Jonas. I don't know why I expected anything more. Or let my hopes rise that he'd actually show up and fix it yesterday while I was at work.

He bailed on us the first chance he got. The day after Jonas graduated high school, he moved to Columbus to start an apprenticeship. He didn't even bother telling Dad or me that he'd gotten it.

It's been almost sixteen years since he moved, and he rarely comes back for a visit. I don't entirely blame him. There's not much to do in this small town. With his plumbing license, he can make a lot more in the city than in rural southern Ohio.

But he didn't just leave to make more money. He left Dad and me. His only family. I can't even get him to come back when we really need his help. It's not like I can change the heating elements on the water heater. I can't even afford to pay someone to do it.

Not if I want to pay for Dad's medicine and keep him fed.

Jonas is just like Mom.

Mom always lied to us—to Dad. And she left us the first chance she got too. Dad, Jonas, and I weren't enough to get her to stay. I guess Dad and I aren't enough for Jonas either.

I should be used to it by now, but I'm not. People who should care the most are always the ones that hurt me the worst. It stings every single time like it's the first time. It's impossible for it not to.

I make my way back down the narrow hallway to the bathroom, where the water is still running. Thankfully, we draw our water from a well, so it's not an expense I need to stress over. It just means the water is colder.

I rush through my shower like my life depends on getting out as fast as possible. I'm already running late, but it's the chill that really has me speeding through my shower routine. I don't even bother washing my hair. I did that yesterday. I can go at least one more day before it becomes a necessity.

Maybe one day I'll get a hot shower again.

It won't be so bad once summer is in full swing. Late April is nice, but hot summer days are still about a month away.

God, please don't let me still be taking cold showers in June.

After getting dressed, I head to the kitchen. The floor creaks beneath my feet the moment I exit the hallway and enter the living room. The floorboards are giving way and it bows with every step I take.

A negative side effect from a leaky roof. This spring has been particularly wet. With all the rain we've gotten, it's been next to impossible to change out the drip buckets fast enough to avoid spillage.

Nothing like adding a leaking roof and rotten floorboards to my long list of trailer repairs. I can barely afford to put food on the table, let alone fix a broken-down trailer that's about twenty years past its life expectancy.

But it's better than nothing, I suppose.

Dad's asleep in his recliner with a book across his chest. He does that a lot these days. His illness and old age take a lot out of him. Between his liver disease and his constant battle over his cravings for alcohol, he struggles with energy. Dad hasn't had a drink in over four years, but he still wants one. He says that craving never lessens.

I give him a quick kiss on the forehead before I head into the kitchen to make sure he has something handy to warm up for dinner. He usually does fine on his own for lunch as long as we have lunch meat and cheese.

Taking quick stock of what's in the refrigerator, I groan. We're running low on everything. There are only two slices of cheese left and enough turkey for three sandwiches. Sometimes Dad eats two for lunch. The mustard is about gone, and we've got less than a gallon of milk.

Looks like I'm stopping at the grocery store after work tonight.

There are still three prepared dinners in the freezer, so at least there's that. I often make up several easy-to-reheat meals on my days off, so Dad is set on the days I work late. I'm rarely home to eat dinner with him. Thank goodness he loves lasagna, chili, soups, and enchiladas. Those freeze easily.

He's got a few snacks left. The chips he likes are getting low. Better pick up more of those. But he still has an unopened box of the granola bars he loves.

I stare at my list and try to think of something different to get Dad. He eats the same things all the time and never complains, but he has to tire of it. Maybe if ground beef is on sale, I'll pick up some of that and make a meatloaf. Dad loves my meatloaf.

And potatoes. If I can swing some store brand cheddar cheese, I'll make up a pan of scalloped potatoes. Those will do well in the freezer too.

Satisfied with my list, I slip it into my back pocket and grab my purse and keys. I have to stop and get gas on my way out of town. I'll grab myself a few snacks at the gas station to hold me over during my shift. I don't want to eat the food my dad needs.

I have a couple of repeat customers on the schedule today, so hopefully my tips will be good. One of them already paid me to come up with a custom design for a full sleeve tattoo. Today I'll lay the foundation for the design. It'll take a few sessions to get it all done. He's paying me in stages. Sometimes that earns me more of a tip. Other times, they hold off on the tip until the entire thing is done.

Fingers crossed, it's the first scenario today. I need the extra cash.

Sliding behind the driver's seat of my old beat up Civic, I send a prayer out to the universe that she starts. My fuel pump is going, but I don't have the money to fix it yet. I need it to hold out until after I figure out how to fix the water heater.

I turn the key and my car sputters and groans but doesn't start. I wait a few seconds and try again.

"Come on, girl. Please do this for me. I need you." I coo and speak softly like that's somehow going to make a difference.

One more month. Please last me one more month. That's all I ask.

The bills are mounting, and I can't afford another thing to go wrong. Not yet. I'm behind on the electric bill and promised a payment by the end of this week. Hopefully that will be enough to keep it on for another month.

Dad's prescriptions need refilling, and my migraine meds are low. There are too many bills and not enough money.

I need time. Lots and lots of time.

If only there were a way to slow time so I could catch up before the floor falls out from under me. Both literally and figuratively.

I give the key another turn, and my car sputters to life. I throw my hands in the air and cheer. One more day that I'll make it to work. Here's hoping I make it back home tonight too.

AFTER FILLING UP MY CAR, I RUSH TOWARD THE ENTRANCE OF Kochs to grab some chips and jerky. The jerky will be enough to hold me over most of the day if I graze at it.

Koch's Pit Stop is one of two gas stations in Beaver. It's not exactly in Beaver, more like on the outskirts near the highway. That it's right off the highway makes it more convenient for me than driving into town to go to the other one.

I hate supporting the Kochs, but sometimes convenience wins out over loyalty to a feud that has nothing to do with me. But in this town, everyone picks a side, and I am firmly on Team Mutter.

The Mutters and Kochs have been feuding for at least three or four generations. It's a story that everyone in three counties knows and loves to gossip about. I believe it was the great-great-grandfathers on both sides that were playing a heated game of poker.

Grandpa Koch was dumb enough to put their land and house on the line. Grandpa Mutter won the hand and, in turn, won the homestead. It caused a rift between the two families that's never settled down.

Tanner Koch, the one I went to school with, owns this place. He's never really paid any attention to me. We ran in different circles in school, and we never connected after we graduated either, which is fine by me.

Before I reach the door to the convenience store, a low rumble fills the air. I glance over my shoulder just in time to see the reason I am firmly on Team Mutter.

Christian Mutter.

I'd recognize his sleek black Ducati and worn leather jacket anywhere. He rarely drives anything else, rain or shine, and he never takes off that jacket until the temperatures reach at least seventy-five. Even then, he wears it when he rides.

After pulling up next to the side of the building, he turns off the bike. The silence that follows is enough to pull me from my daze. I always lose myself when Christian is around. It's hard not to. He's gorgeous beyond words—all the Mutter men are—and his bad boy, *I don't give a fuck,* attitude is like kryptonite to me.

He steps off the bike and lifts his helmet off his head. His disheveled hair falls over his eyes and my hand itches to brush it away so I can see the warm chocolate abyss of his irises. All the Mutter men have the most beautiful, expressive brown eyes.

I quickly turn for the door and continue my way inside before he catches me staring. I've tried like hell to hide my lifelong crush on Christian, but it's been hard. He's just so damn mysterious and intriguing. It's impossible not to stare at him when he enters a room.

Once inside, I rid my head of all thoughts of Christian. Fantasizing about him is just that—a fantasy. And I don't have the time or luxury to indulge in fantasies.

I've got bills and Dad and responsibilities that require my full attention. Like my job. I'm not late for work yet, but I will be if I don't get moving.

One slip up and my dad could suffer the consequences. He has enough issues with health as is. We can't afford to lose out on a paycheck because I can't stop staring at the cute boy in town.

I head toward the cooler to grab a pop when I catch sight of Betty Jo Brigner trying to lift a case of root beer from the top of a stack that's taller than her.

I rush to her side to help. "Here. Let me get that for you."

She turns her eighty-year-old smile on me. "Thank you, dear."

I force a smile in return. "It's no problem. Happy to help."

Betty Jo is spry for eighty. She just might be the most active elderly person in town next to Mila Mutter, Christian's grandmother. But she has no business trying to lift a case of pop off a stack this high. She could hurt herself.

Betty Jo taught history at the high school until she retired a few years ago. She was easily a favorite, despite the boring subject matter. Her ability to connect with people from all demographics and backgrounds is remarkable. Everyone loves her.

She worked way past normal retirement age because she said she had nothing else to do and sitting around waiting to die sounded far worse than going to work. Her husband passed away years ago, and their kids moved and started their own lives before that. They visit her often, but otherwise, she's alone.

She probably taught most of the residents of this town and knows more dirt on local families than most of the families themselves. But she doesn't gossip. That's one of the things I like the most about her.

I turn toward the register where Tanner Koch is leaning against the counter, scowling at something a few aisles over from where I helped Betty Jo. I follow his hard stare to where Christian is standing in the candy aisle.

My gaze meets Christian's, and he winks. He fucking winks at me. He never winks. And I swear there's a hint of a smile lifting his lips. That's something else he never does.

I blink several times to refocus my eyes, and when I look at him again, he's back to studying the candy bars on the shelf with his typical broody expression.

Did I imagine the wink and faint smile? Must have.

I turn my focus back to Tanner and Betty Jo. She's finished paying for her items, so I help her carry them to the car.

"How are you going to get this inside once you're home?" I ask her about the case of pop as I slide it into her trunk.

"My son and his family are visiting today. He'll help me unload the heavy stuff."

I nod, pleased to hear she won't be carrying it inside herself. "If you're sure. Otherwise, I can come by later and do it for you."

She pats my cheek and smiles. "That's sweet of you, dear, but I've got it covered. Promise."

"Okay," I head back inside, but call over my shoulder before I reenter the store. "Call me anytime. I mean it. I'm only a few drives down from you."

She waves me off and slides into her car. Betty Jo lives close to Dad and me, and we've always been friendly neighbors. I've helped her plenty of times with unloading groceries or larger items. If she needed help, she'd tell me.

Once inside, I head to the aisle where they stock the beef jerky. I grab a bag and start for the cooler when I hear Tanner's voice.

"Whatever you're doin', stop it now."

I whip my head around to see Tanner standing next to Christian with his arms crossed over his chest. Christian towers over him like the brooding, sexy god that he is.

"And what exactly am I doing?" Christian growls.

"Can't have you stealing my products. Get what you want and pay for it."

Christian snorts. "I ain't stealing shit and you know it."

Christian turns his back on Tanner and catches me staring. He winks again before he walks away from Tanner like he's not even there. *Huh, maybe I didn't imagine the wink before.*

"Don't walk away from me. This is my store. I'll ban you and all your brothers from shopping here."

"Go ahead. See how much business you lose when you do."

Tanner opens his mouth to refute his claim, but he stops himself. He knows Christian is right. The feud between their families hasn't caused too much of a divide between our community, but there are enough people on both sides that taking action like banning one family from a business would cause quite a stir. Tanner would lose business. No doubt about it.

"Tanner, stop being an ass," I say, sticking my nose where it doesn't belong.

Christian whips around to face me, his brows lift in surprise. It's not like he and I are friends or even talk all that often. I've had a crush on him from a distance.

"Lina, mind your own damn business. This doesn't concern you." Tanner glares at me, and I return his glare, making it clear that his grouchy response doesn't intimidate me.

Out of the corner of my eye, I catch Christian's arm move. He snatches a Snickers bar from the shelf and stuffs it in his pocket. When my gaze shifts to his, he winks. Again.

When I look back at Tanner, he doesn't seem to notice. He's still staring at me.

"Maybe instead of falsely accusing customers of theft, you should pay more attention to the ones that could use your help. Like Betty Jo, for example."

Tanner narrows his eyes on me because he knows I'm right. While he was busy glaring at Christian, he missed out on helping Betty Jo. She may not gossip, but she remembers people's actions. If she picked up on the fact that Tanner ignored her in favor of causing shit with Christian, she'll shop somewhere else.

Tanner nods his head toward Christian. "Grab whatever it is you came here for and get. I don't like it when you're in my store."

Once Tanner is back behind the counter, Christian turns his gaze to me. His eyes quickly flick down my body and back up again. If I hadn't been watching him so intently, I would have missed it.

When his gaze meets mine again, there's something there that I've longed to see in his expression. *Desire.*

He steps closer and drops his voice to a whisper. "Can't say a beautiful woman has ever come to my defense before. Gotta say, I like it."

I feel my face warm, and I inwardly pray my cheeks aren't turning red. From the smile that spreads across his face, I'd say my prayer is useless. The heat that washes over me has me begging for the cold shower that I complained about earlier.

I shrug and try to act like he's not having an effect on me. "His attitude was bullshit. I don't tolerate bullshit, even when it's not being directed at me."

A low rumble of a chuckle escapes him, and I feel it all the way down to my toes. "I've always liked that about you. Kind and generous to those who deserve it, yet you call out bad behavior every time."

I meet his heated gaze. "I didn't know you paid that close attention to my actions."

He lifts his shoulder and rests his hand on the top shelf of the aisle next to us. "I pay attention to a lot of things."

I cross my arms over my chest and lift a brow. I don't miss the way his eyes flicker to my cleavage before he quickly brings them back to mine. I'm not wearing anything revealing, just an old Metallica T-shirt I've had since high school. But it fits snugly, and I'm not lacking in the boob department.

"You sure about that?" I challenge. He couldn't possibly be paying too much attention to me or else he'd have figured out I've had a crush on him for years.

"Oh yeah." He leans closer, and I can smell his woodsy scent mixed with grease and sweat. He smells like hard work on a rainy day. I pinch my lips between my teeth to keep from moaning. "Sometimes I miss things, but not often. I do my best to pay attention when it counts."

I allow myself to lean closer, hoping like hell I'm reading him right. "And what are you seeing right now?"

"Lina Lange," he says my name with a flirtatious lilt. "Are you flirting with me?"

I suck in a breath and step back. I feel my face drop at being called out on my actions. I don't flirt often—more like never—and I didn't expect him to be so direct about it. "If you have to ask, then I suck at it."

"Aw, now. No grumpy faces. I was just teasing." He reaches for my arm and wraps his hand around my wrist like he's afraid I'm going to run away. It's what I want to do, but I don't resist his pull. I like the feel of his hand on me. It sends a warmth through me that leaves me wanting more.

"I'm not grumpy," I say, but my frown deepens.

He chuckles, and I feel it reverberate through his hand and up my arm. "Sure you're not Grumps."

"Don't call me that." Now my brows furrow and my frown turns into a scowl. Truth is, I am grumpy. A lot grumpy. My life hasn't been easy, and I don't have a lot to be happy about. But I didn't expect anyone to notice.

He releases my arm, and I immediately miss his touch. Then he tosses his hands up in surrender in a way that suggests he's going to stop with the grumpy talk. But there's something about the twinkle in his eyes that leads me to believe I will forever be Grumps to him.

Then he shocks the hell out of me with his next words.

"Let me make it up to you and take you out to dinner."

"What?" I shake my head and feel my eyes widen. "Did you ... Um ... Make what up to me?"

"Teasing you." He steps closer. So close I can feel the rise and fall of his chest. His voice drops to a raspy timbre. "Dinner. Friday night. You and me. What do you say?"

A small smile lifts my lips. "Wow. The elusive Christian Mutter finally asks me out on a date. How can I possibly say no?"

Chapter 2

Mistakes and lies

Chase

Wait. What?

Did she just call me Christian?

I just landed a date with the woman I've been pining over since we were in first grade. I'll never forget how she looked up at me on the first day of class when she sat next to me. She wore the biggest smile and the cutest pigtails I'd ever seen. I was a goner for this girl from that day forward.

Just my luck that she thinks I'm my bad boy twin brother.

A shiver runs through me. And not the good kind. It's a warm, late spring day and I feel like someone just dumped a bucket of ice water over my head.

I open my mouth to correct her but stop myself. I look down at my clothing. I'm not dressed in my typical clean cut, somewhat preppy style. I've got on tattered jeans, a holey T-shirt, and Christian's leather jacket. I even rode up on his bike. And she saw me do it.

It's an innocent enough mistake. And one that makes her behavior toward me make so much more sense.

Here I thought it was my lucky day. No matter how much I

wished she'd look my way, Lina Lange has never paid attention to me. Her eye has always been on Christian.

I can't help but wonder if she would have said something to Tanner if I had looked more like myself. Christian and I are identical twins. Even with the differences in how we dress, most people struggle to tell us apart. The easiest differentiation is the fact that he never smiles, and I always smile.

I may not be dressed like me, but I sure as hell am acting like me. I've smiled and winked at her more than once. Christian would never do either of those things. Not even to his girl.

I run my fingers through my hair, smoothing back the messy locks. I know I should correct her. It's not like I intentionally set out to deceive her or anyone else when I borrowed Christian's jacket and bike to run to town.

We're doing construction work to convert the large room above the stables to a private apartment for me. His bike was parked right outside, whereas my truck was in the garage. Borrowing his bike was convenient. Nothing more.

When I meet her gaze, she must sense something's off because she takes a step back. "Is everything okay?"

I hesitate for a moment, internally yelling at myself to tell her the truth. Instead, I say, "Yeah, everything's great." I give her another one of my big, charming smiles. "I just landed a date with a beautiful woman. Why wouldn't I be great?"

She gives me a nervous shrug. "Maybe because you're acting weird now, like maybe you regret asking me."

I take a step closer to her and drop my voice to a whisper. "No regrets. Friday can't come fast enough. In fact, that might be too long. Maybe we should move the date up."

She sucks in a breath, and I fight the tug of a smile that pulls at my lips. She may think I'm Christian, but her physical reaction is to me.

"I can't." Her response comes out breathy and needy. "I work every night this week. Friday is my only day off."

"Damn." I glance toward the counter where Tanner is distracted by waiting on someone. Feeling daring and so unlike myself, I reach for another Snickers bar and slide it into my pocket. "I guess I have no choice but to wait."

Her jaw drops, but I see the hint of the smile she's trying to hide. "You're such a bad boy," she whispers.

"You know it." I waggle my brows and move to walk past her. "Gotta buy some beer. Meet me outside?"

I feel her eyes on me as I walk toward the beer cooler and grab a couple of cases of Bud. Knowing my brothers, they're getting impatient that I haven't returned yet with lunch.

In exchange for their help, I offered all the pizza and beer they could drink. They would have helped me regardless. That's the kind of family we are, but I like to give back to my brothers.

By the time I turn around, Lina has moved to the cooler on the opposite wall. She's grabbing herself a root beer and one of the iced coffee drinks.

I use this opportunity to get a better look at her.

Lina Lange is hands down the most beautiful woman to ever come out of this small town. She's got an exotic beauty that makes her look a little out of place in Beaver, Ohio. Her long black hair and darker skin tone are the opposite of the rest of us from mostly German descent.

I never met her mom before she skipped town, but rumor has it she's part Native American and was quite the looker. It's also where everyone says Lina gets her looks.

She's taller than the average woman, with long legs, curvy hips, a round ass, and tits to die for. I can't stop picturing my hands wrapped around them. They're so full they would spill out between my fingers when I squeezed them.

Feeling a twitch in my dick, I pull my eyes away from her before it turns into a full-fledged erection. I don't need that level of embarrassment.

Avoiding any more small talk with Tanner, I pay for my beer

and head toward Christian's bike. I already picked up the pizza and strapped it to the back seat. I stuff the beer in the storage compartment on the bike. It barely fits and I can't get it closed, but it'll be fine for the short drive home.

Lina still hasn't exited Kochs, so I head toward her car to wait for her.

Despite my nerves and heightened anxiety over the mistake in my identity, I maintain a calm demeanor. I'll figure out how to tell her the truth about who I really am. I just don't want to lose the chance to take her out.

If I tell her now, would she back out of the date? I've been waiting for a chance to take her out for so long and I'd hate to lose that chance before I got to see it through.

But then how pissed will she be if I wait until we're out on the date before I tell her? Would she storm out of the restaurant and vow to never speak to me again? That would suck. Probably be worse than telling her now and having her back out.

But what if she doesn't get that mad? Maybe she'd be fine with the misunderstanding once she sees how much fun we have together. And I would definitely make sure we had fun.

I scrub my hands over my face. Both scenarios sound shitty and could potentially end badly for me. I should have corrected the mistake the moment she said Christian's name. At this point, I'm going to look like an ass regardless of when I tell her.

A few minutes later, she walks out the front door and pauses when she sees me leaning against her car. I don't miss the way her eyes roam down my body. Nor do I miss how her lips tick up like she's enjoying the view.

I may be a mess from a morning of hard work, but Lina likes me this way.

"So," she says when she reaches me. "I take it you haven't changed your mind about Friday."

I shake my head. "Just the opposite. I'm looking forward to it. In fact, let me get your number."

I slide my phone out of my pocket and open a new message thread. She rattles off her number so I can save it to my contacts. Then I type out a quick message. I keep it simple but flirty.

A moment later, her phone dings, and she smiles when she reads it. "Really? 'Can't wait to make you smile, Grumps.'"

My phone dings with a response.

Lina: Already am.

Damn.

The smile that spreads across my face should be all the proof she needs that I'm Chase and not Christian, but she doesn't pick up on it. Instead, she clears her throat.

"As much as I hate to end this conversation, I need to get to work. I'm already running late."

"Oh shit." I step aside and open her car door to let her get in. "I'll text you later with a time."

"Sounds good." She smiles and brushes her hair behind her ear, revealing the full extent of her neck tattoos. Lina has a lot of tattoos, and I've always wondered just how much of her body is covered.

I wish it were my hand touching her like that. Her dark hair is shiny and probably feels like silk. If I'm lucky, maybe I'll get to find out some day. *Soon.*

An awkwardness falls over us that I don't like. Parting ways shouldn't feel so weird.

I give her another smile and a small wave before I turn. Then I stop myself. "Wait, I almost forgot."

I pull one of the Snickers bars out of my pocket and toss it to her. "Save it for a late-night snack and think of me. I'll be saving mine until around nine. If you do the same, we can eat them together."

I toss her one last wink and head to the bike. A bad feeling settles over me and I panic that I've made a terrible decision. I need to tell her the truth now, not later. Later will be far worse.

I turn around, ready to correct my mistake, but it's too late.

Lina has already pulled away from the pump and onto the main road.

I guess I'm telling her on Friday. I hope that doesn't mean I've screwed things up for good and will never get a chance to show Lina Lange how good we could be together.

BY THE TIME I SHUT THE BIKE OFF OUTSIDE THE BARN, I FEEL like the biggest asshole in all of southern Ohio. Maybe even the entire tri-state area of Ohio, Kentucky, and West Virginia.

I should have told Lina the truth. Letting her think I was someone else was a dick move.

At this point, nothing I say or do will make me look like a good guy. I will forever be the asshole that let her believe I was my twin brother.

If I go upstairs with a long face, my brothers will know something is wrong. I never have a long face. I'm Mr. Smiles, all charm and playfulness.

I'm not ready to admit to them the dumbass mistake I made. They'll razz me relentlessly, and I'm not ready for that. I need to formulate a plan before I tell them what I did.

Shaking it off, I grab the pizza and beer and head for the side door that leads upstairs to my new apartment.

My apartment.

This should be enough to put the smile back on my face, and it almost is.

Taking steps to move out of the big house was a tough decision. I longed for my own space but couldn't go far. Not with the responsibilities of the farm on my shoulders.

I love my family and my brothers, but I'm thirty years old. We're all way too old to still live at home. I get why we do. We all like being close to the business, and I think there's a huge part of each of us that relies on the safety our closeness provides. We are each other's ride or die for life. Nothing gets between the Mutter brothers.

But at some point, we all have to do what our brothers Warren and Garret did. Maybe not Warren. He moved to another state and makes it home so infrequently it feels like we never see him anymore.

But Garret put his inheritance to use. He may have moved to his tiny house for all the wrong reasons, but he was still brave enough to take the plunge.

It's not like he went far either. He built his house on his portion of the land. We all get several acres to do with what we please. But Garret is the only one out of the seven of us to do it. Mac is talking about building now that he has Sophia, but he hasn't actually done it yet.

I use the farm as an excuse. I need to be close, but I don't need to live in the big house.

I also worry about Christian. I can't leave him. Not until I'm confident he's truly beaten his addiction and has found peace in his life. He's not there yet.

As the oldest Mutter brother, Liam gets the big house. Grams signed that over to him years ago. Even though Liam manages the garage and I manage the farm, we all co-own both businesses. The land encompassing the businesses was placed in a trust that is divided between the seven of us. No one can make a decision that affects it without the consent of all seven.

I stare at the stables—my new home—and smile.

As stables go, it's really nice. More than half the ground floor contains several stalls that house the large animals—horses and goats. That's also where my office is located, plus several storage rooms for feed and tack and a small bathroom.

We have a barn that houses all the farm equipment. It's not as nice and looks like a typical old barn you see scattered across these hills.

The fact that we already have plumbing running to the stables made it a logical choice to convert the unused upstairs to an apartment.

It's sturdy and large enough—close to two thousand square feet —that I could have put up walls and divided it up into several rooms. But I opted to keep it mostly open for now. That's something I can always do down the road if I change my mind.

I've been excited about my new home for a while, and today, I get to move in. That thought alone makes my smile feel more real.

I started working on these plans months ago without telling anyone. I didn't want to get my family involved until I knew for sure that I could make it work. Once I pulled the trigger, the conversion moved along quickly.

I hear my rowdy brothers before I open the door to the stairs. They may be pains in my ass most of the time, but they're also the first to help when I need it. Today is a perfect example.

I had a few minor things that needed to be finished before I moved in, and every one of them showed up to help. Except Warren since he's in North Carolina. The jobs were small enough that I could have done them all myself, but they insisted.

Even Mac's girlfriend, Sophia, and Clara, a lifelong family friend and Sophia's roommate, came to help. Mac is my youngest brother. He and Sophia started dating toward the end of last year. It really threw Mac for a loop. One look at Sophia and he was a mess until he finally sorted out his feelings and accepted love into his life.

Dating and women have been a struggle for all of us Mutter men. So far, Mac and Garret are the only ones who have found love. Well, and maybe Christian, but he's not ready to admit that to anyone. Not even to me. I'm not even sure if he realizes I know he's been seeing someone.

Call it a twin thing or just my ability to read my brother better than anyone, but I know he's got a girl. He seems to want to keep it a secret though, so I haven't pushed him on it. One day I will, but not yet.

Pushing any of us about women is a dangerous venture. None of us have a great outlook on women. Not with all the drama surrounding our mothers. *Yep. Mothers. As in plural.*

Dad fathered seven sons with four different women. All of them except his first—and only wife—are shitty human beings. Liam, Warren, and Garret share a mom. Unfortunately, Susanne died from cancer within minutes of Garret's birth. Until recently, he blamed her death on himself. Mostly because Dad never recovered from losing her. Garret took Dad's apathy toward him as blame. What Garret failed to notice is that Dad is apathetic toward all of us.

Next came my mom, Christina. She's a real piece of work. She abused Liam, Warren, and Garret for the short time she was here. It sucks to say this, but thankfully, she didn't stick around after Christian and I were born. She had a drug problem back then, and still does. Unfortunately, she lives in town, so we see her regularly. She's also the reason Christian got hooked on drugs.

Needless to say, I'm not a fan of Mom, but I tolerate her for my brother's sake. For some reason, he still wants to see her.

After Grams kicked Christina out—because Dad couldn't seem to do it—he started dating Monika, Ash's mom. True to form, she left right after Ash was born. She showed up several years later and dropped off a daughter she had from another relationship.

Alvera wasn't that old then, but she stayed with us for several years. We all took her in like she was our sister. Then one day, Monika came back and took her away. She hasn't been back here in years, but Ash keeps in touch with her.

Last, there's Heidi, Mac's mom. She stuck around the longest. Then one day, she just left. It really messed with Mac's head, and it nearly cost him Sophia. But she stuck by his side and helped him work through it. He seems to be in a much better place with Sophia in his life.

With the pizza and beer in hand, I make my way up the stairs. When I reach the landing, my smile is wide and bright. The trim is done. I'd opted to keep rough, unfinished walls. I like the barn look. I still had to put up another layer to insulate the space. Otherwise, the elements would make the place impossible to heat and cool.

The dark hardwood floors I put in are clean and shiny. My bed is up and ... Fuck, someone made my bed. With a light blue-gray comforter and ... *Are those decorative pillows?*

I glance up to see Sophia and Clara grinning at me.

"Surprise!" they call out in unison.

"We got you a housewarming gift, and this is it," Clara says as she points to the nicely made bed. It'll probably never look this good again.

My heart warms, and it feels like something is stuck in my throat. I clear it before I speak. "Thanks. This is really nice. It's way better than the old flannel sheets I planned on using. And the color is good. Fits my style."

Clara rushes over to me and wraps me in a tight hug. "I was so nervous you'd hate it."

"Not at all. It's perfect. Seriously."

She beams up at me just as Ash, my second youngest brother, steps up beside us.

"Hey, no stealing my best friend." He teases as he takes the two cases of beer from me.

"You don't dictate who my friends are, mister." Clara narrows her eyes and pokes him in the chest, but it's clear she's only teasing too.

"Pretty boy is back with beer and food!" Ash calls out to the open room like no one else saw me walk in. Then he glances up at me and grins. "Though he's not looking so pretty at the moment. You went in public like that?"

"Fuck off." I playfully punch his shoulder and make my way to the kitchen along the opposite wall.

The plumbing dictated where I put the kitchen and bathroom. The back wall worked out nicely since there's a second entrance on this side. To even out the space, I walled off a lot of that side. To the left of the back entrance is the laundry room and mudroom combined, and to the right is the bathroom. I figured this would make it easy to clean up after a hard day of work on the farm.

I left a short hallway between them for access through the kitchen.

The kitchen is a galley style with a long island to separate it from the rest of the room. Cabinets cover two-thirds of the wall, only breaking where the hallway entrance is. The island spans the same distance.

To the left of the kitchen is just enough space for a six-seater dining table. It makes the perfect spot since there are sliding barn doors on the wall that open up to a small balcony. There's just enough room out there for a couple of chairs. It'll be the perfect spot to watch the sun rise and set.

The dining table is the only other furniture I have so far besides my bed and dresser. And a TV, of course. I can't go without TV.

I'm going to have to make time to do some furniture shopping, so I have some place to sit besides my bed.

I glance over my shoulder after I set the pizza on the counter. Clara is staring at Ash with a wistful look in her eyes. I sigh and shake my head. Will Ash ever see what the rest of us see?

Ash and Clara are the same age and were raised together since they were both old enough to walk. She's had a hard and never-ending crush on him since she was old enough to know what a crush is. He seems completely blind to it.

She's already like a sister to us. I would love to see them get together and make it official. But either she has to be brave enough to tell him how she feels, or he needs to open his damn eyes and see what's right in front of him—a beautiful, funny, caring woman who I suspect loves him dearly.

"My bike okay?" Christian's gruff voice asks from right behind me. I glance over my shoulder and smile. He and Liam have been working on the finishing touches to the bathroom.

"Yeah, she's great. She handles those curves really well. You'll have to let me take her out more often."

His frown deepens and his brows furrow. "Get your own damn bike."

"Nah, you know I prefer my truck. But a bike is fun every now and again."

He stares at me for a minute. I don't know how it's possible, but his eyes narrow even more. Call it twin intuition, but I swear we can read each other's minds. It's one reason I don't worry as much as the others about him having a relapse. If that happens, I'll know instantly.

"What's wrong?" he asks.

I quickly turn away and open one of the kitchen cabinets. The girls put away my dishes and I don't know where anything is. "Nothing. Why do you ask?"

He doesn't answer me as I look in a different cabinet for the plates. It takes me three tries before I find a stack of paper plates to use for our lunch.

When I turn around, Christian is leaning against the counter next to the pizza with his arms crossed over his chest. He's staring at me like he sees right through all my bullshit.

Any minute now, he's going to pull the older brother card. He loves to remind me that he was born a whopping four minutes and twenty-three seconds before me. The closeness of our births earned me my name. It also might be the only funny thing Dad's ever done.

He said I came out so fast after Christian, it was like I was chasing him. Hence, he named me Chase.

"What?" I ask, sounding a little too frustrated. Me frustrated is a dead giveaway that something's wrong.

I sigh as I set the plates down next to the pizza. After taking a quick glance around my new apartment, I relax when I realize no one else is listening to us. I don't have to look at Christian to know he's watching me closely.

"I don't want to talk about it," I whisper. "Just know that there's nothing to worry about."

"Don't want to talk about what?" I cringe at the sound of Liam's voice.

When I turn around, I find him and Garret standing right next to us. Then I turn my glare on Christian. There's no way he missed seeing them walk up to us.

Christian doesn't smile—he rarely ever does—but there's a hint of amusement in his eyes.

Rather than bring attention to the conversation I don't want to have, I plaster a smile on my face and attempt to use my usual charm on my brothers. Sometimes it works and sometimes it doesn't. Let's hope today is a good day.

"Hey, is the bathroom done? I hope that faucet didn't give you too much trouble." My smile is so big my face hurts.

Liam eyes me cautiously, and then he nods. He's picking up that I don't want to talk about it. He and Garret are the only ones of my brothers who I have a chance in hell of letting this go.

"Yep. All set. And Garret fixed that loose step out back." He nods behind him, where Garret is leaning against the counter opposite me.

"Thanks, man. Where's Charlotte?" I ask, looking to further direct this conversation far away from me and my mistake.

"Took Rayne dress shopping. She's got a spring performance coming up."

My grin turns genuine. Garret may not pick on me, but I can't say the same thing about myself. "You didn't want to join them? Dress shopping is right up your alley."

He crosses his arms over his chest, matching Christian's stance, and lifts a brow in challenge. That's my cue to shut the fuck up or else he'll push me to share my issue.

And I am not ready to share.

He of all people should respect that. Especially after how the secret he kept for ten years just imploded on him recently. The dust hasn't even settled yet from that news. To be honest, I'm surprised he's here. He just won Charlotte back.

The news that Garret is Rayne's father just might be the biggest secret anyone in this town has ever kept.

At least he still got the girl when it was all said and done.

Fingers crossed, I can say the same thing when Lina finds out the truth about my true identity.

Chapter 3

Judgment and struggles I can do without, and a date I can't wait for

Lina

I should have stopped for groceries in Chillicothe. At least there, no one knows who I am.

But no.

Like a dumbass, I waited until I returned to Beaver to do my shopping at the local family market.

Foolishly, I thought it'd be safe since it's late on a Sunday night. Shouldn't all the judgment zone people be at evening Church service or at home enjoying time with their family?

Apparently not.

Because they're here, sneering at me and whispering about me like I can't hear them. I hear every single word.

She's so pretty. Too bad she's a child of that bad club.

Beautiful but evil. All those club members are.

She's not good for much, but she sure has a pretty face.

I heard her mom left because the past president wanted to take her as a wife. Steal her away from her family like she didn't have a choice.

I heard Lina was supposed to marry him in her place.

Stupid fuckers.

Sadly, most of it's true. Not the evil part. I may walk around with a permanent bitch face, but I'm not evil. Not even close. I'm also not a member of the motorcycle club, nor have I ever been.

I just don't like most of the hypocritical people that live in this community. They whisper about me like I'm the devil incarnate when they should look inward at their own lives.

I know for a fact one of their husbands is cheating. I see him at Posey's Lounge all the time picking up young and willing girls. When he sneaks out the back door with them, he's not taking them out for ice cream.

But none of that matters. I'm still the scandal of the town.

It's like they think I asked to be born to a member of the Unholy Ghosts MC. I love my dad, but if I could change anything about him, it would be his past career.

Life for a retired MC member is not pretty. At least not for my family. Maybe things would be different now if Mom never ran off and instead acted as the dutiful wife of the MC. Or if Dad hadn't refused my hand in marriage to the former president once Mom was gone.

The MC viewed both events as disobedience and betrayal.

Mom was gone, Dad fell out of favor, and Jonas left home the moment he turned eighteen. Our life has been a slow journey downhill ever since.

For reasons I've never understood, Dad stayed an active member of the MC until his liver disease made it impossible for him to work. Well, that's not true. Once a member, always a member. It's not easy leaving an MC once you're ingrained in club business. It's Dad's loyalty that confuses me.

He's loyal to a fault. Not a bad quality in a man, but also one that's easy to take advantage of. Despite how the past president tore our family apart, he stayed. He continued to do their bidding out of loyalty, obligation, and maybe even as payment for Mom leaving and then refusing my hand in marriage in her place.

I turn down the cereal aisle to move further away from the gossip. Unfortunately, this aisle is a worse fate than the gossip. I come face-to-face with Vicky Lynn Baylor, formerly Vicky Lynn Williams as she likes to tell everyone, and mean girl extraordinaire.

She thinks she's hot shit because her family's name is on the side of this building—Williams Family Market. It's just a stupid small town grocery store. It doesn't make them royalty. But they all act like they are. It doesn't help that most people treat them like royalty too.

Just because her parents are upstanding citizens, go to Church three times a week, and own a respectable business does not make them royalty. Who cares what people accomplish? It's how you treat others that matters the most. And from where I stand, they're all assholes, especially Vicky Lynn.

To make matters worse, we were in the same grade. I had to spend every single school year with her from kindergarten to senior year. She was a bitch even at age six.

"Well, well, well. Look what the cat dragged in," Vicky Lynn says in that sickly sweet, over-the-top sympathetic voice that always makes my bones hurt.

I fight the urge to roll my eyes. That's a sure way to push her buttons and drag this conversation out longer.

"Just getting some groceries," I say, keeping my voice flat and even. I push past her and do my best to ignore her presence.

"There's a sale this week on Frosted Flakes. You know, if you need to pinch your pennies."

I turn a narrowed glare at her. "I'm good. Thanks."

Her eyes flicker down to my neck and then my exposed arms. Her faux look of concern morphs into one of disgust as she takes in all my tattoos. I've covered my body in ink from my neck down to my toes.

I love all forms of art, but tattoos are my preferred medium. It's why I work as a tattoo artist. It's why my body is a living advertisement for my skill and ability.

And it's another reason small-minded people like Vicky Lynn judge me so harshly.

In her mind, my tattoos make me a bad person. It's just fucking art. Art I happen to love dearly.

I whip around and continue walking down the aisle, moving my feet faster than normal to put as much distance between her and me as possible. She calls out something, but I don't hear it. I've already tuned her out.

Before I turn the corner, I quickly grab my dad's favorite cereal and rush to gather the remaining items on my list. The faster I get out of here, the better.

Sometimes I hate my life.

I STARE AT THE PORCH LIGHT OUTSIDE THE FRONT DOOR OF the otherwise dark trailer for far too long. I don't want to go inside.

I love my dad, and I'll do anything for him, but I'm so tired of this life.

I'm sure he's sitting in his recliner watching TV or reading one of the thrillers I got for him from the library. He loves those books and prefers reading to TV most days.

I can't tell from out here, but I know the side table lamp is the only light on inside. It's not very bright and provides a soft yellow light that Dad prefers. That way, he can't take in the sight of the discolored paint on the walls and molding carpet.

Instead, he can get lost in his stories. He can pretend the roof isn't leaking or the floor isn't rotting or that there isn't a stack of bills a mile high that we don't have enough money to pay.

I want to get lost in a story and escape from my life for a while.

I sigh, knowing all too well that will never happen. I'm too pragmatic for that.

Slipping out of the car, I grab the meager bag of groceries I bought. My tips were decent tonight, but not enough that I could splurge on some of my favorite things. I could only get the food Dad needs and a couple of small things for myself.

Looks like it's going to be another hungry week. At least until I get the water heater fixed and get caught up on the electric bill. They haven't cut us off yet, but if I don't make some extra cash fast, they just might. I don't want to live without hot water *and* electricity.

The moon is bright and almost full. It reflects off the lake our small trailer sits next to in rippling waves. The water almost sparkles like the surface is dusted with diamonds.

If only. I'd harvest the hell out of that shit if it were possible. Now who's getting lost in fantasies?

Pee Pee Lake is the only nice thing I can say about where we live. Sadly, we might be the only bad thing about this lake. Well, other than its name. Someone must have thought they were being funny when they decided to name it after the initials P.P. that an early settler, Major Paul Paine, carved onto a tree along the bank. The name draws lots of funny looks from both locals and out-of-towners.

It's not very big, maybe ten acres or so, and we were one of the first ones to build on it decades ago when my grandparents bought this land. They'd used it for camping and fishing, but after Mom and Dad got married, my grandparents signed it over to my dad.

We've lived here ever since, in the same used trailer they bought back then. I'm sure it looked nice at one point, but now it looks like it should be condemned.

Since then, more of the shore has developed, and we're surrounded by custom cabins and luxury homes that constantly remind me just how poor we really are. At least the view on the opposite shore is still undeveloped.

Feeling especially down, I pull out my phone and text my best friend, Jayla.

LINA

Any chance you can come over?

JAYLA

Just got Lucy to bed and Mom's here. So yeah.

LINA

Awesome. I could use some cheering up.

JAYLA

Be there in twenty.

I slide my phone back into my pocket and head inside.

Dad is exactly how I pictured him in his chair reading. He glances up at me when I open the door, but he doesn't speak. His expression is grumpy, and he doesn't look happy.

"Hey, Dad. How's your day been?" I ask, my cheerful tone sounding fake and insincere.

He grunts, which isn't a good sign. Dad practically drank himself to death after Mom left us, and his liver hates him for it.

"Did you take your evening meds?" I ask as I set the groceries on the counter and check his dispenser. Nope, it's all still here. "Dad, you can't skip these."

I dump tonight's pills into my hand and fill a glass with water. He doesn't look up from his book when I hand them to him.

"Dad, you can't forget your meds. Your body needs these to function properly."

He peers up at me and slams his books shut. With narrowed eyes, he takes the offered pills and water.

After he swallows them down, he lets out a long sigh, then asks, "I thought Jonas was coming to fix the water heater?"

"I did too, but apparently, he was too busy to fit us in."

"Piece of shit, son," he mumbles under his breath.

His and Jonas's relationship has always been strained, even before Mom left. Jonas wanted nothing to do with the MC life Dad tried to force on him. Distance hasn't improved things between them, and I'm stuck in the middle, dealing with both their shitty attitudes.

"Yeah, well. I'll figure it out. I always do." Turning away before

I let loose of my anger, I head back to the kitchen to put the groceries away.

"You could stop being so damn stubborn and let the MC help." Dad calls out, not even bothering to temper his tone. He knows I hate talking about the MC. "Edge and a few of the guys stopped by today."

"What?" I whirl around in surprise. He knows I don't want them in this house.

"Lina! We need help." His voice is rough and gravelly, and way louder than he usually talks to me. "I know you're doing your best, and I love you for it, but we're barely hanging on."

"I've got it covered." I insist.

"No, you don't. How long before they turn the electricity off?"

I shake my head because I don't want to answer that question. I have to make a good faith payment by the end of the week, and it better be significant or else we're screwed.

"I don't want their help, Dad. Not after—" My voice cracks. I can't even say the words out loud.

I was fifteen when the former MC president, his club name was Smoke, approached Dad about marrying me when I turned eighteen. He wanted Mom, but since she was gone, he decided her carbon copy was a suitable alternative despite how young I was.

He was forty-seven, hard, and one of the worst humans I've ever met. Dad didn't outright refuse, but he hesitated. That hesitation might as well have been a refusal because it was enough to piss Smoke off.

He left us alone for the next three years, but when I turned eighteen, Smoke approached me himself. By that point, I'd learned how to stand up for myself. I refused without hesitation. He left with a promise to one day own me. For two years, our life was hell on earth.

Smoke purposefully sent Dad on the most dangerous missions for the MC. That's when Dad's drinking got really bad. He'd started when Mom left, but Smoke's actions sent him over the edge. Jonas was already gone by then, and I lived in constant fear of my future and my life.

I'd never been so glad to hear of a man's death as I was the day Dad came home and told me Smoke was gone. Shot in the head by a rival MC. I was twenty and had never been happier.

"You know Edge is nothing like Smoke, right? He's cleaned up the MC. They're almost legit now."

I nod, but I still don't love the idea of accepting their help. Once you let the MC into your life, you're stuck with them. Forever.

I've talked to Edge, the new president, several times at the biker bar they run. Although Posey's Lounge isn't just a biker bar. It's the only bar around, and anyone is welcome.

Dad's right though, Edge isn't a bad guy. But that doesn't change how I feel about accepting their help. I might be stubborn and proud, but I'm also not stupid. Our history with the MC isn't good. It took us years to break away, and the last thing I want to do is let them back into our lives.

AFTER I PUT THE GROCERIES AWAY, I MAKE SURE DAD IS GOOD and head to my room. It's not much, but it's the only room in this house that's a reflection of me.

The room is small and barely big enough for my twin-sized bed, nightstand, and dresser. I stuffed my spinning wheel, knitting projects, and art supplies into a corner. The rest of my stock is in bins in the tiny coat closet in the living room. If I had the space, I'd have an entire room dedicated to my crafts.

My bedding is simple—a black comforter and sheet set. I don't have any pictures on the walls. Instead, I painted them in an abstract mural of the lake we live on. It's bright and colorful and in complete contrast to my typical gloomy mood.

I toss my purse beside my bed and stare up at the ceiling. It's painted to look like a stormy sky with a bright sun fighting to break its way through the darkness. The story of my life.

I'm trapped in an endless thunderstorm with no way to escape. I try to find the positive in life, but sometimes it's hard. Sometimes it feels like there isn't an end in sight to my shitty life.

Needing to drag myself out of my foul mood, I grab my purse and dig out the Snickers Christian gave me.

More like stole from Tanner.

A smile tugs at my lips at the memory. I've got a date with Christian Mutter. Who would've thought I'd catch his eye? I sure as hell didn't.

Lord knows I've tried over the years, but he's never seemed to take notice of anyone. He's a loner, a wounded soul, and someone who knows what it's like to struggle. He's someone who will understand and appreciate why I am the way I am.

Something tells me he wouldn't barge in here and try to fix me and all my problems. Instead, he'd probably encourage me as I work my ass off to fix them myself. I'm sure he'd help if I asked, but he wouldn't try to take everything over and do it for me like I'm incapable of doing it myself. We'd be equals.

He's not a knight in shining armor, but rather a warrior who'd stand beside me. We'd fight our battles together.

That's the kind of man I need and want.

I twirl the Snickers in my hand and remember what Christian said about a late-night snack. He'd be eating his stolen candy bar around nine.

Digging my phone out of my pocket, I check the time. It's a quarter after. I wonder if he's eaten his yet. Does he even remember telling me that?

Deciding to play into the fantasy, I tear open the end and take a bite. I let myself imagine Christian doing the same thing in that exact moment. Both our lips wrapping around our candy bars and taking a bite together.

My eyes slide closed, and a soft moan escapes as my mind

wanders to other things I'd like to feel Christian's lips doing. Kissing my lips, then peppering a trail of kisses down my neck and along the collar of my T-shirt.

My skin instantly pebbles with goosebumps, and I shiver.

"Are you cold, or are you having naughty thoughts over there?" Jayla's voice teases from the doorway of my bedroom. "I can leave if it's the latter."

I frown and toss a pillow at her, hitting her in the chest. She laughs and tosses it back.

"Just get in here and shut the door," I say. "I need to talk."

"Yeah, yeah, yeah," she waves me off. "Would it hurt you to smile every once in a while? Especially when someone's joking around with you?"

"Sorry." I sigh and fall back onto the pillows resting against my headboard. "I'm not in the best of moods."

Jayla chuckles. "Are you ever?"

Jayla and I have been best friends since we were eleven. Her family moved into the house a quarter mile down the road, and we've been inseparable ever since.

We latched together, and nothing has ever gotten between us. She was new in town, and I was ridiculed or ignored because of the drama surrounding my parents. Small towns suck if you have secrets you'd rather no one else knows about. Secrets spread like wildfire in a town like Beaver.

She hands me a bag before she adjusts the pillow I threw at her against the wall my bed butts up against and gets comfortable.

I open the bag and the smell immediately overwhelms my senses with the savory scent of beef. My stomach growls—loudly—in response. "Oh my gawd, what is this?"

"Mom made beef tips and gravy over noodles." Jayla's tone is reprimanding, like she's talking to her eight-year-old daughter, Lucy. I look up to see her eyes narrowed on me.

"What?"

"When's the last time you ate?"

I roll my eyes. Yep, it's lecture time.

I pick up the candy bar I had just taken a bite off of before she walked in. I wave it around like that will satisfy her question.

She snatches it from me and huffs. "This doesn't count. When is the time you ate a meal? Something semi-healthy."

I shrug. "You know I take care of Dad first. I eat whatever's left over."

"Well, that is all yours. I left two more containers in the fridge for your dad. Now eat."

She crosses her arms over her chest and watches me as I take the still warm container out of the bag, along with the plastic fork she'd included. She doesn't relax until I take a few bites.

"This is really good. Please tell your mom thanks."

Jayla nods and leans back on the pillow. "She also made a tray of lasagna. I put that in the freezer. I expect you to eat some of it too. You can't keep starving yourself, Lina."

"I'm not starving myself. I just can't afford to eat like this every day."

She sighs and gives me a sad smile. "I know. But I worry about you. Your headaches have been getting worse."

Jayla's worry is valid. I've always struggled with migraines, and they've been worse now that my diet is all messed up. The doctor was clear that my lack of nutrition was contributing to the worsening of my headaches. Jayla is right. I need to do better.

"I know. The medication the doctor gave me is helping. And I'm trying to do better. As soon as I figure out how to pay for fixing the water heater *and* my car, things won't be so bad."

Jayla shoots up, and her jaw falls open. "I thought Jonas came yesterday to fix that?"

"Me too," I say around a bite of food. "He didn't come. Gave me a shitty excuse and said he would try again some other weekend."

"That worthless, no good, piece of shit."

"My sentiments exactly." I point my fork at her before I take another bite. "I'll figure it out. I always do."

"Yeah, but you shouldn't have to. When do you get to live your life for you? Can't he see how unfair this is to you?"

"I'm sure he can see it. He just doesn't care." I finish the last bite—my stomach feeling full for the first time in days, maybe even weeks.

"Well, I hate him for it."

While I agree with her most days, I shrug it off. There isn't anything I can do about my brother's actions, so I focus on the things I can control. "Speaking of living my life for myself. You'll never guess what happened to me today."

She crosses her legs crisscross style and wiggles in her seat just like she used to do all those years ago when we were teenagers. "Do tell."

She knows how much I've crushed on Christian over the years, and I hope she'll be excited for me. I take a deep breath and look at her through my long, dark lashes. "I have a date with Christian Mutter."

Jayla's smile grows and her eyes light up. "Tell me everything."

Chapter 4

At least farm animals don't talk back

Chase

My eyes blink open. The unfamiliar room is dark. I look around, trying to focus on something I recognize, but it doesn't happen. It's too dark for my brain to register the openness of the space surrounding me.

I'm not fully awake and it takes several seconds before it all clicks into place. Then a slow smile spreads across my face.

My new apartment.

Last night was the first night in my new space. After thirty years of sleeping in the same room, it's going to take me a while to get used to the change.

I grab my cell from the nightstand and check the time. I've got an hour before the sun comes up.

My internal alarm clock is good at keeping me on schedule. As long as I tell myself what time I need to be up the next morning, my body does the rest. I've always been that way. It's a great skill for a farmer to possess.

I toss the covers aside and groan at the ache between my legs. This damn morning wood is a pain in my ass. I haven't been about to get the damn thing to calm down ever since my run-in with Lina at the gas station.

Lina Lange has been the girl of my dreams for as long as I can remember. She's gorgeous—there's no denying that—but there's so much more to her than a pretty face. There's always been something about her soul that drew me in. I know her history, and it's not a good one. A lesser person would have succumbed to defeat, but there's an undeniable strength to Lina. Despite her circumstances, she's a good person with a huge heart. A heart I've always wanted a shot at winning.

Now that I finally have a date with her, it has my body heated.

It also doesn't help that it's been far too long since I've gotten laid. There aren't a lot of options in this small town, and I don't travel enough to meet new people.

I give my dick a light squeeze to relieve some of the pressure. It doesn't work.

"Down boy. I don't have time to fight a boner all morning."

Ignoring my dick, I crawl out of bed and head to the kitchen. I flip on the lights and the brightness is enough of a shock to my eyes that I squeeze them closed. It takes me a moment to adjust.

Once I do, I start the coffee, lean against the counter, and stare out at my mostly empty apartment.

The sparsity of furniture makes the space look so much bigger than it did before I started this project. My chest tightens at the emptiness. I'm happy that I finally have a place to call my own, but this isn't how I'd always imagined it.

I pictured a home full of life, a family—a wife and kids.

What do I have? A bed.

Not exactly the dream life I'd always wanted for myself.

I scrub my hands over my face and push the negative thoughts aside. Thinking about that shit never does me any good anyway. Best to smile and hope for something better.

While I'm waiting for my coffee, I grab a couple of eggs to fry up and pop a couple of slices of bread in the toaster. A quick egg sandwich will be enough to hold me over until I finish my morning chores.

The coffee maker beeps before the toaster pops, so I pour myself a mug. As soon as the hot liquid hits my throat, I feel better.

Once my stomach is full and I've had my caffeine fix, I grab my guitar and head to the balcony just off the dining area.

I take a seat and glance out at the horizon. The faint glow of the sun is lighting up the night sky just over the rolling hills. It won't be long before the sun pushes the darkness away for another day.

I strum my guitar and play a simple melody. It's a tune I can't name but one I recall vividly from my childhood. My mom used to hum it, and it's the only good memory I have of her.

I close my eyes, play a few notes, and allow myself to imagine what my life would've been like had Mom been different. What would things be like had she not been a drug addict and chosen her addiction over her sons?

It's not something I let myself dwell on for long, but I give in to the fantasy for a few moments every day.

Then I push her out of my mind and get to work.

I HEAD DOWN TO THE STABLES BENEATH MY NEW APARTMENT to take care of the large animals first. We don't keep many—a couple of horses, two pigs, and four goats.

I'm still not sure why I added the goats. They're nothing but trouble. But they quickly became my favorite pets. They're fun and seem more like my children most days than useless farm animals.

We also have a few dozen chickens. I've been told my eggs are the best in three counties. We keep what we will eat, and I sell the rest to a few local grocers. They're always asking me for more.

The moment I slide the stable doors open, the goats begin their morning baas and bleats. I keep them in the front two stalls, closest to the exit.

"Good morning boys and girl." I call out as I open the first door.

The boys rush to me like a pack of dogs. I have three rowdy boys in this stall and one sweet girl in the next.

Ramsey, the most playful of the boys, greets me first. He's jumping around next to the gate like the floor is on fire. I chuckle at his excitement and reach over the edge to pet him behind his ears.

"Calm down, Rams. I'll get you outside in a minute where you can run off some of that energy."

Before I'm able to get the gate all the way open, a head rams me in the ass. I don't need to look to know it's Butthead. He's the troublemaker of the group.

"Yo, Butthead. Enough with the ass ramming." I turn around to find him looking up at me with the most innocent look on his face. I swear if he could speak, he'd insist it wasn't him. I slide the next stall open where I keep Tilly.

"Hugo! Tilly!" I call out for the other two to join us since they still haven't come out. "Come on, kids. Let's get you guys outside."

Hugo comes running out next. He's not as rowdy or playful as the other two, but he follows the pack. If Ramsey or Butthead start trouble, he usually jumps in and joins them.

Tilly pokes her head around the side first and looks like she's making sure it's clear before she joins us. She keeps to herself more than the other three. She tends to chill and hang back rather than join them in their gallivanting ways.

They all know exactly where to go once we're outside. The boys race ahead of me toward the gate while Tilly walks beside me, nuzzling her nose into my hand as we walk.

"What is it, sweet girl?" I run my hand down her neck and back and she lets out a low baa. "The boys driving you nuts?"

She lets out a bleat as if to say yes. I chuckle. "I know, but we still love them. They mean well. Most days."

After making sure they have fresh water and hay, I head back inside to take care of my horses, Sunny and Amber. They're both Quarter Horses. Sunny is a buckskin with a few dark patches around his neck, while Amber is a sorrel. They both have dark manes and tails that make their coats look brighter.

Sunny's several years older than Amber and has a calm, easy personality. Whereas Amber is full of spunk. It's one of the things that drew me to her when I was looking to get another horse a few years ago.

I lead Sunny out to the pasture first. He trots along beside me at a slow pace. He's rarely ever in a hurry. I ride him when I need to relax and find peace in this world. He's particularly great when I take the trails through the woods. He handles the hilly terrain like a pro.

Amber, however, loves to run. I've no doubt as soon as I let her in the pasture, she'll take off for the open fields like she's trying to fly.

When I head back into the stables, she's bucking around next to her gate like she can't get out fast enough.

"Calm down, girl. You'll hurt yourself." I reach over the edge and run my hand down her mane. She nuzzles into my touch and neighs.

I grab her bridle and slide it on before I unlatch the gate. She's way too excited for me to risk opening it before I've got a way to hold her back. I make sure I've got a good grip on her reins before I slide the door open.

I can tell she wants to take off, but she contains herself. She's finally learning some patience.

"That's a good girl." I coo in her ear. "Let's get you to the field. Maybe later today, we can ride out and check the fences. Would you like that?"

She lets out a whinny and nods her head like she understands exactly what I'm saying. When I reach the gate to the pasture, she bucks in excitement. Amber is so full of energy and life. She's happy and excited for her day to begin. She's everything I wish I felt sometimes.

Not that I'm *not* happy. But my life isn't exactly where I want it to be.

An image of Lina pops into my mind. I've had a crush on her for so long that sometimes I forget what it is about her that pulls me in.

There's a story behind her expressive eyes. One that we've all heard rumors about. It's impossible to keep anything a secret in this small town. Her family's connection to the motorcycle club, the Unholy Ghosts, is common knowledge, as are the reasons her mother left town never to be heard from again.

I've watched Lina from the sidelines for most of our lives, observing her actions and reactions to situations. She's had a hard life. One that was much harder than mine, and mine wasn't easy. Her life's experiences are what's given her strength like no other and that hard exterior she hides behind. She's stubborn and proud and ridiculously kind under that mask of indifference she always wears.

That kindness is a side of her she doesn't let many people see. I've only seen it because I'm always watching. But will she let me see the real her freely?

Probably not after she finds out I lied to her.

I take a moment and watch my horses run around the field. Would Lina like this life? Farming isn't for everyone. It's hard and demanding and sometimes feels like an anchor. But it's a life I love.

I picture Lina riding Sunny while I ride Amber. Her long black hair flows behind her as the wind whips past us. Would she be smiling? Frowning? Probably frowning.

That image puts a smile on my face. I get why Lina doesn't smile a lot. I've rarely seen her smile, and even then, it's faint. She hasn't had a lot of reasons to be happy.

But I want to change that. I just have to figure out how to break it to her that she's got a date with me, Chase, not my twin brother, Christian.

I slap my gloves to my thigh and head back to the stables.

There are too many morning chores to get done. I still need to feed Clarence and Chubs, our two pigs. And if I don't feed the chickens and gather the eggs soon, they'll riot.

Princess Fluffybutt—that's the only chicken I've named because of her distinct attitude and leadership skills—will have staged a coup if I don't feed them soon. She'll have all my chickens running free.

There's work to be done. Which means there's no time to stand out here and fantasize about a life that may never be.

By late morning, I've finished my chores, showered, and am heading to the garage to see what my brothers are up to.

Now that we've hired Sophia to help, I'm not needed as much to keep the garage going. I still help Ash and Mac with custom racecar builds, but Liam no longer needs me to help with daily customer needs. Sophia and Ash take care of most of that.

This is the change we all wanted and asked for. With the spring and summer demands from the farm, I didn't have enough time to work at the garage too.

But I miss them.

I went from working side-by-side with them every day to my solitary work on the farm. It's an adjustment I'm not even close to being used to yet.

At least I'm about to be too busy to dwell on it much. I start plowing the fields next week to prepare them for planting. I'm sticking with soybeans and corn again this year. Those two crops always have the best return. Plus, they do really well in our fields.

Once those are in the ground, I'll start on the family garden—lettuce, potatoes, tomatoes, carrots, green beans, and various peppers. Grams loves to cook with fresh vegetables, and I try to grow enough for her to can enough to get us through the winter months.

By the time I stroll through the side door of the garage, everyone is elbows deep in work. Sophia is under a car, probably another oil change. Ash has his head under the hood of a racecar, while Mac is behind the wheel revving it up.

Liam is in his office doing whatever he does to keep this place running. Christian's eyes are on me before the door even closes behind me, like he knew I was coming. He's working on a restoration project for some rich dude out of Columbus. He got his hands on a 1948 Indian Chief and hired Christian to restore it to its former glory. I can't wait to see it finished.

Christian studies my expression like he's searching for something. I plaster on a smile, hoping it looks natural enough that he doesn't read anything into it. Then his gaze narrows and I know I'm screwed. Christian can always tell when my smile is fake.

"What's wrong?" he asks.

I chuckle, and it sounds fake even to me. "Nothing. Why would you ask that?"

He lowers his voice as I step closer. "Because I know you better than anyone, and I can sense when something's wrong."

I shake my head. "Not this time. I'm fine. Promise."

He stares at me, unflinching. He doesn't believe me, and why would he? We've always been in sync like that. We're each other's living lie detectors.

"Hey, Chase!" Ash calls out from under the hood. "What are you doing over here today? Shouldn't you be farming or some shit?"

"I had my work done before you even got out of bed, dumbass." I tease, knowing that will piss him off.

"Not all of us have to get up before the butt crack of dawn to work, asshole."

"Just imagine what you'd get done if you did. Might have an entire fleet of racecars ready to go."

"Did you come here just to give me shit or do you need something?" Ash narrows his eyes in challenge.

"Nah." I wave him off. "Came in to grab some tools. I need to change the oil on the tractor and give it a tune up before I start tilling next week."

"Oh." Ash looks disappointed. "And here I thought we'd banter and see who could piss the other off the fastest."

I chuckle, and this time it's genuine. "Not today, little brother. Still got shit to do."

I turn to head toward the back wall where we keep the extra tools just as Liam comes out of his office.

"Hey, Chase, glad you stopped by. Do you have time to look at that Impala you worked on last month sometime this week? Apparently, it's still acting up."

"Sure." I pause and think about my schedule. "Maybe Wednesday? Do you think that'll work?"

"It should. I'll let you know what I find out." Liam turns back toward his office but pauses and spins to face me. "Oh, I heard Clara recruited you for the school bus derby race. How the hell did that happen?"

I shrug. "She said she asked Ash first, but he said he couldn't make time for her, so she asked me. I said sure. It sounds like fun."

"That's not what I said!" Ash yells from behind me. I grin, knowing I riled him up. "I said the racing season was tight, and I didn't want to over commit."

"More like you don't want to lose time with that girl you've been seeing." Mac calls out from where he's sitting.

Ash turns an angry glare at our baby brother. "I'm not seeing anyone."

Mac snorts. "Sure you're not. Don't forget, I'm at all the races with you, and I've got eyes."

"Me too," Sophia singsongs from under the car. "You just don't want Clara to know about it."

Ash scoffs and waves them off. "You guys don't know what you're talking about. To prove my point, I'll be at karaoke on Friday."

"How does that prove your point?" I ask.

"If I had a girl, would I give up a Friday date night to hang out with you assholes at a hole in the wall?"

"Well, I won't be there to find out," I say. "I've got plans."

"What plans?" everyone asks at the same time.

Their fast responses have me nervous, and I rub the back of my neck. I meet Christian's gaze, and he frowns.

"What is it?" he growls.

Well shit. I didn't expect this kind of response. No matter what I say, they're going to question me further. But I'm not sure I'm ready to tell them what really happened.

"Uh, I've got a date."

"With whom?" They all yell, and I shrink into myself. I should've kept my damn mouth shut.

I haven't dated anyone in ages and there's no way I'm getting out of here without telling them. Besides, as soon as we're spotted out, everyone in a fifty-mile radius will know.

"Here's the thing." I hold my hands up in surrender, preparing for the backlash that I know will come. Shit is about to hit the fan. "Don't make a big deal out of this. And I'm going to fix it. I swear."

"Fix what?" Liam asks, taking a step closer to me with a worried look on his face. He's always acting like he has to take care of us. Sometimes I wish he'd just be our brother and stop acting like he's our dad.

"I kinda ran into Lina the other day, and I asked her out." I blurt it out fast, barely taking a breath.

"And she said yes?" Christian asks with a hint of accusation in his tone.

I meet his troubled gaze. He knows as well as I do that she's had a thing for him for years. He's going to kill me when I tell him the truth.

I nod, and his scowl deepens.

"Well, that's great. You've lusted after her for years." Ash teases.

"Don't be a dick." I barked in reply. My expression must say it all because now he's the one tossing his hands up in surrender. I rarely lose my cool, so they'll question my behavior no matter what I say. All I can do now is tell the truth.

"But ..." Christian stares at me with raised brows.

"But ..." I take a deep breath and gather my strength. "She thinks I'm you."

He lets out a deep growl, tosses the tool aside, and stands. He charges toward me, and I prepare for his blow, but it doesn't come. Instead, he nudges my shoulder as he pushes past me and exits the garage.

"Fuck," I mumble. Then I spin around to chase after him. "Christian, wait. I said I'll fix it."

But I'm too late. Christian must have sprinted toward his bike, because he's already started it up. His tire spins in the gravel, kicking it up behind as he speeds away from the garage.

His response only further confirms my suspicions that he has a secret girlfriend. This is a small town, and word will travel fast about Lina and me. Or should I say, Lina and Christian.

It's bad enough that I've made a mess of things for myself. The last person I want to create issues for is my twin.

I kick my foot on the gravel, tossing a few rocks into the air. I need a game plan, and fast. Christian has had enough troubles in his life. He doesn't need me making things harder.

Chapter 5

Oh, that kiss ...

Lina

Fridays are always busy days at the tattoo parlor. My schedule is packed from the moment I clock in. Mostly with my regulars who have scheduled a custom design. Which means they're also my best tippers.

Normally, I'd be hyped to work a double and stay until we close up shop. But not today.

Today, I have a date, and I'm almost smiling about it. *Almost.*

The tattoo parlor I work at is in Chillicothe. It's a city about forty minutes north of Beaver. If I had a choice to work somewhere else, I would. But Country Ink is the only tattoo parlor in the area. I'd have to drive to Circleville before I'd find another one, and that's too far for my old car. It would also break me in gas.

That leaves me stuck working for my lazy ass boss, Rob, at the cheesiest tattoo parlor in existence. At least my chair rental is cheap.

I work solely on commission. He doesn't pay his artists an hourly wage. Instead, we get paid per tattoo. We keep sixty percent of the fee, plus tip. Rob takes forty percent plus the rental cost of the chair and booth. That also means I'm responsible for buying my own gun and inks.

It's not ideal, but it's the only option I've got. Rob knows it too, which is why he can stick us with any charges and fees he wants.

Lately, I've struggled with my ink supply. It's not that expensive, but money has been so tight, I can't afford to replenish my stock. I figure I have about two weeks' worth left of supply before I have to order more.

Trying to budget for supplies is just as hard as budgeting for groceries. My financial woes are a never-ending battle, and it's one I'm beginning to think I'll never conquer.

Thankfully, my car didn't give me any trouble today. She started on the first try. One less thing I have stressing me out at the moment. Lord knows I need a break.

I pull into the back of the parking lot of the strip mall where Country Ink is located. After shutting off the engine, I stare at the entrance. It's still early and we're not open yet.

I love what I do. It's an art form that brings me an insane amount of joy. I just wish I were running my own shop. What I wouldn't do to call the shots in my career.

I close my eyes and let myself picture a different reality. One where life is good, and I don't have any struggles. I can see it so clearly. In big bold letters above the entrance, the words, Beyond Ink, light up the night sky. *My shop.* A place that helps people tell a story with their tattoos.

No more silly hearts or flowers or butterflies that some newly turned eighteen girl comes in to get just to rebel against Mom and Dad. No more *give me whatever is cheapest because I lost a bet.* And no more lazy bosses like Rob who kill the passion behind the art of tattoos.

It would be nothing but custom work. Tattoos are so much more than ink on the body. They tell a story, are meaningful, and should bring the wearer joy for a lifetime. That's the kind of shop I'd run. That's the meaning behind Beyond Ink.

I open my eyes and stare at the sign for Country Ink. A heavy sigh escapes me.

"Keep dreaming, Lina," I mumble as I grab my purse and head inside.

It seems dreams are the only thing I have these days. I should really focus on the positive. At least I have dreams. Some people don't even have those.

A slow smile tugs at my lips as I remind myself of my date this evening. I've dreamed of what it'd be like if Christian Mutter ever asked me out. That's something I never thought would happen, and tonight I get to find out.

"Focus on the positive, Lina. Always the positive," I say under my breath as I make my way to my chair.

"What was that?" my coworker and friend Felix asks. I look up to see him giving me a funny look. Then his brow furrows. "What's wrong with you?"

I drop my smile. "Nothing."

He stares at me for an uncomfortable minute. "I don't buy it. You were smiling when you walked in."

"So." I stuff my purse into my cabinet and pull out my planner. I already know who my first client is, but I pretend to look anyway. "Am I not allowed to smile?"

"Well, yeah." Felix snorts. "But it's not something you ever do. In fact, I can't even remember the last time I saw you smile. You're the queen of bitch face and you know it."

I flip him off and open my cabinet to get my supplies ready for my first client. My action just makes him laugh, which is exactly what I expected.

I've always liked Felix, and we became fast friends when I started working here. He's worked here twice as long as I have and has a client list to die for. Thanks to his help and mentorship, my client list is improving every day. If I keep focused and continue to listen to his advice, I'll have a reputation just as good as his.

I've come a long way in the five years since I started tattooing. At forty, Felix is ten years older than me and has almost twenty-five years of experience. He started tattooing when he was fifteen.

Despite the difference in our years of experience, I'm still the second-best tattoo artist in a hundred-mile radius. Felix is the first, and I'm damn lucky to train under him.

My clients may come from all over the state just to get a Lina Lange original, but his come from all over the country. He even has a few clients who travel from England just to get a tattoo from him.

That's the kind of reputation I want, and if I stay focused and listen to his advice, that will be me one day. I've got the artistic eye and skill. Now I just need the portfolio to back it up.

Maybe then I can open my own shop. Felix is perfectly content to let someone else manage the shop and make sure the doors stay open. Not me. I want to be my own boss in every sense of the word.

I lift the lid on the storage container for my inks and curse under my breath. Then I look over my shoulder at Rob and call out to him. "Rob! Did you let one of the other artists get into my supplies?"

He looks at me and frowns. "No way. You know I don't condone that."

"Then why in the hell are half my inks gone?"

I lift the large bottle of black ink and curse again when I see it's half empty. I just opened that bottle, and it should have been enough to last me a few weeks. Now I'll be lucky if it lasts one week.

Rob marches over to me with furrowed brows. "What's missing?"

"My black is half gone. I just opened this bottle on Wednesday." I dig my hand through my inks and note what's not there. "And my red, blue, and white are gone."

Rob shifts his eyes toward Felix and groans. I look between them, and when Felix nods, I know they know who did it.

"Who?" I bark.

"Now, Lina. Calm down." Rob raises his hands as if he's trying to calm a wild bear. "I'll take care of it. Let me check her supplies and see if they're in her cabinet."

"Her as in Jane?" I ask.

Rob doesn't answer me. Instead, he heads to her cabinet and pulls out her inks. I turn to Felix, ready to lose my shit. I don't have the money to replace inks right now, and I sure as hell know Jane will not pay me back.

"She did an American flag on some dude yesterday," Felix says. "I didn't see her anywhere near your cabinet, but I also wasn't here all day. She could have slipped in when I stepped out to grab lunch."

"She has all three colors." Rob says as he heads back to us. "Are you sure these are yours?"

"Look at the bottom of each jar," I say with my arms crossed over my chest.

He does, and his face immediately contorts into a disappointed grimace. "Fuck."

He holds the bottles up so we can both see the bottom. Clear as day, Lina is etched along the edge, marking those bottles as mine. That's something else Felix taught me early on. *Always mark all your supplies. Too many sticky fingers in joints like these. That way, no one can call you a liar when they steal from you.*

"I'll take care of it." Rob hands me my inks back, then he looks around the shop at all the cabinets for the other artists.

We work on the honor system around here. We're each assigned our own storage space and chair, and we never share. It's understood. That doesn't mean we don't help each other out if we can. All it takes is an ask.

But this isn't the first time something like this has happened. Felix and I have both pushed Rob to update the cabinets with locks. He insists it isn't necessary and that we can trust our coworkers, but clearly that's not the case.

"Take stock of everything that's low and missing." He turns to leave, but I call out to stop him.

"What does it matter? What are you going to do about it?"

"I said I'd take care of it." He grumbles and keeps walking.

When he reaches his desk, he looks back up at me. "Oh, and can you work a double today? We're shorthanded tonight."

"Let me guess. Jane needed the night off." My glare is so intense it could burn a hole through his skull.

"Can you work or not?" He barks, clearly not wanting to discuss the reasons with me. Probably because I'm right. Not only is that bitch stealing my supplies, but she's also bailing on her shifts too.

"Sorry, I can't," I say without hesitation.

Both of their eyebrows rise. They stare at me like they don't recognize me. Can't say I blame them. I never turn down the chance to work more shifts.

"Why the hell not?" Rob says in a tone that suggests he's pissed. He has no right to be. I'll work my scheduled shift without question.

"Got plans." I turn back to my station and get back to organizing my supplies for my first client.

"What kind of plans?" Rob pushes.

I close my eyes and take a deep breath before I lose my shit. I don't need to piss off the owner of this place and lose my chair. Not that I think he'd give me the boot, but I need to maintain a good working relationship with him.

"Not that it's any of your business, but I've got a date."

Rob's frown deepens, but a huge smile spreads across Felix's face. He's been trying to set me up with friends of his for years. He's been happily married for two decades and has three beautiful daughters. He says they make him so insanely happy that he wants that for everyone.

"Anyone I know?" Felix asks.

I shake my head. "Just some guy from Beaver that I've known my whole life."

I say the words like it's no big deal, when everything about this date is a very big deal. I can't bring myself to let my excitement show. Not until I know if there will be a second or even third date.

With Christian Mutter, nothing is a guarantee.

I PULL UP AT THE RESTAURANT RIGHT AT SEVEN O'CLOCK. Christian is leaning against the outside of the building with one leg propped up and his hands stuffed into the pockets of his jeans. Instead of his usual black leather jacket, he's in a dark button-down shirt with the sleeves rolled up. It's not his normal look, but it's still a damn sexy look on him.

Our eyes meet for a second as I park a few spaces down from the entrance, and oh my, his intense gaze makes me feel like I'm fourteen again.

He pushes off the wall and saunters toward me. Just watching the way this man's body moves is enough to make my stomach turn over in excitement.

He wanted to pick me up, but I refused. I can't let Christian see the state of my home, with its leaky roof, sagging floorboards, and musty smell from the worn-out carpet. Not to mention the lack of furniture or anything else that suggests humans live there.

I am not ready to reveal that much about my life. My reality is enough to make me want to leave. I can't imagine how someone from the outside will feel. Let's survive our first date before I expose him to my hell.

He's at my driver's side door and opening it for me before I even shut off the engine. I grab my purse and look up at him. His hand is outstretched, and he's wearing a small smile that makes my heart beat faster than his damn motorcycle at top speed.

His hair is a little disheveled, like he's run his fingers through it several times. Is he just as nervous as I am? God, I hope so. It'll make me feel better if we're both nervous.

I take his hand, and a zing shoots up my arm and straight to my fluttering stomach. He helps me out of the car like a perfect gentleman, but he doesn't step back to make room for me like one. No, he lets our bodies press close together like two lovers who are already familiar with each other. The closeness makes me dizzy.

"Hi," he whispers as he leans down and kisses me on the cheek. I swear that small action makes my heart stop for a few beats.

I squeeze my eyes closed and fight to gain control of my body's reaction to him. I don't need to come off as overly zealous or needy on the first date.

But damn, that's hard when he's so close. His chest is pressed against my arm, and I can feel his heart beating just as fast as mine. *Please let that be a good sign.*

I open my eyes and meet his deep, whiskey brown eyes. They're so beautiful and expressive and full of ... What? Happiness? Excitement? There's a spark in his eyes that surprises me. It softens his otherwise hard, bad boy exterior that I've grown so fond of over the years.

"Hi," I finally manage to say in return. That seems to be enough to snap Christian back to reality, and he steps back. Then his eyes roam down my body. The heat and appreciation I see in his gaze almost makes me smile. *Almost.*

Dressed in all black, I'm wearing my favorite second skin leather pants with an off the shoulder, short sleeve, lace shirt that doesn't leave a lot to the imagination. To my credit, I am wearing a black camisole underneath, but the shirt is a little revealing. It's sexy and fun and shows off my tattoos. I hope it'll tease Christian just enough that he'll want more.

He steps back even further, giving me room to shut my door. But he doesn't release my hand. Christian's hand joined with mine is definitely something I could get used to.

"Shall we go inside?" he asks. He shifts his hand in mine until our fingers are laced together. It's far more intimate than the simple hold he had on me a moment before.

I nod, hoping he can't see the emotions reeling around inside me written all over my face. He doesn't give anything away as he leads me inside to the hostess stand.

The hostess is a young girl that looks like she's barely out of high school. When she looks at Christian, her eyes light up. He's so freaking handsome that he attracts the attention of every woman in the restaurant.

"Can I-I ... help you?" she asks, stuttering a little over her words.

"Reservation for two under Mutter," he says like he doesn't even notice the way the girl is looking at him.

She checks the schedule and nods quickly when she confirms our reservation. "Right this way."

She leads us to the back of the restaurant to a two-seater table by the window. I try not to notice the looks we get as we weave through the tables.

We're at Emery's Steakhouse, which is probably the nicest restaurant in all of southern Ohio. It's much too fancy for the likes of me.

There isn't a dress code, but it's clear the guests and staff are not used to seeing someone like me here. And by me, I mean someone covered in tattoos in leather pants and a shirt she bought at a thrift store.

When I look up at Christian, he doesn't even seem to notice the looks we're getting. He meets my gaze and his smile falters. "What's wrong?"

I shake my head. "Nothing. Just never been here before. It's really ..." I take a moment to glance around before I look back at him. "It's nice."

He stops just as he's about to pull my chair out for me. "Is this okay? We can go somewhere else if you don't like it."

"No, it's fine." I glance around again and catch several people staring at us. They all quickly look away. "I don't think these people are used to seeing someone like me here."

His brow furrows into the bad boy look of his that I've swooned over for years. "What do you mean, someone like you?" His intense gaze rakes down my body again, just like he did when we were outside. "You look gorgeous."

"Thank you," I say, feeling my cheeks blush. Hearing him call me gorgeous makes me feel all warm and fuzzy inside. I can't recall the last time anything made me feel that way. "But I'm not so sure anyone else agrees."

I wave my hand out, and his gaze follows the movement. The eyes are back to staring, causing his frown to deepen.

"Fuck them. They're clearly blind."

As if their looks and stares are inconsequential, he motions for me to sit. Once we're both seated, I finally take in the view from our table.

The restaurant is on the river and the views are beautiful, though we won't be able to enjoy it for long since the sun is already setting. Before long, it'll be too dark to see anything.

As date spots go, this is very romantic. More romantic than I expected from someone like Christian. It both surprises and pleases me in equal measures.

When I look across the table, Christian is watching me with that same sparkle in his eye I saw earlier. His lips tick up into a smoldering grin that causes my heart to flutter, and then he says. "Tell me what you're thinking."

I stare at him, wavering on just how truthful to be. Will he be offended if I admit how surprised I am by this date? Or will he understand?

I take a fortifying drink of water before I clear my throat, deciding to be completely honest. "Well, this restaurant surprises me, I guess. This isn't the type of place I thought you'd pick for a first date. Or any date, for that matter."

His expression drops like I just slapped him in the face. "Would you like to leave? I was serious when I said we can go somewhere else. I just ..." He runs his fingers through his hair, messing it up even more. "I just wanted to take you somewhere nice. Is this all wrong?"

I shake my head. "No, it's fine. Just surprising. That's all."

He gives me a sheepish smile that makes me want to hug him. I don't think any man has ever made me want to hug him before. "You sure? I don't mind if you want to leave."

"I'm sure," I say, even though there's a part of me that wants to say yes to leaving. I glance around and frown when I see several people still staring. But I shake that off and focus on Christian. "It smells too good in here to leave. Let's stay."

"Alright, Grumps. As long as you're sure." He winks as he picks up his menu and starts studying it. I open my mouth to object to the nickname but stop myself. I kind of like it that he calls me Grumps. It shows he sees the real me.

Instead, I follow his lead and pick up my menu. A few minutes later, a server comes by to take our orders. I try not to freak out over the prices of the items. Christian insists I should order whatever I want. So I do—steak with garlic mashed potatoes.

The server suggests a bottle of wine, and Christian says it's up to me. I prefer beer, so I order a stout instead. He does the same.

After the server leaves, silence falls over us as if neither of us knows what to say next. I don't date often, so this is all new to me.

I focus on my hands as I play with the straw in my water glass and try to think of something to say. Before I can settle on a topic, Christian speaks.

"Is it hard letting someone else do your tattoos? I mean, since you're an artist, I imagine you're picky."

I nod. "It is, but I trust Felix. He's my coworker, mentor, and friend. He taught me a lot and is a better artist than me. I designed my tattoos, but he put most of them on me. I did the ones I can reach myself."

"They're beautiful," he says, his words sounding almost wistful. When I look up, he's staring at my exposed arms. "Do they tell a story?"

"Some. They're all meaningful to me in some way."

He tilts his chin toward my right arm where I have feminine

purple and blue feather surrounded by flames. The feather is delicate and beautiful, while the flames are hard and menacing. The two artistic features are in complete contrast to one another, which is entirely the point.

"Tell me about that one?" he asks.

Of course he'd ask me about the most personal tattoo on my entire body. I take a deep breath and run my finger over the edges of the feather.

"The feather represents my heart, and maybe even my looks to a degree. Not to sound conceited or anything, but it's always irritated me that most people only see me for what's on the outside. I know I'm easy on the eyes, as my dad always says, but I'm a lot more than a pretty face. And that's what the flames represent. There was a time that I might have looked like a delicate feather, but I'm anything but. I'm strong and independent. There isn't anything I can't do if I set my mind to it. Just like a raging fire. Once I get started, I'm next to impossible to stop."

When I meet his gaze, I suck in a breath. He's looking at me in complete awe. "That's amazing, and I can totally see it. Do you enjoy working as a tattoo artist?"

"Love it. Well, except when one of my coworkers decides to be an asshole, but otherwise, yes. It's great."

His brow furrows. "What did your coworker do?"

I wave him off, wishing I never mentioned it. I'm not even sure why I did. I'm still pissed over Jane stealing my inks. "Just another artist helping herself to my inks without asking. I wasn't prepared to buy more stock yet."

"She stole from you?" His tone suggests he's ready to go to battle for me, and I have to fight back a smile. I like how it feels to have someone ready to come to my defense.

I wave him off again. "It's fine. The shop owner is taking care of it."

I hope. Knowing Rob, he's already moved on to pretending it never happened. The man hates dealing with conflict.

"You work at Country Ink, right?" he asks.

"Yeah, why?"

He shrugs. "No reason."

The server arrives with our food, interrupting our conversation. Once we're situated with our dinners and the server leaves, I use this opportunity to change the subject.

"So, tell me, what was it like growing up with a twin? You and Chase seem so different."

He immediately starts coughing like he's choking on something. He takes a big drink of water and clears his throat. He takes a moment before the coughing stops long enough for him to speak.

"Sorry about that. Must have choked on my air."

"You okay?"

"Yeah, I'm fine. It happens sometimes."

Once he gets his cough under control, we spend the rest of dinner talking about our families and childhoods in a positive light. There's no mention of how my mom abandoned us or that my dad was a member of the local MC.

I don't ask Christian about his issues with drugs—even though I want to—and he doesn't bring it up. We keep the topics light and fun.

By the time we walk outside, our bellies are full of great food and we each learned more about the other person. Overall, I'd call the date a success.

He walks me over to my car, and we stop next to the driver's side door.

"I had a great time tonight," he says as he rubs the back of his neck.

"Me too. Thanks for dinner. That meal just might be the best meal I've ever eaten."

A smoldering grin covers his face, and it nearly steals my breath. "I'm glad."

I smile in return and lift my hand to his chest. "You're different from what I expected."

"Good different, I hope." He takes a step closer, leaving just a few inches between us.

"Good. Definitely good."

"Does that mean I'll get a second date?" Mischief fills his expression.

"I don't know. I guess you'll have to ask me to find out." I tease in return.

"Lina." He takes my hand in his and links our fingers together. Then he lifts it to his lips and kisses each finger one-by-one. My heart instantly beats faster and pounds in my ears. "Will you go out with me again next weekend?"

I squeeze my eyes closed as I think about my upcoming schedule. If memory serves, I'm booked solid at the tattoo parlor. "I work next weekend, but I should be free the following weekend."

He groans as he leans closer to me. "You're going to make me go two full weeks without seeing you again? I don't think I'll make it."

I run my free hand down his chest, letting my fingers linger over the buttons. "Then I guess you need to think of a way to change that without impacting my work schedule."

His grin makes my heart flutter. Who knew this man could grin so much? "Challenge accepted."

We hold each other's gaze without moving for what feels like an eternity before he finally twirls a strand of my hair between his fingers. "I really want to kiss you. Is that okay?"

I suck in a breath and nod.

With our hands still linked, he lifts his free hand to my face and cups my cheek. My skin burns from his touch and my body aches to feel his heat against me.

He lowers his head toward mine at an agonizingly slow rate, and it feels like his lips will never meet mine. He's so close, yet so far away. My impatience to finally know what Christian Mutter's lips feel like has me wanting to take control. How I manage to restrain myself is beyond me.

When his lips finally brush against mine, I tremble. It's light and gentle and barely there. But that doesn't change the way my body reacts.

Then he shifts closer until our chests touch. He presses my back against my car and applies more pressure with his lips. A deep, guttural moan escapes me and that causes something in both of us to snap.

The kiss quickly changes from sweet and innocent to demanding and sinful. His tongue parts my lips and dives into mine with so much force I feel like I'm going to fall. I clench my hand into his shirt for additional support, but it does nothing to keep me from melting into him.

Before I know it, both of his hands are around my head and gripping my hair in tight fists. My arms wrap around his waist and my fingers dig into his back.

Our bodies are pressed together. His heat is my heat, and I can't tell where he ends and I begin. Then he rotates his hips. And oh. My. God. His very hard erection pokes me in the stomach. Heat pools at my core and I lose all sense of self control.

"Christian," I breathe into him as I lift my leg around his hips so I can feel that erection press into me somewhere else.

Then he freezes.

He releases me and takes a couple of steps back, taking all his heat with him. His sudden retreat leaves me cold and confused. The lust-filled look in his eyes vanishes and is replaced by something resembling guilt.

"What's wrong?" I whisper.

He shakes his head but doesn't look at me. His gaze is focused on the ground between us. "Just don't want to get out of hand in the parking lot."

I don't believe him. Something is off and I can't pinpoint what. How did we go from an intense, feverish kiss to something that feels a hell of a lot like regret?

"It's okay. I should get going anyway." I spin around and dig my keys out of my purse. I suddenly want nothing more than to get as far away from Christian as I can.

"Wait!" He steps up behind me and rests his hands on my upper arms before he leans close to my ear. "I'm sorry. I freaked out. That kiss was ... Hell, Lina. That kiss was everything."

I nod, feeling the exact same way. "Yeah, it was intense."

He brushes my hair away from my neck and face and nuzzles his lips against me. "Can I still see you again?"

Leaning into him, I sigh. "I'd like that."

"Good." He kisses my cheek and steps back. "I'll call you, or better yet, I'll figure out a way to see you as soon as possible without impacting your work schedule."

That makes me smile. I glance over my shoulder to find he's smiling too. "I look forward to it."

He steps toward me and presses a quick kiss to my lips before he backs away. "See you soon, Grumps."

With that, he spins around and heads toward the back of the parking lot. I slide into my car and take a deep breath.

Holy hell. That kiss.

He wasn't kidding when he said it was everything. No kiss has ever made me feel that alive and wanted.

Christian Mutter was full of surprises tonight. Good surprises.

And I'm looking forward to seeing him again so he can surprise me more.

Chapter 6

We are the way we are for a reason

Chase

My phone buzzes from somewhere inside my apartment. It's buzzed a few times this morning, but I've ignored it. After taking care of my morning chores, I showered and have been sitting on the small balcony staring out over the farm ever since.

I haven't even bothered with breakfast and coffee yet.

This is usually when I play my guitar, drink coffee, and enjoy the view of the land I tend to. But I haven't allowed myself to have that joy. I don't deserve to be happy right now. I deserve an ass kicking.

Life is so fucked up, and it doesn't help when I do stupid shit to fuck it up even more. Like I need any help to complicate my life. I'm a Mutter. We were born with complications.

But I went off and complicated things anyway.

More like seriously fucked up.

It's been fourteen hours and twenty-six minutes since I had my lips on Lina's, and I can still feel and taste her. All I can think about is tasting her again.

I'll be one lucky son of a bitch if she lets me. I've done some seriously stupid shit in my life, but this one just might win the stupid prize.

I yawn and rub my hands down my face. I really need that coffee.

I didn't sleep much last night. I couldn't. All I could think about was how much I want to see Lina again, and how much I want to feel her heat next to mine with no barriers.

And then whatever joy I feel from our date is crushed by the realization that she'll probably hate me when I tell her the truth.

Because I have to tell her the truth the next time I see her. I've already let this misunderstanding go on longer than I should have. Hell, I should have corrected her the second she called me Christian.

But nope. I'm a selfish bastard who finally got a date with the woman I've pined over for years. So I let her think she went on a date with my twin brother. I let her think she fucking kissed him. And it was the best fucking kiss of my life.

Screwed, that's what I am.

My phone buzzes again. On a sigh, I push off the railing and head inside. Might as well see who keeps texting me.

Christian's name pops up on the screen. It's Sunday. And not just any Sunday. It's the first Sunday of the month, which means it's time to visit Mom.

Before I go through his messages, I see I have two from Lina. A smile tugs at my lips. I open the message and my small smile turns into a full-faced grin.

LINA

> I know I'm not supposed to reach out so soon after our date. I should follow some stupid dating rule like wait three days or some shit like that before I make contact. I'm sure texting you the minute I wake up makes me look eager or desperate or something else that's not good. And maybe I should play hard to get. But I don't care. I'm not like most girls. I play by my own rules. I had a great time last night, and I thought you should know.

> Also, I don't think I thanked you for dinner. Did I? I don't remember. My brain was scrambled after that kiss. Thank you. It was the best meal I've had in a really long time.

I fall back on my bed and prop my head against a pillow. With my legs crossed, I type out a reply.

CHASE

> I don't care about rules. Fuck rules. I do what I want, and like that you do too. Seeing this message from you put a huge smile on my face. And I mean HUGE. I think my cheeks hurt from smiling so much. I had a great time too, and it was my pleasure feeding you. I'll take you out to eat as often as you'll let me.

> And that kiss ... WOW! It kept me up all night.

LINA

> I like your smile. You smile more than I expected. You're always so broody and serious when I've seen you out before. What's up with that?

> And I didn't sleep much last night either.

I bang my head against the headboard of my bed and groan. Of course she'd pick up on how much I smiled at dinner. I smile. A lot. Christian doesn't. I can't even recall the last time I saw him smile, and he's my fucking twin.

CHASE

What can I say? You bring out the best in me. Do you like ice cream?

LINA

What kind of question is that? I love ice cream. Doesn't everybody?

CHASE

You'd be surprised at the stupidity of others.

LINA

Stupid people never surprise me. I'm surrounded by them.

CHASE

We need to change that. Let me take you out for ice cream one day this week.

LINA

I wish. I work every night this week. All late shifts. I'm not off again until next Monday.

CHASE

You're killing me. I don't want to wait eight days before I get to see you again.

LINA

Then I guess you better get creative.

CHASE

You like tossing out challenges, don't you?

LINA

Maybe.

CHASE

Alright, I'll figure it out then. Not sure how yet, but I'm on it.

LINA

Can't wait.

Have to go. Time to drive to work. Text me later?

CHASE

Yes. Have a great day. I'll be thinking of you.

I close out the message thread with Lina and start to open the one from Christian, but there's a knock at my door.

Tossing my phone aside, I get up. When I open the door, I'm surprised to see Christian on the other side.

"Hey, what's up?" I ask as I wave him in.

"You're not answering my messages," he growls out in response.

"Yeah, sorry." I rub the back of my neck. I never ignore my brother. "I've been distracted this morning."

He squares his shoulders and crosses his arms over his chest. He glares at me like he already knows he's not going to like how this conversation ends. "You didn't tell her the truth."

He doesn't have to ask. He can read me better than anyone.

Dropping against the wall, I rub my hands down my face. "I couldn't. I had every intention of telling her, but I couldn't. We were having such a great time, and I didn't want to ruin it."

"Dammit, Chase." He grounds out. "I can't have rumors spreading around that I went out with Lina."

"I know!" I yell.

His shoulders drop and his hard expression turns to something closer to confusion. "Fuck!"

He turns around and mimics the action I just made by rubbing his hands over his face. Then he turns to me with a deep furrow in his brow.

"How long have you known?"

I shrug. "A while. A long while. But I don't know who it is. I take it she means a lot to you."

He nods. "She's everything. I can't lose her because you're a chickenshit."

I stare at my brother like I'm seeing him for the first time. I knew he had a girl, but I didn't pick up on just how serious he really is about her. "Does this mean you love her?"

His gaze shifts to the floor. "Don't know. Not sure I'm capable of love. But that doesn't mean I can lose her."

When he looks back up at me, I know what he's thinking. He's not thinking about heartbreak or what his life would be like without her. He's thinking about how the loss could push him in a direction he never wants to go again. A direction that could end his life.

That's not something I can let happen ever again. I almost lost Christian twice to his addiction, and I'll fight my way through hell and back to make sure we never end up there again.

"I hear you. I'll fix it the next time I see her. I promise."

"Thanks." He steps toward the door with a nod. "See you at Mom's later?"

"Yeah. See you later."

Then he's gone, leaving me alone in my turmoil.

I blow out a puff of air and curse, knowing I'll do whatever it takes to protect Christian from his demons. Even if it means I'll lose the only woman I've ever really wanted.

Per our unspoken agreement, I arrive at Mom's apartment a couple of hours before Christian said he'd be here. Christian has been clean for a few years now, and I refuse to let anything tempt him into using again. Especially our mother.

Mom still uses and is the one that got Christian hooked in the first place. We were fourteen the first time Christian used. He was having trouble sleeping and Mom said she could help. Within a few months, he was hooked on pills. A year later, he was hanging out with the MC right beside Mom and took his first hit of cocaine. It was all downhill from there.

Rather than knocking, I use my key to let myself in. It'll piss Mom off, but I don't care. I pay her rent. I can come and go as I please.

Besides, she doesn't need a warning that I'm coming. She'll

hide her stash and then offer it to Christian when he gets here. I refuse to let that happen.

Mom's apartment is in the only small complex in Beaver. There aren't very many units and they're all low-income. They were nice when they first built them about ten years ago, but now they're rundown and look twice as old. Probably because people like my mom live in them.

I'm immediately hit by the stench of rotten food, musty carpet, cigarettes, and stale beer.

Despite it being almost one in the afternoon, the apartment is dark. There are no lights on, and the curtains are shut tight.

The first thing I do is open the living room curtains. I frown when I see the mess. Mom must have had a party—maybe several—and didn't clean a damn thing.

I close my eyes and sigh when I see her stash on the coffee table. Or at least what's left of it. She knows we come every first Sunday, but it always seems to slip her mind. At least it makes it easy for me to clean her out.

I grab the small bag of pills and whatever is left of the cocaine dumped out on the broken picture frame glass.

I don't see a separate bag for it, so either she's hidden it somewhere else, or this is all of it. I'm going with the latter. She's not smart enough—or sober enough—to hide her drugs. This is probably what's left from whoever joined her party last night and shared.

I take the pills and cocaine to the bathroom and dump it into the toilet before I search the apartment for more. I check all her usual storage places and a few new ones. I find Mom passed out on her bed with her head buried in her pillow. After I confirm she's still breathing, I head back to the bathroom and flush the toilet.

I know she'll have more drugs before the night ends, but at least she won't have these when Christian gets here.

It's not that I don't trust that Christian has his addiction under control. He does. I'm so proud of the progress he's made these past few years. Getting sober and staying sober was something he wanted this time. Of course, we all wanted it for him too, but this time he made the decision. We didn't make it for him.

I'll be damned if anything tempts him.

To spare my brother the temptation, this is what I do the first Sunday of every month. I arrive at Mom's apartment early, dispose of her stash while she's still passed out, and then clean her fucking apartment.

I start with the trash. There are enough empty beer and liquor bottles here to serve a bar. I really hope multiple people helped Mom drink this shit, and it's not all from her. If she's drinking this much, she's got even bigger issues than just drug abuse.

Once all the bottles are cleared away and in the dumpster outside, I clear out all the rotten and moldy food. She's got half empty takeout containers stacked on the kitchen counter and floor. It's so filthy and gross I can't believe she's not infested with bugs or rodents.

After that's cleaned up, I open her windows to let some fresh air in. It's a warm spring day with a nice breeze. It should help clear out the stench in no time.

Even with all the garbage out, the apartment is still a disaster zone. Every dish in the place is dirty and stacked on the counter and tables. Her cabinets are empty and so is the dishwasher. I wouldn't be surprised if the last time it was run was last month when I did this.

I roll up my shirt sleeves and fill the sink with water. Most of these dishes are going to need to soak before I load them up to wash.

While the first batch is soaking, I gather up the rest of the dishes littered around the apartment and stack them in the kitchen. Then I grab the bottle of disinfectant spray—the bottle that doesn't look like it's been used once since I put it under the sink—and get to work cleaning off every surface in this place.

I work tirelessly for what feels like hours before I finally make headway on the place. Thank fuck it's only a one bedroom, one bathroom apartment or else this would take days.

I scrub the bathroom until the counters, tub, and toilet shine white again. The living and dining room are clean and look presentable. I've got one load in the dishwasher, and then I mop the bathroom and kitchen floors.

Now that all the trash is out and the dirty surfaces are clean, it smells better. At least I can breathe through my nose without gagging.

Mom is still passed out on her bed, so I gather her laundry while a sink full of dishes soaks. It doesn't look like she's done laundry this past month either.

I take all her dirty clothes and towels to the small closet just off the kitchen where there's a stacked washer and dryer. I get the first load started and then wash the dishes I'd left in the sink.

Once her kitchen is spotless, I lean against the counter. Rubbing my hands down my face, I sigh in exhaustion.

How the fuck can anyone live like this? This isn't living. I'm not even sure it's surviving.

Doing this every month drains the life out of me. I've been taking care of Mom like this since I was fifteen. Back then, I did it for her. I did it because I thought I could be the reason she stopped using. And if she stopped using, then so would Christian.

That never happened. There hasn't been a single time in my thirty years of existence that Mom hasn't used.

When I finally figured out that she'd never give up her drugs, I stopped doing this for her. Now I do it for Christian.

"God dammit!" Mom's tired and slurred voice calls out from her bedroom. That means she's figured out I'm here and that her drugs are likely gone.

I rest my hands against the counter and drop my head, bracing myself for her anger. A few moments later, I hear her footsteps come down the short hallway. I feel her presence before I hear the huff expel all the air from her chest.

She doesn't speak, and I'm sure if I turn around, she'll be leaning against the doorway with her arms crossed over her chest, glaring at me. No matter how old I get, she still tries to reprimand me like I'm a child.

I ignore her and go back to washing her fucking dishes.

"Did you get rid of it all?" she finally asks, her words laced with frustration.

"Don't know why you're asking. You know I did."

A low growl escapes her, followed by the sound of a chair crashing to the floor. I glance over my shoulder just in time to see her shaking hands run through her hair.

There was a time when Mom was a beautiful woman. When I close my eyes and let my childhood memories break free, I see her long, dark, shiny hair flowing in the wind. She had a stunning smile and amber-brown eyes that sparkled. Everyone says I got her smile. It's not a compliment. Not anymore.

Now she's haggard. Her hair is always a tangled mess. Her eyes are dark and sunken without a sparkle in sight, and her skin is dull with a gray tinge. She looks worn hard and completely spent. Whatever beauty she had faded a long time ago. All that remains is a shell of a woman addicted to drugs and bad men.

"You have no right to be here and throw away my stuff."

The anger and hatred I see in her eyes should upset me, but it doesn't. Not anymore. Mom never showed me love. I never gave into her demands and temptations like Christian. Therefore, I was disobedient and unruly.

"Since I pay the fucking rent on this place and it's my name on the goddamn lease, I'll come and go as I please. I'll also throw away anything and everything that I find in here that I don't like."

I don't know why I bother to say all that. It's the same damn speech I give her every month. It's like the two of us are stuck in a loop that neither of us knows how to get out of.

Instead of arguing with me about it—because she knows I'm

right—she spins around and leaves me alone in the kitchen to finish doing *her* dishes.

It doesn't matter how pissed Mom gets at me for coming in here and cleaning up, she can't do a damn thing about it. The landlord knows the deal, as does Ricky, our local law enforcement.

I close my eyes as I let my head fall back. *I'm doing this for Christian. Not her.*

I repeat those words over and over again until my heart rate calms, and my frustration subsides. Getting mad at Mom doesn't help. That's what she wants. She loves to piss me off, hoping that will make me leave and never come back.

But she doesn't take into account just how much I love my brother. I'll do anything to protect him, even put up with her bullshit.

As soon as Christian arrives, Mom is all smiles. She's always shown Christian more affection than me. Even when we were little, she preferred him.

I try not to let it bother me, but it's hard. She treats him like the beloved son she always wanted, and me like I'm a nuisance.

There were times when she'd try to divide us, make one hate the other. But she underestimated the power of our connection. We're twins. It'll take a hell of a lot more than a manipulative parent to divide us.

While I always come over and clean, Christian brings groceries. We try to buy enough non-perishables to last her for a month, but I doubt that happens with as many parties as she hosts. I wouldn't be surprised if all the assholes she lets hang around here eat it all within a week.

Once Christian is able to extract himself from Mom's embrace, he brings the groceries inside. I try not to let it bother me that Mom never hugs me. She doesn't even act like she's happy to see me. Ever.

"You alright?" Christian asks as he sets a couple bags on the clean counter.

I nod but don't speak. I can feel his eyes on me before he turns and heads back out to his truck to get the rest of the groceries.

I unpack what he brought in to keep me busy. Mom steps into the kitchen and takes a seat at the dining table. "Why can't you be more like Christian? He brings me the things I need rather than throwing it all away."

I ignore her as I continue to put the food away. He bought all the fixings for spaghetti and meatballs, so I leave that out. I always make her dinner before we leave. At least I know she gets one good meal out of everything we bring.

"Answer me," she barks.

I lift my eyes to hers, doing everything in my power to look unaffected by her words. "What do you want me to say, Mom? That I'm sorry for flushing your drugs down the toilet? Grams taught us not to lie, so I'm not going to lie."

"You have no right."

Choosing to ignore her, I go back to the groceries. "Spaghetti and garlic bread tonight?"

She doesn't answer me, so I look over my shoulder at her. She waves her hand at me in disgust just as Christian walks in with his arms full of more groceries.

Christian looks between us and sighs. He knows how hard these visits are on me, and he also knows I do it for him. If it weren't for him, I'd never see Mom again. I wouldn't pay her rent or clean up her shit or even bother giving her the time of day. Not after everything she's done to hurt Christian.

Despite all of that, he still loves her. Then again, he would. She's always loved him back.

"This is the last of it," Christian says as he sets them on the counter and starts unpacking them.

"I told Mom I'd make spaghetti. You good with that?"

He nods. "With the meatballs that I like?"

"Yep. And the garlic bread. I figured that would also leave her with some leftovers for tomorrow."

"Sounds good. I also got a brownie mix and some eggs. We can make those up too. Brownies are her favorite."

"Will you two stop talking about me like I'm not here? It's rude."

I snap my eyes in her direction. "Rude? You have some nerve to call *us* rude. You've been nothing but rude and hateful to me since the day I was born. You should be grateful we even care enough to check on you, let alone feed you."

"You're not the one feeding me. Christian is. You just annoy me."

"Mom," Christian sighs. "Chase paid for these groceries too. They're from both of us."

Mom opens her mouth like she's going to say something else—probably another insult at me—but then stops. Then she lets out a huff and leaves the room. A moment later, her bedroom door slams shut.

Christian looks at me with sadness in his eyes. I wave him off. He always makes excuses for her behavior, but that's all they are. Excuses. I'm tired of hearing excuses. I'm tired of having to listen to him defend her when she's never done anything good for either of us.

All she's ever done is hurt us. Albeit in different ways. Him through drugs and me through verbal abuse.

Nothing we do or say is ever going to change her. I accepted it a long time ago. I just wish Christian could do the same.

Chapter 7

I can take care of myself

Lina

"I'm here! I'm here!" I call out as I run through the front door. My car gave me a shit time starting again. It took so long to start, for a long, hot minute, I didn't think I was going to make it at all.

"Lina!" Rob's voice bellows through the open room. "Is that you?"

"Yeah, it's me. Sorry. My car wouldn't start." I rush to my station, not sparing a glance at anyone. I'm never late, and today I missed my first appointment. Thank goodness it was with a repeat customer whose number I had. He graciously understood, and we rescheduled his appointment before he even showed up. Which meant Rob didn't have to deal with an upset customer.

When I reach my station, I stop. My mouth drops open and my eyes widen. "What's all this?"

In front of my cabinet is a new, sleek black cabinet about the same size—maybe a little bigger—with double doors on the front that lock. Stacked on top are several boxes. Taking a closer look, the boxes contain several bottles of ink. And not just any ink. Some of the best ink in the business. Taking quick stock, it looks to be at least three or four months' worth.

I spin around to see Felix staring at me with raised brows and a small smile, while Rob is glaring at me.

"Where did all this come from?" I ask.

"I was hoping you could tell me," Rob grumbles. "This was all delivered to you about an hour ago. Having the inks sent directly here is fine, but a fucking cabinet? I told you I'd take care of it."

"I didn't order this!" I say a little too loudly. "You know I can't afford a cabinet like this. Hell, even this much ink is out of my budget."

"Well, someone took it upon themselves to take care of you. I don't like it." Rob moves past me and starts removing my things from my old cabinet. I don't know what to say or do, so I just stare at him.

When he moves the old cabinet away from the wall, I finally snap out of it. "What are you doing?"

"What does it look like I'm doing?" He growls.

"Rob, stop. I don't know where this came from. I can't use it."

"Why not?" His brows furrow as he eyes me, but he doesn't stop moving the old cabinet away from the wall.

"Because it's not mine," I say. I'm still at a loss for words and that's the best I can come up with. It's a very nice cabinet, much nicer than the ones Rob put in years ago, but I don't know where it came from.

"Box has your name on it." He grunts as he positions the hand cart under the cabinet and starts hauling it away. I hadn't even noticed he had the cart with him. "Besides, it's a nice cabinet. I think I'll replace all of them with the same style. Make them all match."

"But ..." I press my hands to my cheeks, trying to snap out of my shock. This can't be happening. Nothing like this ever happens to me, and I can't decide if it's a good or a bad thing.

"Snap out of it," Felix says as he wraps his arm around my shoulder. "This is some nice shit. Did you find yourself a sugar daddy or something?"

I glare up at him. "You know better than that. I'm nobody's arm candy, especially some douche of a man who has more money than sense."

Felix knows how I feel about men who only date women because they look good on their arm. I've been propositioned one too many times by men who only want to date me because they think I'll make them look better. They don't always have money, but typically they do.

My looks were the only reason the former MC president wanted to marry me. That, and I was young and untouched. The whole idea of only wanting someone because they look good or have money makes my stomach turn.

"Well, someone is trying to impress you." Felix waggles his brows. "Or maybe they're just looking out for you. That might not be such a bad thing, Lina. You could use a break."

"But who?" I sift through the first box of ink. There are several bottles of black, and a full range of colors. I can create so much beautiful art with these inks without the worry of having enough to get me through the next week.

This is a very generous gift. Too generous. I need to know where it came from before I use them. I don't like or want to be beholden to another person. I can't pay them back for this. I've got nothing to give.

Rob returns and positions the new cabinet exactly where he wants it. Then he helps me put all my stuff into it. I stuff the box of new inks on the bottom shelf. I'll worry about those later.

"Um, just so you know, Jane is replacing all your inks." I look up to see Rob rubbing the back of his neck. "She's also on warning to never touch anyone's supplies again. If she does this again, she's gone."

"Thanks for dealing with that for me." I give him a tight-lipped smile that's not even really a smile. It's too forced to even pass for a smile.

"Well, I figured it was better me than you. No need to have your temper blowing up this place."

"Hey!" My frown deepens and my brows furrow. "I have every right to be pissed."

Rob holds his hands up in surrender. "No one's saying you don't. I'm just trying to keep the peace. You're a great artist, and I want to keep you here."

His words surprise me. Rob acts like he doesn't need any of us or care if we stick around. It's good to hear otherwise.

"Thanks. I better get set up for my first client. He should be here soon."

Rob leaves me to it while I get out the designs and notes for my client. It's a custom design of a wolf's head, baring its teeth and surrounded by trees. This art will cover his left shoulder and wrap around his arm and eventually be worked into a full sleeve. Today is day one of at least three sessions it will take to complete.

Jobs like this are my favorite. They're the ones that pay the most and bring me the most joy.

While I'm organizing the inks I need to lay the foundation for this tat, my mind wanders over the past week of conversations I've had. Aside from my coworkers, I've only discussed my ink supply issue with two people.

One was Jayla, and there's no way she did this. She can't afford it any more than I can. She's a single mom, living with her parents and working at Walmart. She can't even afford her own place, let alone supply me with ink.

That leaves one other person. And he just might have done this.

Christian Mutter.

But why?

We went on one date. We've texted several times since then and even agreed to a second date, but it's not like we're a couple.

I sigh and drop back into my chair.

I knew it was too good to be true. That kiss was too amazing, too life-altering, to be real.

Men only ever want me for one thing—my looks and sex. Okay, maybe two things. And many of them have been willing to buy their way into my pants.

Is that what Christian is doing? Preying on my weakness? Buying me things he knows I desperately need just so he can get me naked?

It wouldn't be the first time, and with my luck, it won't be the last.

Well, shit. I thought he was different. Was I that wrong about his intentions? It is odd that he suddenly noticed me. I've watched him for years, and he never looked in my direction until that day at Kochs.

I scrub my hands over my face just as the bell over the door dings, letting us know a customer has arrived. I look up to see it's mine.

I push to my feet and wave him over. I'll have to deal with Christian later. For now, I need to keep my frustration and internal accusations in check. No need to let myself get too pissed until I talk to him.

As soon as I slide behind the driver's seat of my car, I shoot off a text to Christian.

LINA

Did you buy me ink and a new cabinet?

I toss my phone into the passenger seat and start my car. Or rather try to. I've got to figure out where I'm going to find the money to get my car fixed before she dies on me completely. If that happens, I won't be able to get to and from work.

I drop my head back and growl while I wait a few moments before I try starting her again. My phone buzzes.

CHRISTIAN

Hmm? Ink and a cabinet? Are those things you need?

I sense a teasing nature to his words, and that pisses me off even more. I don't need bullshit right now. I need honesty.

LINA

Don't play dumb with me. Did you do it or not?

CHRISTIAN

Am I missing something? I know this is just a text, and I'm trying not to read too much into it, but you sound pissed.

LINA

I am pissed.

CHRISTIAN

Why? Because someone did something nice for you?

His response has me seeing red.

I slam my phone down in the seat beside me and try starting my car again. This time, the engine purrs on the first crank. I quickly fasten my seatbelt and pull out of the parking space and head toward the highway.

I hear my phone buzz a few more times, letting me know he's sending me more text messages. Every buzz makes me press my foot harder against the accelerator. I'm driving way too fast through town, and I can't bring myself to give a damn.

When the last light just before my highway exit turns red, forcing me to stop, I take a deep breath. I've got to calm down. The last thing I need is a speeding ticket.

I close my eyes and drop my head to the steering wheel. Why

do I let shit like this get to me so badly? So what, he bought me some ink and a cabinet?

But we only went out on one date. *One. Date.*

This is too big a *gift* after only one date.

My phone rings, dragging my eyes up to check the light. It's still red.

I pick up the phone, not bothering to check who's calling before I bark out my hello. I already know it's him.

"Will you please explain to me what's happening here?" Christian's voice sounds frustrated and confused.

"Did you do it?" I ask with way too much venom in my tone. The light turns green, and I gun the gas. My engine revs up way too much, and I back off out of fear of messing up my car more than she already is.

"Do what?"

I let out a low growl. "Buy me the ink and locking cabinet."

"Is it such a bad thing if I did?"

"Yes!" I yell. "We've been on one date. This isn't the kind of thing you do for someone you've only gone out with once, unless you have ulterior motives."

"Ulterior motives?" He barks out an incredulous laugh. "What the fuck, Lina?"

"Just answer my fucking question. And don't you dare lie to me, Christian."

"I'm not Chr ..." He suddenly stops talking and lets out a low huff. I imagine him shoving his free hand into his hair and pulling on the strands. That's something I've seen him do a lot when he's frustrated or nervous.

"You're not what? Finish that statement."

He's silent for a few more beats before he takes a deep breath and sighs. "I'm not lying to you. How can I when I haven't even answered your question?"

"Then answer it."

"I feel like I'm going to lose no matter what answer I give you."

"I just want honesty." This comes out so much softer than anything I've said since we got on the phone. My vulnerability is showing, and I don't like it.

"Yes," he says with defeat. "I sent you the ink and the cabinet."

"What the fuck for?"

"What do you mean, what for?"

"It's too much. I can't accept this."

"It's not too much. And you have to accept it. I bet the cabinet is already installed."

I open my mouth to argue with him, but I've got nothing. I may not have touched the ink, but Rob replaced my old cabinet before I even had a chance to fully wrap my brain around what was happening.

"I can't control my boss, but that doesn't mean you can't still take it back."

"I'm not taking it back. It's a gift."

"No one gives gifts like this unless they have an ulterior motive."

"There you go again with that damn ulterior motive." He growls, and it sends a shiver down my spine. He sounds so sexy when he's angry. I scold myself for having such thoughts because I am supposed to be mad at him, not turned on.

"You know what, fuck it!" he says, causing me to straighten in my seat. "You're right. I do have an ulterior motive."

"I knew it!" I yell.

"Be quiet and let me speak." His command booms through my phone. His voice is so demanding and authoritative, I have no choice but to obey. It's hot and sexy and I'm surprised by how much I like it.

"My ulterior motive was to make you smile—to wipe out the negative thing that happened to you. Someone stole your belongings, and I wanted to fix it."

"It wasn't your problem to fix," I interject.

"Lina," he says my name in a low growl. A growl that says I am not to interrupt him again. "This is what people who care about you do. They help you fix problems when they arise. I had the means to fix this, so I did. If that pisses you off, well, get over it. I'm not sorry I did it."

"But it's too much. I can't afford to pay you back for this."

"I don't expect or want you to pay me back. It's a gift."

"This is hardly a one date gift. You know that, right?"

"Yeah. I know. But I don't give a shit." We're silent for a few beats before he asks me another question. "Would you have been pissed if I sent you an embarrassingly large bouquet of flowers?"

I open my mouth to say yes but stop myself. Would I? I would've thought it was too much, but my gut tells me it would have made me happy.

"I don't think so," I answer honestly.

"Flowers aren't cheap. The bouquet I would've sent you cost almost as much as those inks cost. I opted for practical because it's what you needed. That's not to say I won't ever send you flowers, but I wanted to do this for you instead. Be pissed all you want, but I don't regret doing it."

I blink, focusing on driving for a moment. I've been on autopilot ever since I took the highway exit, and I'm not paying any attention to where I'm going. I'm already past the halfway mark to home.

"I'm not used to people doing nice things for me unless they want something from me. And it's usually something I don't want to give."

His sigh is so heavy I feel it in my bones. "I do want something from you."

"Oh yeah?" I say with a little too much anger. "And what's that?"

"I want another date, Lina. And a kiss. I'd definitely love another one of those kisses. I also want to make you smile. If that's not something you want, then I guess we're through before we even really begin."

He sounds so sincere and dejected. It makes my chest ache. Whatever anger and frustration I carried toward him a moment ago are gone. I can't deny him what he wants because I want it to.

I answer him with a single word. "Okay."

"Okay what?"

"Okay, I want that too. I want to go out on another date, and I'd really, really like for you to kiss me again. I liked that very much."

"Thank fuck." He sighs in relief.

"Just promise me no more gifts like this. I don't need you to take care of me."

He lets out a deep, playful laugh that does not sound anything like something that would come from Christian Mutter.

"I cannot and will never make that promise."

"Christian!" I scold. "You can't do—"

"I can and I will." He cuts me off. "I already told you. I take care of those I care about. And I care about you. So go right ahead and prepare to be pissed at me a lot because it's happening."

I growl, and he laughs.

"I like it when you growl, Grumps. It's sexy."

"I'm not trying to be sexy right now. I'm pissed."

"Still like it." His tone has shifted to playful and happy. I smile without even realizing I'm doing it. I want to stay mad at him. His gift makes me nervous and fills me with a sense of obligation. I don't want to be beholden to anyone. Ever.

"Then you're in luck. I growl and frown a lot. That you don't surprises me. You smile and joke around a lot more than I expected."

He's quiet for a moment. So quiet, I don't think he's going to respond. But then he does.

"Is that a bad thing?"

"No." I answer before I have time to think about it. And it's true. I like his sense of humor and easy smile. It gives him charm I didn't know he possessed. "Your smile makes me feel better."

"Good. That makes me happy."

We talk until I reach my driveway, falling into easy conversation. It's like we've been doing this for years when it's the first time we've ever talked on the phone.

I've always had a crush on Christian, but now I can see that crush developing into something so much more.

I just hope he's looking for the same things I am. If not, my heart may not survive.

Chapter 8

There's way too much pretending going on around here

Chase

Rather than eat breakfast alone in my apartment again, I decide to head to the main house to see what Grams is making for everyone else. I finished all my early morning chores, and I've got some time to spare before a meeting I have before lunch. I could use some of Grams's cooking. Plus, I miss my brothers.

I love having my own space, but I miss my family far more than I thought I would. I still see them every day, but living apart from them makes it different somehow. Like there's a distance between us that I'll never be able to eliminate again.

I don't like it, but I'm thirty fucking years old. It's time I live on my own.

Garret managed to move into his own place, and he survived. Granted, he's a grumpy bastard who likes solitude. I like people. Hell, I need people around me in order to feel human.

This living alone thing is definitely going to take me some time to get used to.

I hear the low rumble of my family before I even open the back door. Everyone is probably around the large dining table in the kitchen, joking or razzing each other about something stupid one of them did.

And I'm missing out.

I jog the last few steps to the back door and pull it open. After kicking off my shoes, I march into the kitchen, same as I always did after finishing up the morning farm chores.

All my brothers, except Garret and Warren, are sitting around the table laughing and eating. Grams is at the stove, and I don't see Dad.

My heart lurches when I see a plate set at my usual seat at the table. I look over at Grams and she nods. It's as if she could read my mind and knew I'd be here.

I pull out my chair and plop down. My brothers are already eating—eggs, bacon, and toast. Before anyone even acknowledges that I'm there, Grams scoops some scrambled eggs onto my plate, and I grab a few pieces of bacon from the dish on the table.

"Don't forget we've got those Euchre scrimmages next week. Are you prepared for it?" Grams asks with a hint of concern in her voice.

"Yeah, I remember. And I will be there. Don't you worry."

As if I could ever let Grams down. None of us enjoy these Euchre tournaments we play in with Grams, but it's important to her, therefore it's important to us.

We take turns each year playing with her, and this year is my turn. At least it's an opportunity to kick the Kochs' asses at something else. That's something none of us Mutter brothers will ever pass up on.

The Kochs have been our rivals at everything ever since their great-great-grandfather lost this land and house to ours in a poker game. Talk about cocky and stupid. They've been trying to goad us into a game ever since in an attempt to win it back. As if any of us would ever be that stupid.

"You going to tell us how that date with Lina went, or keep us guessing?" Ash asks with a shit-eating grin on his face.

A loud clunk sounds from the stove, and when I turn around, Grams is staring at me with wide eyes. "You went out with Lina? Like on a real date?"

"Yeah, is that so surprising?"

Grams's eyes shift between me and Christian with nothing but confusion written all over her face. She knows Lina pretty well. They both meet up almost weekly at the community center for knitting club.

"But ..." She presses a hand to her chest and watches me like she's waiting for clarification.

"How did she react when you told her it was you and not that asshole?" Mac asks while pointing at Christian.

I wince and Christian growls. He's the only one I've talked to about how I didn't come clean with Lina.

"She still doesn't know," I say under my breath, and then promptly stuff a bite of eggs into my mouth.

The kitchen falls so silent, all I can hear is the pounding of my heart. When I glance around at my brothers, they're all staring at me with wide eyes. They don't need to tell me how stupid I am. I see it written all over their faces.

"What doesn't she know?" Grams barks from right behind me.

I open my mouth to tell her, but Ash beats me to it. "Lina thinks she went out with Christian, and this asshole didn't correct her."

Grams doesn't speak. Instead, she whacks me upside the head the same way she did when we were kids and acting like little assholes.

"It was a mistake. I didn't intentionally mislead her."

"Yet you still misled her?" Grams asks with enough anger in her words that they sting far more than the whack upside my head.

I sigh. "I'm going to tell her the truth. I just didn't know how to bring it up."

"How about, oh by the way, I'm not Christian, I'm Chase?"

Ash suggests, still grinning at me like he's having the time of his life.

"You listen to me." Grams pokes me in the shoulder, and I instinctively pull away from her. She may be a tiny woman at only five-foot-three, but she's feisty and could take every one of us Mutter men down. "Lina has been through enough. She's had a rough life, but she's a good girl. Do *not* hurt her."

"I don't want to hurt her." I toss my hands up in surrender. "I like her. I want to date her. I didn't know she thought I was him when I asked her out." I point at my twin. He's still frowning at me like he doesn't give two shits about my mistake. He just wants me to fix it. "When I realized she'd mixed us up, I didn't know what to say. I was stunned into silence and confused. Then I was afraid she'd cancel because it's me instead."

Grams lets out a heavy sigh. Before she has a chance to say more, a timer goes off. It must be whatever deliciousness I smell baking in the oven.

"Are you at least acting like you around her?" Liam asks.

I look up at him and nod. "She's made a few comments about how much I smile and joke around. Seems surprised by it."

"But does she like that side of you? It's not like you two are anything alike." Liam adds.

"She says she does." Now it's my turn to let out a heavy sigh. "But it doesn't matter. She's going to hate me when I tell her the truth."

"Why do you say that?" Mac looks at me with a furrowed brow.

"Because I lied to her. She doesn't take too kindly to liars."

"Oh, she'll be pissed alright. Probably will want to put you in a grave." Gram singsongs from across the kitchen. She fucking singsongs. Grams never singsongs.

"Thanks Grams. Much appreciated." I push to my feet, suddenly no longer hungry despite the fact that I think those are her famous cinnamon rolls she just pulled out of the oven.

"Sit!" she barks out the command. And like the twisted, sad puppy dog I am right now, I listen.

"Will there be a second date?" Grams asks.

I nod.

"Then she likes you. There's hope." Grams grabs a stack of small plates and places one in front of each of us. "But you better tell her the truth before she finds out from another source. Don't make her look like a fool publicly. Got it?"

"Yes, ma'am."

Thankfully, the subject shifts away from me and we enjoy the rest of our breakfast. Grams packs up a couple of extra cinnamon rolls for me and an entire tray for Garret.

"How come Garret gets a whole tray and we each only get one?" Mac complains.

"Because he'll be sharing that tray with Charlotte and her family. Besides, I've got another one ready to go in the oven. You boys will get more than your share. Don't worry."

"Thanks, Grams." I kiss her on the cheek and clear my place at the table.

"You leavin'?" she asks.

"Yeah. I've got a meeting about the school bus derby this morning. Can't be late. Clara doesn't have a lot of time between classes. I guess this was the only time everyone could make the first meeting."

"I still don't understand why she asked you instead of Ash," Liam says with furrowed brows as he stares at Ash. "I mean, she's your best friend."

"She did ask me, and I told you, I don't have time," Ash says. His tone is off from his usual playful nature. He sounds almost frustrated. "I'm too busy with races and building cars. No time to play with a school bus."

"That doesn't make any sense." Liam adds. "You never pass up an opportunity for fun. Plus, it's for Clara. Since when do you refuse to help her?"

"I'm not refusing anything. I said I don't have the time. Why is that so hard for everyone to believe?" Ash pushes to his feet and grabs his dirty dishes. He quickly rinses everything off and shoves them into the dishwasher. Then he leaves without another word.

His behavior has all of us staring after him in disbelief. Ash never gets worked up over something like this. Out of all my brothers, he's the most like me. Fun. Playful. Charming.

Something is definitely bothering him.

"On that note, I'd better get going before I'm late." I say a quick goodbye to my brothers and kiss Grams on the cheek before collecting my container of cinnamon rolls. I toss one last wave in the air and head back to my apartment.

It's time to go have some of that fun Ash seems so determined to avoid. A school bus derby between all the county high schools may not be a necessary distraction, but it sure as hell will be a good time.

Especially with me involved.

Per Clara's instructions, I park my truck in the parking lot behind the school, close to the side entrance. Just as she said, the door is propped open so I can walk right in.

The door opens to a small meeting room where Clara and two other teachers are sitting at a small table talking. I've seen these two with her before at Posey's Lounge for karaoke night, but I don't really know them.

"Hey, Chase." Clara smiles up at me. "I'm so glad you could make it."

"Of course." I lean down and give her a hug. "Happy to help."

It's still unclear to me why Ash isn't the one helping her out. He is her best friend, after all. I know he said he was too busy with the racing schedule, but I know that's bullshit. I worked that schedule for years while running the farm. He could make it work if he wanted to. I hope she and Ash didn't have a fight. I'd hate to not see her around as often.

"Have you met Karla and Trevor?" she asks.

I shake my head. "I've seen them with you at the bar, but I don't believe we've ever been introduced."

"Well," Clara starts, "this is Karla Keller. She teaches PE and coaches the softball team. And this is Trevor Martin. He's a math nerd. Teaches calculus and geometry."

I hold my hand out to each of them, taking Karla's hand first. She is a beautiful woman, but not my type. She's petite and blond and I like tall and brunette like Lina. Or maybe Lina is just my type, and no other woman compares.

Trevor has dark hair similar to mine, but with a mess of curls on top. He's tall. Not as tall as me, but I'd say he's close to six feet. He wears dark-rimmed glasses that suggest he embraces his inner nerd.

"Nice to meet you both. I'm Chase Mutter."

"Same," Trevor says. "I assume you're our mechanic?"

"Yep." My grin is wide. I love projects like this. No stress or business consequences if things go wrong. Just some good old-fashioned fun. "Clara asked me to help you turn this bus into a racing machine. Let's hope I can deliver."

"You're being modest," Clara returns my smile with an eye roll. "Chase's cars always win."

"I lose sometimes." I nudge Clara with my elbow. "But not often. I'd say the odds are in our favor."

"There's the cocky Mutter that I've grown to love." Clara teases. "Keep that attitude and nothing will stop you."

"So now that we've established that we can't lose, what are we up against?"

"There are five teams for each school district. Eastern, that's us of course, Pike CTC, Piketon, Waverly, and Western. Each team is allowed six members and no more. If we bring anyone else in and get caught, we're disqualified."

"There's only four of us here," I say.

"We have two more members. Mac promised to drive. I figured you could serve as the mechanic and direct us on race day. Karla has some knowledge of cars, so she'll help you. That leaves—"

"Sorry I'm late. Had to help my dad this morning. It won't happen again." Lina comes running through the back door. When her eyes meet mine, she freezes. "What are you doing here?"

I give her a huge smile and try not to let my surprise show. From the way she asked that question, I'd say she thinks I'm Christian.

"I'm a mechanic. What role are you serving?"

Lina's eyes shift between me and Clara. I see the moment she begins to question whether I'm Christian or Chase. Thankfully, Clara steps in and clears it up for her.

"Chase, you know Lina, right? She'll head up the art team. Trevor and I will help her. We've got to decorate the bus as part of the race."

"Of course I know Lina. We went to school together." I force my grin so wide it hurts. There's no way I can let her find out like this that I'm the one she went out with. "Plus, I see her at Posey's a lot."

Lina's gaze meets mine again, and the air suddenly feels heavy. Her eyes narrow as she studies me.

My heart rate kicks up several notches as something dangerously close to recognition flashes across her expression. This is too much. Too much tension. Too much pretending. And way too many opportunities to fuck this up. I've got to fix this mix up between us, and fast.

Thankfully, she shakes her head and focuses on Clara.

My shoulders relax, but only slightly, as the meeting kicks off. My focus is on high alert. I cannot let her find out this way that I've lied to her.

She'll never forgive me if she does.

Chapter 9

Grumps gives it away

Lina

My gut is screaming at me that this is not Chase, but Christian. My body is aware of him in the same way it was when we ran into each other at Koch's Pit Stop and again on our date.

There's something about his eyes that's so familiar and telling. The slight sparkle that always lightens his chocolate brown eyes calls to me. I know those eyes. Even his smile—though much wider than normal—is familiar.

Is this a twin thing? They are identical.

I shake my head and try to focus on the reason I'm here. I may have known Christian and Chase my entire life, but it's not like I've spent a lot of time with either of them until recently.

It definitely has to be a twin thing.

"Lina, have you met Karla and Trevor?" Clara says, dragging me back to the here and now. I push my confusing thoughts aside and focus my attention on her.

I don't normally volunteer for things like this, but when Clara asked me a few weeks ago, I couldn't say no. She joins our knitting club off and on, and I quickly figured out she's a good person. Not everyone in this small town is.

I also don't have a lot of friends, so when someone kind asks me to help them or join them in an activity, I have a hard time saying no.

Not that I expect Clara and me to become friends after this, but it would be nice to have a few more people in this town on my side. I don't make friends easily. Mostly because I don't trust many people. The sins and actions of my parents make that hard for me.

While Clara explains the groups we'll be divided into, I study my other team members. I've seen Karla and Trevor around, but this is the first time I've met them. Karla comes across as confident and outgoing. She smiles and laughs a lot.

She'll work with Chase on the mechanics. While nothing compared to Chase's resume, she's got some experience working on old muscle cars with her dad growing up. That bit of knowledge spurs a side conversation between the two of them.

"Oh, yeah?" Chase asks. His smile is so big it lights up the entire room. Oddly, a pang of jealousy rushes through me because he's giving her that smile and not me. "What's the last car you worked on?"

"A Pontiac GTO." Karla smiles back. "It's a sweet ride. Dad kept that car. He sold all the others."

Chase presses his hand to his heart and looks up at the ceiling in awe. "I've worked on a few of those over the years. Only ever test drove them after rebuilding the engines. I always wanted to open them up on the racetrack and see what they really have, but never had the chance."

"Well, Dad doesn't race. Ever. He barely drives the Pontiac at the speed limit. He treats that car like a precious, fragile child."

"Yeah, not sure I'd be that way if I owned it. I'd be too tempted to race it."

"Then it's a good thing we brought you on the team," Clara says. "We need power and speed if we want to win. Unfortunately, this is a bus, not a muscle car. Just tell me you can handle it."

Chase winks at her, and another wave of jealousy washes over me. It's confusing and has me scolding myself. "Of course I can. There's not much that I can't handle."

Then he looks at me. His smile grows, and he gives me the same wink he just gave Clara. My belly does a little flop and my insides warm.

That's weird, right? I'm sort of dating Christian. He's the twin I'm into. Can my body not distinguish the difference between them?

Chase turns his gaze back to Clara and focuses on what she's saying. I take this opportunity to study him.

He's what I'd call a clean-cut, pretty boy. He's wearing dark jeans that look brand new. I'd guess that they've never seen a hard day's work. His light blue button-down is crisply ironed. His hair is combed to one side without a strand out of place.

He and Christian may be identical twins, but they dress nothing alike. Except Christian dressed a hell of a lot like *that* on our date. I shake my head and focus on the man in front of me.

There's no denying he's a gorgeous man, but he's not my type. I like the bad boy, rough and rugged look that Christian wears like he was born in it.

A little messy and *a lot* bad. That's Christian Mutter.

I close my eyes and picture him sitting on the back of his bike, wearing his black leather jacket. He takes his helmet off and his hair is disheveled. I run my fingers through it and tug on those locks just before his lips crash into mine.

Oh, that kiss. I can't wait until our next date so I can kiss him again.

I open my eyes and study Chase some more. He doesn't look like he knows how to cause trouble if trouble hit him in the face. That doesn't seem to change how my body reacts to him. My body is charged with need and desire. I've never had a reaction like this to a *good* boy.

Maybe that's my problem. I need to stop categorizing men as good or bad. I've only ever dated one so-called good boy, and that was back in school. Hell, it wasn't even a date. I wasn't old enough to date yet. But that didn't seem to matter to the asshole. He lured me into his car, making me think he liked me.

Fucking Charlie Fisher.

That didn't turn out so well. He only wanted me for one thing, and when that didn't happen, he hit me. Hard. He left me with a black eye and a cut across my cheek from where his class ring scraped my skin. I still have a faded scar. That was the first and last time a man ever laid a hand on me.

Charlie is from a good, wealthy family. His dad's a retired congressman and Charlie is following in his footsteps. Charlie is the kind of man that's never had to work for a damn thing in his life. Mommy and Daddy handed him every opportunity he's ever had.

He's several years older than me, and when he asked me out, I thought I won the lottery. A rich, handsome man wanted to go out with a poor daughter of an MC member. I'd said yes without giving it a second thought and took him up on his offer to drive me home.

That drive ended in violence. I may have gotten hurt, but he didn't get what he wanted from me. He got a hard kick in the groin instead.

I still see Charlie around town, and he still looks at me with those creepy eyes that say he'd take what he wanted from me if the opportunity ever presented itself. I've made damn sure there's never been any opportunities.

It doesn't matter that he's married with a kid. I know he cheats on his wife. Poor Hannah. She's a sweet woman. She joins the knitting club sometimes. It's not often because I think Charlie keeps a tight rope around her. Based on her behavior—and my past experience with Charlie—I think he beats her.

Damn shame too. She's one of the good ones. She doesn't deserve a piece of shit like Charlie.

I shake myself out of my memories. I need to pay attention

since Clara asked me to lead the art team. I need to know what's going on if I'm going to lead these people in this effort.

We talk about the game plan. The art of choice for this is graffiti, and of course, no one has any experience with that except me. I'll have to give Trevor and Clara some lessons before we start, since they'll be helping me with the art. Neither of them knows anything about engines.

I agree to come up with a design that fits our school's mascot—Home of the Eagles.

Then the conversation shifts to driving and who's going to do it.

"Chase, are you sure you don't want to drive on race day?" Clara asks.

He shakes his head. "I'm not much of a driver. I build cars. I don't race them."

"But you know how to drive?" I ask with a little too much sass. I don't know why I'm irritated with him, but I am.

He stares at me with raised brows. "Um, yeah. But driving is not the same thing as racing. It's a different skill. Since we have room to add more team members, Mac can do it. He already said he would."

"Isn't that an unfair advantage to the other teams?" I ask with a hard glare directed at him.

"How so?" Chase's grin grows as he crosses his arms over his chest and leans back in his chair. His charm is blinding.

"Mac is a professional driver." I growl. "Feels like cheating."

"Oh, come on Grumps. What good is it to have connections if we don't use them?"

My eyes widen and he flinches. "What did you just call me?"

"Nothing. Let's get back to planning." He turns his attention to Clara. "There's nothing in the rules that limits Mac from driving, right?"

Clara shakes her head. "We're good. If everyone is okay with it, let's go with Mac."

I stare at Chase, unable to get his words out of my head. He called me Grumps. No one has ever called me Grumps before.

Except ... That means either the man sitting across from me is really Christian—which I highly doubt—or I didn't go out on a date with Christian.

I went out with Chase.

My participation in the meeting stops. I don't even hear anything else they discuss. Instead, I study Chase's every move, action, and expression. His mannerisms and expressions match those of the man I went out with.

There's a chance that Chase and Christian share all the same mannerisms, but I doubt it. I may not know them well, but I grew up with them. They've always been opposites in everything.

Maybe Christian told Chase about the nickname he gave me, but I doubt that too.

My instincts tell me the man sitting across from me is the man I went out on a date with, and he is, in fact, Chase Mutter.

I always trust my instincts, and they are screaming at me.

Chase lied to me.

Unable to sit here and hold in my anger a moment longer, I push to my feet and rush out.

Clara calls after me, but she doesn't follow. I'm almost to my car when I feel a hand wrap around my wrist. I jerk it free and whip around. Chase is right behind me with a look that can only be described as fear on his face.

"Lina, please."

"It was you!" I yell. "All this time, and it was you."

I'm not asking. I know the truth and there's nothing he can say that will change that.

He steps closer to me, effectively pinning me against my car. He lifts his hands and cups my cheek. My brain is screaming at me to push him away, but my body betrays me. Every ounce of my being wants him close.

Everything happens so fast, and his lips are against mine before it registers what he's doing. And just like after our date, I melt into him. I'm powerless to pull away, even though I know I should. I want his lips and his hands and his touch.

His tongue darts out and licks the seam of my mouth, and my lips part. He's soft and gentle and yet demanding of what he wants. And I let him take it.

When our tongues tangle, my legs wobble and my body goes limp. I've kissed plenty of men in my life and no one has ever made me feel like this. This is *not* normal.

But this is also not Christian. That realization is enough to finally give my brain the strength to take back control of my body. I press my hands against Chase's chest and push hard.

He stumbles back, looking just as surprised as me from that kiss. He feels exactly what I feel, and that pisses me off even more. I don't want to feel anything where Chase Mutter is concerned.

"I told you to never lie to me!" I yell, not caring that we have an audience. Clara and the others are standing just outside the door, watching us.

"I didn't lie. Not really."

"I'd say tricking me into going out with you instead of your twin is the very definition of a lie."

"I didn't lie!" He yells. "I just didn't correct you when you called me Christian. I never once said that I was him."

"You are not getting off on a fucking technicality. That's still a lie, *Chase*." I say his name with so much venom that he stumbles back. "How could you do this?"

"How could I?" He has the audacity to look mad, and that only feeds my anger more. "Fuck, Lina. How could I not, is more like it? When I asked you out, I thought you knew it was me. Me!" He pokes himself in the chest. "I was on top of the world with that answer. I've wanted to ask you out for so long, and for the first time since I've known you, you showed a fucking interest. *In me.* And then you called me Christian. Talk about a slap in the face."

"You should have corrected me."

"Yeah, I should have. Not going to deny that I made the wrong decision. But then what? Would you have canceled?"

"I guess you'll never know."

He sighs and runs his hands through his hair. "I was going to tell you."

"When?" I cross my arms over my chest like that's somehow going to protect me from his closeness.

"I don't know. I hadn't quite worked that out yet."

"Well now it doesn't matter." I reach for my door handle to leave, but he stops me.

"Lina, please." He pleads. "Don't walk away from this. There's something between us. I know you feel it. Don't you want to see where this could go?"

"I did. Now I want you to leave me alone and never speak to me again."

"I'm sorry. I made a mistake." The hurt in his eyes causes my throat to tighten. No man has ever looked at me like that. It's almost enough to deflate my anger, but not quite.

"Yep, you sure did. And now we'll never know what could have been. From this moment forward, you and I are enemies."

I don't give him a chance to say anything else. I hop in my car, and thank fuck, she starts on the first try. I drive off, but like a fool, I look back.

He shoves his hands in his hair and tugs at the ends like he's frustrated. I even think he curses as he watches me drive away.

I don't think I've ever seen someone look so dejected in all my life. But right now, I can't bring myself to care. Chase Mutter committed the worst possible crime against me.

He lied.

Chapter 10

It's all fun and games until it's not

Chase

It's been five days since Lina found out about our little mistaken identity issue. I've called. I've texted. I've even tried to catch her outside of Country Ink. She refuses to talk to me.

I can't say I blame her, but I refuse to give up on us.

There's no denying the way she makes me feel. I know she feels it too. It's evident in the way she kissed me back. Both times.

She may have thought I was Christian, but she reacted to *me*. I just need to figure out how to get her to give me a chance to prove that to her.

A sharp jab to my ankle pulls me from my thoughts. When I look down, Princess Fluffybutt is pecking at my leg.

"Sorry girl." I drop some feed at my feet, and she immediately starts pecking at the ground instead. Now that she's distracted by food, I rub behind her neck. This chicken may be a pain in my ass, but she's my favorite. She's got so much personality and spunk. Exactly how I like my women.

I finish feeding the chickens so I can gather the eggs without getting overrun. My girls are greedy when it comes to feeding time. Probably because I've spoiled them. Only the best for my girls.

Not only does it make them happy, but it ensures they produce the best eggs. That means Grams's cooking is top-notch. Selfish, yes, but we all win in the end.

I'm back in the barn, sorting the eggs into cartons, when I hear shuffling behind me. I glance over my shoulder to find Grams leaning against the wall, watching me.

"Hey, what are you doing out here this morning?" I ask. "Need some eggs? I'm going to have to run to town and sell some of these before they go bad. The fridge is full."

I keep a refrigerator in the barn for egg storage. I have enough chickens that it doesn't take long to fill it up. About once a week, I take most of them to the market in town to restock their shelves. They usually sell out of our eggs within two days.

"Nah, got plenty for now. You go ahead and sell those."

There's something in the tone of her voice that I don't like. I meet her gaze and see worry looking back at me. "Everything okay?"

"Dunno. You tell me."

"Uh, not following." I turn to face her and lean against the counter. Something is on Grams's mind and I'm not getting out of this conversation until she says her peace.

"I haven't seen you all week. Not once." She raises a brow as if to challenge me to deny there's meaning behind my absence. She's not wrong, but I deny it anyway.

"You know this time of year is busy. Had to get the fields planted. Also been working on our private garden."

"Bullshit." She growls out and shakes her head. "Been doin' that for years and that's never stopped you from eating breakfast, lunch, and dinner with your family. What's goin' on Chase?"

"Nothing." I lie. "Until now, I've lived at home. Got my own apartment now. Working on learning to feed myself."

She narrows her eyes and studies me. Then she takes a step closer, shaking her head. "Not buyin' it. Somethin's wrong. There's sadness in your eyes. You're never sad."

"Nope, not sad." I insist, even though she's not wrong. I've never been very good at hiding my feelings. "I got several new peach trees this week," I say, hoping to change the subject. "Gonna plant them along the fence line behind the house. Should make for some great cobbler or preserves in a few years once they fruit."

"That's great. Can't wait," she deadpans. "But I don't want to talk about fruit or gardens or eggs right now. I want to know why my happy-go-lucky grandson is sad."

"I said I'm not sad."

She gives me a knowing stare that says she knows me better than I know myself and that I am definitely sad.

I sigh, knowing she's not going to let this go. "I'm fine, Grams. I swear."

"Is it Lina?"

"Now, why would you ask me that?"

"Because you've had a crush on that girl since first grade. I'm guessing it didn't go over so well when you told her the truth."

"What? ... How? ..." I scrub my hands down my face. "Grams, what are you talking about? It was just one date. No lifelong crushes going on over here."

"Again, bullshit." Grams puts her hands on her hips and stares me down like the little menace she can sometimes be. She's not letting me out of this conversation. "Tell me what happened."

"She found out before I had a chance to tell her myself. She didn't take it so well."

"Imagine she didn't." She sighs and glances out the open barn door at the newly planted fields before she looks back at me. "How you gonna fix this?"

"I don't know yet. She won't take my calls or answer any of my messages. I've tried catching her outside Country Ink, but she ignores me. Any suggestions?"

Grams studies me again before she speaks. "Lina's a complicated woman with a complicated life. She doesn't trust easily. Not gonna lie to you. Breakin' her trust will be hard to overcome. But it's doable. If you really care about her and want a shot, you're gonna have to be persistent."

"Persistent? I don't want to be a nuisance. I already feel like a stalker."

"I'm not talkin' about calls or messages or following her around. You need to let her see who you really are. You're a good man, Chase. The best. I've no doubt if that woman lets you love her, it will be the best love she's ever seen or felt."

"No one said anything about love, Grams. I want to date her first."

"Yeah, well. Dating leads to love. But before you can date her, show her you're worth the risk."

"And how do I do that if she won't talk to me?"

"You're a smart and resourceful man. Figure it out."

With that, Grams spins on her heels and leaves me standing alone. I stare after her, clueless to how I'm going to *figure it out*.

"Not a lot of help there, Grams," I mumble as I turn back to sorting the eggs.

I do my best to push all thoughts of Lina from my mind and pour myself into the farm. I've got enough work that needs to be done to keep three people busy.

Maybe if I work myself to death, I won't think about how she feels. Or how sweet her lips taste. Or how my body lights up with anticipation and need when she's nearby.

Unfortunately, it doesn't work.

THE ROAR OF LOUD ENGINES CAUSES MY EARS TO RING, AND the smell of dust and smoke overpowers my lungs. I cough to clear my throat and chest.

It's the spring tractor-pull, and Mac just finished his first race. He won, but just barely. Jason Koch, the youngest of our lifelong rivals, finished a dangerously close second.

Even though Jason never causes us any problems, Mac will still be pissed he almost beat him.

Jason is the only Koch that doesn't seem to give a shit about the feud between our two families. Well, he and his sister Amelia. She never participates in feeding it either.

I'm crowded around the first row of the bleachers with the rest of my brothers near where Mac will head once he accepts his winnings. He doesn't get much. It's just a cheap metal figurine of an old-time tractor.

But the prize isn't the point of winning at tractor-pulling. It's about the thrill and bragging rights.

Tractor-pulls are nothing like racing fast cars on a perfectly paved track. In fact, there is no track. It's just an open, dirt field surrounded by bleachers. Most of the time, the field is smooth and even from recently being graded.

But sometimes, like tonight, it's rough with deep ridges. After a hard rain, the field can get pretty messed up. It takes several rounds of grading to smooth it out again. Or some hard racing.

I prefer nights like this when they leave it rough. It makes for more interesting and exciting races.

The souped-up tractors line up on one end with trailers loaded with weights and debris attached to the back. As they race across the field to see whose tractor will win, the rough ridges cause a lot more bouncing around. Sometimes they even get stuck. Watching drivers try to maneuver their hauls free is entertaining as hell.

The surrounding arena lights kick on, illuminating the field more. I hadn't even realized that the sun was setting. We've probably got another thirty minutes of daylight left.

This also means its intermission. About half the races are held prior to sunset, and the other half after.

After dark is when things tend to get more exciting. There's no meaningful difference between the races or the entries. The order of the races is purely by the luck of the draw.

It's more of a mood shift in both the crowd and the entrants.

Most of the families with kids leave at intermission and the rowdy crowd comes out to play.

Just as Mac heads our way with a stupid grin on his face, country music blares through the speakers. Sophia runs past us and jumps into Mac's waiting arms. She doesn't care that he's covered in sweat and grime. She kisses him hard and deep.

A pang of jealousy washes over me at the level of affection and intimacy they share. I'm happy they found each other. Lord knows they both deserve their happiness. But I want that for myself.

"Get a room!" Ash calls out from behind me.

I turn around to find all my brothers laughing and having a good time. Even Garret has a smile on his face. Then again, why wouldn't he when he has a woman like Charlotte wrapped up in his arms?

Liam steps up next to me with a huge grin on his face. "Your tractor did good. Mac didn't get stuck once."

"Of course it did good. I only build the best." I chuckle and squeeze Liam's shoulder. "You didn't think I'd build crap, did you?"

Liam shakes his head and laughs. "And modest. You're very modest too."

"You know me well, bro." I scan our surroundings to see who's still around and who's taken off before the second half of the night begins.

Gerald Mayer, aka Jerry, the resident drunk, is heading our way. He's happy and smiling which isn't normal for him. He's usually walking around with a scowl on his face and tense as all get out.

"Hey, Jerry," I say as I slap his back in a friendly gesture. "You're looking good tonight."

His smile widens, and he nods his head vigorously.

"Good night tonight," he says, and I catch a whiff of the alcohol on his breath. He may be in a good mood, but he's still drunk as a skunk on moonshine.

"You don't say." I take a step back to put a little distance between us. From the way he smells, I'm going to get a contact buzz. "What makes tonight better than another?"

"All this noise." He waves his hand around us in a large sweeping motion. "It keeps the deer away."

I can't help but chuckle. This man has been terrified of deer ever since he hit one while riding his bicycle while drunk. He killed the deer and landed himself in the hospital. Ever since, he swears the deer are conspiring against him.

"At least all this noise is good for something besides entertainment." Ash teases. He winks at me as he takes over the conversation with Jerry. "Did you get yourself a corn dog yet? Frank's food truck always makes the best ones."

"Well, no, I haven't, but I've heard they're good."

"Come on, let's go get you one." Ash wraps his arm around Jerry's shoulder and leads him toward the food trucks.

My brothers and I have taken it upon ourselves to keep an eye on Jerry. He may have a drinking problem and draw a lot of suspicious stares around town, but he's a good man. He spends too much of his money on alcohol, so we make sure he has plenty to eat when we see him.

Jerry and Ash disappear behind the bleachers, and my eyes catch a pair of deep blues staring at me. Lina is standing at the end of the bleachers where we're sitting, and her eyes are locked on me. Not Christian, who happens to be right next to me, but *me*.

She worries her bottom lip between her teeth, and I swear I see something resembling desire reflecting back at me. Then the little girl standing next to her pulls her attention away. I recognize the girl as Lucy, Jayla Smith's eight-year-old daughter. Jayla also went to school with us, and she and Lina have been best friends for as long as I can remember.

I watch Lina interact with Lucy for several minutes. She smiles and laughs at Lucy a lot. The two of them are clearly very close.

Their relationship almost seems more like aunt and niece instead of friends.

I like seeing Lina interact with Lucy. It's obvious she loves the girl very much. And she's good with her.

Does Lina want kids of her own someday? That's something I've never let myself think about before. I've daydreamed about a life with Lina, and maybe I've pictured kids in that life, but I've never asked myself if kids are something Lina wants.

I've always wanted kids of my own. Kids are fun and bring so much joy to life. I find myself hoping that it's something Lina wants too.

Her eyes lift and meet mine again. This time her gaze is softer, almost forgiving. And it gives me hope.

I smile for what feels like the first time in two weeks.

"There's our brother!" Ash jumps onto my back like I'm going to give him a piggyback ride and ruffles my hair.

I shove him off me with my elbows and growl. "What the hell are you talking about?"

Every one of my brothers looks in Lina's direction. Only now her gaze is cold as ice. Even her deep blue eyes have an icy sheen to them.

"Let me guess," Liam says. "You didn't tell her the truth yourself."

I rub the back of my neck as I watch Lina walk away with Jayla, Lucy holding each of their hands, swinging between them.

"I didn't get a chance."

"Remind me again why you didn't tell her when you were on your date?"

"Because I'm a dumbass."

Liam tosses his head back and laughs, and then he slaps me on the back. "Ain't that the truth?"

I growl, feeling worse than I did before. Fixing this is not going to be easy, and I don't have a clue where to begin.

Chapter 11

One day it's gonna get better. It has to

Lina

I roll over for the hundredth time this morning. I'm restless, but I can't find the energy to drag myself out of bed.

It's later than I usually sleep in, but I don't have to be at work until one this afternoon. It's not like there's anything good waiting for me if I get up early.

A crash followed by a slur of curses comes from the kitchen. Dad must be up and trying to make himself something to eat. I usually do that, but since I've refused to get up, he's on his own.

I try burying my face under my pillow, but after a few minutes, guilt consumes me. I toss my covers back and sit up. My head feels dizzy and instantly aches. I had another migraine last night that left me sick to my stomach. While I feel much better this morning, I sat up too fast.

I also need to eat something. I went to bed last night without dinner.

Opening the side table drawer, I check the quantity on my prescription. If I don't get too many migraines, I have enough meds to last me another month. Maybe two if I'm lucky.

That would require me to reduce stress and eat a healthier diet.

My doctor's words taunt me.

I've always been prone to headaches, but my migraines are primarily brought on by poor diet and stress. Two things I can't really do anything about.

Another crash has my feet moving. Whatever Dad is doing, he's struggling with it.

"Dad! What are you doing?" I ask before I even make it to the kitchen.

I find him standing at the stove with shaking hands. He's trying to make some oatmeal.

He lets out a low growl and tosses the small packet on the counter. "My damn fingers won't work. I can't rip this open."

"Here, let me." I take the packet from him, rip it open, and pour it into the waiting bowl on the counter. The tea kettle is on the burner heating, but it's not quite ready. "Anything else you need while you wait?"

He grumbles something under his breath that I can't make out and shakes his head.

"Dad, it's okay." I rub his back as he turns away from me. "I'm here to help."

"That's the problem, Lina. You should be out there living your life. Being young. Instead, you're stuck here taking care of me. It's not fair to you."

"I'm not stuck. I want to take care of you."

He growls and waves his hand at me as if he thinks my words are bullshit. They are and they aren't. I do feel stuck. He's not wrong about that. Even if I wanted to move, I can't afford to live anywhere else but here. But that has very little to do with him. I'd stay and care for him even if I did have somewhere else to go.

"Did you take your morning meds?" I ask even though I know he did. I already see his pills are gone. It's more a way of changing the subject.

"Yeah," he mumbles as he heads to his recliner.

"Do you want more coffee?" I ask before I rinse out the carafe to make a fresh pot.

He picks up his mug from the end table and looks inside it before he answers me. "Another cup would be nice, doll. Thank you."

I smile at his softer tone. This is how it always goes. He gets frustrated with himself when he can't do something on his own, lashes out about how I shouldn't have to care for him, and then settles down once I do just that.

There isn't anything I wouldn't do for my dad. His MC lifestyle may be responsible for our current situation and a lot of my past pain, but he protected me when no one else would. He stood up to Smoke and refused to let that man anywhere near me. A lesser man would have given Smoke what he wanted to save his own skin.

Life was hell for dad after that, but he never wavered in my protection. He committed the ultimate sin against the MC. He put his daughter first.

The tea kettle whistles, so I finish up Dad's breakfast. Or maybe it's lunch. It's almost eleven now. I really did sleep late.

Once Dad is settled with his food and more coffee, I search for something to feed myself. We don't have much. I need to go shopping again.

I finally decide on a packet of beef flavored ramen noodles. The sodium content isn't going to do me any favors, but it's cheap and fast. It will also hold me over for a few hours. I still have some beef jerky left that I'll eat for dinner, along with an apple.

As I eat my noodles, I flip through the stack of bills on the counter. It just keeps growing and growing. The cable bill is paid, so that's one less thing I have to worry about. I'd let it go if it weren't for Dad. He's stuck here all day, every day, and needs some form of entertainment besides books.

The medical bills taunt me. With Dad's health, they're never ending. Aside from his medication and primary care physician, I can push most of those aside for now. It's the electric bill that has me worried.

I made a payment, but it wasn't enough. If I don't make a hefty payment by next Friday, they're going to shut it off. Whatever savings I have is going to have to go to it.

Which means no hot water for a few more weeks. I also have to push off work on my car a little longer.

And then there's the matter of paying Chase back for the supplies. There's no way I can accept the ink and cabinet as a gift now that I know the truth.

I can easily figure out the cost of the ink since that's something I buy all the time, but I've no clue how much the cabinet cost. He won't tell me either.

Maybe Rob can figure it out since he's considering upgrading all the other cabinets now to match.

I let out a low puff of air. *How is this my life?*

Despite how bad things are here at home, for a moment, I was happy. I had such a great time on my date with Chri—no, *Chase.* Chase Mutter. I can't believe he tricked me like that. It makes no sense.

His words from our confrontation echo through my mind.

When I asked you out, I thought you knew it was me. I was on top of the world with that answer.

I've wanted to ask you out for so long and for the first time since I've known you, you showed a fucking interest.

And then you called me Christian. Talk about a slap in the face.

He couldn't possibly mean any of that. He made it sound like he's wanted to go out with me for a long time—pining after me. That can't be true. He's never once given me any indication that he even noticed me, let alone liked me.

I've asked myself more times than I can count what I would've said if he corrected me at the time of the mistake. If I'm honest with myself, I would have canceled. I've had my sights on Christian for so long, I know I would've been overcome with disappointment and bolted.

Because that's what I do when things get tough and awkward. I bolt.

Maybe it was an honest mistake on his part, and maybe it wasn't. I guess I'll never really know.

A lie is a lie. I've been betrayed too many times in my life to let this one slide. I was willing to forgive him for overstepping with the supplies he gifted me, but this is too big. How could I?

How could I not?

His other words ring through my ears. Those were some of the first words he spoke when I asked him why he did it.

How could I not?

I've always thought of Chase as the confident, cocky Mutter brother, always so sure of himself. He always smiles and jokes around like life is all fun and games. It's a quality that's always turned me off from people. Not that I don't like to have fun—I do—but I prefer the serious, contemplative type over jokesters.

But he wasn't all fun and games on our date or the few times we talked. We had a fun time, but we also had some great talks. Is it possible there's another side to him that no one ever sees?

"Of course there is Lina," I say to myself. He's a Mutter. They've dealt with just as many problems at home as I have. They're just as broken as I am.

Maybe that's why this stings more than it should. He knows my trauma, and he still lied.

I rub my temples, fighting back the onset of a headache. I'm too stressed about this. If I'm not careful, I'm going to get a migraine.

That's the last thing I can afford right now.

———

MY SHOULDERS SAG AS SOON AS I STOP IN FRONT OF MY workstation. There's an embarrassingly large bouquet of colorful flowers. It's so large, it's the first thing anyone sees when they walk through the front door. The bright colors pop against the mostly black and white decor of the shop.

I don't need to read the card to know who they're from. He warned me about this. But I read the card anyway.

Lina,

A flower petal for every second that I've thought of you and wished I handled things differently.

Please forgive me.

Yours,

Chase

"Who's Chase?" Felix says from right over my shoulder.

I slap the card to my chest and glance back at him. I was so absorbed in the card that I didn't hear him walk up behind me.

"Nosy much?" I growl.

He shrugs. "Been curious who they were from since they arrived this morning. No one's ever sent you flowers before and these, well ... This is something."

Ignoring him, I turn back to the card and read it several more times before I slip it into my back pocket. *Flower petal. He said petal, not flower.*

I study the bouquet and there's at least three dozen daisies and carnations with a few other flowers scattered in. Two flowers with lots and lots of petals. That's a lot of seconds.

Felix plops down in my chair and crosses his legs at his ankles. "Talk to me, Leens. Who's Chase? Is that the guy you went out with?"

I nod. "Only he led me to believe he was his twin brother. I thought I went out with Christian, not Chase."

Felix lets out a low whistle. "Ouch. That stings."

"Yeah, no shit, Sherlock." I grumble.

"Is this the same guy who sent you the replacement inks and locking cabinet?"

I nod but remain silent as I prepare to start my day. I've got about thirty minutes before my first client arrives.

"Can't be all bad if he did all that for you."

I rub my temples and take a few deep, calming breaths. "He lied to me about his true identity. He literally tricked me into a date. I consider that bad."

Felix narrows his eyes and studies me, clearly not satisfied with my response. Felix isn't going to let this go until I tell him exactly what happened.

"Explain," he says after a few beats of silence.

I drop my face into my hands and sigh. Then I turn around, lean against the cabinet, and tell him exactly how it happened. I don't leave out a single detail from our interaction at Koch's Pit Stop to our date and then follow-up conversations. I even tell him how I've had a crush on Christian since we were in high school.

Felix just stares at me with the same narrow, assessing eyes he always uses when he's searching for the hidden truth behind a story or a person's actions. Felix is the ultimate people watcher. Not much gets past him when it comes to others' motives or intentions.

"Well, say something," I finally say when his stare reaches the point of discomfort.

"Hmm." He pushes to his feet and moves to his workstation next to mine. His inks and supplies are already prepped for his next client, but he fiddles with his gun anyway. I cross my arms over my chest, ready to push him some more when he finally gives me his thoughts. "This guy, Chase, he knows you better than you realize. And he also really likes you."

"Knows me?" I scoff. "If he really knew me, he'd know not to lie. I can't tolerate liars."

Felix nods and gives me a look that suggests he understands and agrees, but then he says, "And he also knew you had a thing for his twin. You would've canceled the date if he told you the truth."

"You don't know that."

Felix raises his brows with a look that says, *the hell I don't.* "Did you have fun on the date?"

His question throws me off. I wasn't expecting such a quick shift in the conversation. I hesitate, not really knowing what to say. So I say nothing.

"I'll take your silence as a yes."

"The fact that I had fun is irrelevant. I thought I had that fun with Christian."

"The fact that you had fun is the only thing that matters." He turns to face me. "Let me ask you this. Do you think he only lied about his name, or did he also try to act like his twin?"

"Why does that matter?"

"It matters a lot, Leens. Was he himself when he was with you, or was he also changing his behavior to match his twin? How far does his deceit run?"

I think about that for a minute. Chase smiled a lot more than I expected, and he was quick with jokes and saying things that made me smile. There were even times when I caught a twinkle in his eye that confused me. I thought I was seeing a different side of Christian that he doesn't show to just anyone. When in reality, I was seeing Chase.

"I think he was being himself." I admit. "He let me believe he was Christian, but he didn't change his behavior. I was with Chase."

Felix steps up to me and takes me by the shoulders, looking me in the eye. "Think about that for a minute. You had a good time on that date. Even said yes to a second date. You like Chase."

I open my mouth to argue, but Felix presses a finger to my lips to stop me from disagreeing. "Don't argue. Think. Use this smart brain in your head to really process how he makes you feel before you push him away completely."

Felix walks away, leaving me alone with my thoughts while I finish setting up for the day.

My head hurts too much for this. I don't want to think about Chase and his lie. I want to go back in time and keep to myself that day at Koch's. If it never happened, then I wouldn't be feeling the way I feel.

Confused. Angry. Needy. Three emotions that are making my head hurt worse.

I try to avoid taking my meds on the days I work because they can make me sleepy, but I can't afford to miss work if this headache gets worse. So I take half a pill in the hopes it will keep the headache at bay.

I just have to get through this day. With any luck, I'll be too busy to think about Chase and the way he makes me feel.

As soon as my eyes land on the bouquet dominating my work-station, I know that's an impossibility. I'll never get him out of my mind with these as a constant reminder.

By the time I make it back to Beaver after my shift, my car smells like a florist shop. I had to strap the bouquet into the passenger seat with the seatbelt just to get it to stay put. Petals tickled my arm the entire drive home.

I pull into a parking spot outside the community center and stare at the monstrosity, debating on taking it inside with me and leaving it on one of the front tables. It'd make for great decoration and the visitors would love it.

But tonight is knitting club. Which means Chase's grand-mother, Mila, will be here. That woman sees and knows everything. If she sees these flowers, she'll know who gave them to me, and she'll question me about him.

Hell, she's going to question me about him at some point regardless, but I don't need to give her more ammunition to use against either of us.

I like Mila, and she's always treated me with respect. But that doesn't mean she wants me to date one of her grandsons. She's a fiercely protective woman. If she doesn't want me dating Chase, she'll interfere.

I let out a deep groan.

"Why do you even care, Lina?" I say to myself. I'm not dating, nor will I ever be dating, Chase Mutter. I don't care what Felix said. Chase lied to me, and I can't forgive him for that.

Opting to leave the flowers in my car, I grab my knitting bag from the back seat and head inside.

Knitting club is a small crowd, though we've grown from our original founding group of four regular attendees to seven or eight. Every now and then, a random guest will come with one of the founders, but not often.

The regulars are Mila, Mrs. Engles, who owns the hair salon in town, Mrs. Hoffman, the principal of the high school, and me. Sometimes Clara Zimmerman comes. Grams dragged her along several years ago to teach her to knit. Clara has been a lifelong friend of the Mutter family and practically grew up as a sibling. She's always been nice to me, unlike some others.

Charlotte Weber and her niece Rayne have started coming regularly now that she's moved back to town. Charlotte went to school with me, but we were never friends back then. She was the homecoming and prom queen that everyone loved while I was the class outcast.

As popular girls go, she was never mean to me. That role was owned solely by Vicki Lynn Baylor. I swear Vicki only took up knitting and started coming to our weekly meetings just to piss me off.

But I like Charlotte. She's a good person, and she fits in with the rest of our misfit group just fine.

I'm a little early tonight since my last client couldn't stay for the entire session, so I'm one of the first to arrive. The only other person in the meeting room is Hannah Fisher, Charlie's wife. She's a few years older than me and has always been kind to me.

"Hey, Hannah, glad you made it this week." She jumps at the sound of my voice and presses her hand to her chest like I terrified her. "Sorry. I didn't mean to startle you."

She shakes her head and waves off my apology like it's fine, but her expression suggests she's anything but fine. "I was just lost in my thoughts. I didn't hear you come in."

I watch her carefully. Her eyes keep darting past me like she expects someone to barge in and grab her. "You okay? You look a little … flustered."

I want to say scared, but I don't want to spook her worse than she already is.

She gives me a forced smile. "I'm fine, really. Like I said, I just didn't hear you come in."

"If you're sure." I give her a comforting smile. It can't be easy for a sweet woman like her to be married to an asshole like Charlie. I never understood what she saw in him. Especially considering she dated Liam Mutter before she started seeing Charlie. Liam is twice the man Charlie could ever be.

"I'm sure." She holds her smile like she's practiced it for weeks but still can't figure out how to make it look real. Then she adjusts in her seat, winces, then presses her hand to her back.

"Hannah, are you in—"

"Do you think you could show me that special cast-on technique again?" She holds up her needles and yarn, which are a tangled mess. "I've been trying to get it right, but I just can't. Maybe if you show me again."

"You mean the Middle East wrap that I use for toe-up socks?"

"Yes, that's the one."

"Sure." I sit down next to her, knowing this is just a distraction, so I'll stop asking her if she's okay. Because she is not okay. Something's wrong, but she doesn't want to talk about it.

My gut tells me it has something to do with her shithead husband. But I don't push her. Instead, I show her how to do the cast-on technique again. By the time we're done and she's knitting the toe of her sock, the rest of the group is here. Unfortunately, that includes Vicki.

Vicki takes the seat opposite us and turns her nose up at me like she's too good to even breathe the same air as me.

"Hey, Lina," Charlotte says before Vicki can toss insults at me. She always does, and she'll find a way to work them in before the night ends. Putting me down seems to make her feel better about herself. Who am I to deprive her of something that makes her so happy? "You'll have a booth at the spring art festival in Chillicothe, right?"

"Yeah, I'll be there selling my work."

"Is it true you're going to offer a class this year for kids?"

I nod. "There will actually be two one-hour classes. One in the morning and one in the afternoon. Why do you ask?"

"Rayne wants to learn to paint. Would this be good for someone her age?"

"It'd be perfect for her. Just let me know, and I'll put her name down."

Charlotte looks over at Rayne and smiles. "You wanna do it?"

"Yes!" Rayne bounces in her chair.

"Consider it done," I smile.

"Just let me know how much it is. Happy to pay whatever the price."

Before I can tell her, Vicki sneers. I glance over at her and roll my eyes. Oh goodie. It's time for the immature part of the evening where Vicki acts like we're still in high school.

Her eyes roam over my clothes. I don't have a lot of nice clothes, and what I do have, I don't wear to work. My everyday attire consists of ripped jeans and old T-shirts. Some of which I've had since high school.

"Something wrong?" I ask.

"What is all over your shirt?" she asks with way too much disdain in her tone.

I look down and see a large ink stain on my gray T-shirt. It's been there for so long, I don't even notice it anymore.

"Ink," I say without elaborating. I think I spilled this on it about a year ago when I was giving myself a tattoo on my left arm. I wasn't paying attention and knocked over the ink when I shifted in my chair.

She scoffs. "You need new clothes. You bring down the overall aesthetics of our group."

The words fuck off are on the tip of my tongue, but I bite them back. I open my mouth to put her in her place using less colorful word choices, but Mila beats me to it.

"You need a new attitude. Your mouth brings down the overall joy of our group."

Vicki's mouth falls open, but Mila gives her the sweetest smile. Someone looking in from the outside would think Mila loves Vicki.

I laugh it off with the rest of the ladies. Vicki just gives everyone a tight smile and pretends we're not all laughing at her.

I may be laughing, but I find this anything but funny. I'm tired of people like Vicki, and I want it to stop. I've done my time. High school is over and I'm ready for the good life.

One of these days, I won't have to deal with people like her or liars or shitty MC presidents or run down trailers or cold water or bills piled so high I can't see the top.

It has to get better. This can't be all there is to my life.

Chapter 12

Persistence is the key to winning, every time

Chase

There's a pep in my step, and I'm whistling like a lovesick fool. I've no real reason to be in such a good mood. In fact, everything in my life has gone to shit.

One of my goats is sick, and I had to call the vet. The chickens ripped one side of the coup apart and four chickens got loose. Probably the work of Princess Fluffybutt. She's a little rascal and is always causing trouble.

The tractor broke down in the middle of seeding the field yesterday. By the time I had it up and running again, it was too late to finish up. Now I need to figure out when to get it done.

By all accounts, I should be frowning. Instead, I can't stop smiling.

Today is our next team meeting for the school bus derby, which means I get to see Lina. Who wouldn't be excited about that?

We still haven't spoken since the last meeting. All my calls and text messages have gone unanswered. But I'm a persistent son of a bitch, determined to win a second chance with her.

But first, I have to swing by the garage to borrow some tools. Clara said the bus currently doesn't run. Apparently, that's part of the challenge. It's not enough to supercharge it for racing. We've got to get it running first too.

Good thing that's what I do best.

The garage is busy when I walk in. Liam is talking to Sophia about a car she's working on. Mac and Ash have their noses buried in a racecar they're building. I offered to help, but they want to do this one on their own. It'll be their first build without me.

I feel a slight pang of jealousy over missing out on the project. I love building cars. But I love farming more. It wasn't easy to step back from the garage, but it had to be done. I needed to do it if I wanted to maintain my sanity—at least during the spring and summer when I've got to plant the fields and get them to survive to harvest.

Christian sees me first. As usual, he's working on a custom motorcycle build. That's about all he does anymore. He's highly sought after and is damn good at what he does. Plus, it's what helped to get and keep him clean.

Once he poured himself into building bikes, it kept his focus on something he loved far more than the high he was always chasing with drugs. Motorcycles saved him where nothing else could.

He meets my gaze, and I grin. He lifts a brow in silent question.

Why are you so damn happy?

I get to see Lina today.

She talking to you yet?

Nope, but I'm about to change that.

My grin widens, and Christian's frown deepens. He sympathizes with me, but he also thinks I've messed things up to the point of no return with Lina. He hasn't said as much, but I see it in his expression.

Maybe I have screwed things up too badly, but I refuse to give up without a fight. Not after the way Lina's lips felt against mine. My body still shudders every time I think about it.

"What are you doing here?" Liam asks once he sees me. "Thought you still had fields to plant."

"Can't today. I've gotta meet Clara and the team to check out the bus for the derby race. Apparently it needs a lot of work to get it running. Came by to borrow some tools."

"Isn't Lina on that team?" Ash asks with a teasing grin. He loves picking on me more than my other brothers. Probably because I'm the one always giving him shit too. You reap what you sow.

I grin, refusing to let anything get me down today. "Yep. It's gonna be a good day."

"Heard she's pissed. Like volcanic eruption level pissed. You might not survive the aftermath if she blows."

Ash is not wrong, but all I can do is smile. Lina's got passion, I'll give her that. All I have to do is figure out how to redirect that passion into loving me instead of hating me.

I pause at that thought and my grin grows wider. We're a long, long way from love, but I'd enjoy that journey if she let me in. Something inside me swells with excitement, and my determination to win her over intensifies.

"Yeah," I say with a sigh. "I'm looking forward to absorbing whatever she throws at me."

Ash gives me a funny look. One that suggests he doesn't recognize the fool standing in front of him. If he's thinking I'm a fool, he's not wrong. I am one hundred percent a fool for Lina. Always have been. I only just now got my chance to let it all out.

"Dude, she's gonna tear you apart," Mac says as he walks up beside me, wiping grease from his hands. "Lina's tough. She doesn't take shit from anyone."

"Her strength is one of my favorite things about her." Against my will, my mind strays to Mom and how weak and pathetic she is. I could never date someone like her. I need a strong, independent woman who knows her self-worth. Lina is exactly that.

Ash cackles. "Well, I'm gonna pop some popcorn and kick my

feet back and enjoy the show. Watching her tear you apart is going to be fun."

"Not as much fun as it's gonna be for me to let her." I slap him on the shoulder and push past him.

All I can do is smile. If I let his words sink in, they'll fester and eat away at my confidence. I need all the confidence I can get if I'm going to pursue Lina with any level of success.

Needing to take the attention off me, I turn to Christian. "You and Garret playing in the next poker match?"

He nods. "Liam is thinking about playing too."

I turn a surprised expression to our oldest brother. He rarely ever plays. In fact, Christian and Garret are the only ones that ever do. "What brought this on?"

Liam shrugs. "Figured it was time to have some fun. I miss playing."

"Well shit." Ash rubs his neck and stares at the ground like he's thinking harder than he's used to doing. "I'll have to change my plans so I can be there. No way I can miss three of you kicking Koch ass at poker."

"What plans you got?" Mac stares at him with a furrowed brow. Ash and Mac spend the most time together since they work so closely on the racecars. I used to be right there beside them before I stepped back. I miss the assholes.

"Um." He scans the room with a nervous gaze. "I've kinda been seeing someone."

"What?!" This comes from Sophia, who has been quietly working since I arrived. Should've known she was listening in on everything we're saying.

She rolls out from under the car she's working on and scowls at Ash. "As in a *girlfriend*?"

Ash lets out a nervous chuckle. "Yeah, a girlfriend. Her name is Andrea."

We all stare at him like he just grew two heads.

He takes a tentative step back like we're going to pounce on him. "Why are you looking at me like that?"

Sophia steps past all of us and right up into Ash's face with her hands on her hips. She's a natural redhead and can be a force of nature. "I thought you were just messing around."

Ash shakes his head. "Nah, I really like her. Met her at a race a few months ago. She lives in Chillicothe."

The garage goes completely silent as we all absorb this information. From everyone's reaction, it's safe to say no one knew about this.

Ash scowls. "What's wrong with you assholes? Is it that shocking that a girl wants to date me?"

Sophia crosses her arms over her chest and glowers. "Does Clara know?"

Something a hell of a lot like fear flashes across Ash's eyes. He shakes his head. "Wanted to make sure it would stick before I brought it up. Seems to be sticking."

"You're an idiot." Sophia punches him in the arm and spins around. She goes back to work, mumbling under her breath. I'm pretty sure I heard her call Ash a few choice names, but I can't be certain.

Ash looks dejected and confused. "I don't get it. Why is everyone looking at me like I've done something wrong?"

Liam steps up to him and squeezes his shoulder. "You're fine, man. We're just surprised, is all. If you like this girl, we're happy for you. Bring her with you to poker night. We'd love to meet her."

Ash nods, still looking forlorn. "Yeah, okay. I think I will. Andrea is a nice girl. I think you'll like her."

"Good." Liam gives him a gentle smile while the rest of us are still staring like he's given us the worst news ever. "Looking forward to it."

Ash ignores us and heads back to the car. Liam looks between the rest of us, giving us a look that says to drop it. He's always the peacemaker and fierce protector of us.

He may have encouraged Ash to bring his new girl around, but I can tell he's thinking the same thing we are. Ash is an idiot and Clara is going to be hurt.

That girl has been in love with Ash since they were kids, and he's completely blind to it. I think the only thing that keeps giving Clara hope is Ash never brings girls around. I don't think either of them has openly dated other people around each other since high school. Almost like it's been some kind of unspoken rule in their friendship.

This has disaster written all over it.

I can only hope Sophia will give Clara fair warning so her heart doesn't shatter when she sees him with another woman for the first time.

By the time I make it to the shop behind the high school, the rest of my team members are already there. They're huddled over a table in the corner looking at designs Lina's come up with for the bus.

Since no one has seen me enter, I take a moment to look around the old building I haven't been inside of in over twelve years. Being a gearhead, I spent as much time in this shop as was allowed back in school. I had no interest in English literature or math or any kind of science. All I ever wanted was to farm my family's land and tinker with cars.

While most of my classmates were applying to colleges and dreaming up a life far away from this small town, I was already living my dream. Graduating from high school was just a formality for me.

If Grams hadn't demanded we all graduate, I'd bet half of us Mutter men would have dropped out. It's not like it would have changed a thing about our lives. I'd still be farming. Liam would still manage the garage. Christian would still make custom motorcycles. And Ash and Mac would still be racing cars.

Warren and Garret are the only ones that have done something different with their lives. Not that Garret needed his high school diploma to be a handyman, but he runs his own business separate from the family.

Warren is the only one that went to college. He went all the way, earning his bachelor's, master's, and PhD degrees in some kind of mechanical and automotive engineering. It's all way too smart for me. All I know is he's some big important racecar designer in North Carolina.

He may have fancy degrees and be smarter than the rest of us, but he's still a gearhead at heart. He loves fast cars just as much as the rest of us.

Clara spots me first and gives me a little wave. I take this as my cue to join the team. So I slip into the space right next to Lina and lean down close to her ear. "Love the eagle. Those claws look deadly."

She jerks back, bumping into Trevor, who's standing on her other side. She glares at me while he chuckles as he steadies her.

"What?" she says. Her eyes narrow. She's trying to look pissed, but that one word comes out breathless. My smile grows.

I point at her sketch for the design. "I said I liked the claws. *Deadly.*"

"Deadly?" She looks confused by my word choice.

"Yeah. It screams don't mess with me. Like it's a challenge that no one can resist."

By a challenge, I mean her. And by no one, I mean me.

From the way her eyes widen, I think she gets what I'm putting down. I give her a wink and turn my focus to the drawing on the table.

"Do you do a lot of street art? Graffiti and such?"

She's silent for a beat and then lets out a deep sigh. "I've participated in some organized events, but not often, no. Graffiti isn't exactly legal. I try not to do things that could land me in jail."

I raise my brow and give her a devilish grin. "I didn't take you for a good girl, Grumps."

She turns to face me directly and crosses her arms over her chest. The action squishes her breasts together and accentuates her cleavage. Lina is very blessed in the boob department and it's hard to keep my eyes trained on her face. Everything inside me is screaming at me to look down.

"Maybe because you don't know me at all. You can't say what kind of girl I am."

"True enough." I waggle my brows, refusing to let my smile waver. "We can change that if you like."

She scoffs. "Not on your life. You lied to me, remember?"

I toss my hands up in apology. "It was a misunderstanding. One I'd really like to make up to you."

She quirks a brow. "Misunderstanding? That's what you're going with?"

"Yes." I step closer to her until her arms brush against my chest. I don't care one bit that Clara and the others are watching us in amusement. I like Lina, and I refuse to give up on her. There's something there with her, and I know she feels it too. "Because it's the truth. My goal is not, and never was, to lie to you. All I want is another date."

"Never gonna happen." Lina is still glaring at me, but she can't hide the slight tick up in her lips. She's not completely turned off by me.

My smile grows so big I feel it hit my eyes. "Don't be so sure, Grumps."

"Oh, I'm sure." She snorts to hide the fact that she was about to laugh. She's caving even though she really doesn't want to. "You're not my type, Pollyanna."

I press my hand to my chest and toss my head back in a laugh. She's clearly trying to piss me off, but it's having the opposite effect. The more she pushes back, the more I want her. "Aw, Grumps. How sweet of you to give me a pet name too. Step one toward relationship zone."

Her frown returns and deepens like I've never seen it before. "There will be no relationship."

I hold my ground and my smile. I give her arm a gentle nudge. The slight touch is enough to send a zing up my arm and straight to my cock. She sucks in a breath, suggesting she felt it too.

"Come on, Grumps. Don't say that. Anything is possible if you open yourself up to it."

She shakes her head. "Not this time there's not."

"We'll see." I wink, and she scowls.

Rather than continue down this path, I turn my attention to the others. "So, where's this heap of junk of a bus? Let's get under that hood and see what we're up against."

Chapter 13

Hands off the goods

Lina

"**G**irl, we should do this more often," Jayla says from the seat next to me.

"More like you should join me more often," I say in response.

Jayla and I are hanging out at Posey's Lounge for the first time in months. Posey's is the only bar near our small town, and it's owned and run by the Unholy Ghosts MC.

I frequent it often, but only because there's nowhere else to go out for a drink, and it's dirt cheap. But I mostly come to get away from home.

There's nothing to do at home except sit with dad and stare at the falling down ceiling. It's not like I can drink a beer or even think about bringing it anywhere near the trailer. Not with Dad's addiction. He's been clean for years now, but I will not be the one to tempt him just because I want a drink.

So I go to Posey's instead, even though I hate the MC that owns it.

Besides, home is depressing. I need an escape from my thoughts and the taunting pile of bills that awaits me there.

Jayla gives me a sad smile. "I know. Sorry. It's hard to make it out with work and Lucy. Both keep me really busy."

I nudge her shoulder, not meaning to make her feel bad. "I was just joking. Didn't mean to make you feel guilty or anything."

She spins on her stool and rests her arm on the bar. "So tell me. What do you typically do when you're here?"

"Honestly," I take a healthy drink of my beer. "You're looking at it."

Her shoulders slump. "Seriously?"

I nod. "Sometimes I play darts or pool, but I typically keep to myself, have a few drinks, and people watch. People watching in this place can be a hoot."

"Oh yeah?" Her face lights up. "Give me an example."

Jayla likes to people watch just as much as me. It's what we always did back in high school at events. While everyone else was participating in the dance or game, Jayla and I were watching and taking notes. We studied behaviors and words and actions. How our fellow classmates treated each other and how we didn't want to be.

It's something that's stuck with me, and I still do it today.

Looking around, I tap my finger to my chin. "Let's see. Well, if it were karaoke night, I'd be internally making fun of everyone who got up on stage. Like Jojo and Steve. Give those two a few drinks and they think they're Sonny and Cher. Neither can carry a tune in a bucket."

Jayla chuckles at the image of two of our former classmates. "When's karaoke night again?"

"That's on Fridays, so last night. Tonight's poker night. Game should be starting soon."

"Ooh, poker. Do you ever play?"

I shake my head. "Can't afford the buy-in. Too rich for my blood."

"But you watch?"

"Of course I watch. Christian always plays. And you know ..."

I lift my drink and take another big gulp. I don't need to remind Jayla of my crush. She knows.

"Any more from Chase?" Her voice is tentative as she asks.

Her question has me downing the rest of my beer and signaling to the bartender to pour me another. I've tried not to think about Chase, but he's made it impossible. Especially after how he acted toward me at the derby meeting.

Every word he spoke had my body coming alive. But nothing lit me up more than his teasing and gentle touches. My body has been tense and needy for days. All because of Chase Always-Fucking-Smiling Mutter.

Jayla nudges my side. When I look in her direction, her smile grows. "That good, huh?"

"He's not going to give up easily. He seems determined to get me to go out with him again."

"You should do it," she says casually like he didn't do anything wrong. I whip my head in her direction, gaping.

"Are you fucking kidding me?" I ask a little too loudly.

She takes a slow, measured drink of her wine. Jayla isn't a fan of beer like me. She typically thinks before she reacts, whereas I fly off the handle before I even allow myself time to process what's happening. We are opposites in a lot of ways, and yet we see the world similarly. It's why we've always been such good friends.

Based on the look on her face, that's about to change. She's going to push me to forgive Chase.

"Lina, you know I love you like you're my blood, but sometimes your stubbornness hurts you."

"Stubbornness? You're messing with me, right? He lied to me. About his identity. I can't forgive him for that."

"Sure you can. You just don't want to." She pins me with a serious stare. "You and I both know that you really like the man who took you out on a date. He had you feeling things you haven't felt in a really long time. That man was Chase. Give him another chance."

I'm shaking my head before she even finishes speaking. "You know I can't. Lying is a deal breaker for me. And this isn't just some simple white lie. He lied about his identity. That's huge. I can't let that kind of behavior into my life."

"Whatever you say." She slips off her stool and pats my back. "I'm going to the restroom. Be back in a minute."

I watch Jayla walk away before I take a moment to scan the bar. It's a little early for the poker crowd. There are a few regulars huddled around tables, but it's mostly just us and a few MC members. I imagine the Kochs and the Mutters will be here soon. A few of them play poker and the rest always come to heckle the players.

"Here you go, doll," Sally, the bartender, says as he slides a fresh draft in front of me. I'm not a huge fan of Bud, but they keep Sam Adams lager on tap. That's much more to my tastes even though it is more expensive.

"Thanks." I nod in Sally's direction. I can't help but smile as he heads to the other end of the bar to pour another drink.

Sally is one of the oldest members of the club, and one of the few from my dad's days as a member that's always been kind to me. He's getting close to seventy, but unlike my dad, he's still as spry as ever. I've no clue what his real name is. Everyone has always called him Sally because of his obsession with the actress Sally Field.

From the jokes I hear tossed around some nights, he makes the younger members watch all of Sally Field's older movies. I don't think they're fans, but they appease Sally because they respect him.

Jayla's bar stool shifts and I turn to face her. Only it's not her taking the seat.

"Edge." I frown at the current MC president. He's nothing like Smoke, but his presence still makes me uneasy.

"Lina." He nods in Sally's direction and within moments a whiskey neat is in his hand. He takes a heavy sip before he turns his steely blue-gray eyes on me. "Did your dad tell you we stopped by?"

My entire body tenses at his words. Not because I'm afraid of Edge—I'm not—it's because I want nothing to do with the MC. I don't care that he's a better president or that he's one of the best-looking men in this area. I don't want their help.

I don't know how old he really is, but he has to be in his early fifties. He's one of those handsome men that just keeps getting better looking with age. His hair is still dark, but his short beard is mostly gray. Add in his large muscular build, tattoos, and firm abs, and he's hard to not stare at. I kinda hate him more for it.

My hand tightens around my mug, and I sit up straight. I refuse to let him intimidate me. "He did."

"And he told you I want to help?"

I let out a frustrated huff. "I refuse to be indebted to the club. I can't accept your help."

Edge lifts his hand in surrender. "The debt is all ours. Your family was unfairly treated by the former president. I want to make it right."

"We're fine." I snap. "There's nothing we need you to do."

He raises his brows, calling my bullshit. "You have no hot water, the ceiling is falling in on you, the carpet is moldy, and you can barely stock food in the kitchen. You're not fine."

I internally growl about the fact that Dad shared our struggles with him. I don't want others to know how bad things are. "I'm handling it."

"How long before the electricity is shut off? You can't keep this up, Lina. And you shouldn't have to. The club takes care of their own. Current and retired."

My eyes snap to his, and there's fury burning deep within. "Since when did the club ever take care of us?"

"Lina." He sighs in exasperation and rubs the bridge of his nose. "I wish I could change how Smoke treated you and your family. I can't change the past, but I can pay the debt owed to you and your family because of those actions."

He picks up his whiskey and downs the rest in one swallow, and then he turns his gaze back to me. It's cold, but non-threatening. "I'm a patient man. I'll give you a little more time to get used to the idea, but mark my words, I will fix this with or without your approval. I can't sit back and let you struggle. You deserve better. Your father deserves better."

He pushes to his feet and leans into the bar. "Sally, her tab is on the house. Whatever she and her friend want. I've got it."

Sally nods and Edge charges off before I can object. And I definitely want to object to it all. My pain and pride refuse to accept anything from the club. Even free drinks.

But the decree has been made, and Sally will not take a penny from me tonight. He'll keep our drinks coming even if we don't order them. No one defies the club president. Not even one as fair and decent as Edge.

The front door opens, and I drag my eyes in that direction. My gaze meets Chase's. It's as if all the air is immediately sucked out of the room. His gaze is heated and hard and full of intention.

I turn back to the bar and down half my beer. I knew he'd be here tonight with his brothers, and I thought I prepared myself for it. But I was wrong.

The effect he has on me is intense. I never understood what others meant when they said they could feel someone's eyes on them. But now I do. I don't need to look at him to know he's watching me. I feel everything. It's like he's burning a hole right through my thick wall of armor with his fierce stare.

I don't know how to process this, and even if I did, I'm not sure I can handle the answers I'd find.

THANKFULLY, CHASE AND HIS BROTHERS HEADED STRAIGHT for the game room after they arrived, and I haven't seen any of them since. As long as it stays that way, I should make it through the rest of this night without seeing him again.

Aside from the brief conversation with Edge, the evening has been fun. The drinks have been plentiful, and Jayla and I have laughed at each other's antics. All in all, it's been a good evening.

The bar has picked up since we arrived. The front door opens, and the Koch brothers crowd the entrance. Without bothering to acknowledge the crowd, they file into the game room. That must mean the poker game starts soon.

That knowledge should relax me. That means Chase will likely be occupied watching the game. But I'm anything but relaxed. My senses are on high alert and the hairs on the back of my neck stand up as if I'm being stalked.

Jayla's smile quickly fades as her eyes narrow in on something behind me. Or should I say someone?

"Well, well, well." Charlie Fisher's low rumbling voice causes goosebumps to prickle across my skin. And not the good kind. "If it isn't my favorite beauty from the past."

"Go away." I grit out, not wanting my decent mood to be squashed by the likes of him.

He sidles up on the opposite side of me from Jayla and leans close so she can't hear him. "Oh, now don't be like that. We both know you want what I've got." He runs his finger down my arm and I swat him away.

"Don't touch me."

His smile grows, and it sickens me how relaxed and easy it is. He looks like he's settling in to have a good time with an old friend. He and I are not friends.

"Why don't you and me sneak out the back door? I've got my truck. We can finish what we started all those years ago. You owe me, sweetheart."

"Not a chance in hell, and I don't owe you anything, except maybe a punch in the junk."

His easy grin turns into a playful chuckle. It's as if he's completely unaffected by my words.

"Come on, Lina. We could have fun together."

My gaze narrows and my nostrils flare. This man has some nerve talking to me like that. Charlie Fisher may have most of this county fooled, but I see right through him. He showed me his true colors all those years ago.

He is not the decent, God-fearing man he leads this county to believe. He's the devil in an expensive suit and nothing more.

"And what would your *wife* say if she found out you had *fun* with another woman?"

His smile fades, but only slightly. It's the shift in his eyes that has me scooting back in my seat, fighting for distance. There's a threat hidden behind his smile, and I don't like that it's directed at me.

"This isn't about Hannah. Besides, what she doesn't know won't hurt her. A man in my position needs to have his fun and blow off steam." His eyes rake down my body, and I suddenly feel naked in my tight T-shirt and ripped jeans. "And I'd really like to blow off that steam with you."

"Ew, gross." I wrinkle my nose in disgust. "Go away before I pay you back for what you did to me."

He holds my gaze and leans in closer. "Can't pay me back when nothing happened."

"Is that how you keep your pretty wife in check? Tell her all kinds of lies and hope she believes you? Or do you hit her too?"

His jovial expression turns hard and dangerous. His lips turn up on one side in a snarl and his nostrils flare. "Watch it, Lina."

"No, you watch it." I poke him in the chest, effectively pushing him back. I breathe a little easier at the distance it puts between us. "Need I remind you of how you hit me? You gave me a black eye because I refused to fuck you. That ain't nothing, Mr. Mayor."

"What was that?" Chase's deep, gravelly voice booms from behind us. When I turn around, there's fire in his eyes and his jaw is tight.

Charlie's smile returns. He looks at Chase as if he thinks Chase is being funny rather than about to rip him in half. "Hey, Chase. Been a while since I've seen you around. Where've you been hiding?"

Chase takes a step toward Charlie and gets right up in his face. "What did you say to her?"

Charlie tosses his hands up in surrender. "Nothing that concerns you. This is between Lina and me."

"If I find out you laid a hand on her, I will personally make sure your hands never work again. Is that clear?"

"Are you threatening a public official?" Charlie chuckles. If Chase's threat makes him nervous, he's not showing it.

"Yes." Chase barks out through gritted teeth. "You stay away from her."

"Good luck trying to stop me." Charlie's grin turns sinister. "Why don't you ask that older brother of yours how well that worked out for him and Hannah? Last time I checked, she's *my* wife."

With that, Charlie turns around and heads back toward the entrance. He's gone before I even have a chance to catch my breath.

When I turn back to Chase, his eyes are studying me, but they're softer now.

"You dated Charlie in school." It's not a question, but rather a statement of understanding. But he's got it all wrong.

"No. He asked me out. Didn't like it much when I rejected him."

Chase steps closer to me. He lifts his hands as if he's going to cup my face, but he stops himself. Instead, he clenches them into fists and presses them into his sides. "What did he do to you?"

"Nothing." My shoulders sag. This isn't something I want to get into with him.

"I don't believe you. He hurt you." Again, it's not a question.

"No, Chase. He didn't hurt me. Now leave it be."

He studies me. His eyes roam over my features. First my eyes, then nose, mouth, and back again. He gives me a slight shake of his head before he says, "I still don't believe you. And I can't leave you be. You may be pissed at me, but that doesn't change the fact that I care. Tell me what he did. Please."

I drop my head back and groan at the way he tossed *please* at the end of his little tirade like that's somehow going to soften me up. It doesn't work.

"It's none of your business," I whisper.

He crowds my space, leaning in close, same as Charlie did. Only the effect on me is very different. My heart rate speeds up, and my breath catches in my throat. I feel his closeness all the way to my bones and it has me trembling with the need to feel more of him.

"Lina," he says my name like it's a promise. "Let me make it my business."

I hear Jayla let out an adoring sigh. She would find this interaction swoonworthy. I take a cleansing breath and force my face into a neutral expression. Then I gather up all the strange emotions swirling around inside me, stuff them in a box, lock it, and bury it deep in the recesses of my mind.

I hold his gaze and say the only thing I know to keep me sane. "I can't."

Chapter 14

It's just a friendly game of pool

Chase

The look in her eyes causes me physical pain. Not because of her own pain that I see hiding behind her deep blue gaze, but because of the need she's trying so hard to fight. Lina wants me, but she doesn't *want* to want me.

All because I did something I never should have done. I added to her pain rather than easing it. Pain—no doubt—that Charlie Fisher added to as well. The last person I ever want to be lumped in with is that asshole.

He walks around this town acting like he's everyone's savior. Like he's going to make everyone's problems go away and make Beaver a better place to live. He may have fooled most in this town, but he's not fooling me or anyone in my family.

We all saw his true colors when he betrayed Liam and stole Hannah from him. For years, Liam and Charlie had been best friends. They were just as inseparable as the rest of us. We brought him into our fold and treated him like a brother.

I'm not sure how it all went down. But one day Hannah was Liam's girl, and the next, she was dating Charlie. Liam and Charlie have hated each other ever since.

I look past Lina to see Jayla is fighting back a grin. It causes my own lips to tug up. Does this mean Jayla is on my side and encouraging Lina to give me another shot? Fuck, I hope so.

Without a word, Lina hops off her stool and pushes past me. I take her hand in mine and tug her back. "Not so fast, Grumps. We're not done here."

"Oh yes we are." She pulls at her hand, but I lace our fingers together and squeeze. Her eyes slide shut, and she takes in a shuttered breath. I fight back my smile.

I want to pull her body flush against mine and kiss her senseless, but as long as she's fighting against me, that would be a terrible idea. Instead, I come up with a brilliant plan.

"Come on." I turn to Jayla and grin. "You too. I think it's past time we all have some fun."

Jayla hops off her bar stool and grabs both of their drinks. Then she looks at me and smiles. "Lead the way."

"What? No!" Lina objects, but we both ignore her. With my hand still linked with hers, I lead them both to the game room and toward one of the empty pool tables in the corner.

I love playing pool and so does Lina. I've watched her play many times, and she's a damn good player. But so am I. I'd go so far as to say we're evenly matched.

I also know that Lina loves a challenge, especially one she thinks she can win.

Tonight, we're going to find out just how good she really is.

"What are you doing?" She tugs at her hand again, and this time I let her go. Now that we're next to the pool table, she's less likely to run. Plus, I see the curious look behind her wary gaze. Whether she likes it or not, I've got her attention.

I grab two cue sticks from the rack and turn to face her. I give her a huge grin. "Challenging you to a game of pool."

Her eyes narrow. "I'm not playing pool with you."

I step closer to her and hand her a stick. "Why not? Afraid I'll beat you, Grumps?"

"Stop calling me Grumps." She growls. "And no. You can't beat me."

I chuckle and shove the stick at her. This time she takes it. "Then prove it."

"I don't have to prove anything to you."

"No, you don't." I dare another step toward her. Our chests are almost touching. Instead of backing away, she straightens her back and holds her ground. Her determination and strength make my smile grow. "But you want to."

She lets out a low huff. "Do you ever stop smiling?"

I shrug. "Sometimes, but not often. Do you have a thing against smiles?"

"Yeah, I do. They're suspicious and fake."

"Ouch." I press a hand to my chest and toss my head back. "You wound me, Grumps."

"You annoy me, *Pollyanna*." Her retort has me laughing.

"Pollyanna?" a deep, playful voice calls out from behind us. I turn around to find my brothers in a line, watching us in amusement. At least the ones that are already here.

"She calls you Pollyanna?" This comes from Mac. He's got his arm around Sophia's shoulder and is grinning like he just won first place in a race. "That's awesome."

Sophia playfully slaps him on the chest. "Leave them be. Can't you see they're having a moment?"

Mac shrugs. "Then they should take it somewhere private if they don't want us interrupting."

Sophia rolls her eyes and I wave off her concern as I glance at my brothers. They all look amused, even Christian and Garret. Liam is also here, but I haven't seen Ash yet. He must be running late.

"It's fine," I say as I meet each of their gazes. "Shouldn't some of you be playing poker?"

Liam, Garret, and Christian all shrug.

"Paused the game," Garret says. "This looks a hell of a lot more interesting at the moment."

I flip him off, and he laughs. It makes me smile in return. It's good to see Garret happy. "I've just challenged Lina to a game of pool, but she's refusing to accept. Thinks she can't beat me."

"I never said that." She scoffs. "I *know* I can beat you. I just don't want to play with a liar."

"Ooo, burn." Mac chuckles.

Christian nudges him in the side and grumbles, "Leave 'em alone."

Then Christian looks at me, and in a matter of seconds, we hold a silent conversation.

"Are you sure you know what you're doing?" he asks.

"Not a clue, but I've gotta try something."

"Why her?" He nods his head in her direction.

I shrug. "It's always been her. Can't say why. It just is. Gotta find out what's there."

"Just be careful. She has the power to hurt you."

"Yeah, yeah. I know."

"What are you playing for?" Mac asks, choosing to ignore my twin.

"We're not playing," Lina says at the same time I say, "We haven't established that yet."

She turns to face me, her eyes hard and determined. Heat builds in my chest and a wave of desire rushes through my body. *Please tell me she feels this too.*

"I'm not playing with you," she says, but her voice wavers as if she's not as confident in her answer as she was a few minutes ago.

"Scared?" I waggle my brows.

"No." She scoffs.

I lean down close to her ear and relish the way she sucks in a breath at how close my lips are to her skin. "Then *play* with me."

I don't wait for her to answer. Instead, I walk to the opposite end of the table and rack the balls. Before I finish, Clara comes rushing in and takes a seat next to Jayla.

"What did I miss?" she asks, her eyes filled with amusement.

"Chase challenged Lina to a game of pool, but she keeps refusing to play," Jayla answers her. "Lina's still in denial. She's afraid that if she plays, Chase will break through her protective walls."

"Jayla!" Lina shouts. Her friend ignores her.

"Aw," Clara nods. "Still hanging on to her anger?"

"Yeah, she's stubborn like that." Jayla waves a hand in the air and rolls her eyes.

Lina places her hands on her hips and glares at Jayla. "You know, I'm right here."

Jayla tosses her a teasing smile. "Yep. And I intended for you to hear every word. Give the guy a chance."

"No," she says so quickly it makes me wince.

"He's right." Jayla chuckles. "Grumps is the perfect nickname for you."

"Don't you start too." Lina glares at her friend.

"Are we going to play or what?" I interrupt their exchange. I lift my grin to the grumpiest of grumpy faces I've ever seen. It makes my smile grow.

She narrows her eyes and shakes her head. "Prepare to have your ass handed to you, Pollyanna."

I lift the rack off the balls and wink. "I'm looking forward to it."

She rolls her eyes and heads to the table to get her drink. Then she casually leans against the table and rests one hand on the edge while lifting her beer to mouth.

She's purposely moving slowly and never once breaks eye contact with me. When her mug reaches her lips, she licks the rim before taking a slow, seductive drink. I watch her every move with rapt attention.

My body heats and I shift on my feet, subtly attempting to

adjust myself without drawing attention to my growing problem south of my waist.

Unfortunately, she notices.

The smile that spreads across her face cuts off all blood flow to my brain, and I can't think. Hell, I can't even breathe.

"Problem?" she teases, and fuck me, I like it.

I shake my head and speak at the same time. "Nope, I'm just fine."

She chuckles, and damn, her laugh is better than her smile. They both do things to me I've never felt before. If she refuses to give me another chance, I'm screwed. All I want is her—grumpy, smiling, or laughing. I'll take it all.

Our eyes lock, and something shifts in her gaze. It's still playful, but I see the same heat that's coursing through my veins looking back at me.

She clears her throat and hides her face behind her mug. "I'll let you go first. Something tells me you need a head start."

Now it's my turn to give her a teasing smile. "Not until we establish the rules of the challenge."

She stiffens, all humor vanishes from her expression, and I'm graced with a glare. "Rules? You're pushing your luck, Pollyanna."

Making my way around the pool table, I stop when I'm right next to her. I mimic her lean against the edge, and then I drop my voice to a whisper. "I didn't challenge you for fun. I want answers, Grumps."

Her eyes widen. "Answers to what?"

I lean down close until I'm eye level with her. "I want to know more about you."

"Like what?"

"Well, for starters, I want to know why Charlie Fisher threatened you."

A gasp sounds beside us, dragging our attention to the small table next to us. Clara is staring at Lina with wide eyes. "Charlie threatened you?"

She says this loud enough that it draws the attention of my brothers, and the next thing I know, we're surrounded by an angry wall of testosterone.

"Fuck," Lina whispers as she covers her face.

I'd been so wrapped up in our exchange that I forgot we weren't alone. I wince and squeeze my eyes closed, knowing I need to make this right and get my brothers to back down.

"Back off, bros," I say, meeting each of their angry glares. We all despise Charlie and will do whatever it takes to protect those we care about from assholes like him. "Who doesn't Charlie threaten? No need to get all worked up. I've got this covered."

One by one, my brothers nod and back off. When I turn back to Lina, she lifts her eyes to me in a questioning look. "You do?"

All I see is surprise within her blue depths. No anger or frustration. Just genuine surprise mixed with a healthy dose of curiosity. It puts my smile back on my face. I lean down close so only she can hear me. "You bet your hot ass I do."

She sucks in a breath, and I relish how good it makes me feel that I have this effect on her. She turns her face toward me, so her lips are close to my cheek. Now I'm the one who can't breathe.

"And how exactly do you have it covered?" she whispers.

"You're going to tell me everything. Once I know the story, I'll devise a plan to deal with Charlie. Either way, he'll never threaten you again."

She pulls her head back, so our eyes meet. "And why will I tell you everything? You're not exactly my favorite person."

This woman. She has me all tied up in knots. She has no idea how much her feistiness turns me on. "Because we're playing for answers, and I'm gonna kick your ass at pool."

She snorts. "Doubtful. But I'm looking forward to watching you try." Then she pushes against my chest, putting distance between us. I immediately miss her heat. "Break the rack, Pollyanna."

My grin grows as I slowly back away and head to the front of the pool table to kick off our game. Just as I lean over to position my stick in front of the cue ball, Ash rounds the corner and enters the game room with a pretty brunette next to him. They're close, with their hands linked. My eyes immediately dart to Clara.

The hurt that takes over her expression has me cringing. Ash is such an idiot.

Before anyone can say anything or even acknowledge that Ash is here, Clara pushes to her feet. "I've gotta go. I forgot my mom asked me to help her with something."

She pushes past Lina and is almost to the doorway when Ash grabs her arm. "Don't go. I want to introduce you to my girlfriend."

Clara forces a smile and looks at the woman beside him. "Sorry. Please forgive me, but I have to leave. Maybe next time."

Clara pulls her arm free and disappears into the main room of the bar before Ash can stop her. He turns to us with a confused look on his face. "Is she okay?"

Sophia shakes her head. "Ash, you are truly a blind dumbass."

Then she takes off after Clara.

"What did I do?" he asks, looking even more confused than he did a moment ago. "What just happened?"

"Nothing, man. Nothing." Liam rubs his hands over his face to stifle a groan. Then he smiles and walks toward them with his hand held out. "It's Andrea, right?"

"Yes." She smiles and takes his offered hand. "It's so nice to finally meet you all. Ash has told me so much about his family. I feel like I know you already."

Ash makes the rounds, introducing Andrea to everyone. We all welcome her, despite the impact her presence had on Clara. It's not Andrea's fault Ash is an idiot.

Lina steps up next to me and leans in close. "Is this a Mutter thing?" she asks.

I raise my brows, not following her train of thought. "Is what a Mutter thing?"

"That you're all dumbasses? Anyone with eyes can see that Clara has a thing for him. He has to know that."

I sigh. "Sadly, he doesn't. And no, it's not a Mutter thing. It's a man thing. We're all dumbasses."

"Clearly." She shakes her head and then shoves my cue stick at me. "Come on, Pollyanna. Let's get this game started so I can kick your ass."

I press my hand to my chest and scoff. "You wound me."

She rolls her eyes. "I did no such thing. Now break 'em."

Lina moves to the opposite end of the table while I lean over to position myself for the break. Instead of watching the ball, I lock my eyes with hers. She's trying to hide it, but there's a hint of humor dancing behind that stare. She's enjoying herself and that pleases me immensely.

I take my shot. The cue ball hits the rack with a loud crack and the balls spread out around the table. Three go into various pockets —two stripes and a solid.

"Looks like it's stripes for me." I grin as I take my next shot. I make the next two shots before I miss.

Lina steps up to the table, calling out her first shot with barely a glance at the position of the balls. Before that shot even hits the pocket, she's calling out her next shot like a practiced pro. She does this over and over again until all her balls are in the pockets.

She turns to me and grins. "Eight ball, corner pocket."

She points her stick in the motion she intends to send the ball and then leans over in front of me, pointing her ass right at my crotch. She gives it a seductive shake, causing me to groan. A deep, throaty laugh escapes her right as her stick hits the cue ball. The cue ball ricochets off the side rail and hits the eight ball with a loud clunk. Seconds later, the eight ball sinks in the corner pocket.

Lina turns to me with a wide, victorious grin on her face. She's never looked more beautiful. Then she shoves her stick at my chest, forcing me to grab it. "Sorry, Pollyanna. No answers for you today."

She spins on her heels and heads out of the game room without a glance back. I hear my brothers hooting and hollering, but I don't pay them any attention.

I can't take my eyes off the direction Lina vanished. She may have left, and I may have lost. But tonight was progress.

I'm one step closer to getting that second chance. I feel it deep in my bones.

Chapter 15

Wearing me down

Lina

"Oh, honey, how about this one?" A woman who looks to be in her early forties smiles up at the man next to her whom I assume is her husband. She beams as his smile grows to match hers.

"I like that one. It'd look great over the dining room table." He motions with his hands as if to frame a location on a wall. "You know the spot I'm talking about?"

"I do." She turns back to the painting they're admiring. A look of confirmation covers her expression. "And the colors are just perfect. Can we get this one and the smaller set over there?"

She points to a set of three small square paintings of abstract wildflowers in a meadow. It's a set I painted in soft watercolors last spring just as the wildflowers bloomed in the field next to the trailer.

It's not always easy, but I try like hell to capture beauty even in the ugly. There's nothing beautiful about my home. Most people would never even look past the rundown, broken trailer to see the speckled field of pinks, purples, blues, and yellows.

But I do. In fact, most of my paintings are of the nature

surrounding my troubled home—the field of wildflowers, the sparkling lake, the seasonal shift in the trees, or the ever-changing sky. I paint it all, and it wipes my mind of the reality of my life.

"We'll take these," the man says as he hands me the larger painting while his wife collects the set of three. "I take it you're the artist?"

I meet his gaze, and all I see is admiration and respect. It's a look I wish I got everywhere and not just when I sell my work at a street festival like this one.

If there's one thing I'm confident about, it's my artistic ability. Dad always said I was born with a paintbrush in my hand. Painting and sketching are something I've done since my earliest memories.

Despite my natural talent, I would have loved to have gone to college for fine arts. I had my eye on the Columbus School of Art and Design throughout high school, but even with financial aid, I couldn't make it work. The private school tuition was just too steep.

So I had to settle with whatever education I could get from my high school art teacher, which means I'm mostly self-taught.

I'm sure a trained professional could see the flaws in my work, but art enthusiasts like those who frequent these summer art festivals don't seem to notice. If they do, they don't care.

Even if they did, it wouldn't stop me from painting. I love it too much. It always brings me calm, even when my life is nothing but chaos.

"I am." I smile as I take the painting from the man and set it on the table behind me.

"Your work is amazing and unique. Each one evokes an emotion. It's all really beautiful."

"Thank you." I have to force a smile. This is the part of selling my work at events that I struggle with. I don't take compliments well.

To hide my discomfort, I focus on wrapping up the first painting. If I keep busy, hopefully they won't notice. Thankfully, they keep the small talk to a minimum as we finish up the transaction. It's been a good day so far, but this sale turns it into a great day.

I mostly sell the smaller pieces at these events, especially in smaller cities like Chillicothe. They're cheaper and easier for people to carry out. Selling a large piece like this is rare, but when it happens, it makes my entire summer. I can rest assured that Dad will have all the medication he needs for the next few months and plenty of groceries stocked in the kitchen. If I'm lucky, there will be enough left over to fix the damn water heater.

"Sorry, we're late." Jayla says as she and Lucy make their way around the makeshift counter. "I had to park four blocks away."

"You're fine." I feel my smile turn more genuine now that they're here to provide a distraction. "I still have plenty of time to set up."

Jayla usually takes care of the customers while I restock or organize the shelves as we sell items. But for this event, I agreed to do two art classes for the kids. She'll run the booth for me while I teach a bunch of kids to love art as much as I do.

"Where are you setting up?" she asks.

I point to a row of tables underneath a pavilion not far from my booth. "Just over there. I won't be far if you need anything. And I can always send Lucy over to help too."

I look at Lucy, who's wearing a huge smile. She loves these events and can spend hours walking through all the booths.

"You ready to go paint?" I ask her.

"Yes!" She bounces on her feet. "Are we painting the sunset and trees?"

"Yep. That's the one you liked the best, and I think it will be an easy one to teach."

A light breeze passes over us, and I close my eyes, breathing in the fresh air. May is coming to a close, and while it's not too hot, the sky is clear, and the sun is bright. It's a beautiful day, but I'm glad the event coordinator could secure a covered area for the classes. It will make it more comfortable for everyone.

"You guys go have fun." Jayla surveys the area before she turns her smile to me. "I'm sure I'll be fine. I've helped you enough at these things that I can almost pretend to be you."

I snort. "You'll have to work on your frown more to pass as me."

"Or ..." She nudges my arm. "You could work on your smile and be less grumpy."

"Never gonna happen," I say in a low, grumbly voice. I give her a wave before I pick up the tote full of art supplies. "I'm heading over. Come on, Luce. Let's go have some fun."

We make it to the pavilion at the same time as Sharon, the event coordinator. She's setting out paperwork and a case of water bottles at the end of one of the tables.

"Hey, Lina. We've got a full house for you. Every slot is filled in both classes," she says with a huge grin.

I can't hide my smile at this news. I wasn't sure what to expect from a class like this, especially at twenty dollars a pop. That's not a lot for a one-hour class that includes all the supplies, but I can never tell with these small-town people. It's not like any of us are swimming in cash.

"That's great, especially for the first year."

"I have a feeling the community is going to ask for more of these. I had to turn people away."

"Really?" I look at her with wide eyes. "And here I thought we'd struggle to fill half the class."

"You underestimate how well known your skill is, Lina. You're a local artist. Everyone who loves art, and even a lot that don't, know who you are. Parents jumped at the chance for you to teach their kids."

My frown deepens. I'd never thought about whether people knew who I was. I've been doing these street fairs for years. Some of my artwork is even hanging in local businesses. But to know me by name? That's mind boggling to me. I'm nobody.

"Aunt Lina, can I set up the stations?" Lucy asks, dragging me back to reality.

"Aunt?" Sharon asks. "I didn't know you had a niece."

"Well, not by blood. This is Lucy. She's my best friend's daughter."

Sharon turns her smile to Lucy. "Are you an artist the same as your aunt?"

"Yep. I wanna grow up and be just like Aunt Lina."

Her words send a chill through me. I'm glad she loves art, but the last thing I want for anyone is for them to grow up and be just like me.

"Well, Lina is a great role model. You couldn't have picked a better person to want to be like."

I visibly cringe at Sharon's words. She notices and laughs it off. "Looks like we're making your aunt uncomfortable with all this praise."

Lucy rolls her eyes. "She's always like that."

Before either of them can say anything else, a voice calls out over a walkie talkie on the table. Sharon lets out an audible sigh. "That's my cue to leave. Grab one of the staffers to hunt me down if you need anything."

"I'm sure I'll be fine."

Sharon takes off to deal with whatever emergency she was called to away for, while Lucy and I set up the table.

I've done a lot of prep work to save time. The watercolor paper is already taped to a board, and I made up small palettes of paint with each color they're going to use. All we really have to do is set everything out and wait.

I take one of the water bottles and fill each rinse cup half full. Just as I finish placing the paint brushes out, the hairs on the back of my neck stand on end.

I know that feeling, and it's one that's created way too much internal conflict inside me over the past few weeks. I don't have to look to know the reason for the sudden shift in my body's reaction, but I do it anyway.

Glancing over my shoulder, I find Chase Mutter standing right behind me and he's not alone. He has Rayne, Garret's ten-year-old daughter, with him.

Our eyes lock. His deep brown gaze instantly lights up with little flickering flames that send a rush of heat through my veins. I hate the effect he has on me.

I swallow hard and quickly turn my gaze to Rayne. "You painting with me today?"

She nods with a huge smile. "I've never done this before."

Her enthusiasm and honesty drag a smile out of me. "Well, let's see if I can turn you into an artist in one hour."

Rayne rushes to take a seat at the front of the table right next to where I'll be working. Which means Chase will be standing close behind the entire time.

Lucy takes the seat next to her, and they fall into an easy conversation. Lucy's a couple of years younger than Rayne, but they seem to get along just fine. Something about that pleases me far more than it should.

"You look good," Chase says from next to me. His voice is low and gravelly.

I chance a glance up at him and immediately regret it. He looks so handsome with that goofy smile that I didn't know I liked until him. He hasn't shaved in a few days and has the start of a short beard growing. It's a different look for him.

"I like the scruff," I say without meaning to. I immediately cover my mouth with my hand.

Of course, he gives me a cocky grin. "Glad to hear it. Should I keep it?"

I shrug, trying to play it off like it's an innocent topic of conversation. "Your call. Makes no difference to me."

He leans close to my ear, so close that his lips brush against the lobe. "But your opinion makes a difference, Grumps. It makes *all* the difference in the world."

The next thing I know, his hand is on my lower back in the lightest of touches. Then his lips press a gentle kiss to my neck, just below my ear. My heart stops and I can't breathe. Flames lick my skin and I feel like I'm about to combust from this one simple touch.

I am in so much trouble, and from the way he chuckles, he knows he's got me.

"This isn't over, Grumps." He reminds me again. Then he steps back and leans against the pole behind us as if he's completely unaffected by what he just did. But I don't miss the way he discreetly adjusts himself to hide what's growing between his legs.

I turn back to the table and scrub my hands down my face. Taking a few deep, cleansing breaths, I push all thoughts of Chase out of my mind. I've got a class to teach and a table full of kids.

In the short time he distracted me, most of the students who signed up arrived.

One hour. I can survive one hour with him behind me, watching me with those heated, sexy eyes.

Lies, all lies.

With him near, my heart can't seem to slow the fuck down. With every grin and small act of affection, this man is wearing me down.

I squeeze my eyes closed and press the palm of my hands into my eye sockets. I'm tired, hungry, and running late. The last thing I need is a headache on top of all my other problems.

It's been a few weeks since one of my debilitating migraines hit me, and this feels like the early onset of exactly that.

Poor eating habits aside, this always happens to me when I overextend myself. My days have been nonstop ever since the street fair last week. Preparing for those always wears me out. If I can't take a couple days off work after one, it feels like I can't ever catch up.

Digging the bottle of Tylenol out of the cabinet, I take two, hoping it will be enough to stave it off. I'm getting low on my prescription meds and can't afford to buy more.

"You feeling alright?" Dad drawls as he walks into the kitchen. The look on his face is one of concern, yet I see a hint of relief hidden behind his knowing blue gaze.

"Just the start of a headache. Not bad. Hopefully, I can keep it at bay." I kiss his cheek before I grab him a mug and pour him some coffee. "You're looking good this morning. The new meds working out?"

"I feel good. I don't know how you managed it, but thanks, doll. I can't remember the last time I felt this good."

Despite the pain in my head, I give him a broad smile. "I'm so glad to hear that. The doctor said it should help a lot with your energy."

"He ain't wrong. I feel good enough to get out of this house. Maybe go on a walk."

My smile slips. "Don't overdo it too soon. It's only been a week since you started this medication."

Dad chuckles and pulls me in for a hug. I wrap my arms around his waist and let myself lean into his embrace. We don't hug often, but when we do, it always makes me feel better.

"Don't you worry. I'll go easy. Promise." He kisses the top of my head and releases me. "I'm feeling good. Let me enjoy this while it lasts. You take care of that headache of yours."

I fight the urge to roll my eyes. "It'll be fine, Dad. Promise."

He eyes me for a moment like he doesn't quite believe me, but then he says, "Well, then. I guess we're both just gonna have to trust the other's promise, aren't we?"

"Yeah, I guess so."

Dad gets started on making himself something to eat while I go through the status of this month's bills. I used most of the money I made from the street fair to get dad these new meds and made a hefty payment on the electric bill. Unfortunately, that didn't leave enough to fix the water heater, but one good night of tips at the parlor and I should be able to swing the fees.

We really couldn't afford this new medication, but Dad's doctor has been recommending it for a while. It's new, which means there isn't a generic on the market yet and our insurance doesn't cover it. I had to pay for it in full.

But seeing how good Dad looks makes it all worth it. I can live with cold showers if he keeps getting better.

I just hope my payment to the electric company is enough to hold them off for another month. With any luck, I'll also be able to swing the repairs to my car this month too.

"You got the day off?" Dad asks as he whisks a couple of eggs in a bowl.

"No." I sigh. "I've got a meeting for that school bus derby I told you about. We're going to work on the design today. Then I work the late shift at the parlor."

The Saturday night shift is always iffy. I don't get too many of my regulars coming in or scheduling appointments that late in the day. My chair is typically filled with first timers or drunks who lost a bet at the bar.

Sometimes tips are good, and sometimes they're just shit. It's not my favorite shift to work. Thankfully, Rob only asks me to work one Saturday night a month. He usually saves the crap shifts for the newbies.

"You sure you're up for that?" Dad eyes me over the rim of his mug.

I pat his chest and give him a kiss on the cheek. "Yeah, I'll be fine. Better get going before I'm late."

Before Dad can question me further, I grab some snacks and my water bottle before I rush back to my room to finish getting ready. Dad knows me too well, and he can spot all the signs of a bad migraine coming on.

Unfortunately, I don't have time to get sick. I've got obligations and work and bills coming out of my ears. I'll do what I always do and work through it and hope it doesn't get worse.

As soon as I step outside into the bright sunny day, my head sings a different tune. There isn't a cloud in sight, and the light from the sun immediately causes my head to pound.

I dig my sunglasses out of my purse and slip them on. They help, but not enough.

Thankfully, my car starts without issue. Good thing, considering I'm already late for today's meeting. It's scheduled to be a long one, starting this morning and lasting through early afternoon.

Today is all about teaching Trevor and Clara how to spray paint art. They're both eager to learn, which normally would make me insanely happy, but today I just want to crawl back into bed and call it quits.

I could call in sick. We've got plenty of time for the decoration portion of this project. I'm sure getting the bus running will take most of our summer. But I hate to bail on obligations.

Fifteen minutes later, I park my car next to Chase's truck in the back parking lot of the school. I check the time and breathe a sigh of relief when I see I'm only five minutes late. That's way better than I thought it would be.

Trevor and Clara are sitting at a picnic table next to the rundown bus that looks like it should have been dumped for scraps at least twenty years ago. Chase and Karla have their heads under the hood, already hard at work.

Seeing the others waiting for me sends a pang of guilt through me for being late.

I grab my supplies from my trunk and make my way to my waiting team. "Sorry I'm late."

Clara waves me off with a smile. "You're fine. I just got here myself."

I shift my gaze to Chase. Clara must see the confusion on my face because she adds, "Oh, don't pay any attention to his state of filth. He got here early. Been at it at least an hour already."

Chase straightens and turns to face us. He gives me a soft smile that has my belly twisting up in knots. I haven't seen him since the street fair, and as much as I hate to admit it, I've missed him.

It also doesn't help that he looks damn good standing there covered in grease. He's wearing an old T-shirt that I'm guessing used to be white, but now it's covered in stains with holes ripped throughout. Some holes are so big I can see the hard ripples of his chest and abs beneath. It makes me wonder why he even bothered to put it on.

His jeans are also stained and full of holes. They hang low on his hips, revealing a hint of his black boxer briefs.

His forearms have smears of grease covering them in long streaks and swirls. I suddenly have a strong urge to cover his arms in tattoos. He hasn't said as much, but something tells me he's ink free. I'd really love to change that and be the first to turn his skin into art.

When I shift my gaze back to his, he's frowning. It's such an unusual look for him that it has me taking a step back.

"What's wrong with you?" I ask.

He shakes his head and softens his expression. "I was just about to ask you the same thing. You're pale."

I wave him off. "I'm fine. Just late, and I hate running late."

"You're not late," Clara says as she jumps up from the table. "Here, let me help you with those."

She takes the box from my arms, leaving me with two bags hanging on my shoulder. We take them to the table, and I organize the supplies.

I make the mistake of glancing over at Chase to find he's still watching me. His knowing gaze suggests he doesn't believe my excuse. Somehow, he can see right through me and all my bullshit.

If I want to hide my pain from him, I seriously have to work on my game face.

Then again, maybe it's not so bad that he sees me. *The real me.* I've never truly let a man into my life. When I thought he was Christian, I was more than ready to do just that. His lie sent me running.

But his persistence and constant attempts at making up for his mistake have the armored walls erected around my heart cracking.

Chapter 16

I call bullshit

Chase

The hot June sun beats down on me, and I'd do just about anything for a breeze to kick in and cool this sweat off my back. The air is unusually stagnant today, making it feel warmer than it really is.

I wipe my brow with the back of my hand, most likely adding another streak of grease to my face. I've done that so many times this morning, I doubt I can even see the color of my skin anymore.

Karla and I got an early start, so we'd have time to run out for supplies if needed. After a thorough investigation, I determined the engine was fine. It really just needs a good tune up. Once we replace the spark plugs and give this old lady some new oil, we'll be ready to see if she starts.

Once the sweat is cleared from my eyes, I tighten another bolt. I glance over at Karla and smile. "I think that's almost it for now. You got those?"

She nods and tightens her grip on the wrench. "Yep. I got it. I can finish these up if you want to clean up for lunch."

I grab the industrial hand soap from my toolbox and head to the side of the building where the water hose is located. Working under the hood of cars is a dirty job, and this bus definitely made me dirty. Every inch of exposed skin is covered in grease and grime.

After stripping my useless T-shirt off, I turn on the hose and hold it over my head. I suck in a sharp breath as cold water hits my heated skin. Not caring if my clothes get wet, I let the water run over my head and down the entirety of my body as if I were standing in a shower.

Once my skin is wet, I grab the soap and squirt a large dollop in my hand. It's going to take a lot of this shit to get the grease off me.

I start with my arms and then rub the citrus scented soap over my face and chest. The white liquid quickly turns gray as it strips the grease away. I'm sure I'll still have plenty on me, but it should be good enough to eat without contaminating my lunch.

Once I'm satisfied that I've scrubbed enough of the grease away, I pick up the hose again and rinse off. By the time I'm done, my jeans and boots are soaked through. I probably should have taken my boots off first. Guess I'm dealing with squishy feet until I get home.

"Can I use some of that?" Karla asks as she steps up beside me.

"Here." I hand it to her. "Use as much as you need. Got plenty."

"Thanks." She nods toward the bus. "Someone can't seem to take her eyes off you. Then again, what woman could with the shower show you just put on for us?"

Instead of turning back to the bus, my eyes snap to Karla. "Shower show?"

She snorts. "Oh, come on. Don't act dumb. You know you look damn good shirtless and covered in grease like a bad boy hot mechanic. Add in the spray of water, and it's every girl's fantasy." She looks past me, and her smile turns teasing. "I'd say that's especially true for Lina."

I glance over my shoulder, and sure enough, Lina is staring at me with a look on her face I can't quite decipher. Is she pissed off or turned on? Maybe a little of both.

"I think she's jealous." Karla adds.

"Jealous? Of what?"

"Me," she says with a cheerfulness to her tone.

I frown. "Why would she be jealous of you? We're not together. Hell, we're not even flirting."

"Doesn't matter." She shrugs. "You're spending time with me. Shirtless, I might add. It also doesn't help that I'm close enough to touch those strong hard muscles that she hasn't been able to keep her eyes off of. She's fighting it, but that girl has it bad."

That spark of hope that I've been fighting to hang onto intensifies. Nothing would make me happier than to know with certainty that Lina wants me.

I glance back and she's still watching us, only this time her eyes look dazed and unfocused. Maybe even a little hurt.

Well, shit. I don't want to hurt her. Jealousy means she cares, but pain? That's not something I want any part of.

But then she rubs her temples and squeezes her eyes closed. I study her for a moment. Even in the shadows of the bus, I can tell she looks pale and there's a tenseness to the way she's carrying herself.

Maybe that hurt I see has nothing to do with me and everything to do with the fact that she's hiding something.

"Come on." I pat Karla's arm. "Let's eat before we lose the afternoon. I want to get those spark plugs in before we call it a day."

Rather than sitting around the picnic table that's in the full sun, we gather around a large oak tree in the nearby field. The shade is a welcome treat after standing in the sun all morning.

Clara, Trevor, and Karla start in on some drama that's going on at the school. Something involving the boy's baseball coach and two cheerleaders. They're talking in code so as not to outright say what the coach did, but it doesn't take a rocket scientist to figure out it wasn't good.

Sounds like someone might be going to jail. It also leaves a gaping hole in the coaching staff following a winning year. The boy's baseball team won state last year. Nobody wants to follow up a year like that with a scandal.

Lina settles into a shaded area just across from me. I study her while she's busy opening the small bag in her hands. She's definitely not feeling like herself. She's always frowning, but there's something different about the way her brows are drawn together today. There's tension there that typically isn't visible.

I shift my gaze to the bag in her hands. It's a snack sized bag of peanuts—the cheap kind you buy at the gas station when you need a quick snack. The only other thing I see with her is a bottle of root beer.

"Is that all you brought to eat?" I ask.

Her eyes snap to mine. Her expression causes my entire body to tense. She's not scowling or glaring at me like I've come to expect. She's in pain.

"What's wrong?" I push.

"Nothing." Her voice is low and soft and so unlike my Grumps. "I'm just not that hungry."

"We've been working for a few hours. How can you not be hungry?"

She shrugs but doesn't answer me. Instead, she slowly eats one peanut at a time like she's trying to make them last.

I open my lunch box and grab one of the two peanut butter and jelly sandwiches I made. Then I set one on her knee. "Eat this."

This time, anger flashes in her eyes when she looks at me. "I'm not taking your lunch."

"No, you're not." I state matter-of-factly. "I made two sandwiches. Plus, I have chips and fruit." I open the container of cut up pineapple and orange slices and set it between us. "I have more than I can eat. It's called sharing."

She stares at the container of fruit. Her eyes go wide like she's seeing food for the first time. It causes something inside me to break. I know Lina has a tough time at home. She doesn't have much, but the thought of her not having enough food to eat tugs at my insides. It makes me want to drag her to Grams and let Grams do what Grams does best—feed her.

Nobody goes hungry with Grams around. It didn't matter how little we had growing up, Grams always made sure we had good food on the table.

I see the moment she gives in. Her shoulders drop and she lets out a slow breath.

"Thanks," she whispers, then reaches out and plucks a small piece of pineapple from the container.

"Any time," I say. "I always pack too much. I can't eat all of this myself." I lie.

Truth is, I eat a lot. Way more than the average person. I'm always on the go. Plus, working outside burns a lot of calories. I need to eat a lot to replenish my strength. But I'll go without if it means Lina gets to eat.

I start to offer her all the fresh vegetables and fruits she wants once our crops are in, but Clara cuts in before I get the words out.

"Chase, tell them you can sing," she demands.

"Uh?" I turn a confused gaze to her. I'd been so focused on Lina that I completely tuned their conversation out.

"We're talking about Tide Waters and her amazing singing voice." Trevor cuts in. "I said there's no one in this county that could sing with her. Clara says you can. Is that true?"

I snort. "Fuck no. That woman sings like an angel."

"Oh, come on." Clara scolds. "You're being modest. You have a great voice. You should duet with Tide sometime."

"You can sing?" This comes from Lina. I meet her stare. The curious and needy look in her eyes has me nodding.

"Just at home and when no one is around." I admit. "I just mess around on my guitar for fun. It relaxes me. No one ever hears me."

"But Clara has?" Lina pushes. If I'm not mistaken, I hear a hint of pain and disappointment in her tone.

"That's just because she's like a sister to us. She's always hanging around the house with Ash."

"Not anymore," Clara says under her breath.

I inwardly cringe at my mistake. After Clara stormed out of the bar when Ash showed up with his new girlfriend, I should have known better than to mention him.

Thankfully, Trevor keeps the conversation moving. "You should sing at karaoke night. I bet the crowd would love it."

I wave him off. "The only way any of you are hearing me sing is if you sneak out to my house at sunrise and spy on me. Otherwise, it ain't happening."

"Boo! You're no fun," Karla teases.

"Spying it is." Trevor jokes. "Just don't go calling the cops when it happens."

I flip them off and go back to eating my lunch. A few moments later, Lina gathers up her trash and pushes to her feet.

"Thanks for the sandwich," she whispers, so only I can hear. I nod and then stare at her ass as she heads back toward the bus.

After an hour, a few new scrapes on my hands, and countless f-bombs later, Karla and I are finally putting in the last new spark plug. This old beast decided to be difficult with us on this last step. It took us most of that time getting the old plugs out. They were so corroded and covered in grime, they didn't want to budge.

"Now what?" Karla asks as she pops in the last one.

"Now we change the oil filter and get some clean oil in this thing. Then we'll see if she'll start."

"Sounds good, boss."

I grumble at the nickname she started calling me after lunch, and she laughs.

"Don't you already have an asshole boss?" I ask. "You don't really want another one, do you?"

She smiles broadly. "You mean Linden? He ain't so bad."

"Ain't so bad?" I raise a brow. "Surely, you're not talking about the same Linden Koch that's been at odds with my family since before he was born."

"The one and only."

"Then you need to get your head checked. He is definitely that bad." While she finishes up with the spark plug, I grab the oil pan to prep draining whatever oil might remain in the bus. "Linden is the worst of the Koch brothers. He goes out of his way to start shit with us."

She shrugs. "Yeah, he's intense, but ..." her brow wrinkles like she's thinking about how to explain. "He's different at work than he is when he's out. I'll admit, he's pretty bad when I see him at Posey's. But at school, he seems almost ... happy."

I snort. "Linden? Happy? I don't think I've ever seen the man smile. Ever!"

Karla chuckles. "He smiles all the time at work. And believe it or not, he's really good with the kids."

I stare at her like she's telling me state's secrets. Then I shake my head. "Nope, I don't believe it. Hell will freeze over before I ever see that man smile or show any kind of emotion other than being perpetually pissed off."

Karla's shoulders shake with laughter. "You'll just have to take my word for it."

We work in silence for several minutes while I slide under the bus to open the drain on the oil pan. When I stand back up, I catch a glimpse of Lina. She and Clara are standing by the picnic table looking at what Lina drew.

Lina is explaining something to her, and Clara is listening with rapt attention. I glance around, looking for Trevor, but I don't see him. Then he steps from behind the bus with a poster sized board in one hand and a can of spray paint in the other.

"How's this?" He holds it up to show it to Lina.

There's a large block letter E in the middle. It's mostly white with a black outline.

Lina squints at it and nods. "Much better. See how the faint shading makes it pop?"

Trevor beams at her like she just told him that he won first prize. She's been teaching them how to do graffiti paint, and from the looks of it, they're catching on.

She's a good teacher. I was impressed with how well she did with the kids at the street fair. She's patient and knowledgeable. Teaching is definitely a strength of hers, and it's something she should do more often.

"She's still standing there, Romeo." Karla teases.

"Huh?" I pull my eyes off Lina and look back at Karla.

She chuckles and shakes her head. "You two are disgusting. I catch her looking at you just as much as you look at her. She may act like she hates you, but she doesn't."

"Yeah, I know." I look back at Lina. I know she doesn't hate me. She wants me just as much as I want her. I can feel it every time she's near me. Okay, maybe she doesn't want me as much as I want her, but she *does* want me.

She's stubborn and hangs onto her values like they're the only thing she has. I can't fault her for that. Especially since I'm the one in the wrong. It just means I have to work harder to prove myself to her if I want a chance at her heart.

"Does she look pale to you?" I ask as I wipe my hands on a towel. It doesn't get all the grease, but it gets the worst of it off. I'm not nearly as dirty as I was before lunch.

Karla steps up beside me and watches Lina carefully. "Yeah, maybe. Watch her hands." Karla points in Lina's direction. "They're shaky."

"I noticed that too." I rest my hands on my hips with my eyes focused on Lina's expression. "She keeps wincing and rubbing her head."

Lina says something to Clara and Trevor, and then they grab a few cans of paint and their boards. They disappear behind the bus. I assume to practice whatever technique Lina just taught them.

Lina brings both hands to her face, and her body sways.

"Hey, Lina," Karla calls out. "You feeling okay?"

Lina's eyes snap to us in surprise. Almost as if she forgot we were here. "Yeah, fine. Just getting a headache. It happens."

I start walking toward her before she even finishes speaking. "What do you mean, it happens?"

She stares up at me like she's confused why I'm even here. "Headaches. Ever heard of them? Some people get them regularly. I am some people."

Her words are clipped, and a little slurred, like she had to work hard to get each one out.

I frown and furrow my brow. "Don't be a smartass, Grumps. I just want to make sure you're okay."

"I'm not, and I'm fine." She turns away from me so I can't see her face.

She sways again and this time she has to brace herself against the picnic table to keep from falling.

"Bullshit. You're not fine." I insist. I step up behind her and rest my hands on her shoulders. She shudders under my touch.

"Yes I am. Now fuck off." She growls out, but there's no real force behind the words. She's trying to hide from me, and I don't like it.

She pushes against me and takes a quick step forward like she's desperate to put space between us. The movement is too much for her—too fast—and her legs give way. She crumbles to the ground, but I swoop in and grab her before she makes contact.

"Lina!" I call out, but she doesn't respond. She's out cold.

I gather her up in my arms and her forehead falls against my neck. She feels cold despite the fact that it's a warm spring day.

"I'm getting her out of here," I say, more to myself than anyone else.

"What's going on?" Clara calls from behind me, but I don't stop to answer her. Karla can fill her in.

I open the passenger door to my truck and set her down. As I'm pulling the seat belt around her, her hand brushes across my arm.

"My meds," she mumbles. "Need them."

"Where are they?" I ask, trying not to let the worry come out in my tone.

"Purse." She points toward the picnic table. When I look back, I see Clara gathering up her things.

"Okay." I kiss her forehead and she lets out a soft sigh. "I'll get it."

By the time I turn around, Clara is already heading in our direction. She has Lina's purse and her water bottle in hand.

"Thanks," I say as I take them from her.

"Is she okay?" Clara's worried voice does nothing to calm me down. Mostly because it's not a question I can answer.

"Lina, tell me what you need." I dig into her purse despite how wrong it feels. Grams preached to us as kids that a woman's purse was off limits. I push Grams's voice out of my head and do it anyway. Thankfully, I find a prescription bottle quickly.

When I lift it up, Lina nods.

"How many?"

She holds up a single finger.

I hand her a pill, then help her take a drink of water to swallow it down. As soon as she does, she relaxes into the seat as if this one little pill will make everything better.

Meanwhile, I'm filled with panic. I don't recognize the name of the drug, and every worst-case scenario imaginable is running through my head.

Is Lina sick? Like life-threatening sick? If she is, she's done a hell of a job at hiding it. No one keeps secrets for long in this small town.

"Where are you taking her?" Clara asks.

"My place. She'll be comfortable there," I say as I rush around to the driver's side of my truck.

Clara nods. "I'll arrange to get her car to you then. That way it's not stuck here all weekend."

"Thanks, Clara." I slap the roof of my truck as I slide inside. Without a glance back, I rush out of the parking lot and head home.

Lina appears to be asleep now that she's taken her meds. I only hope that when she wakes up, she'll tell me what the hell is going on. This panic I feel inside me is too much. I only hope her truth can calm it down rather than feed it.

I'm not sure I can handle it if she's not okay.

Chapter 17

No more running

Lina

My eyes slowly flutter open to a dimly lit room and an unfamiliar, soft bed. I'm also tangled in the arms of a very hard body.

I squeeze my eyes closed as I run through the events from earlier. My headache had reached unmanageable pain levels. It was to the point where my vision blurred, talking was a challenge, and my stomach was twisted in knots.

Chase had noticed it all.

He notices far too much when it comes to me. Something tells me I won't be able to hide anything from him moving forward.

Especially considering my leg is weaved between his, my arm is hugging his waist, and my head is resting on his shoulder.

His arms are wrapped around me in a protective hold, and his hand is lightly brushing up and down my arm.

I look up and meet his worried gaze. He gives me a gentle smile before he lifts his hand and brushes my hair from my face.

"Hi," he says. His voice croaks on the word, as if he's gone far too long without talking.

"Where am I?" I ask as I look around the room.

It's large and open. There's not much furniture in the space.

There's a beautiful kitchen opposite the bed and what looks like a balcony overlooking green fields. It must be late because the sky is no longer light blue. Instead, it's a mix of deep purples, dark blues, and oranges.

Chase clears his throat before he answers me. "My apartment."

"You have an apartment?" My eyes snap back to his.

"Yeah, it's new," he says as he draws lazy circles on my back. "Just moved in a few weeks ago. I wanted my own space but couldn't exactly go far. Need to stay close to the farm."

"So, we're on your family's farm?"

He nods. "Converted the top floor of the stables into this. It's not much, but it's enough for now."

I glance back at the kitchen. There isn't much light, but there's enough to tell that his kitchen is way nicer than anything I've ever lived with. It's new and fresh and stylish. I'd kill for a space this nice to call home.

I glance back at him. His eyes are locked on me like he's studying my every move. He's worried, and I can't recall the last time anyone besides my dad and Jayla worried about me.

"I passed out on you, didn't I?" I ask as bits and pieces from earlier in the day come back to me.

His arm around me tightens while the fingers on his other hand brush down my cheek. "Yeah. I was worried. You okay now?"

I nod. "It was just a migraine."

"I figured that out." He winces and squeezes his eyes closed. "Please don't be mad, but I looked up your medication. I had no clue what I was dealing with or if I needed to take you to the ER."

I cup his cheek. He still hasn't shaved, and I like the feel of his short beard. "It's okay. I would've done the same thing if I were in your shoes."

"Do you get them often?" His voice is low and cautious like he's almost afraid to ask me. I can't blame him. Not with the way I've pushed him away.

"Yeah, too often actually."

He hugs me closer, tucking my head under his chin. The safety I feel in his embrace has my chest fluttering and a heat building between my legs. That's when I realize I'm not in the clothes I had on earlier. My jeans are gone and I'm wearing a large, baggy T-shirt. But I'm still in my bra and panties.

A small smile tugs at my lips at the image of Chase changing me out of my clothes while I'm passed out and sleeping off my meds. Something tells me he was a gentleman the entire time.

"These aren't my clothes," I say in as gentle a tone as possible.

He stiffens around me, then he tightens his hold like he's afraid to let go. "You were a mess. Especially after I carried you to and from my truck. I was covered in grease and some of it transferred to you."

"Thanks," I whisper.

My one-word response relaxes him. His hand slides around my neck and his fingers twine around my hair. "I washed your clothes after I showered. I got all the stains out."

This time I stiffen as reality hits. I try to sit up but his hold on me is too tight. "Let me go. I have to work. What time is it?"

"Shh. It's okay," he whispers before he kisses the top of my head. "I called the parlor. Talked to your coworker, Felix. He said he'd call all your clients and reschedule."

"You did?" I let myself relax into him even though the thought of missing out on the money from a shift makes me anxious. I can't afford to miss work.

"Yeah. Might want to call him later. He sounded worried."

I lift my chin. Our faces are close. So close that I can feel his breath brush across my cheek. "You took care of me."

He cups my face and nods. "If you let me, I'll always take care of you."

Well crap. How am I supposed to hold on to my anger at him for lying about his identity when he says shit like that?

His eyes lock mine in place. There's so much need and desire flickering in his expressive brown eyes. But it's more than just lust.

He cares, and for the life of me, I don't understand why. No one cares for me like this. Like ever.

Dad tried in his own way, but he wasn't capable of seeing to the needs of a daughter, let alone fulfilling them. He did his best after Mom left, but it was hard. Especially with how the MC treated him after he refused the former president's demands.

I've had so few people in my life that I can truly count on that it's always been easier to take care of myself. Giving up that control to someone else, even if I need the help, is scary.

"Lina," he whispers my name. "Tell me what you're thinking."

"You scare me," I say before I can stop myself. He's being honest and open with me right now. I owe him the same.

He nods like he understands, then he presses his forehead to mine. "What can I do to help you not be scared?"

"I'm not sure there's anything you can do. This is something I have to work on."

He tightens his hold on me as if I just told him I was leaving while I figure out my feelings. We went from me being snuggled up while I slept off my migraine to our bodies being pressed together in a very intimate embrace.

He feels good next to me like this. Very good. And as close as we are, it's still somehow not close enough.

Sensing his hesitation, I slide my hand around his neck and pull his mouth to mine. The zing of energy that rushes through me from this simple, gentle union of our lips has me melting into him.

He lets me control the kiss, taking my lead. Only parting his lips when I part mine. It's slow and innocent and yet somehow it makes me feel things I didn't know my body could feel.

But when my tongue darts out and brushes across his lower lip, everything changes. A low rumbling growl builds up from his chest and fills me with more need than I've ever felt toward a man. That one small move unleashes the beast inside him, and he takes control.

He rolls me over, parting my legs with his knee. His tongue

dives into my mouth, stealing my breath as his very hard erection presses against my core. I'm in nothing but a thin pair of cotton panties, and he's still wearing his jeans. That will not do.

I want to feel him—all of him. While his hands twine with my hair, I let mine roam down his body. My hands cup his ass and press his cock into me. I moan at the feel of his rough jeans rubbing against my clit. But that's not what I want.

I want to feel him with no barriers between us. I reach around to the front and quickly unbutton his jeans.

Apparently, that was the wrong thing to do, because he pulls his mouth from mine and stops my hand from moving inside his jeans to grip him.

"Lina," his raspy voice says my name like a plea.

"What's wrong?" I search his face for the answer, but I don't find it. He clearly wants me. I see it in his eyes and feel it in his body.

"Fuck," he grumbles and extracts his body from mine. He scoots to the edge of the bed and sits with his elbows propped on his knees and his head buried in his hands.

"Chase, talk to me." I sit up and reach out to rest my hand on his shoulder but stop myself. His rejection stings and leaves me confused. "I thought you wanted me like this?"

"It's not that." He glances back at me, and the pain in his eyes causes my breath to catch. "I don't want to screw this up more than I already have. I really like you, Lina. I always have. Doing this right with you is important to me."

The relief that washes over me at his admission lights me up inside. Nothing can stop me from doing what I do next.

I crawl across the bed and sling my body around him until I'm straddling his lap. "You're not screwing this up. I want this. I want you."

Before he can object or remove me from his lap, I clench my fists in his shirt and kiss him hard.

Thank God he doesn't stop me. Instead, he leans into the kiss and digs his fingers into my ass as he presses my center into his erection.

Even through our clothes, my body sings from the closeness. His hands trail up my thighs, past my waist and under the T-shirt he put on me. I relish the feel of his rough hands against my bare skin.

"More." I breathe against his lips just as his hands reach my breasts and squeeze. I gasp at the intensity of his grip because he's not gentle.

He pulls away from my mouth and rips the shirt over my head. Then he loops his fingers through my bra straps and pulls it down, effectively securing my arms against my side.

His eyes roam over my bare chest with an odd mix of reverence and jealousy. "You have tattoos on your breasts?"

His voice is rough and gravelly as his eyes snap up to mine. I nod. "I've covered most of my body in ink."

His nostrils flare, and his fingers dig into my skin. "Who gave these to you?"

I raise a brow at the demanding tone of his question. "Some of them I did myself, but Felix did most of them."

"Felix? Your coworker." His jaw is tight and his fingers flex against my skin as he rakes them back up my body. His hand cups my heavy breast and lifts it to his waiting mouth. Then he licks and sucks on the nipple, sending a rush of heat to my core. "I don't like that he touched you here."

I snort. "You're not the first man to see me naked. You know that, right?"

He growls out his displeasure before his mouth descends on me. This time, he sucks my nipple between his teeth and bites down. I toss my head back and moan at the pleasurable pain he's giving me.

I want to shove my fingers into his hair and lock him in place, but I can't move my arms. My bra is still wrapped around me, making it hard to move.

"More." I pant as he switches to my other breast and gives it the same deliciously rough attention. "I need more."

With one hand gripping my hip, he slides his other around my neck and shoves his fingers into my hair. He fists his hand and pulls my head back, lifting my chest higher.

"Fuck," he groans, and then licks and kisses his way up my chest as if he's tracing the lines of my ink. When he reaches my neck, his kisses turn to nips. It feels so good that I buck my hips into him, loving the feel of his hardness between my legs.

"Please, Chase." I beg. "More."

The word has barely passed my lips before Chase flips me around to my back and pushes me down on the bed. He settles between my legs, pressing his cock into me while his hand wraps around my neck.

His thumb brushes along the line of my chin, and his fingers gently squeeze. It's a show of his strength and control over me. I fucking love it.

I thrust my hips to meet his erection and moan. "Yes. More of this."

But he doesn't move. Our eyes are locked in a heated stare that says we both want the same thing—his cock buried deep inside me.

His lips hover mere millimeters from mine and I lift my head to kiss him. He stops me by tightening his hold around my neck and pinning me to the bed.

My lips tug up in a grin. "Oh, this is going to be fun," I rasp.

"How so?" he growls.

"We both like control."

"Hmm." His eyes shift to my mouth as his thumb brushes across my bottom lip. I dart my tongue out and flick the tip, causing his eyes to darken. Then he pushes his thumb into my mouth, and I suck it hard. His cock twitches between my legs and a string of curses escapes him.

"Lina," he says gruffly. "Before we continue, we need to get one thing straight."

He pulls his thumb from my mouth, effectively loosening his hold on me. I take this opportunity to flip us over.

But he's ready for me, and I'm unsuccessful. A devilish grin covers his face as he reaffirms his hold around my neck. His grip on me is tight, but not painful. "Nice try, Grumps."

I shrug. "Can't blame a girl for trying."

His expression turns serious as he studies me. "No more running."

"What?" His statement surprises me. I don't know what I was expecting him to say, but this isn't it.

"If we do this, you will stop running from me. I need you to promise to give us a fair shot."

"And by fair shot you mean—"

"A relationship." He demands. "You and me. No more running. No more pushing me away. Agree?"

The tone of his voice leaves no room for debate and no doubt about what he wants. It's also so very unlike the jovial, easygoing Chase I know him to be.

"And if I don't?" I ask. His demand scares the shit out of me, but I mostly ask because I'm curious about what he'll say. *Mostly.*

"Then I remove my hand from your throat and let you go."

"Just like that? No fighting? No trying to change my mind?"

"Nope. You either want this with me or you don't," he says matter-of-factly.

"It'd be that easy for you to just let me go?" I wiggle my hips against his very hard erection. He lets out a low growl and drops his forehead to mine.

"No. Nothing about this is easy for me, babe." He brushes his lips to mine before he continues. "But I can't do this with you unless I know you're staying. I need you for more than just one night. You also need to understand that I'm terrified that one night with you will be my undoing."

I lift my arms to tug him closer, only to discover I can't. My bra is still wrapped around me. I meet his expectant gaze and smile. "If I say yes, will you free my arms so I can touch you?"

He raises a brow. "That depends on what you're saying yes to."

I huff. "A relationship! Isn't that what you're demanding from me? Although you should know, I've never really been in a real adult relationship. I've kind of run from those like the plague."

A slow smile spreads across his face. "You mean to tell me I get to be your first relationship?"

I narrow my gaze. "Don't sound so smug."

"Oh, but I am." He presses his lips to mine before he sits up, straddling me. Then he reaches around me and unhooks my bra.

As soon as my arms are free, I reach for him, wrapping my hands around his neck and pulling his mouth to mine.

I kiss him hard and deep. His tongue tangles with mine as we war for dominance. There's a part of me, albeit a very small part, that tells me I should let him win. But I don't. I love control too much. I even love fighting for it.

But he's stronger than me. He extracts himself from my grasp. The smile that spreads across his face as he sits back on his heels takes my breath away. He's happy, and I made him that way.

I'm not sure if I've ever been responsible for that kind of smile before. I decide I like it, and I want to find more ways to make him smile.

He reaches for his jeans and unbuttons them. Then he drags down the zipper, freeing his thick, hard cock. I can't pull my eyes away as he strokes himself. A small bead of pre-cum forms at the tip and I lick my lips.

"You want this?" he asks.

"Yes," I say without taking my eyes off him pleasuring himself.

"Fuck, Lina." He growls. "I love how you look at me."

I quickly sit up and knock his hand away. Then I push his jeans further down his hips. With the way he's still straddling me, it makes it easy for my mouth to wrap around his cock. I take him deep, sucking him hard.

He bucks into me, clearly unprepared for my mouth on him. I gag when his tip hits the back of my throat and I pull back slightly.

"Fuck, I'm sorry." He rasps.

Then he lifts his hands and cradles my head while I take him in and out of my mouth. This is a vulnerable position. If he wanted to, he could fuck my mouth hard and there wouldn't be a lot I could do about it.

But he's gentle, letting me set the pace.

I slide my hands around his ass and pull him closer. I lick and suck and take everything he's willing to give me. His dick twitches and then thickens even more.

"Baby, fuck." He thrusts into me once more before he jerks away, pulling himself from my lips with a pop.

"Not like this." He pants. "The first time I come with you, it will be inside you."

He pushes to his feet and grabs a roll of condoms from the top drawer on the table beside the bed. Then he loses his jeans and boxer briefs. He strokes his cock a few more times before he sheaths himself with a condom.

Then he grabs my ankle and pulls me to the edge of the bed. I fall back, my arms tossed above my head like an offering. I'm still in my panties, but nothing else.

His eyes roam down my body, taking his time like he's studying every inch of me. "Your body is so fucking beautiful."

His fingers trace the lines of my tattoos on my stomach before he loops them through my panties and yanks them from my body.

"Spread those pretty legs," he demands.

When I do, his eyes darken as he takes in my heat. His hands grasp my inner thighs, and he pushes my legs even further apart as he lines his tip up with my entrance.

We both let out a low moan when he pushes inside me. He's only given me an inch, but I feel so full.

"Baby. Watch us." His tone is soft, almost like he's in complete awe of us coming together. "You look so beautiful taking my cock."

I press up on my elbows and stare at where we're joined. When I see how little of his cock is inside, my walls clench. He's barely given me anything and yet I feel like I have all of him.

"I feel you tightening around me," he says as he pushes deeper inside. "Fuck, baby. You feel so good."

I hold my breath as he pulls out before he slams all the way in. I cry out as he hits me deep and spreads me open. The sting I feel from the sudden invasion is quickly replaced with pleasure as he slowly moves in and out of me.

"Tell me what you want, baby. I'm not going to last long, and I need you to come first."

"Harder." I moan as he pushes all the way inside me. "Fuck me harder."

"Shit." His grip on my thighs tightens as he stills. He's as deep as he can get, and it feels so good. "You're killing me."

I chuckle. "Not yet. But if you don't fuck me harder, that might happen before the night is over."

The smile that spreads across his face takes my breath away. He drops to his hands and presses his lips to mine. I wrap my legs around his hips and draw him closer to me.

He gives me what I want, and we lose ourselves in each other's arms. When I come apart, everything around me fades into the shadows, and there is only him and me and this aching feeling in my chest.

As much as I try to ignore it, this ache makes me think my heart no longer belongs to me.

EVERY INCH OF MY BODY ACHES IN THE BEST WAY POSSIBLE. I can't help but smile as I stretch my arms over my head. But that smile quickly fades when I roll over and find I'm alone in bed.

I glance around the large open room, and I don't see him. The sun is already up, so chances are high he's taking care of the farm.

He told me he'd have to get up at sunrise, but the disappointment in his absence still surprises me.

I roll over onto my back and stare at the ceiling. Last night was amazingly unexpected. After the first time we had sex, he got up and made me something to eat. What should have been a simple grilled cheese sandwich ended up being some sort of fancy grilled cheese with a mix of cheese, tomatoes, and basil. It was so good I stole some of his sandwich.

Then we showered together. That ended up being the hard fast fuck I begged him for when he had me in his bed.

I reach up and wrap my hand around my neck and smile. Chase is so much more demanding and controlling in bed than I expected. *Dominating.* That's the best way to describe him.

After he'd meticulously washed every inch of my body, he pressed me against the shower wall and wrapped his hand around my throat. That's how he held me in place. With one hand around my neck and the other pressed against the shower wall, he slammed into me over and over again until I cried out his name in pleasure.

It's not how I pictured him. His personality led me to believe he'd be more tentative, slow, and caring during sex. Caring, yes. But tentative and slow? He is anything but.

I can still feel his grip around my neck. It was firm, powerful, domineering. But I never felt pain or fear in his grasp. Only wanted and revered.

I loved every second of it.

I've always been the one in control. I thought that's what I liked and wanted from a partner. Someone who'd let me take the lead and set the pace. But Chase proved otherwise last night.

I was more than willing to submit to him. It was hot and exciting and the best sex I've ever had.

That thought sends a shiver through my body and goosebumps pebble my skin. I've never let myself be so vulnerable with another person before. I learned a long time ago to never give someone the upper hand. Because if I did, I'd lose everything I fought for.

My independence and freedom cost me a lot. It cost my dad everything. My life may be mine and mine alone, but it's never been easy. But it's far better than the alternative.

If I had given into the demands of the MC all those years ago, I wouldn't be struggling with bills, a barely running car, and a rundown trailer. I would have been taken care of in all the ways I struggle now, but I wouldn't have been free. I would have been Smoke's property, and that's something I could never live with.

The soft sound of a strumming guitar drags me out of my morose thoughts. I glance in the direction of the sound and notice the balcony door is cracked.

Tossing the sheet back, I grab the T-shirt he'd given me to wear last night and pull it over my head, and then make my way across the large room. Disappointment washes over me when I discover the balcony is empty.

Where is he?

Stepping outside into the cool morning air, I take in the amazing view of his family's land. The sun is still low in the sky, casting a muted light across the horizon. The shadows of the rolling hills and the hazy light from the low fog have me wishing I had my paints and a canvas. This is exactly the kind of view I love to paint.

The music picks up again, and I search the area closer to the stables. I find Chase sitting on a stump, guitar in hand, singing to his goats. My heart gallops and I have to press my hand to my chest to catch my breath.

I didn't think I knew what swooning was. Hell, it's not something I ever thought I'd experience. But right now, I am swooning over the man singing to his goats while they're bouncing round him like playful children.

I swallow the lump forming in my throat and press my hand harder against my chest. My heart is so not prepared for a man like this. I've guarded my heart for so long because I've always known that if the right man came along, I'd give him everything.

Giving someone everything is dangerous.

Chase Mutter is that kind of man. Which means he's a man that could completely break me if I'm not careful.

Chapter 18

This is how it works

Chase

I take another deep breath before I strum my guitar again. I should probably head back upstairs and see how Lina is doing, but I'm kind of freaking out.

I finally got the girl of my dreams, and I'm terrified I won't be able to keep her. Losing her would ruin me.

Maybe I'm being paranoid, but I can't shake the feeling that I'm not the kind of man she really wants. Sure, she made me promises last night. She agreed to a relationship. But for how long?

Will she be done with me in a week? A month? A few months? Hell, she could wake up this morning and decide it was all a mistake.

Lina doesn't want a man like me. She wants a bad boy like Christian. She made that very clear from the beginning.

But I relentlessly pursued her anyway.

Because I had to have her.

One night with her is nowhere near enough. I want more. I want everything. Family. Kids. Love. The forever kind of love that I can't live without or else I'll stop breathing and cease to exist.

That's what I've always wanted. And I want to figure out if

she's the one who will give me all of that and let me give it to her in return.

I let out a slow breath and struggle to calm my pounding heart. Panicking over something that hasn't happened and may very well never happen is just stupid. Our relationship isn't even a day old and I'm already freaking out over how I'll handle it when she leaves me.

Because chances are high she will leave me. I've already fucked things up royally, and she doesn't take too kindly to fuck ups.

I'm not quite as cynical as my brothers when it comes to women. We've all watched our moms walk away from Dad, leaving him to become nothing more than a shell of a man. But I know not all women are like that.

Look at Grams. She's the best woman I know, and she and Grandpops had an amazing marriage and a great life together.

I know that the forever kind of love exists. I'm just not sure I'm good enough to keep Lina and make her happy. But I'm certainly going to do everything in my power to try.

I feel her walking up behind me before I hear her steps.

When I glance over my shoulder, my heart trips over a beat. She looks stunning with the way the sun glimmers off her dark silky hair. It's a little messy from our night in bed together and hangs over one shoulder in loose waves.

She put her jeans back on, but she's still wearing my baggy T-shirt. The neckline is so big, it hangs off her shoulder, revealing her bra strap and all those glorious tattoos I traced with my tongue last night. She tied it in a knot at her waist, showing off a hint of her midsection.

When she gets close, I set my guitar to the side and reach for her. She willingly steps into my arms and lets me pull her down on my lap. With one arm around her waist, I cup her neck and pull her in for a kiss.

"Did you sleep okay?" I ask.

She pulls her bottom lip between her teeth and nods. "What little sleep you let me get."

I grin and bury my face in her neck. This is quickly becoming my favorite place to be. "I'd apologize, but I am not sorry about anything we did last night. Even the fact that I kept you up most of the night."

She wraps her arms around me and rubs her hands down my back. It feels so good to have her like this that I tighten my hold.

"You sing to your goats," she says with a hint of amusement in her tone.

I chuckle. "I do. They like music."

"It was ... *cute*." I feel her smile in her words.

"Are you making fun of me?" I poke her in the side, making her squirm. I'd learned last night that she's ticklish if I get her just right.

"No! Just making an observation." She laughs, and the sound steals my breath. Lina's smiles and laughs are hard earned, and the fact that I get to see her like this is monumental.

I stare at her in amazement for so long that she stills in my arms.

Her smile fades, and her laughter dies away. "Everything okay?"

I nod, then brush her hair away from her face, tucking it behind her ear. "I love seeing you like this. Happy and carefree."

She gives me a gentle smile before pressing her lips to mine. "I like feeling like this."

"Good." I breathe her in and kiss her neck. "You smell like me."

"Because you spent most of the night marking me with your scent," she says with a heavy dose of sass, but there's nothing but humor in her eyes.

"You liked it."

"Maybe." She shrugs, looking away to hide her smile. Her eyes narrow as she stares down at her leg. "Are those ladybugs?"

I follow her gaze and smile. Sliding my finger along her thigh, I pick up the two ladybugs that landed on her. "They are. You know what this means, right?"

She shakes her head.

"It's a sign of good luck to come. Two means double the luck."

She raises a brow. "You don't really believe that, do you?"

I scoff and mock shock at her skepticism. "Of course I do. Ladybugs always bring good luck. They're a sign of protection, healing, and good fortune. They're life-givers. Just look around." I wave my hand toward the field in front of us. "My fields are covered in ladybugs. That means I'm going to have a great harvest."

She studies me for a moment. Her expression softens. "Why is that exactly?"

"Ladybugs ward off pest insects, so my crops are healthier. My soybeans will flourish, and my corn will be sweeter because they're here."

"Hmm." She wraps her arms around my neck. "I didn't know that."

"Glad I could teach you something." I squeeze her ass before I give it a light slap. "Come on. Let's get inside. I'll make us some breakfast."

She lets out a low groan. "I can't. I need to get home and check on Dad. Plus, he's probably worried about me. It's not like me not to come home."

"Okay," I say, trying to hide my disappointment. "I'll drive you."

She shakes her head. "Just take me to my car. I need to get it anyway."

"Your car is already here. It's in the shop."

She pushes back from me and glares at me like I just insulted her. "Say what?"

I furrow my brows. "Yesterday, Christian and Mac went and grabbed your car from the school. They had trouble getting it to start and discovered you needed a new fuel pump, so I had them take it to the shop to fix it up."

"No!" She jumps off my lap. Whatever happiness I saw a few moments ago is replaced with anger. "I can't afford to pay for that yet. Please tell me they haven't started on it."

"Baby, don't worry about it." I reach for her, but she pulls away. "It's no big deal. We had the part already and Sophia said she'd come in and change it for you."

"You made Sophia fix my car?" Her voice rises, startling my goats.

"No, I didn't *make* her do it. She offered. Mac had plans at the track with Ash and she was free."

She shoves her hands into her hair and huffs. "Is it ready? I need to get out of here."

I shake my head. "The hoses were brittle. We didn't have the right size. Liam will pick those up in town tomorrow."

"Tomorrow!" she yells. "I can't go without my car, Chase. How am I supposed to get home? I have to work."

"I'll take you." I keep my voice calm even though her reaction is causing a whirlpool of anxiety to build inside me. When I reach for her hand, she jerks away and rushes toward the stables.

"The hell you will." She grumbles under her breath.

I rush past her and pull her close to me. She struggles against my hold, but I refuse to let her go. "Why are you so mad?"

"Let me go." She struggles harder and pounds her fist against my chest.

I run my hand up her back and cup her neck, forcing her to look up at me. "Not until you talk to me and tell me why you're so mad."

Her breathing is heavy and the angry look in her eyes cuts through me like daggers, but I don't back down. If I do, I'll lose her.

She closes her eyes and slows her breathing. Then she lets out a barely audible sigh and drops her forehead to my chest. "I can't afford to fix it yet. I needed to wait until next month."

"Lina, baby." I slide my hand into her hair and hold her tighter.

"You don't owe us any money. I told you, I want to take care of you."

"Why?" Her whispered question is so quiet I almost don't hear it. "People don't do things for me without expecting something in return."

"I don't expect anything in return for this. This is how it works when someone cares about you." I place my fingers under her chin and lift her face to mine. "I care about you. Deeply. Despite how much you try to hide from the world, I see the real you. The kind, loving, funny woman who hides behind a scowl and that tough girl persona."

For a moment, I think she's going to give in to me. But then her expression hardens, and she pushes against my chest. This time, I let her go.

"You're wrong. I'm not kind or loving. And I certainly don't take handouts. Will you please take me home? I'd appreciate it."

I nod. My shoulders slump as she spins around and heads back toward my apartment. I shove my hands into my hair and tug at the strands as my frustration builds.

So much for being happy and carefree. That version of Lina is gone.

With one act of kindness, her walls are back up. I only hope this time they're not as strong, and I'm able to break them down faster than last time.

LINA IS QUIET AS WE MAKE OUR WAY TO MY TRUCK. SHE doesn't look at me when I open the door for her, and she refuses my hand when I offer it up to help her in.

I shut the passenger door a little too hard after she's settled. My frustration is near the boiling point.

If I'd thought for one second she'd be this pissed off about her car, I would've asked her first. But I thought I was doing her a solid.

I get that she's used to dealing with shit on her own, but she doesn't have to anymore.

Hell, she never should have had to deal with all this on her own in the first place. No one should.

I make my way around my truck and slide into the driver's seat. I sit there for several beats, staring at the space in front of me. I'm at a loss about what to say to her to make this right. It's not like I can ask Sophia to unfix her car. She already installed the new fuel pump. The hoses were trashed, so until the new ones are put in, her car is parked.

"Are we just gonna sit here all morning, or do you think you can start this truck up and drive me home?" She snaps out her question, clearly annoyed. Her tone only manages to piss me off.

"Can you kill the attitude?" I snap my gaze to hers, and she flinches. "I didn't fix your car to piss you off or control you or to get something from you. I did it because you're my girl and I hated the thought of you getting stuck somewhere when it finally died. It wasn't something that cost me a lot of money *or* time. I really don't see what the big fucking deal is."

"It is a big fucking deal." She tosses her hands in the air. "And I shouldn't have to explain that to you. Just take me home. Then we can go our separate ways and forget last night ever happened."

"Fuck!" I slam my hand on the steering wheel before I slide my seat back. I reach for her so fast she doesn't have time to fight me off before I have her in my lap with her body held tightly against me.

I wrap my hand around her neck and hold her face close to mine. "There's no way in hell I can forget about last night. Ever." I bark out. "You said you wouldn't run. So no fucking running."

She pushes against me, but I hold her tighter. "Let me go."

"I can't." My voice cracks as I pull her mouth to mine. All it takes is one swipe of my tongue and she immediately softens. She opens her mouth and gives just as good as she takes. Our mouths devour each other in a hungry, angry kiss that says there's no way in fucking hell that we're walking away from each other.

She can be pissed all she wants, but she's mine. I'll spend the rest of my life proving that to her if that's what it takes.

When I break the kiss, we're both panting. I'd been so focused on kissing her into submission that I didn't even notice she'd rotated until she was straddling me.

"Dammit, Chase." She cups my face and pulls my mouth back to hers. "I want to be mad at you."

I growl and squeeze her ass. When I do, it pushes her center closer to my hardening cock. We both moan at the friction. "Be mad all you want, just don't fucking run, babe."

"Okay." She breathes against my mouth before she sucks my bottom lip between her teeth and bites down.

I groan and thrust up as my cock thickens. "If you keep that up, I'm not taking you home."

"I have to go home." Her voice is raspy and sexy and so ready to give in to me.

I squeeze her ass one more time before I give it a light pat. "Then I suggest you slide back to your seat and buckle up."

"Party pooper." She pouts.

She starts to move from my lap, but I tighten my grip on her hips. Her eyes shoot to mine. "I'm sorry. I should have asked you about your car first. I won't make that mistake again."

She nods and presses a light kiss on my cheek. "Thanks. I appreciate that. And I'll try to manage my temper. If you haven't noticed, it's bad. I don't always think straight when I get mad. And maybe ... I shouldn't get so mad when all you're trying to do is help."

A broad smile spreads across my face. "Look at us, talking it out like adults."

She rolls her eyes and playfully slaps my chest. "Don't be such a goof."

"Can't babe." I slap her ass, this time with a loud smack, as she lifts off my lap. "Goof is my middle name."

"You don't have to come in," Lina says as she rushes out of the truck before I even get it in park. I ignore her and hop out anyway.

"Nonsense. I need to officially meet your dad." I grin as I wrap my arm around her shoulder.

"Chase." She shoves my arm off her and turns to face me. Then she plants a firm hand on my chest. "Now might not be a good time. I don't know what he's doing."

Rather than let her push me back, I place my hand over where hers is pressed against my chest and tug her flush against me. "I'm sure a quick introduction is fine."

She shakes her head. "He might not even be dressed. Sometimes he's slow to move in the morning."

"Okay." I drag out the word. "Does that mean he's likely sitting inside naked or just in his pjs? 'Cause I gotta tell you, baby. Thinking about your dad walking around naked in front of you is kinda weird."

Her eyes slowly fall shut with a look of exasperation, and I can't help but chuckle. "This is not funny, Chase. My dad is a sick man."

I wrap my arm around her waist and kiss her forehead. "I know, babe. I just want to meet him. As your boyfriend. If he's not interested in having a guest, I'll leave."

She growls and fists her hands against my chest. Then she grumbles something under her breath that I can't make out.

"What was that?" I ask as I nuzzle my lips into her neck. I love her neck. It's soft and sweet and feels damn good against my lips. I also love the way she shudders and sucks in a breath every time I kiss or nibble on her skin just below her ear.

She looks up at me with an expression I can't quite read. "I said I've never introduced Dad to someone I'm dating."

The smile that covers my face almost hurts. "You mean, I get to be the first at this too?"

She rolls her eyes. "Your smiles annoy me."

I chuckle and plant a light kiss on her lips. "No, they don't. You just wish your smile was as awesome as mine."

She snorts. "Hardly."

Before I have a chance to defend my smiles further, the screen door on the trailer creaks open. I shift my eyes to the man walking out onto the small landing.

"Lina," his gruff voice calls out. "Everything okay out here?"

She extracts herself from my arms and then takes my hand before she turns to face the man. "Yeah, Dad. Everything is fine."

He looks at her for a moment with a hard stare before his gaze softens. Then he looks at me. "You're one of them Mutter boys, right?"

"Yes, sir." I squeeze Lina's hand and lead her to the steps. I offer him my hand. "I'm Chase. And you must be George Lange, Lina's dad."

He stares at my hand for several beats with a furrowed brow. I'm not sure if it's because he's not happy he found me with my arms around his daughter or because he's not used to people offering him a handshake. Either way, I keep my hand out and wait.

He finally takes it and smiles. "It's nice to meet you, son. Forgive my surprise. Can't say Lina's ever brought a boy home before."

"Dad," Lina groans, bringing another big smile from me.

"Yeah, she told me that. I think she's nervous." I tease.

She slaps my arm and frowns. "I am not nervous. Just ..."

Her voice trails off. Then her shoulders slump as if whatever excuse she was going to give doesn't make any sense.

"Well, you two might as well come in. I just put on a pot of coffee." George opens the screen door and then waves us in.

"That's not necessary. I think Chase needs to get going," Lina says quickly.

"Nonsense." I squeeze her hand to let her know I'm not going anywhere. "I can spare a few minutes to talk with your dad."

As soon as we're inside, Lina stiffens next to me. I glance around and immediately understand why she didn't want me to come inside.

The place is a dump. Actually, dump might be too nice of a word. It looks like it should be condemned.

The musty smell of mold and something rotting is overwhelming. The ceiling sags and there are large water stains on the carpet. There's not much in the way of furniture inside. Just a recliner and a small table positioned in front of an old TV.

The living room opens up to the kitchen, where I see a pharmacy worth of medication spread out on the counter. The countertops are chipped, the appliances are old, and the cabinet doors barely close.

Every instinct in me wants to pack up all her shit and drag her out of here caveman style. I almost don't care that it would piss her off. No one should have to live like this.

I must stare at the counter full of prescription drugs for too long because George clears his throat and explains without my asking. "Too many years of hard living and drinking. I don't recommend it. 'Fraid I did a number to my liver."

Lina lets go of my hand and rushes to the kitchen. "Why don't you sit Dad? I'll get you your coffee. Did you take your meds this morning?"

He waves her off but does as she said. "Yeah, yeah. First thing. I can take care of myself, doll."

"I know you can," she whispers, but keeps doing what she's doing. A moment later, she walks out with a cup of coffee for her dad. She hands it to him and then says, "I'm going to walk Chase out. I'll be back in a few."

He nods and squeezes her hand before she passes me without a glance and walks outside.

I turn to her dad and smile. "It was nice meeting you, George. Have a good day."

"You too, son." He lifts his coffee to his lips and then picks up the TV remote. I head outside and find Lina leaning against my truck.

"Hey," I say when I reach her, but she keeps her eyes focused on the ground. I place my fingers under her chin and lift her eyes to mine. "Talk to me."

She squeezes her eyes closed and sighs. "I didn't want you to see any of that."

"I figured as much." I gather her into my arms and hold her close. "I'm not judging you if that's what you're worried about. But I'm not gonna lie. The thought of you living like that has me raging like a wild beast."

"Chase, it's fine." She scrubs her hands over her face. I assume to hide her embarrassment.

"Baby." I drop my head so I'm eye level with her. "You need help. You can't manage a sick father and a falling down trailer on your own. Where's your brother in all this? Why isn't he helping you?"

Her embarrassment quickly shifts to frustration. "He's in Columbus, living his life. And always way too busy to help."

This news causes my frown to deepen. "What about you?"

She furrows her brows. "What about me?"

"When do you get to live your life? How come all this falls on your shoulders?" I wave an arm at the trailer that should be condemned.

"Who says I'm not living?"

I raise a questioning brow, and she scowls. "Don't look at me like that, Grumps."

"Oh, so no more baby?" she asks. "I'm back to being Grumps?"

I ignore her and continue. "You deserve better than this."

She shakes her head. "We're not all fortunate enough to be born into wealthy families. Or even families that have stable, steady incomes. You, of all people, should understand that. This is the life of a sick, retired MC member and his forgotten daughter. Just because you've seen behind the curtain doesn't mean anything is going to change. *This* is poverty. *This* is life. *My life.*"

I move my hands to her face and cup her cheeks. "First of all, *you* are not forgotten." My voice cracks on the words and I clear my throat. Hearing her say that has my heart aching for her in ways it's never ached before. "Your mom leaving the way she did was a really shitty thing to do, but that doesn't mean others don't see you. I see you. I always have. Now, I'm going to help you."

She pushes me away for what feels like the millionth time over the past two days, but I don't let her go. "I don't need you to fix this."

"Too bad. I'm helping you," I say as if it's a foregone conclusion.

"Chase, taking care of me and fixing my messes is not your job."

I growl, beyond frustrated with her constant rejection. "Newsflash, Lina. I wasn't born into a family with money either. Anything and everything we have, we worked our asses off for. My family life is far from perfect too. And in case you forgot, my mom is the town drug addict and the one responsible for her son's addiction. Christian is a recovering addict because our mother is a worthless piece of shit who reveled in dragging her sons down with her. I almost lost my twin twice because of her, and I worry every day that he'll relapse. So don't talk to me like I don't know what a hard life is like. Because I do. The only difference between you and me is I had others standing beside me to help pick up all our messes. Now you have me. I *will* help you."

She sucks in a long, ragged breath and her eyes well up with tears. When one breaks free, I wipe it away with my thumb.

I drop my forehead to hers and sigh. "Tell me you understand, baby. I'm gonna help you and it'll be a lot easier on both of us if you don't fight me on it."

She gives me a slight nod as a few more tears break free and slide down her cheeks. My body immediately lets loose of the tension that had my shoulders bunched and my chest tight.

I press a light kiss to her lips and whisper, "Thank fuck."

***

AFTER LEAVING LINA, I SHOULD HAVE GONE HOME. I SHOULD have done some work around the farm or gone to the main house to see what my family was up to for the day. I should have literally done anything else except what I did.

Seeing her living conditions was too much of a reminder of Mom and her inability to care for herself.

So instead of doing something that made me happy, I drove to her apartment to check on her.

Big mistake. Maybe one of the worst mistakes I've ever made in my life.

Because Mom's apartment looks worse than it ever has, and she's passed out on the floor on her stomach with her head lying in a pile of vomit.

At least she's still breathing.

After standing outside for what felt like an eternity, catching my breath and getting a tight hold of my anger, I head back inside. I grab her stash that's sitting in a small bag on the coffee table and take it to the bathroom. I don't care that it looks like a week's worth of blow. I flush it down the toilet. Then I turn on the shower so it can warm up.

Picking Mom up off the floor, barely conscious, is its own kind of hell. There's no love lost between us at this point in our relationship, but that doesn't mean seeing her like this doesn't hurt.

Because it does. It cuts so deep into my wounds that I prefer to pretend it doesn't exist. Life is easier if I plaster on a smile and make jokes rather than dwell on all the shit that festers in the recesses of my mind. That shit won't solve anything. And it certainly doesn't make me feel good.

I place Mom under the showerhead, letting it hit her in the face. She lets out a loud *oomph* sound when I sit her down. Probably because it was more like a drop. I should be gentler, but after the morning I've had, my temper is begging to be let loose. Mom's lucky I'm even doing this much for her.

She sputters and spits, then lifts her hand to wipe the water away from her face. Once her head is mostly cleaned off, I push her back so she doesn't drown or choke under the spray.

I let out a low snort. She just sits back against the tub, eyes closed, like she's going back to sleep without a care in the world.

Maybe I should turn the water to cold. That might wake her up.

Deciding to leave her, I head to her bedroom and get her some clean clothes. Only I can't find anything clean. She's already dirtied up everything I washed the last time I was here. I'm stuck picking out the cleanest shirt and sweats I can find. At least she still has clean towels. Likely because she rarely bathes.

No son, at any age, should ever have to give his addict mother a shower and then dress her in clean*ish* clothes. I've done this more times than I care to count and for more years than is survivable.

And yet, here I am, doing it again.

Once she's settled in her bed, I head back out to the living room and get to work. There's so much garbage scattered around the apartment that I use up all the remaining trash bags to take it all out.

I clear out all the rotting food and load up the dishwasher with as many dishes as it can hold. And there's still a counter stacked high with dirty dishes.

I'm about to fill the sink up with water when my phone buzzes in my back pocket. I groan when I see it's from Grams reminding me of the Euchre practice match that starts in five minutes. Good thing she reminded me.

I type out a quick reply, letting her know I'll be there, then I shove my phone back in my pocket.

After a quick glance around the apartment, I head to the door. It's still a mess, but it's a lot cleaner than it was when I arrived. Mom probably won't even notice.

For a man who just shared the best night of my life with a woman I've wanted for years, I'm in one hell of a shit mood.

When I slide behind the wheel of my truck, a heaviness weighs me down. Hopelessness and defeat. I've spent my entire life caring for a woman who doesn't care that I do it. Hell, she doesn't even acknowledge my existence. And she's my fucking mother.

Am I setting myself up for failure by trying to do the same thing for Lina?

She said she doesn't want my help, and yet I keep insisting. Unlike my mom, I want to take care of Lina. I *need* her to *want* to rely on me.

I can't tell if her resistance is stubbornness or that she really doesn't want me the same way I want her.

Either way, I'm already in too deep. All that I can hope for is that Lina is truly in this with me too.

If she's not, it just might destroy me.

Chapter 19

Stubbornness and pride that run a mile wide

Lina

There's a hint of guilt nibbling at the fringes of my thoughts, but I push it back for what feels like the hundredth time.

Okay, maybe it's not a hint. More like a large neon sign flashing before my eyes that says *STOP! Don't do it.*

But I'm predictably stubborn. And I don't stop.

I bummed a ride from my neighbor after I received word that my car was fixed and ready to be picked up.

And now, I push right past that glaring imaginary sign trying to get my attention, and march into Mutter's garage.

I walk right past Sophia, who's standing next to an old Buick with a greasy car part in her hand. Christian pushes to his feet from where he was sitting next to a bike he's building. I see a few other bodies move in my peripheral vision, but I ignore those too.

I head straight for Liam's office.

"Lina." He pushes to his feet, surprised to see me. "I told you we'd drop it off for you. You didn't need to come down."

"I know, but I wanted to make sure *I* paid you for the work."

He furrows his brow and stares at me like I spoke a foreign language.

"I can't take your money," he says in a low, almost threatening tone. It causes my already tense nerves to tighten even more.

"Of course you can. Now tell how much I owe you," I demand as I pull my wallet out of my purse.

This is going to hurt and might even cost me our electricity, but I can't take this level of charity from Chase. I thought the inks and new cabinet he bought me for work were too much, but this takes his so-called help to a whole new level.

I'm not a dummy. I know how much a fuel pump for my car costs. The part alone is over three hundred dollars. The labor I was quoted to replace it was even more. I can't afford this—not even close—but I can't let him do this for me.

I run through my mental checklist of all the bills I still haven't paid this month, and I start to feel ill. I owe the electric company a payment soon, and this will eat away at what I've saved. It also means I still won't be able to fix the water heater.

Looks like it's another month of cold showers.

At least it's getting warm outside now that we're working our way into the summer months.

Thank goodness my sales at the street fair were so good and I was able to stock up on Dad's medication. If that hadn't been the case, I'd be screwed on an unbearable level.

I pull my bank card out of my wallet and hand it to him. He tosses his hands in the air and steps back like I'm shoving a poisonous snake at him.

"I said, I can't take your money."

I growl. "And I said, I'm paying for my damn car. Now tell me how much I owe you."

I see movement behind me and a moment later, Christian is standing beside me.

"Chase insisted on taking care of this," he says in a low growl that sounds almost as frustrated as mine.

"I don't give a shit what Chase said. I am paying for my car."

I feel Christian's eyes on me, but I keep my determined gaze focused on Liam. He's the man in charge and the one I need to convince to let me pay.

I've no clue how long we remain in this weird sort of standoff, but it feels like forever. They can both stare at me with those angry scowls all day long. It won't cause me to back down. After the life I've lived, those looks don't scare me.

"Just take her money," Christian mumbles and shakes his head. "It's clearly not gonna work."

I snap my gaze to his and furrow my brow when I see something resembling disappointment on his face. "What does that mean?"

He steps closer to me and drops his head so he's eye level with me. His brown eyes turn to ice and a chill washes over my body. "You and Chase. It's not gonna work. Leave him before you hurt him."

"What?" I say at the same time Liam says, "Christian," in a low rumbly threat.

Christian turns to Liam and gives him the same icy stare. "She clearly has no clue who Chase is or she wouldn't be acting like this. Take her money and get her out of here." Then he turns his gaze back to me. He looks me up and down with derision and irritation. "I don't want her in my garage."

"*Our* garage," Liam says.

The brothers share one more glare before Christian saunters back into the garage and gets back to work on his bike. I can't help but watch him in disbelief. What an ass. I can't believe I had a crush on him for so long. If that's how he always acts, we would have killed each other in a matter of minutes.

I turn back to Liam and shove my card at him again. He lets out a resigned sigh and takes it. "You ready to deal with Chase when he finds out about this?"

"Are you?" I ask with a raised brow. This earns me a chuckle.

"No, but I can handle my pissed off brothers. Don't let Chase's jovial personality fool you. He's got an angry streak in him that can rival his twin."

"You should see me pissed off."

He raises both brows as if to ask me if I'm not pissed off right now. I am, but this is nothing. He hasn't seen a truly pissed off Lina Lange. But if his brother keeps it up with all these expensive acts of kindness, he'll see just how pissed off I can get.

"Fine." He picks up an invoice and studies it for a moment before he looks back at me. "Would you believe me if I said it cost a hundred dollars?"

I snort. "Hell, no. That doesn't even cover the parts."

He huffs. "Okay, then I'm only gonna charge you for parts. Labor is on the house."

"I can't let—"

He raises his hand. "Lina. This is already gonna cause shit between me and my brother. You're going to take this deal or give us nothing. Got it?"

With a curt nod, I back down. I don't like it, but at least he's giving me something.

"Maybe think about *not* telling Chase I paid. Save us both the headache."

His glare turns from irritation to anger, and I can't help but smile. All the Mutter men have a growly dominant side to them that adds to their hotness factor.

"You clearly don't understand how our family works," he says as he takes my bank card from me.

I shrug, resting my hands on my hips. "And you boys clearly don't understand how I work. So we're even."

For the first time since I marched into his office, Liam smiles. "There ain't nothing even about this deal. You just wait and see."

FELIX'S REACTION TO HOW I HANDLED MY CAR HAS LED TO A boatload of guilt on my part. It's festered and grown as the day wore on. I was so certain I was doing the right thing by paying for the repairs myself. Isn't that what every man wants in a woman? Someone independent and capable? Not a mooch.

When I told Felix what happened, he was so shocked by my response that I'd rendered him speechless for about ten minutes. It takes a lot to make Felix go quiet, and yet I managed it. It made me wish I could take back telling him what Chase did, and how I responded.

When he finally spoke to me, his words made me cringe.

You made a mistake. Apologize.

That's it. Five words. Then he went back to work, not saying another word to me about it the rest of the day.

At first, I couldn't see why Felix thought my decision to pay for my car was a mistake. Hadn't I told Chase I wasn't his responsibility? I'd been very adamant about that. As far as I'm concerned, he has no right to be upset with me for taking care of myself.

No one does. I've managed just fine in my adult life. I don't need someone stepping in now and taking over.

Giving up control of one's life never ends well. I saw that first-hand for years from the MC. How many women married into the club just to lose their lives? Not literally, but they had no independence, no individuality, and no control over anything that happened to them. They were treated like property.

I refuse to be put in that position.

But as the day went on, I started to see Felix's point. And maybe even Chase's.

He's not trying to take over my life. He's trying to help make it easier. Better.

At least that's what I think he's trying to do. I've never been good at relationships of any kind. That's why I don't have them. A couple days into this one, and I may have already screwed it all up.

Which is how I find myself sitting in Walmart's parking lot texting my best friend after I got off work.

She responds to me almost immediately, letting me know where I can find her. If anyone can help me make sense of all these feelings over what's happening with Chase, it's Jayla. She knows me better than anyone and often can put how I'm feeling into words better than I can.

I find her repricing some shelves in the cosmetics aisle. She gives me a gentle smile as soon as she sees me approach.

"Hey, Leens." She pulls me in for a hug before she turns back to the tags she's hanging. "Gotta talk and work. I need to finish this section before my shift ends in ..." she glances down at the time on her phone, "fifteen minutes."

"I think I screwed up with Chase." I blurt out. "I mean, he keeps doing all these things for me—things that cost a lot of money—and it's ... Nice."

Jayla looks at me out of the corner of her eye as she moves an entire section of concealer to a new rack. "And ..."

I let out a low huff and lean against the shelf. "I don't like it. You know how I like to take care of myself. I can't have someone dropping into my life and taking over."

"Gawd, babe. There are so many things wrong with everything you just said."

"What?" I glare at her.

She gives me a side eye glance and rolls her eyes. "First of all, who doesn't like it when someone helps them out? I sure as hell would love to meet someone who cares about me and wants to help make my life better. Of course you can take care of yourself. We all can. But that doesn't mean we have to. And accepting help from someone doesn't mean they're taking over your life. Chase isn't a member of the MC. He's not treating you like property. What he's doing is called caring. I know that's a foreign concept to you, but if you're going to date him, you're going to have to get used to it."

"Caring is *not* a foreign concept to me." I scoff, not only at my words but at the fact that this is the only thing I can think of to say to refute her. She's not wrong. Aside from her and my dad, I've not had a lot of people in my life who actually cared for me.

She gives me a look that says she's calling my bullshit. Then she shakes her head before turning back to her work. "Leens, let me ask you. Do you like Chase? Like butterflies in the stomach, you can't wait to see him again and have his arms wrapped tight around you, like him?"

I look away from her and stare at anything except her knowing glances. She really does know me too well. Which means my only option here is honesty.

"Yeah," I sigh. "I really like him."

"Have you told him that?"

"Not in so many words. But I did agree to date him and give this a shot. Does that count?"

"No." She chuckles. "Use the words. Tell him how you feel. Stop hiding behind all those protective walls you've built around yourself and let him in."

"Ugh," I groan and drop my head back against the shelf with a thud. "I don't know how."

"Then tell him that too. If you want this to work, tell him all the things. Help him understand your struggles. And he will understand. I'm sure of it."

"How do you know that? For all we know, he's just playing me."

This time she gives me a *you're a dumbass* look. "He's a Mutter. They don't *play around* with their women. They have their faults just like the rest of us, but they only date when it's serious. It's not who they are."

I drop my hands into my face and fight back a scream. "Why do you have to use logic on me? You know I hate that."

"Because I love you and I want you to be happy." She laughs. Then she turns to face me and all humor is gone. "Listen to me and listen real hard. You don't have to fight everything and everyone.

Things have been tough for you for so long. I think you've forgotten how to accept something good in your life. Chase is good. And it's okay to like him. Let him in and tell him how you feel."

"Arg," I growl out my frustration. "Why is this so hard for me? What do I even say?"

"Try sorry, I was an ass. This is new for me. Please be patient. Oh, and I like you. Like really, really like you."

"You make it sound so easy."

"Because it is easy." She gathers up the remaining labels before she points a finger at me. "You're the one making this hard. You need to get out of your own head and let those feelings flow out of you for a change. Keeping everything bottled up inside you is toxic."

"I don't keep everything bottled up inside me." I insist.

She stares at me like she thinks I'm an idiot. Probably because I am.

"Okay, fine." I toss my hands up in surrender. "You're right. I need to let myself feel more often. And I'll talk to Chase ... *Eventually.*" I add at the end like an afterthought.

Because I know myself. I won't talk to him right away. This is something I'll have to prepare for and give way too much consideration before I finally broach the subject. But I will do it at some point. Hopefully before it's too late and I screw up my chances with Chase.

Jayla lets out a long, tired sigh. "I know you will. Now walk with me. I need to put this stuff away and grab my purse. This shift is over."

I nod and loop my arm through hers, hoping this means this conversation is over. "What are your plans for the rest of the evening?"

"Promised Lucy we'd watch a movie. Mom is making that caramel popcorn we love. Wanna join us?"

"Sure. That sounds like fun."

"Great. Lucy loves it when you come over. She hasn't stopped talking about the art skills she picked up from you. I can't keep enough supplies on hand for her. I have piles and piles of paintings."

For the first time all day, I have a genuine reason to smile. "I'm glad. And I can't wait to see them."

"Oh, and that reminds me." Jayla opens an employee only door and waves me through ahead of her. "Any chance you can watch Lucy on Tuesdays for a while? Mom's shift changed at the clinic, and she has to work until seven. I don't get off until ten."

"I have my knitting group on Tuesdays. As long as she doesn't mind hanging out with us, it should be fine."

"She'd love that. Knowing her, she'll insist on learning to knit too and pick up another hobby she loves that I can't afford."

I laugh. "I should probably feel bad about that, but I don't."

"You should," she says as we enter the employee break room. She unlocks her locker and grabs her purse. "Anyway, Mom can pick Lucy up from knitting night if you prefer."

I wave her off. "I can drop her off at home once we're done. I love spending time with her."

"Thanks. I really appreciate it." She wraps her arm over my shoulder as we head out. "Now let's go eat too much popcorn and watch cheesy age appropriate rom-coms with my little girl."

Chapter 20

Mine to protect

Chase

Other than a few text messages and late-night phone calls, I haven't seen Lina since the night we spent together. She's had to work most days and nights—taking on double shifts—and I've been busy working the farm.

It's been impossible for us to find time to get together.

And I'm in a shit mood because of it.

Partly because my gut is telling me Lina is avoiding me. I believe her when she says she's working, but I can't help but wonder if she's taking on all those double shifts so she doesn't have to see me.

I pushed her hard about my need to take care of her when she was here. She definitely wasn't ready or happy about that.

At least I didn't have to push her too hard about being in a relationship with me. She didn't argue with me about that.

It's only been a week, but it feels like months. I miss her. And the level at which I miss her has me terrified. I'm in deep, and I'm afraid she's not really in this at all.

Talking and texting is not enough, but she's refused to give me time. It's that refusal that has me tied up in knots and throwing shit around the barn.

I toss another bucket that tries to trip me behind me and growl. I hate being in shit moods. When I get like this, it's like a vicious cycle that feeds on itself, making me feel worse. I don't know how to stop it when it starts.

"What did the bucket do to you?" a deep voice asks from the barn doorway. I glance over my shoulder to find Liam leaning on the frame with his arms crossed over his chest.

I've been avoiding my family all week. It was a matter of time before one of them hunted me down. Figures they would send Liam. He's probably going to go all dad-mode on me, and I'm definitely not in the mood for a lecture.

"Got in my way," I mumble.

He doesn't respond for a moment, and I don't stop cleaning up the mess I made yesterday when I knocked all this shit down in a fit of frustration.

"You haven't been to the main house all week. That's not like you."

"Been busy. Always am this time of year."

"Sure." His one-word response says so much. I hear the call of bullshit in his tone. "That's never stopped you from joining us for breakfast and dinner before. And now you've done it twice in the past month. So either we've pissed you off or something else is wrong. I'm going with something else because nothing has ever stopped you from speaking your mind with us before. So talk."

"I'm not in the mood for this right now, so fuck off."

Liam lets out a full-bellied laugh that causes my anger to spike even more. "Since when does that matter in this family? Is it Lina?"

My body visibly tenses at the sound of her name. "I said I don't want to talk about it."

"Too bad. I'm not leaving until you do."

"Don't you have a garage to manage?" I bark.

He chuckles. "It's Saturday. We close early on Saturdays."

I rub the bridge of my nose before I toss my head back and groan. I am not getting out of this conversation. "I've been in a shit mood, and I don't want to take it out on anyone else. Just let it go."

"You know I can't do that." He pushes off the edge of the doorway and steps toward me. When he reaches me, he places his hands on my shoulders in the way a father would just before he's about to let his son have it. "That's not how this family works, and you know it. So you can either talk to me and I can ward off the others, or the entire family will barge in here demanding answers. Your choice."

I sigh, resigning to talk. Because he's not wrong. If he leaves here empty-handed, Grams will drag all my brothers over and demand answers. After Warren left the way he did, she's never let anyone else get away without a fight.

"Lina's being distant, and I don't like it."

My older brother gives me a sympathetic look. "Has she given you a reason why?"

"She's been working a lot, taking on extra shifts. Her dad is sick, and she worries a lot about money. Which is why I wish she wouldn't fight me on helping her so much. Her family's association with the club jaded her."

Liam's eyes fall shut, and he lets out a slow breath like he's struggling to keep his body from tensing.

When he opens his eyes and meets mine, I see something resembling regret. It's confusing and causes my brows to furrow.

"I can see how that would bother you," he says.

"It's frustrating as fuck," I say. "I don't know what to do to convince her that I want to help because I care. But she keeps fighting me on it like she thinks I'm full of shit."

"Chase, you know better than anyone that you can't force your help onto someone. It's not your job to fix everyone's problems. I've watched you practically kill yourself cleaning up your mom's shit to protect Christian. Don't think for a second that I'm going to sit back and watch you do the same thing with Lina."

"Lina's different. You can't compare me helping her to saving my brother's life. Those two examples aren't even in the same playing field."

"I get that, but you can't take on everyone's problems as your own. Especially if they don't want your help."

"But Lina *needs* my help. And I do think she really wants it. She just doesn't know how to let me take on some of her burdens. If I give up on helping her, then I give up on her. And I can't do that."

"Okay, I'll give you that. But what about your mom? When was the last time you cleaned up her shit?"

I groan, not wanting to answer that question.

"Chase!" Somehow, he manages to chastise me with just my name.

"I know!" I scrub my hands down my face. "But I can't help it. She's a complete mess. If she keeps this up, she's going to kill herself. I can't let Christian find her like that. It'll kill him. And if that happens, I won't survive."

"None of us would, man. But at some point, you're going to have to trust Christian. We all are. He's a big boy, and he's been clean for a few years now. I know it's hard, believe me, but you have to learn to trust that. Trust him. You can't protect him forever."

"But I want to. He's my brother. My twin. My other half."

"I get it, but Christian is doing good. Besides, I'm keeping an eye on him. If anything seems off, you'll be the first to know. I promise. You need to put yourself first for a change."

Now it's my turn to laugh. "Hell, man. I've never done that before."

He shrugs and shakes his head. "Neither have I, but that doesn't mean it's not good advice. One day I've no doubt I'm gonna need one of my brothers telling me the same shit. So learn now so you can teach me later."

I squeeze Liam's shoulders. "Why not start learning now? We don't need you taking care of us anymore."

He raises a questioning brow as he looks around at the mess I've made of my usually well-organized barn. "You sure about that?"

I laugh and it feels real and good. It's also something I needed.

By the time I finish cleaning up the mess I made of the barn, it's late afternoon and my stomach is growling like an angry bear.

My brother's visit didn't exactly make me feel better. If anything, he made me realize I'm more screwed than I thought. I'm not going to be able to stop myself from helping Lina. It's who I am. And if she fights me every step of the way, I don't know where that leaves us.

When I step inside my apartment, my mood is worse. I don't even know how that's possible. Maybe I'll feel better once I eat.

I'm also in desperate need of a shower. After cleaning up after the animals and stirring up all the dust in the barn, I'm covered in dirt and grime. I rip my shirt over my head and use it to wipe the worst of the filth off my arms and face. It doesn't do much. Only hot water and soap will get me clean.

But then my stomach growls again, reminding me how long it's been since I've eaten. I never go this long without food, and if I don't eat something soon, I'll regret it later when I'm feeling weak and fighting off a headache.

Food first. Shower second.

Opening the fridge, I find a few containers of leftovers that weren't there before. I shake my head and grumble, knowing one of my family members snuck into my apartment and put them here. I don't mind the food, but I don't like them coming in as they please.

"I knew leaving a key with Grams was a bad idea," I mumble as I pop the top of what looks like meatloaf and mashed potatoes.

Shoving it in the microwave, I heat it up before I take it to the small balcony that overlooks the farm. It's a hot June day, and there's not much wind to speak of, but I feel too dirty to sit inside.

I'm so hungry that I scarf down half of it without tasting a bite. Just as I take the first bite I actually taste, there's a knock at my front door. It's light, almost timid, which is a clear indication it's not one of my brothers. Then again, if it were, they'd probably use the damn key.

There's a second knock before I have time to stand—this one louder than the first.

"Coming!" I call out after dropping my lunch off on the kitchen counter.

I swing the door open and freeze. I don't know who I expected to see, but it wasn't Lina. Not with how distant she's been this week. Besides, she's always made me come to her. That she came to me causes my insides to light up and a wave of need to spread from my chest to my dick.

Damn, this woman always makes my body sing.

Her eyes widen as they rake down my bare chest, and if I'm not mistaken, I see lust darkening those gorgeous blues I could get lost in.

"Dammit," she mumbles just before she really surprises me and launches herself at me. She wraps her arms around my neck and pulls herself up and around me. Her legs wrap around my waist and tighten like she's hanging on for dear life. Then her mouth crashes into mine.

There's nothing gentle about the way her mouth attacks mine. It's frenzied and needy on a level I've never experienced before.

Her tongue plunders my mouth, and her fingers dig into my scalp. Both earning her a groan from deep within my chest.

Without thinking—because let's be real here, the only part of my body thinking right now is my dick—I close the door and pin her against it. I grind my swollen cock into her center. The moan she lets out from the pressure I put on her clit is positively painful. My cock hardens even more, and the additional pressure against the zipper of my jeans might leave a permanent mark.

Somehow, rational thought takes over and I pull my mouth from hers. We're both panting, and from the painful look on her face, we're both desperate for more.

"Baby, I need a shower." I manage through ragged breaths. "I've been working outside all day."

A slow smile lifts her lips and something inside me breaks. A smiling Lina is my kryptonite.

"I can tell," she whispers. "You're irresistible when you look like this. All dirty and sweaty. I couldn't stop myself from kissing you."

I chuckle. "Men covered in barn dirt and maybe even a bit of manure turns you on?"

She shrugs. "Maybe. Or maybe it's because I missed you. Like, way too much."

I drop my forehead to hers and sigh at her admission. Knowing she missed me like I missed her calms a lot of the worry I've been carrying around all week. "I missed you too."

I press a gentle kiss to her lips so in contrast to how she just attacked me that it causes her to whimper. Then I slide my hands around her ass and lift her closer to me. Spinning around, I carry her through my apartment and into my bathroom.

Sitting her on her feet, I turn on the shower and adjust the temperature before I face her.

With a broad smile, I demand, "Strip."

She raises a brow and watches me as I reach for the button on my jeans and slowly undo it. Her eyes heat and she nibbles on her bottom lip as she tracks my every move.

"Baby!" I snap. Her eyes flash to mine as her breath hitches. "*Strip.*"

This time my one-word command registers and she listens. She rips her shirt over her, revealing the sexiest black bra I've ever seen. It's see-through, giving me a clear view of exactly what's contained underneath. Her nipples are hard and begging to be sucked. So I do exactly that. I don't wait for her to take off her bra. I drop my mouth to her chest and bite her through the thin material. She cries out in excitement and digs her nails into my forearms.

That's enough to snap me out of it, and I release her. "God, baby. You fry my brain when you're near."

While she's panting and shooting daggers at me, I strip off the rest of my clothes and step into the shower. When she doesn't immediately join me, I poke my head around the curtain.

"If you hurry it up and get in here, I'll do that again." She shakes her head and gives me a lust-filled look. I wink with a cocky grin that I learned a long time ago drives women crazy. "Just let me wash off first."

I shove my head under the spray of water to soak my hair, then grab the shampoo. By the time she steps into the shower with me, I've finished lathering up my hair and rinse it off.

"I reject your plan." She states firmly as she presses her hand to my chest, shoving me further under the shower head until water runs over my shoulders and down my chest. "*I'll* wash you off first, then you can do that again."

I grin as she grabs the bar of soap and steps close to me. She reaches around me and retrieves the washcloth hanging on the bar. Once it's lathered up, she steps closer until her body is almost flush with mine. That movement alone is enough to make my dick twitch, but when she runs the washcloth over my hard chest, my dick throbs in pain.

"Baby," I groan and place my hands on her hips, tugging her closer so my dick pokes her in the stomach.

She knocks my hands away and shakes her head. "Not yet. No touching."

I toss my head back and growl. When I do, water runs over my face, snapping me out of it. She chuckles and drops to her knees as she drags the washcloth down my abs and then squeezes my cock. She strokes it a few times, lathering it up with soap, before she runs the washcloth down one leg and up the other.

Once my front is thoroughly washed, she turns me around so the shower can rinse me off. She gives my backside the same treatment. By the time she's done, there isn't an inch of me she hasn't touched.

"My turn," I say as I take the soap and washcloth from her. Then I flip us around so she's the one standing under the shower head.

"But I'm not dirty. I showered before I came over."

"Don't care." I drop to my knees the same as she did and lather up the washcloth. "After the way your hands felt on my body, I need to touch you in the same way."

"Oh God," she moans and drops her head back until her hair is soaked while I press the washcloth to her flat stomach. "It's so nice to feel hot water again."

My hand freezes at her words. "What does that mean?"

She cringes but doesn't answer me.

"Lina?" I growl.

She sighs and drops her head into her hands to hide her face. "Our water heater doesn't work so great."

I fight the urge to yell at her for not telling me this sooner, but I bite back my frustration. Instead, I ask, "Doesn't work so great, or doesn't work at all?"

She drops her hands to my cheeks and stares down at me with a regretful gaze. "Does it matter?"

Wrapping a hand around her wrist, I force myself to stay calm. "It does to me."

We hold each other's gazes for several minutes before she finally nods. "Yeah, okay." Then she lets out a long, fortifying breath and answers me. "It doesn't work at all. Jonas keeps saying he'll come and fix it, but he hasn't yet. I'll take care of it as soon as I can."

I shake my head before she even finishes. "I'll fix it for you. Just tell me what's wrong, and I'll get it done."

"No! I can't let you do th—"

I press a finger to her lips. "Baby, when are you gonna learn? There's nothing you can do to stop me from taking care of you."

"Chase." She drops her forehead to mine and sighs.

Before she can object further, I lift the washcloth to her throat and brush it down her chest and between her breasts. Her breathing quickens, causing her breasts to heave. I can't help but lift up and flick her nipple with my tongue.

Her soft moans have me wrapping one arm around her waist while sliding my hand holding the washcloth between her legs. I'm not gentle as I stroke her, pressing the textured cloth against her clit.

She does me in when she digs her fingers into my hair and arches into me. It's all I can do to spin her to the wall and lift her leg over my shoulder. I drop the washcloth so I can run my finger down her center and slowly press inside her. Her grip on my hair tightens when I add a second finger just before I wrap my lips around her swollen clit.

She bucks against me, and I finger fuck her harder. With each lick and suck from my mouth and thrust of my fingers, she's pushed closer to the edge. I groan and suck her clit harder when I feel her body clamp around my fingers like she's trying to suck them deeper inside her.

"I'm coming," she pants and clenches her fingers into my hair and pulls while simultaneously pushing me harder into her.

The moment her orgasm hits her, I push my fingers as far inside her as I can reach, curving them into her. Then I flick my tongue against her clit. Her body bends forward and her legs buckle, and I have to wrap my arm around her waist to keep her from falling in a puddle at my feet.

I continue to pump my fingers inside her until her body stills and she tosses her head back against the shower wall. Hot water sprays over us and steam fills the air. She's completely sated, gasping, and has never looked more beautiful.

Wrapping my hand around her neck, I pull her mouth to mine and kiss her deep and hard. Her body may be limp from her release, but she kisses me back with the same level of fierceness that I kiss her.

"Fair warning." I mumble against her lips. "I'm fixing your water heater."

She shakes her head. "I can't let you do that."

"Baby, I'd like to see you try to stop me." I pump my fingers again while my thumb brushes across her clit.

Her protesting groan comes out more like a weak whimper and it makes me chuckle. "You're not playing fair."

My lips turn up in a grin. "How so?"

"Thanks to that orgasm, I'm too weak to fight you right now."

"So what you're saying is, if I keep giving you orgasms, you'll be too weak to stop me from helping you?"

"Probably. Maybe. I don't know. I can't think right now."

My shoulders shake with laughter, then I scoop her up in my arms and turn the shower off. "How about I take you to bed and give you more orgasms until you agree to everything I say?"

"Okay," she whispers as she buries her face in my neck and wraps her arms tight around me.

"I'm gonna remind you that you said that."

I kiss the top of her hand before I lay her on my bed. Her legs fall open and I groan at how deliciously gorgeous she looks. Her center is swollen and ready for my aching cock.

I quickly roll on a condom and position myself over her. I slide in with ease, filling her up completely. We both moan.

I spend the rest of the afternoon fucking my girl until she's promised to let me help her.

Is it wrong to use orgasms to get my way? Probably. But I don't care. I need to take care of her, and I'll do whatever it takes to get her to accept my help.

Chapter 21

Maybe I could get used to this

Lina

The heavy weight pressing down on me is foreign yet comforting. It's warm, like I'm wrapped up in a human blanket designed to protect and love me. And it's something I've never felt before in my life.

I can't believe I'm thirty years old and experiencing this feeling for the first time. The last time I spent the night with him, he was gone by the time I woke up. I had no idea this is what I was missing out on.

My back is pressed against Chase's chest and his arms are wrapped around me in a tight hug. His leg is tossed over mine and curled around the front like he's afraid I'll slip away if every inch of his body isn't touching every inch of mine.

Then his lips press to my shoulder, and a shiver runs through me.

"You're awake." His voice is rough and sexy and has me melting into him.

I glance over my shoulder to find he's watching me. Despite being filled with sleep, his eyes are bright and alive with something I've never seen before. *Love?* Surely not. I'm too difficult to make a man like Chase fall in love with me.

"Morning," I whisper as I fight to turn around in his embrace. He doesn't make it easy for me since he doesn't loosen his hold. But I manage. As soon as I'm turned around, he slides his hand down to my lower back and tugs me closer. His cock is hard and presses against my soft belly.

"Did you sleep okay?" he asks.

I nod. "Maybe the best ever."

He smiles and kisses the tip of my nose. Then he playfully slaps my ass. "Good. I've got to go take care of the animals. Get some more sleep."

He tosses the covers back and slides out of bed before his words even register. My mouth waters when I take in his perfectly toned, naked body. Everything about Chase's body is perfect. Tall, muscular, tanned. He's got just the right amount of dark hair dusting his chest. His abs are defined, and his legs are thick and strong. But my favorite part is his arms. So hard and built with muscles that could tear me apart if he wanted to. Instead, they keep me warm and safe.

His tight, firm ass is nice too, but that view disappears when he pulls his boxer briefs on. It's enough to shake me out of my moment of pure admiration for his form.

"I'll get up and help." I insist.

"No, babe." He leans over me, pressing my body back into the bed. "It's too early for you to be up. Get some more sleep. I want you rested for when I get back."

He plants a quick kiss to my lips and pulls away before I'm able to wrap my arms around him and pull him down with me. I let out a low growl in frustration, which only manages to make him laugh.

"Growl at me all you want, babe. It only turns me on more."

I narrow my eyes at him. "Your cheerfulness is infuriating on a good day. I can't handle it first thing in the morning."

His laugh shakes his entire body. "Then we're in for some fun mornings. I always wake up happy."

I grab the pillow from his side of the bed and press it over my face to muffle my groan. His deep throaty laugh gets louder, then is followed by the rustling of clothes. When I remove the pillow from my face, he's already covered that gorgeous body of his with an old, tattered pair of jeans and a black T-shirt.

I immediately miss seeing him bare. Without thinking or really knowing where the thought comes from, I blurt out. "I want to put some ink on you."

His eyes snap to mine with raised brows. "What?"

I swing around until I'm up on my knees and crawl to the edge of the bed so I can reach him. His eyes darken as he takes in my naked form. But unlike him, my body is covered in ink.

"You don't have any ink. Ever considered getting a tattoo?"

He shrugs. "Not really. Not sure I'd even know what to get."

I run my hands up his chest and then around his neck. His hands find my hips and his fingers dig in like he's struggling to maintain his control.

Leaning in close to his ear, I whisper, "Would you let me give you a tattoo?"

He's silent for a moment, and I'm not sure if it's because he's trying to find a way to gently tell me no or if he's seriously considering it.

I pull back and look into his deep brown eyes. He presses a kiss to my lips, then says. "I don't know. Will you stop fighting me and let me help you?"

My brows furrow. "Are you bribing me?"

His smile grows, then he slaps my ass. This time so hard it stings, causing me to yelp.

"If it works as well as the orgasms, you better believe it." He releases me, grabs his boots, and then heads toward the doorway through his kitchen. Just before he passes through the door, he turns around to face me, taking the last few steps backward, and calls out. "Baby, I just might do whatever it takes to get you to accept my help. Even let you cover my entire body with your art."

He disappears before I can respond. I want to be angry. I want to argue with him and tell him no way. But I can't deny the warm and fuzzy feeling I feel in my chest.

Chase Mutter has officially gotten under my skin and worked his way into my heart.

I know I'll still fight him on helping me—I won't be able to stop myself—but it won't be with the same level of conviction as before.

I IGNORE CHASE'S ORDERS TO STAY IN BED TO GET MORE SLEEP. There's no way I can miss an opportunity to see him work. He loves this farm and the animals, and I'm aching to learn more about it. Growing up in a small town surrounded by farmland, it's impossible to not to know a little bit about farm life. But I've never experienced it firsthand.

As soon as he leaves, I get out of bed and throw my clothes from yesterday on. Aside from being wrinkled from where I tossed them on the floor, they're still clean. I'd only had them on for a couple of hours before I arrived at Chase's apartment.

I stop by the bathroom to freshen up before I head outside to find him. I really want a cup of coffee but I'm afraid if I make coffee first, I'll miss seeing the animals.

When I reach the bottom of the stairs, I poke my head around the open stable doors. A broad smile immediately covers my face. Nothing could have prepared me for what I see.

Chase is running in circles while two goats chase after him. One of them catches up to him and playfully bumps him on the leg. Chase laughs and the goat makes some kind of noise that almost sounds like he's laughing too.

"Ramsey! Chill out, dude. If you keep acting like this, we'll never make it outside."

Chase scratches the goat he just called Ramsey behind the ear and a second one nudges his way between them like he's jealous. The chuckle that leaves Chase warms my insides and makes me a little jealous. I like it when Chase touches me behind my ear too.

"Come on, boys. Let's get you outside. I'll come back for Hugo and Tilly in a minute."

Chase takes a few steps toward the stable doors before he looks up and sees me. His smile grows and the playfulness in his eyes turns to desire. *Gawd.* When he looks at me like that I melt inside.

He steps up to me and looks down at me. I can't tell what the look in his eyes means. Either he wants to punish me for not listening to him or press me up against the wall right here and fuck me. Maybe both.

Then he lifts his hand to my cheek and presses a chaste kiss to my lips.

"I thought I told you to stay in bed," he says softly.

I shrug and lean into him. "Wanted to see your animals. I really like animals."

He pulls his head back with a look of surprise. "You do?"

I nod. "Always wanted a dog, but never had one. Do you have dogs too?"

He shakes his head. "Nah, my goats are my pets."

A wave of disappointment washes over me. When I was a little girl, I begged my mom and dad for a puppy. I'd seen kids with dogs in movies and they were like their best friends. I didn't have a lot of friends growing up, so I thought a dog would be the next best thing. Maybe even better than a friend.

But my mom hated animals. She'd cringe anytime a dog or cat got near her. She always said they were disgusting creatures. After she left us, I'd thought about asking Dad if I could get a dog, but I never worked up the courage. Besides, they just make me think of her and how much I hate her for how she left us. I don't need the constant reminder.

"You don't like dogs?" I ask, deciding I need to know why a farm boy like him doesn't have dogs. Dogs seem like a normal thing to have.

"No, I do. We had several dogs when we were kids. Don't really know why we don't have more now. Garret has a dog, Rocket. She's around a lot, so she fills that role, I guess."

I nod, fiddling with the hem of my shirt. I'm oddly relieved by his answer. Dogs aren't something I've thought about in a long time. And I certainly haven't considered getting one. Couldn't afford one anyway. But it makes me happy to know he's not opposed to them.

He slides his arm around my waist and pulls me against him. "What's that look mean? I can't tell if you're disappointed or relieved."

I look up at him and wrinkle my nose. "Maybe both. I like dogs and always wanted one. Relieved you like dogs, but sad you don't have one, I guess."

He opens his mouth to say something but is cut off when one of his goats pushes his way between us. Chase growls as he releases me.

"Butthead! Should have known you'd be a cock blocker."

I chuckle. "Butthead? Please tell me that's not his name."

"Oh yeah. That's his name alright. He's nothing but trouble." He plants a quick kiss to my lips and then takes several steps backward. "Come on, boys. Let's get you in the field, so I can get your brother and sister."

I fall against the side of the stable and sigh. Watching him run with his goats is oddly sexy and makes me like him even more. He talks to them more like they're his kids than his pets. And they chase him and cling to his side with equal affection.

"He's really taken with you," a strong, raspy voice says from beside me. I jump in surprise and press a hand to my chest. I smile when I see it's his grandmother.

"Mila! I didn't see you walk up."

She waves and makes a tsk noise. "Please, girl. You know better than to call me anything other than Grams."

I nod, and she places her hands on her hips before she looks up at me with a narrowed gaze.

Mila Mutter may be a small woman, but she's still intimidating. She's only five foot three with shoes on. Her white hair is short and spiked on top, making her look like a total badass. She cusses almost as much as her grandsons, and she always speaks her mind. From the way she's looking at me, I'd say I'm about to get a piece of her mind this morning.

"Now, about my grandson." Her words are firm, almost threatening.

I glance over my shoulder to find Chase is still in the field, running around with his goats. "What about him?"

"He's got it bad. Don't want to see him get hurt."

My chest tightens at her words and my eyes fall shut. I've known Mila my entire life. She knows my history, and we spend time together on knitting night. She just might know me better than Chase.

"I don't want to hurt him either. I like him."

She takes a deep breath, causing her nostrils to flare. "Yeah, I can tell. You've got it bad too. It's just ..." She trails off and looks past me to where Chase is now walking toward us. Her expression softens as she watches him. "He's a good man, Lina. One of the best. You both have baggage. Don't let it get in your way."

"He's a very good man. Treats me well. And I'll try. But it's hard for me."

Her eyes come back to me, softer now. "I know dear. Just don't forget that you're a good woman as well. Also one of the best."

My throat feels tight, and I feel my eyes heat with tears. I clear my throat and drop my head so she can't see the emotions she's evoked. The last thing I want to do is cry.

She squeezes my arm. "Now, none of that. He's almost here. If he thinks I upset you, he'll give me hell."

That makes me chuckle and instantly dries up the tears threatening to spill over. I always loved Mila and her ability to bring humor to any situation.

"Hey, Grams," Chase says before he kisses her cheek. Then he turns to me and presses a quick kiss to my lips like it's the most normal thing to do.

I stiffen and jerk back, surprised by the display of affection in front of his grandmother. He laughs with a wink, and then he slaps my ass.

"Chase!" I gasp, but he ignores me, turning his gaze to Mila.

"What brings you out this early?"

"Been baking. Need more eggs," she says matter-of-factly.

"Fridge inside is empty." Chase points behind him. "Took everything into town yesterday. Haven't collected this morning's eggs yet. How soon do you need 'em?"

"Can't make breakfast without 'em. I'll go collect them since you've got company."

"You sure? I can get 'em after I let Hugo and Tilly out."

She waves him off. "I'm sure. You just make sure you bring Lina over for breakfast. Don't you be keepin' her all to yourself."

He snorts. "She's my girlfriend. I can keep her to myself if I want."

Mila narrows her eyes at him. "I dare you to try."

"Now, Grams. Don't go gettin' your panties in a bunch." He leans down and kisses her on the cheek again. "You know I will."

Mila's frown melts away and turns into a soft smile. "You're a good boy, Chase." Then she turns to me and her smile grows. "I'm happy you're here. See you at breakfast."

I wave as she heads toward the chicken coop like a woman on a mission. Mila Mutter is locally famous for her cooking, and I've always wondered what it'd be like eating a meal at her house. With her rowdy grandsons, I bet it's nothing but jokes and laughter. I guess this morning I'll find out.

I turn to Chase to find he's still watching his grandmother walk away. I nudge his shoulder and ask. "Who're Hugo and Tilly?"

He gives me a wide grin and winks before lacing his fingers with mine and leading me inside the stables. "My other two goats. Come on, I'll introduce you. Tilly will love you."

AFTER PUTTING ALL THE ANIMALS OUT IN THE FIELD, IT takes Chase another thirty minutes to give the stalls a quick clean and lay down new hay. No matter how many times I tried to get him to let me help, he refused. Instead, I make mental notes of everything he does so I can help him do this at some point.

When he finishes, he turns to where I'm leaning against the stable walls with a heated look in his eyes. Then he stalks toward me with so much purpose in each step he takes that it has me standing up straight.

His hands come to my face and cup my cheeks. Then his lips crash into mine. It all happens so fast that I stumble from the surprise. But the strength of his body supports mine.

My back hits the wall as he pins me to it, taking the kiss deeper. His tongue dives into my mouth, exploring like this is the first time he's kissed me. His kisses often feel like that—*the first time*.

Our lips and hands turn frenzied and the next thing I know, he's pulling my shirt over my head and I'm undoing his jeans. Just as my hand slips inside and grabs his swollen cock, he tugs my bra down and sucks one of my nipples into his waiting mouth.

"This is why I wanted you to stay in bed." He mumbles after releasing my breast and switches to the other, giving it the same hungry treatment.

"Why is that?" I ask through pants and gasps for air.

"I knew I wouldn't be able to resist fucking you here. Having your eyes on me while I work is too damn tempting."

He thrusts into my hand, dragging a deep moan from my chest. Then he steals another deep, hard kiss before he pulls away.

His eyes rake down my body, and he frowns when he reaches my jeans.

"Take those off." He demands as he reaches for his back pocket. He pulls out a condom and then frees his erection.

I watch with excitement as he quickly sheaths his hard, thick length. "Do you always carry condoms when you do your morning chores?"

A sly smile spreads across his face. "Only because you're here. I knew you'd defy my order to stay in bed."

I quirk a brow. "Defy your order?"

"Yeah, baby. Just like you're defying me now. Your jeans are still on." He takes a step back and my body whimpers for him to be closer. "Off. Now."

I comply without hesitation. Within seconds, I'm standing before him, completely naked, while he strokes his cock.

"Fuck, you're beautiful. Your body is a work of art."

Before I can respond and tell him how much I admire his body, he charges me. His mouth covers mine as he lifts me up and presses me against the wall. My legs wrap around his waist and his cock finds my entrance like it knows where it wants to be.

I expect him to thrust into me hard. I'm prepared for it. My body is wet and more than ready for him. I want him to fuck me hard.

But that's not what I get. His kiss may be hard and frenzied, but he oh-so-slowly pushes inside me. It's so slow it's agonizingly painful. I want all of him. Need him. Crave him. Yearn for him in ways I've never yearned for anything.

A sudden rush of fear washes over me at how true all those feelings are. I've never felt this connected with someone before. I've spent my entire adult life avoiding relationships. I saw first-hand through my parents how much a broken relationship can destroy a person. I'm not convinced my dad ever really got over losing my mom. I never want to feel his pain, and letting Chase in opens me up to that kind of pain.

But it's too late to go back now. He's rooted in me. Whether or not I like it, he owns me in a way I hope I own him too.

Once he's completely seated inside me, we both moan.

"Please tell me that you feel this." He breathes into me. "You feel so good. Too fucking good to be real."

"I'm real," I pant as I swivel my hips, desperate to take him even deeper. "This is real."

He drops his forehead to mine and watches as he slowly pulls in and out of me. His movements are so controlled and steady. It's almost as if he's trying to commit every feeling and movement to memory.

"Please." I beg. "I need more."

He shifts his eyes to mine and cups a hand around my cheek. "More what, baby? I'll give you anything."

"More of you." I gasp as he pulls out, leaving just his tip at my entrance.

"You have me. All of me," he says, then slowly slides in until he hits me so deep it sends a tremor up my spine.

"Then fuck me harder."

"You got it, babe."

He pulls out of me again as he slides his hands under my ass. I wrap my arms around his neck and brace myself for his next thrust.

And it's everything I need and want. Chase fucks me hard and fast. I come almost as hard and fast. My body tightens around him. I toss my head back and cry out at the intensity of the pleasure.

Somewhere in the recesses of my mind, I remind myself that we're outside—in the stables—where anyone could walk up and find us. Hell, they can probably hear my cries inside the main house with as loud as we're being.

But I can't bring myself to care. Especially when Chase's orgasm follows mine and pushes me right into another one.

When he captures my mouth and swallows my cries, it's then that I admit to myself just how lost to this man I really am.

Chapter 22

An open arm welcome and a warning

Chase

Lina fidgets with the hem of her shirt as we approach the back door to the main house. She's been nervous ever since we got out of the shower and started getting ready for family breakfast.

A nervous Lina is an adorable Lina. She's always such a badass. If she's been nervous around me before, she hid it well.

I pull her to a stop just outside the door and tug her close. "I've got to be honest, babe. I'm really torn about how to feel right now."

Her brows furrow as she tightens her hold on my hand. "Care to explain that to me?"

"You're nervous. I don't want you to be nervous about eating a meal with my family. But I'd be lying if I didn't tell you that seeing you nervous right now makes me feel fucking awesome."

She snorts. "You feel good about me being nervous?"

I shake my head. "Not good. Amazing. It means you care. I like knowing that you care about me, even if you don't say it out loud."

Her face softens, and she leans in to press a kiss to my lips. "Of course I care about you. I wouldn't be here if I didn't."

Some of the worry and tension I've been hanging onto ever since we started dating fades away.

"You have no idea how much I needed to hear those words." I pull her into me and wrap my arms around her in a tight hug. Then I kiss her temple. "Now let's get inside before Grams sends out a search party."

Lina chuckles. "She wouldn't."

"Oh, she would." I grin as we step inside and through the washroom.

"She would what?" I turn just in time to see Mac standing in front of us.

"I was just telling Lina that if we didn't hurry it up, Grams would send a search party to find us."

"For sure." Mac turns his grin to Lina. "I'm the search party. She just asked me to come find you two."

Lina's eyes widen, and I chuckle as I squeeze her hand. "Don't worry. You know everyone here."

"I know," she leans into me and whispers. "But I've never eaten a meal with my boyfriend's family before. This is a first for me."

"A first of many, I hope," I say as I give her a chaste kiss.

"We seem to be sharing a lot of those." Some of the nervousness in her expression is pushed away and replaced with happiness. My chest warms.

"Oh, good. You're here." Grams's voice breaks through our moment. "I need to steal Lina for a sec."

I give Grams a questioning look. "Steal her for what?"

"Knitting problem," she says and waves me off like my question is ridiculous. She looks at Lina and smiles. "Come with me. This won't take long."

Lina gives me a shrug before she follows Grams out of the kitchen. Apparently, I stare after her for so long, my brothers start heckling. When I shake my head and scan the table, Liam, Ash, and Mac are watching me with various looks of humor and surprise.

Christian, however, looks concerned. Maybe even a little pissed.

"No Garret this morning?" I ask, ignoring my twin's glare as I take a seat next to him.

"Nah," Ash answers. "Now that he has Charlotte, he never joins us anymore."

Liam snorts. "It's not like he joined us much before her. Now he just has a good excuse."

My oldest brother is not wrong about that. Garret's been a grumpy bastard for as long as I can remember. He moved out of the house the first chance he got and only came over when Grams insisted he show up. If not for her, we'd probably never see him, even though he lives on the property.

We may not see Garret at breakfast anymore, but we see him more often for dinners and other events thanks to Charlotte and her family values. She's been good for him and has softened his hard, grumpy personality.

Now, if we could figure out how to get Warren to move home, all my brothers would be close.

I make the mistake of glancing over at Christian and find he's still glaring at me. I make an even bigger mistake by asking him why.

"Spit it out, man. I know you've got something to say."

He leans on his elbows and narrows his eyes before he whispers, "You're in deep."

I sigh and run my fingers through my hair. I expected one or more of my brothers to call me out on my feelings for Lina, but I didn't expect it to be Christian. Nor did I expect him to do it when she's in the other room.

"Yeah, I am." I admit.

"Be careful. I'm not convinced she's in it as deep as you are. You're going to get hurt."

"Chill. No one is getting hurt."

He shakes his head and his nostrils flare. "You will if you're not more guarded. I don't trust her."

I rear my head back. Now it's my turn to glare. "Well I do. She and I are on the same page about our relationship. I don't need you deciding it's time to step up and play the protective brother."

"That's not what I'm trying to do." He growls. "I just want you to be careful."

"Listen, this is new. Give us time to actually date and figure this out before you doom our relationship to fail."

I push to my feet, but Christian grabs my arm, holding me in place. "It may be new, but I know you. She means more to you than you do to her."

I shove his hand away and push back my chair. "Maybe so, but one day that will change. I'd appreciate your support rather than whatever the hell this is you're doing."

Before he can say anything else, I head across the kitchen to the coffee pot. I can feel everyone's eyes on me as I pour myself a cup. I'm sure the rest of my brothers heard our conversation, which means at some point, the others will say something to me too.

That's fine. They can say whatever the fuck they want to me as long as they don't speak a word of their concerns to Lina. She's enough of a flight risk without those assholes putting doubts in her mind.

I've finally got her.

She's with *me*.

She *wants* to be with me.

And I refuse to let *anything* or *anyone* ruin what we've started.

It's ridiculous how happy holding Lina's hand in public makes me. It's a seemingly little thing to most people, I'm sure. But to me? It's huge.

Lina is not big on public shows of affection, not even of the hand holding variety. That she's given me this is a major boost to my ego *and* my heart.

She even let me pick her up and drive us both to the school for a day of working on the derby bus. She's so damn independent that I expected her to tell me no when I offered. The smile that spread across my face when she agreed nearly split my face open.

I was already struggling with my disappointment over her refusing to come over last night and stay with me. I've seen her almost every day this past week, even if it was only for a few minutes before she headed to work.

She only stayed with me one night. She doesn't like leaving her dad alone, which I respect. I haven't been able to work out if that's because of his health or their poor living conditions. If something were to go wrong with the trailer, there's no way her dad could handle it on his own. I'm hoping once we get that fixed, and it's a safe place to live, she'll relax and stay with me more.

Assuming she doesn't kick me to the curb for stepping up and taking care of this for her. I haven't worked out all the details, but I have a plan brewing.

I squeeze her hand and lift it to my mouth, kissing her fingers. My chest warms when she smiles at me.

Clara, Karla, and Trevor are sitting at the picnic table laughing when we walk up. They're so engrossed in their conversation that I'm not sure they even heard us arrive until we step into view.

"Oh, hey," Clara says as she hops off her seat and pulls me in for a hug. After she releases me, she does the same for Lina. Lina stiffens slightly, but she doesn't retreat. *Progress.* "I didn't hear you guys pull up. We were just talking about school stuff until you got here."

"Anything worth sharing?" I tease.

"Not really. Unless you want a reminder of all the dumb shit teenage boys do to get girls' attention."

I nudge her shoulder and grin. "You say that like we don't still do dumb shit when we're grown men. I can tell you stories that prove otherwise."

"You mean like pretending to be your twin brother just to get a date?" Lina deadpans.

I turn my grin on her and wrap my arm around her waist. "Yeah. Exactly like that."

Then I plant a kiss on her lips. I expect her to recoil at the affection, but she doesn't. Instead, she kisses me back. My girl is full of surprises today.

"Aw!" Clara sighs. "You two are so cute."

Lina rolls her eyes and scoffs while I laugh.

"Alright, I'm outta here." Lina pats my chest and extracts her hand from mine. "I'm gonna get started on painting."

Before she escapes my reach, I give her ass a playful slap. She turns her glare on me, making Clara laugh along with me. Her eyes may be narrowed and her lips turned down in a frown, but I see the gleam in her eyes. She can pretend all she wants, but she likes all forms of my affection.

Once she's out of earshot, Clara says, "Glad to see you two finally figured things out."

"Yeah, me too. She's not made it easy on me, but she's worth the fight."

"Lina's got a huge heart under that tough exterior. You just got to chisel your way through to get to it. It takes a lot to earn her trust and very little to lose it, so be careful."

I turn my gaze to Clara. "Since when did you become an expert on Lina?"

"Knitting night." She shrugs. "I've gotten to know a bit about her since I started going. I like her, and I like her for you. I think I like you for her even more. She needs someone with your light-hearted personality and Mr. Fix-It mentality."

I snort. "Light-hearted? That's not exactly how I'd describe myself."

"Okay, how about a playful personality? She's always so serious. She needs someone who's going to make her smile."

I wrap my arm around her shoulder and give her a side hug. "That I can do."

"I don't doubt it. You are always the life of the party." She lets out a wistful sigh like she's thinking about something else rather than the conversation we're having.

"You okay?" I ask.

She shrugs. "Just thinking it's time I put myself out there. Seeing you and Mac, and even Garret, dating has me wanting more for my life."

I watch her for a moment, knowing who she's really thinking about. Clara's crush for Ash runs deep and long. I don't think she's ever even considered another man before in her life. And Ash is a damn fool for not seeing it years ago like the rest of us.

"He doesn't deserve you or your loyalty," I say, catching her off-guard.

Her eyes snap to mine, all wide with surprise. "Who?"

I tighten my hold on her, wanting her to know how much she means to our family despite my dumbass brother. "Ash. He doesn't see what the rest of us see. He's an idiot."

"What? ... I ..." She lets out a long breath and drops her face into her hands. "Is it that obvious?"

I chuckle. "Yeah. At least to me and everyone else who isn't Ash."

She lets out a low groan and peeks at me through her fingers. "Just tell me he doesn't know. Please."

I shake my head. "I wish he did and would do something about it. You're practically family already, and we'd love it if you were our sister-in-law. But ..." I trail off, searching for the right words.

"But what?" She drops her hands with a look of panic on her face.

"You've been pining over him your entire life. I can't recall you ever dating anyone. Not even when you went to college."

She shakes her head, and her eyes glisten behind her dark-rimmed glasses. The last thing I want to do is make her cry. But she shakes it off and takes a deep breath.

"It's never been easy for me to make friends, let alone find a boyfriend. I'm too awkward and nerdy. Hiding behind a book is easier than talking to people."

"You are not awkward. Shy maybe, but not awkward."

She chuckles. "But I am nerdy. Is that what you're saying?"

"Oh, you are definitely nerdy." I bump her hip with mine. "But nerds are so cool. And smart."

She rolls her eyes. "That's just what every man wants. A cool, nerdy girl that's smarter than him."

"Hell yeah. Don't underestimate the power of a beautiful, nerdy girl. Put yourself out there and you might be surprised. You're a catch, Clara. If Ash is too dumb to open his eyes and see it, then it's his loss. You deserve to be happy in love."

"Yeah, maybe." She shrugs and stares at the ground where the toe of her shoe is digging in the dirt. "I'll think about it. I just don't know where to begin. It's not like there are a lot of single men in Beaver."

I sigh. "No, there's not. Waverly or Chillicothe maybe?"

She wrinkles her nose. "Would I have to go out to a bar to find them?"

My chest tenses at the thought of Clara hanging out in bars to find dates. "I don't know. Might need to give this more thought."

"I guess I could try a dating app. Isn't that how people do it these days?"

That idea makes me feel even more protective of her. "That sounds even worse. Maybe we can just conk Ash over the head and knock some sense into him."

This earns me a laugh. "If only it were that easy. I might have tried that years ago."

"Wouldn't we all." I give her another side hug and tug her toward the bus. "Come on. Let's get to work painting this bus. Get your mind off him."

Chapter 23

Good news and bruises

Lina

Tuesday knitting nights have always been one of my favorite nights of the week. Especially in the summer when Vicki Lynn Baylor rarely comes because her husband takes her on a summer-long vacation. Her absence alone creates a calm that I desperately need.

But now that Lucy is coming with me, it's no contest. Knitting night is the highlight of my week. She brings life to our misfit group that's never been here before.

She and Clara nerd out over books for at least twenty minutes before they start knitting. Last week, they spent most of the evening discussing Harry Potter and how Neville Longbottom is the true hero of the series. This week, Clara handed her a few books and whispered something to her that had her eyes going wide.

Then Lucy settled in next to Mila and the two of them knit together like old friends. Since then, Lucy has bounced around to each member, chatting and making them laugh. But she has spent most of this evening curled up next to Hannah.

I've never seen Hannah smile so much in all the years I've known her. That haunted look that I sometimes catch in her eyes hasn't appeared once tonight. It's good seeing her happy for a change.

"Aunt Lina," Lucy calls out, dragging my eyes up from my knitting. "Can I have another cookie?"

"You've already had three. Your mom is going to kill me if I send you home on a sugar high this close to bedtime."

"Just one more." She clasps her hands together in front of her chest, pleading. "Mom will never know. And I promise I won't act too excited when I get home."

I raise my brow, ready to hold firm to my no, when Mila cuts in. "Here you go, dear. One more won't hurt."

Lucy jumps up, clapping her hands, while I narrow my eyes on Mila. She grins at me and winks in the same playful way Chase always does when he knows he's pushing my buttons and enjoying it.

"Oh, Lina! I almost forgot to give you this." Mrs. Hoffman smiles at me with her hand outstretched. She's holding a white envelope, sending a wave of relief through me. "It was a good week. Might want to think about a restock. We're almost out of your hand-spun yarn."

"Really?" My eyes widen as I take the envelope from her. Taking a quick peek inside, my jaw drops when I see how many twenties are inside. There's even a hundred-dollar bill. When I look back up, Mrs. Hoffman's smile is wide and bright.

"Like I said, it was a good week. Sold three pairs of your hand-knit socks and several skeins of your hand-spun."

"This is great. Thanks." I stuff the envelope in my purse and take a mental note of the stock I have at home that I can bring. I have more than enough hand-spun yarn to sell, but I'd like to add more completed projects. I don't sell many, but when I do, it's a nice boost in income. "I'll bring in some more stock this week to replenish."

"That'd be great." Mrs. Hoffman shares a look with Mrs. Engles. The suspicious gleam in their eyes has me glancing between them. Those two are known to plot and spread gossip like an out-of-control wildfire. My defenses immediately go up.

I'm almost afraid to ask what that look means, but I do it anyway. "Is everything okay?"

"Oh, yes. Everything is fine." Mrs. Hoffman gives me a gentle smile.

"We were talking to Sharon. The woman who organizes the Chillicothe street fairs," Mrs. Engle says. She looks over at me and waits for my confirmation that I know who she's talking about. "Well, she told us how successful your little art class was and, well ..." She pauses and takes a deep breath. "We were hoping you'd be interested in doing something like that here."

"You want me to teach classes? At the community center?"

"Yes," Mrs. Hoffman says without hesitation. "You know how we take a survey every year and ask what the community would like to see? An offering of classes was at the top of the list. We'd love it if you'd consider taking that on and teaching the first round of classes." She looks over at me with a hopeful gaze. "If you have the time."

"Um ..." I glance around the room, surprised by how excited everyone looks about this prospect. "But I don't have any formal training. I didn't go to college."

"Pish posh." Mrs. Hoffman waves me off. "If there's one thing I've learned over the years working in the school system, it's that college isn't everything. Life and career skills can be learned anywhere. You're talented and, from what I hear, a skilled teacher."

"She's the best!" Lucy chimes in. "She's taught me everything I know about art."

I smile at her excitement. "What kind of classes did you have in mind?"

"Oh, I don't know," Mrs. Hoffman says. "Maybe some painting and knitting classes to start. Anything that you're comfortable teaching. If those go over well, which I suspect they will, I'd like to expand. Turn the back part of this building into an art wing or studio. I've been looking into some grants that would allow us to buy supplies and equipment. We may be a small community, but we're a creative one. There's a strong interest in pottery and wood-working too."

"I've never done either of those things."

"That's okay. I'm sure we can find someone willing to teach some classes. But let's start with your skills. Once you've found a good groove, then you can look into adding other types of classes."

"Me? You want *me* to look into other classes?"

"Well, yes. I want you to be the art director. It'll be a part-time job. But if we get this grant, someone will have to take it over."

"So you've already applied for a grant?" My heart is beating wildly, and my mind is racing trying to keep up with this conversation.

"We did. Even worked in a salary for a director. You're our first pick to take on the role, but if you're not interested ..." Mrs. Hoffman trails off, staring at me with wide eyes.

"You're offering me a job?" I press my hand to my chest. The pounding of my heart reaching my hand.

"Yes. It wouldn't start until the fall, but we wanted to give you plenty of time to think about it."

"When will you know if you got the grant?"

"We've already been told we made the first rounds of approval. Now it's really just paperwork. As long as nothing changes regarding the funding source, it's a done deal. Three years of funding with the opportunity for renewal."

"Are you sure I'm the best choice? I mean, with my—" I cut myself off, not able to bring up my family history or the way so many in this community look at me. I want this, but I can't let myself get excited about something that I'm a terrible fit for.

"Lina, there isn't anyone else we want filling this role. You're the perfect fit." Mrs. Hoffman leans over and squeezes my hand.

"Let's schedule a time to talk next week to discuss specifics. Think about it and give us an answer after we talk more."

I nod, glancing around. Everyone is smiling at me with looks of encouragement. "Okay, sounds good."

Everyone turns back to their knitting like I wasn't just offered a life-changing opportunity. I'm sure the pay won't be a lot, but the opportunity to teach classes on top of running the program will add some much needed income to my bank account.

Who knows, maybe it will result in more sales for completed projects too. Sometimes getting to know the artist leads to increased chances of a sale. That's why street fairs are usually more successful for me than selling on consignment.

I glance over at Lucy, who's curled up next to Hannah, working on the scarf I'm teaching her to knit. The pure look of happiness on Hannah's face makes me smile. It's good to see her happy for a change. For the longest time, she never smiled. I'm glad Lucy brings this side out of her.

Hell, even I'm smiling more than I used to. But my smiles are not because of the little girl sitting across from me. It's not even because of the job I was just offered.

All my smiles are because of Chase. Three months ago, if someone had told me I'd be in a relationship with Chase Mutter before summer's end, I would have laughed in their face and called them a liar. Now I can't imagine my life without him.

And I'm trying really hard not to let that fact freak me out.

I HEAD DOWN THE LONG HALLWAY OF THE CONVERTED SCHOOL with Hannah. Lucy's grandma picked her up on her way home from work so I didn't have to drop her off, which meant I gotta stay a little longer.

"Evenin', Lina. Hannah." Ricky, the local law enforcement and Elvis impersonator, nods at us as we reach the door.

"Hi, Ricky," I say. "Quiet night tonight?"

"The best kind," he answers with a drawl. "You ladies have a good night and be safe drivin' home."

Hannah and I are still smiling when we step outside, and I'm about to say goodbye when she stiffens next to me. I follow her gaze. The chill that surrounds us feels like someone dumped a bucket of ice water over our heads. Gone is the warm summer evening. It might as well be the dead of winter with the way the air temperature dropped.

"You're late," Charlie says. His tone is cold and decisive. "Mind telling me why you're late?"

"Honey, knitting night ends at nine. I'm sure I told you that." Hannah's voice trembles at the end. In fact, her entire body is shaking, and it's not because of the chill that consumed us when Charlie appeared. She's scared.

He takes a step closer. "And I told you I wanted you home by eight. Now get your ass in the car. I'll deal with you at home."

"God, you're an asshole," I say, dragging Charlie's glare to me.

I hold his stare, but out of the corner of my eye, I see Hannah rush off toward her car. Charlie reaches out and grabs her arm, pulling her into him. Her body goes rigid, and she squeezes her eyes closed like she's bracing herself for a blow. He whispers something to her, and she nods quickly before he lets her go. She runs to her car.

I cross my arms over my chest, making sure he understands that I'm not scared of him. "We were just knitting."

"I don't give a fuck what you were doing. When I tell *my wife* what time to be home, I expect her to listen."

"Is that the only way you can get off? By scaring people? Or in your wife's case, hurting her."

His eyes flare, and he charges me. Before I can wrap my head around his intentions, he has me pinned against the side of the building with his arm pressed over my neck. "Choose your next words wisely, Lina."

"Or what?" I grab at his arm and dig my nails in, hoping it'll get him to loosen his hold. It doesn't. "You gonna show me how powerful you are? Hurt me like you hurt Hannah? I dare you."

Moving quickly, I work one of my arms free and try to jab him in the eye, but he's faster. With his other hand, he grabs my wrist and presses it over my head. His fingers hurt as they dig in tight, ensuring I can't break free.

"You never could keep your mouth shut. It got you in trouble when you were a kid, and it's going to get you in even more trouble now."

"Get. Your. Hands. Off. Her." Chase's cold, threatening voice booms around us. Each word spoken slowly and with so much anger, it makes me tremble.

Charlie ignores him and presses his arm tighter against my neck. I struggle to take in oxygen. "This doesn't concern you, Mutter."

"Wrong answer." Before Charlie can respond, he's ripped away from me and tossed on the sidewalk. I crumble to the ground, gasping for air. Chase charges Charlie, lifting him up by his shirt and getting in his face. "I warned you to never touch her. Payment time."

"Chase, no!" I cry out. Thankfully, he turns to me and the anger in his eyes fades. "Don't do it."

"He hurt you." It's not a question. It's more of a plea. He wants to protect what's his. He wants to protect me. And Charlie just threatened me.

"I'm okay. He's not worth it."

He shakes his head and turns his glare back at Charlie, but before he can take action, the doors behind us swing open.

"What's goin' on out here?" Ricky drawls.

"He attacked me!" Charlie yells. "Came out of nowhere."

Chase tosses him back to the ground and doesn't hesitate to kick him in the gut in front of Ricky.

Charlie moans. "See. He's violent. Arrest him."

Ricky looks back and forth between us. His eyes finally settling on me. He studies me for a moment before his eyes go wide. "Mind telling me what happened to your neck since the time you walked out of that building? It's really red."

My hand immediately covers it. It hurts and I'm sure I'm going to have one hell of a bruise with how hard he pressed against me, but it must be bad if he can already see it with all my tattoos.

"Charlie. That's what happened."

"Do I need to arrest *him*?" Ricky asks.

"No," I say at the same time Chase says, "Yes."

Chase's nostrils flare and his eyes go wide. Ricky shakes his head. "Well, which is it? You gonna press charges? If you are, I'll take him in."

"No, I'm not pressing charges." Chase objects, but I hold my hand up. Then I step close to Charlie. Close enough that he and Chase are the only ones that can hear me. "Not this time. But you touch me again, and you will pay a price that I can guarantee you are not willing to pay. Same goes for Hannah."

"You don't get to tell me what I can and cannot do with my wife," he says through gritted teeth.

"Don't say I didn't warn you."

With one last growl, he crawls to his feet and stalks to his car. No one says a word until his car is out of sight.

"Mind tellin' me what happened?" Ricky says, finally breaking the silence.

"I think he beats Hannah," I whisper. I feel their eyes on me. "I don't have proof, but she's scared of him. She flinches every time he's near. Sometimes she winces like she's in pain when she shifts in a chair, and at others, I swear I can see hints of bruises hidden under a thick layer of makeup."

"Well, fuck." Ricky groans. "I'll drive by their house tonight and check on her. Make sure she's okay. Won't leave until I see her."

When I look over at Chase, there's a look in his eyes that I can't quite read. Like he's lost in some deep, far-off thought.

I place my hand on his arm and give it a gentle squeeze. "I'm okay. I promise."

He shakes his head and pulls me into his arms. "Come on. Let's get you home."

For once, I don't argue with him. I don't insist on driving myself home even though my car is here. I give in to him and let him lead me to his truck. I'll worry about getting my car later.

After what just happened, he needs this. Hell, I need it too. Being in his arms sounds good and safe. It's the only place I want to be.

Chapter 24

It's not a fucking request. It's a demand

Chase

Lina doesn't say a word as I walk her to my truck. I don't say anything as I help her up and shut the door behind her. Hell, neither of us speak as I pull out of the parking lot and head toward the highway.

Lord knows, I'm too amped up to control my words right now. There are no words to describe the anger and emotional rage pulsing through me when I saw Charlie's hands on her.

He was hurting her, and for that, I wanted to kill him.

I don't know what I would've done if she hadn't stopped me. Part of me is glad she did. Ricky was there. No matter how wrong Charlie was in his actions tonight, nothing good would've happened to me if I beat the shit out of a man in front of law enforcement. I'm damn lucky Ricky didn't arrest me after I kicked Charlie in front of him.

But then there's a part of me that's still boiling over with so much pent-up rage over how I found them that I wish I took a swing at him. Just one. My fist connecting with his jaw would bring me so much satisfaction. That would've taught him a lesson he'd never forget.

Then again, with Charlie's money and power, he'd find a way

to make me pay for taking a swing. There's still a chance I'll pay for that kick.

That's tomorrow's problem. Right now, I need to take care of my girl.

It isn't until it becomes clear that I'm driving her to my apartment that she finally speaks. "Chase, I need to go home."

I shake my head. "You're staying with me tonight."

"I can't. I need to check on my dad." Her voice is so much gentler than what I'm used to hearing from her when she doesn't want to do something I want, and it catches me off guard.

"Fine. But I'm staying with you."

"No!" Her protest is quick and fast, and it has me looking over at her in concern. I don't miss the hint of panic in her expression before she schools her emotions.

I reach for her hand and squeeze it as I pull it over to my lap. "You know I don't care about where you live. I don't judge you, and I never will."

"It's not that," she says, but from the way her shoulders are bunched I don't believe her. "Dad is really sick. He doesn't like guests."

I snort at her lame excuse. It's cute that she thinks I'd fall for that. "Your dad loves me."

She rolls her eyes. "Not everyone loves you, you know that, right?"

I smile for the first time since seeing Charlie's body pressed against hers. "True. But your dad does."

I pull into a random driveway and turn around. She shakes her head like she's irritated with me, but then adjusts herself so she can rest her head on my shoulder. "Cocky isn't an attractive look for you."

"Liar," I say as I plant a kiss on the top of her head.

It doesn't take long to reach her trailer. It's dark. The porch light isn't on and there are no lights shining from inside. Lina fidgets next to me. I glance over at her after I put my truck in park.

"Everything okay?" I ask.

"Yeah, why wouldn't it be?" she says in a rush.

"Oh, I don't know," I say with a little too much sarcasm. "Maybe because as soon as the trailer came into view, you tensed. Now you can't even look me in the eye."

She retreats to her side of the truck like she's trying to escape me. My body sags at her reaction.

"Maybe you coming inside isn't such a good idea," she whispers.

I reach for her hand and thank fuck when she doesn't flinch from my touch. "Lina, look at me." I wait until she turns her beautiful blues to me. "What are you hiding?"

"Nothing!" she says with way too much infliction in her tone. "It's just ... Dad's sick. He's probably sleeping and doesn't want to be disturbed."

I lift her hand and kiss her knuckles. "Then we'll be quiet."

Before she can object, I turn off the truck and slide out. She rushes after me. "Chase, please."

I ignore her plea and head straight for the door. It isn't until I reach the doorknob that I notice the flicker of light through the window. I pause because it looks like a candle burning. Stepping aside, I nod my head for Lina to open the door. She hesitates for a moment before she finally sighs and unlocks the door.

"It looks like that last payment to the electric company wasn't enough, doll." A gruff voice calls out before we even make it inside. Lina's eyes fall closed and her body sags. She didn't want me to hear that.

"Dad." There's a hint of begging behind how she speaks. It makes me want to pull her into me and hug her close. Tell her it will be fine. "Are you okay?"

"Yeah, yeah. Just hotter than a sinner in hell." He waves her off as he pushes to his feet. "Chase. I didn't see you there behind her."

I reach my hand out to shake his. For someone she insists is too sick for company, his grip is firm. His palm is clammy and as soon as he releases me, he takes a paper towel to his brow. It's then that I notice just how warm it is inside.

"How long has the power been out?" I ask as I head toward the window to slide it open.

"A few hours. Just after I warmed up dinner. At least I got that done before they flipped us off."

"Why didn't you call me?" Lina asks.

"What for?" Her dad's raspy voice comes out loud and with far more authority than I expected. "You had your knitting. It's not like you could have done anything except sit here with me."

"I could have called the electric company." She insists.

"They're closed. Ain't nothin' happening until tomorrow."

I look around the small space until my eyes land on a pile of bills. I head straight for it. As soon as my hand lands on it, Lina calls out.

"No!" Her hand slams on top of mine before I can pick up the bill on top. "What do you think you're doing?"

"Helping," I say, keeping my tone flat. Then I pull her hand off mine and sift through the stack until I find what I'm looking for. Most of what's here are medical bills. A lot of them. I knew she was struggling, but this looks far worse than I thought.

Once I have the electric bill in hand, I stuff it in my back pocket. "I'll take care of this first thing in the morning."

"No, you won't. I can take care of it myself."

"Then why is your power off?" I snap, immediately regretting how the words come out.

"Because someone forced me to fix my car before I was ready to pay for it." She slaps her hand over her mouth like she didn't mean to say that.

I narrow my gaze as I decipher what her words mean. "*I* took care of your car."

Her shoulders sag, and she drops her head. "I made Liam take my money for it."

I close my eyes and swallow back the string of curse words that want to break free. I take a few deep breaths to calm myself before I open them and stare at a worried-looking Lina. "My brother and I are going to have words about that. I told you I had it covered."

"And I told you I couldn't accept your help." She barks her reply.

"Too stubborn for her own good." Her dad cuts in. "Won't accept help from no one. Not even the MC, and those fuckers owe me. Edge keeps trying to replace the water heater, and she refuses. More stubborn than her damn mother."

I turn my angry gaze to Lina. She covers her face with her hands like that's going to hide her from me. "You still don't have hot water?"

She shakes her head.

"You told me you had it covered."

"Damn thing hasn't worked in months," her dad says. "Getting tired of those damn cold showers, but this one," he points at Lina, "keeps waiting for her useless brother to fix it. Like that's ever gonna happen."

"Dammit, Lina." I place my hands on my hips, struggling to keep hold of my anger. "You could've used the money you paid my brother for your car to get the water heater fixed."

"Yeah, well, I didn't do that, did I?" she yells. "This is my life, Chase. This is what I have to deal with every single day. Don't you dare come in here and get all pissy with me because I didn't do what *you* wanted me to do. You do not get to dictate my choices."

I can't stop the growl that boils up from my chest and slips right past my lips. Is that what she thinks of me and my help? That I'm trying to control her? That's the last thing I want to do. I just want to take care of her. Make sure she's safe and has the basic needs that everyone should have to survive. She's got this all wrong.

Rather than correct her, I pull her into my arms and hug her tight. She fights me at first, but when I tighten my hold, she relaxes into me.

"Baby," I whisper in her ear. "I just want you to be safe and have the things you need."

"And I keep telling you that I'm not your problem to fix."

I lean back so I can look her in the eyes. I cup her cheek and give her a chaste kiss. "Part of what you're saying is right. You *are not* a problem to fix. You're my girlfriend. Someone I care very much about. If you think I can sit back and watch you struggle without helping, you're mistaken. I thought we settled this already. You agreed to stop fighting me on this."

She huffs. "I know, but I couldn't let you pay for my car. Please don't be mad at Liam. I didn't exactly give him a choice."

I stare into her determined eyes. Her strength is impressive, and I admire the hell out of her tenacity. But I cannot and will not sit back and watch her struggle like this. Not when I love her as much as I do.

My eyes fall close at how easily that thought came to me. I love Lina. She's mine, and I'll fight for her until my last breath.

"Okay," I say. "Let's forget about the car. But I'm taking care of your electric bill."

"No! I can't let you do that."

I shrug. "And you can't exactly stop me either. You've got enough on your plate with the rest of that pile. I'm not fucking asking anymore. I'm doing this for you."

She opens her mouth like she's going to object but stops herself. After a few beats, she finally nods. "Thank you."

She looks like those words caused her pain to say out loud. It drags a small smile from my lips. "When are you gonna learn, baby? I'll do anything for you."

Her eyes widen at that admission. Before she can make a big deal out of it, I kiss her again and say, "Go pack a bag. You're staying with me tonight."

She shakes her head and pulls away from me. "I can't leave Dad alone without power."

"Sure, you can," her dad interjects. "No use in both of us suffering."

"Fuck," I grumble as I wipe my hands over my face. In the heat of the moment, I'd forgotten about her dad. I look between them as they're having their own stare down. Seeing the determined look on her dad's face, I'd say he's just as stubborn as his daughter.

"Okay, fine," I say, breaking up their staring match. "I'll be back soon."

I rush past Lina and head toward the front door.

"Chase!" Lina cries. "Where are you going?"

I spin around and pull her into me, giving her a hard kiss. I don't even give a shit that her dad is watching. "To get some things. I'm not asking you to let me help you anymore. I'm just gonna do it, and you're gonna accept it. I'll be back."

I release her and rush to my truck. When I start it up, she's standing in the doorway, looking a little dazed and dumbfounded.

I kind of like that look on her. It softens her hard edges. It also means she's not fighting me, and that's progress.

I need to make progress with her. Because one day very soon I'll tell her exactly how I feel. I just hope she loves me too.

Chapter 25

Giving into this man feels too good

Lina

"Doll, if you don't stop pacing, you're going to wear a hole in this carpet. It's in bad enough shape as it is. It doesn't need help from you."

I spin around and face my dad. He's sitting in his recliner with a wide grin on his face. "Why do you look so happy? Need I remind you we have no power?"

"Temporary problem." He shrugs. "Can't be upset about that when my daughter is in love with a good man."

"Love!" My eyes widen. "I am not in love with him."

It's been almost an hour since Chase left me standing in the doorway, stunned by his declaration. I've paced around the small space of the living room ever since. I don't know why I'm so stunned. His insistence on helping shouldn't surprise me at this point. It's right on brand for the man he's proven himself to be.

I've spent so much time over the past couple of months either pushing him away or refusing his help. He ignored me every step of the way.

And yet he keeps surprising me in more ways than one. I've always seen him as a goofball that doesn't take anything in life seriously. I'm right about the goofball, but not the other.

Chase might be one of the most serious people I've ever met. He's also one of the most dependable. If he says he's going to do something, he does it. That's a quality I like very much.

It also scares the shit out of me.

Because it makes me *like—not love—*him far more than I'm willing to admit to myself. Sure, he's stirred feelings in me I didn't know I could feel. But love? I'm not even sure I know what that is.

Dad chuckles. "Sure you're not. Just like he's not in love with you."

I scoff. "He's not. He couldn't possibly be. I mean … It's not like I make this relationship easy on him. If anything, he …"

He what? I pause, thinking about how to finish that thought. I rack my brain for every possible negative emotion Chase could feel toward me and I come up empty-handed. Because I know he likes me. He wouldn't do the things he does for me if he didn't.

But love? Could he really love me? Could I love him? I let that thought roll around in my head and when I settle on an answer, I close my eyes. "Fuck."

Dad's soft chuckle surrounds me like a welcomed hug. "Don't sound so annoyed. Lovin' a good man isn't a bad thing, doll."

"It's not that." I sigh. "I'm not saying I love him, but my feelings for him are far deeper than I realized. Do you think he knows?"

Dad snorts. "Not with the way you're acting. I'd be surprised if that man wasn't second guessing everything about you."

I let out a deep groan, making Dad laugh even harder. "Am I a bad person?"

"No." He stops laughing and frowns. "You're a stubborn pain in the ass. That's for sure."

"Gee thanks."

"Let me finish," he scolds. "But you have a heart of gold. You protect it, rightfully so I might add, which makes it hard for some to see it. But I'd say that man has already figured that out about you. He sees your heart, and he loves you for it."

"How do you know he loves me?"

"Doll, all you gotta do is look at the way he looks at you. His eyes sparkle." Dad wiggles his fingers in front of his eyes in an exaggerated motion. "Even when you're pissing him off, his love for you shines through."

I nod, taking in everything he's saying. If I think about it and look back on all the time I've spent with Chase, I can see it. He always looks at me like I'm the best thing he's ever seen.

"I've never been in love before, Dad. I don't even know what it really feels like. What if I screw this up?"

He studies me for a moment. I can't tell if it's because he's studying me to figure out if I've already screwed this thing up with Chase or if he's thinking about his own mistakes. I'd be lying if I said his failed marriage to my mom hasn't influenced my views on love. Because it has. Mom left us without hesitation. She walked out that door and never looked back. Dad never recovered from the loss.

"Well, that's the thing about love. If it's the right kind of love, it'll last forever no matter what mistakes you make. If it's wrong, well ... it's doomed anyway, and your mistakes won't make a difference." Dad pushes up from his recliner and comes to me. He rests his hand on my shoulder. "I know what you're thinking. I loved your mom in the beginning. Would've done anything for her. I did, even after we fell out of love. I made great sacrifices for her that almost cost me my life. And she left us anyway. It was the wrong kind of love. We were never really meant to be."

"What?" I gape at him. "But ... You never got over mom."

He waves a hand in the air as if to shoo away my words. "Not true. If it were right, she'd still be here, and I'd still love her. But she's not, and I don't. Truth is, we fell out of love long before she left. You kids kept her here for a while, but after some time, even that wasn't enough. Sometimes love is just wrong."

"Dad." My entire body sags as the weight of my emotions pushes down on me like a ton of bricks. "How do I know if this is the right kind of love? I mean, what if it's wrong, but I move forward like it's right, and one day I wake up and realize we don't fit together?"

"You listen to your heart, not your head. You can't overthink love. You have to feel it." Dad presses his hand over my heart and whispers. "What does your heart tell you, Lina? That's what you have to listen to and learn to trust."

"What if I can't do that?"

"Then you'll lose that man. Ask yourself how that would make you feel. I suspect that will give you a clue about your true feelings."

Before I can ask Dad more questions, headlights illuminate the living room. I glance out the window to see two trucks pulling into our driveway. One is definitely Chase, but I'm not sure about the other.

Seeing Chase's truck causes my heart to beat faster and my stomach to feel light. Is this how someone's body reacts to the person they truly love? I wish I had all the answers, but I don't. I'm too new at relationships to decipher it yet. But I'm determined to figure it out.

Chase walks around the front of his truck just as the person driving the second one climbs out. Christian.

I haven't seen Christian much since Chase and I started dating. But based on how he glared at me when I had breakfast with his family, Christian isn't happy about it. I know it's not because he's jealous or likes me romantically. I'm getting hate vibes. When I asked Chase about his reaction, he told me not to worry about it.

Like that worked. It made me worry more. How is a relationship going to work between Chase and me if his twin brother can't stand me? Those two are close, and I can't be the one to come between them.

That concern is pushed to the back of my mind when Chase and Christian head to the door, each carrying two bags of ice.

I pull the door open before they knock, and Chase walks right in. He leans down and kisses me on the lips as he passes me and heads to the kitchen, with Christian trailing behind him.

"This ice should help keep everything cold while the generator catches up," Chase says as he stuffs two bags into the freezer and the other two in the fridge.

"Generator?" I ask.

Chase nods. "It's in the bed of my truck. Christian can help me get it hooked up. It's a big one. Should keep you with power until I can settle things with the electric company."

I cringe at his words, and this time it has nothing to do with his declaration to help. I don't want his family knowing how hard things are for me. The fewer people who know my struggles, the better. I don't need more small-town gossip.

Chase must sense my thoughts because he pulls me in for a hug and whispers in my ear. "It's okay, baby. Christian is the last person who would ever judge you. You're safe with us."

I squeeze my eyes closed to fight back the tears. Between the conversation I just had with Dad and Chase's comforting words, I'm an emotional mess.

"Thank you," I whisper back as I wrap my arms around him in a tight hug.

Chase relaxes against me in a way I've never quite felt before. Then he kisses the side of my head. "Anything for you."

I watch as they head back outside. Christian walks around the trailer with a flashlight and reappears a moment later. He points toward one side, then Chase hops into his truck, backs it out, then turns around so he can back the bed up in the direction Christian pointed.

It takes both of them to get the generator out of the truck and positioned on the side of the house. About ten minutes later, a rumbling sound fills the air, and the lights flicker on. Dad's window air conditioner kicks on next.

I shut the window Chase opened earlier, and then head to the kitchen. Even though I hear the fan running on the refrigerator, I make sure it's working.

A few minutes later, I hear a truck start up, followed by the sound of tires running over gravel. I hold my breath and wait, not letting it out until I hear the front door open.

"You should be good for the night, George," Chase says to my dad. "There's extra gas next to it. I'll refill it in the morning before I leave for work. Hopefully that will get you through until the power is back on."

"Thank you, son. I appreciate you helping us out. That's mighty kind of you."

Chase looks at me and smiles. "It's no trouble at all. Glad I was able to help."

"Well, I'm gonna go get ready for bed," Dad says as he pushes to his feet. "Probably gonna sleep in the recliner since it got so hot in here. No lecturing me, Lina."

Dad waves over his head as he heads down the hallway to his bedroom. Once his door clicks shut, I relax. Normally I'd give him shit about sleeping in his recliner. He gets better rest in his bed. But with the power being out for so long, his room is no doubt too hot to be comfortable.

The window unit in the living room isn't enough to cool the entire trailer, but it usually takes the edge off the heat in the other rooms. Tonight will not be one of those nights.

Chase takes my hand and drags me toward my bedroom. He stops to grab a bag I hadn't noticed him bring in with him.

"What are you doing?" I ask.

"Taking you to bed. You're exhausted."

"No, I mean what's with the bag?"

He looks at the bag in his hands with a furrowed brow. "I packed a few things before I headed back over."

"Chase, you don't have to stay with me. I'm sure it's hot in my room, and I only have a twin-sized bed."

He stops and pulls me flush against him. "Baby, I am not

leaving you tonight. Not after the day you've had." He lifts his hand and traces his finger along the bruises on my neck that I still haven't seen. Between my tattoos and the darkness from having no power, my dad couldn't see them. I hope he never sees them. "I'm staying."

I nod in understanding. Coming home to no power pushed the events from earlier out of my mind. I'd momentarily forgotten about the run in with Charlie.

I'd prefer to forget about it anyway.

We get ready for bed in silence. Chase uses the bathroom first, taking his toothbrush with him. I change into sleep shorts and a thin tank top that will be cool. I'm already sweating, and I imagine it'll only get hotter once we're both crammed together on my tiny bed.

I stare down at it and try to picture us curled up together. It's going to be a tight fit, and if it were cooler, a cozy fit. But as it is, we're going to turn into a puddle of sweat.

Being early June, the night air still gets cool. Hopefully, that's the case tonight. I dig the box fan from out of the closet and clear the few things I have sitting on the windowsill out of the way.

"Let me do that," Chase says as he steps up behind me. I turn to face him and my heart flutters at the sight of him. He's in nothing but a pair of dark blue boxer briefs. Every clean muscle from his shoulders to the waistband is on full display. My mouth waters and I have to clench my thighs together from the heat pooling between my legs.

"Baby, don't look at me like that when I can't do anything about it." His voice is rough and gravelly.

"What do you mean?" I step closer to him and run my finger along the tight rows of muscles down his abs. I linger at the ones just above the edge of his boxers, right where I'd put a tattoo if he'd let me. "I'm right here. You can do whatever you want."

He shakes his head. "Not in your father's home. I can't. That's disrespectful."

I roll my eyes. "I'm a grown woman and my dad knows I'm not innocent."

"Don't care." He leans in and kisses me, then he slaps me on the ass. "Now go finish getting ready for bed. I'll get the fan situated."

By the time I make it back to the bedroom, the overhead light is off. The small lamp next to my bed is the only light on. He's stretched out on my bed with his back against the wall. The room is already cooler with the fan running. Maybe it won't be as bad as I thought it'd be.

He pats the narrow spot next to him, then lifts his arm over his head. I can't help but smile at how good he looks. Chase is tall and slender but very well defined. I don't know if he works out or if he owes his firm body to working on the farm.

His body is tanned with hints of those farmer tan lines I've seen on others. With as tanned as his chest is, I can only assume he works outside without a shirt on most days.

Curling up next to him and keeping my hands to myself when he looks so damn delicious isn't going to be easy.

I click the door shut behind me and step across my small room. After flicking the lamp off, I crawl into bed, facing him. One arm wraps around my back, hugging me close, while his other hand slides up my body. His touch is so gentle it almost tickles.

His palm lightly presses against my throat and his fingers brush across my neck, right where Charlie's arm held me against the wall.

"Does it hurt?" he whispers, just before he kisses my forehead.

I want to tell him no—save him from the anger I know he'll feel from the truth—but that would be a lie. I need to be honest with him. *Always*. Even if it hurts him.

"A little." I look up at him to gauge his reaction. "My wrist hurts more from where he grabbed it."

His jaw tenses, and I immediately cup my hand around his cheek.

"I'm okay," I say. "I promise. In fact, I kinda wish he really had hurt me."

He pushes up on his elbow and glares down at me. "Why would you say that?"

I take a deep breath, debating on how much to tell him. He's not going to like my truth, but I think he needs to hear so he understands me better. That night with Charlie shaped the person I became just as much as my mom leaving and the nightmare with the MC. I just hope he doesn't lose his temper and do something stupid, like take revenge on my behalf.

"I need you to promise me you won't do anything."

His eyes narrow. "This is already starting off poorly for Charlie. Why do I get the feeling I'm gonna want to put him six feet under?"

"Chase." I warn. "Promise me you won't touch him, or I won't tell you."

He holds my gaze for several seconds before he finally lets out a slow breath. "Fine. I won't touch him unless he lays his hands on you again."

"Fair enough." I run my fingers through his hair, mostly as a stalling tactic, but also because I know he likes it. Then I take a breath, digging deep for my strength. "I was fourteen and—"

His entire body goes stiff with those few words. He knows exactly how much older Charlie is than me. Charlie went to school with Liam, Chase's oldest brother.

"So he was nineteen," he says, more as a statement than a question.

"Yeah. He was the cute, charming, older guy who seemed like local royalty to dumb little girls like me. And he asked me out on a date. I wasn't old enough to date yet. Dad said I had to wait until I was sixteen."

"Smart man." Chase grumbles.

"But I wanted to say yes. Badly. All the girls in my class had a crush on him, like he was a movie star or something. It made me feel special. That wasn't something I was used to feeling. Not with the MC and how they treated all the women and girls like property. To everyone but my dad, I was just a pretty face. Someone that would look good standing by their side."

I cringe at the memory of how Smoke made me feel. His creepy eyes were always looking at me like he was imagining me naked.

"Anyway." I shake off the memory and focus on an equally bad one. "I told Charlie that I wasn't allowed to date yet. He said he'd wait and ask me out again in a couple of years. He was sweet, and I believed him. Then he offered to drive me home."

"Fuck." Chase sits up and shoves his hands into his hair. "I don't like where this is going."

I join him, tossing my legs around him until I'm straddling his lap. "It didn't go where your mind is thinking. I promise. But he did hurt me."

Chase drops his head to my chest, and I wrap him up in a tight hug. "As soon as I got in his car, he came onto me. He tried to get my clothes off me, but I fought him. When I refused to have sex with him, he called me a tease and then hit me. Said I had no business looking the way I did if I wasn't going to let men take what they wanted. He was no different from the men of the MC. That was the day I started hating my appearance. I wasn't just some pretty face that men like him could do what they wanted with. It's what first started my obsession with tattoos. I own my body, and no one touches it unless I say they can."

Chase is quiet. It's almost as if he isn't even breathing. But then he looks up at me. I expect to see anger and rage. But I don't. His eyes glisten from the pain he's feeling for what happened to the fourteen-year-old version of me.

"Just when I thought I couldn't hate Charlie more, you prove me wrong." His words are meant in all seriousness, but they still make me chuckle. "I'm being serious. I wish I could take back my promise I made to you."

"I know." I smile and press a kiss to his lips. "I like seeing you like this. All worried and protective and caring. No one has ever cared for me like this before."

He brushes my hair back from my face and deepens the kiss. His tongue licks across my lips and brushes against mine. Then he pulls away, leaving me wanting more. "I'll always be here to keep you safe. I promise."

My instinct is to tell him to not make promises he can't keep, but I swallow back those words.

Instead, I focus on the conversation I had with Dad. I focus on my feelings. Being held by this man makes me feel safe. His words make me feel safe. The combination of the two makes me feel loved.

Maybe he loves me, and maybe he doesn't. But right now, that's not what matters. He's here, and he's holding me so tight it feels like he'll never let me go.

A girl can hope—maybe even dream.

For now, Chase Mutter is mine. And that's enough.

Chapter 26

Assholes, surprise visitors, and secret deals

Chase

Things with Lina this past week have been great. Really, really great. On her evenings off, we cooked dinner together for her dad. I stayed the night at her place on those nights. The rest of the time, she stayed with me.

I fixed a few things around the trailer that were easy to fix. I tackled that damn water heater that's on its last leg. It won't last long, but at least they have hot water again.

I took care of her electric bill and ensured they'd never go without power again. Even if things don't work out between us, that's something she'll never have to worry about. I took care of a few other household bills, so all she has to focus on is her dad's health.

The best part is Lina didn't fight me on it once. In fact, she welcomed my help. She didn't even complain when I showed up with enough groceries to feed an army. She's letting me take care of her, and I love it.

She's been so much more relaxed and happier now that some of this pressure has been taken off her shoulders. She's lighter, more carefree, and has smiled more this week than I've seen from her in the entire time I've known her.

Fingers crossed, my next plan doesn't cause the opposite reaction. Lina is a proud woman. It could go either way.

But first, I need to deal with my brother. I've put it off for too long, and I need to clear the air between us before my anger becomes a permanent fixture in my mind.

The garage is bustling with noise and excitement when I enter the back door, but I ignore all of that and head straight for the office.

"Liam," I call out. "We need to talk."

I find him standing next to his desk with his phone in his hand. He looks up at me and gives me a huge grin. Shit, he's in a good mood. Too bad I'm about to ruin that.

"Hey," he says. "I was just about to text you."

"Why the hell did you take Lina's money?" I cross my arms over my chest and glare at him, ignoring the happy vibes filling up the garage. I need him to know how pissed that makes me.

He sighs. "I wondered when or if she'd tell you about that."

"*You* should have told me. What the hell, man? Did I not make myself clear when I said under no circumstances were you to take money from her?"

"You were, but ..." He runs his hands through his hair. "She's very convincing. And kinda scary."

I scoff and shake my head. He's not wrong about the scary part. When Lina sets her mind to something, it's best to just get out of her way and let her do what she wants. Otherwise, she'll take you down as she plows over you.

I study my brother for a moment. He looks so out of place in the garage, dressed in clean khakis and a pale blue button-down shirt. He rolled his sleeves up, revealing his tattoos on his arms. If not for those tattoos, he'd look like a preppy boy.

"That's beside the point," I say. "You should have refused her and told her to talk to me. I would've calmed her down."

"How was I supposed to know that? I assumed your relationship wasn't that serious. Lina doesn't do serious."

The growl that comes out of me causes Liam to take a step back. His brows furrow as he studies me.

I regain the distance he put between us and then some. I don't stop until my arms bump into his chest. "When do I ever bring a girl to the house? Let alone to breakfast. With. My. Family."

"You don't." He huffs. "But this was before, and I just assumed—"

"That's your problem." I cut him off. "Don't make assumptions. Ever. She's my girl, and I'll take care of her. So when I tell you, or anyone else in this family, that I've got it covered, then that means I do. No exceptions. Is that clear?"

I expect Liam to fight back—to give me shit for being so aggressive with him—but he doesn't. Instead, he smiles.

"Wow. Look at you putting aside the smiles and jokes and being commanding and serious." He pats my arm and steps around me. "It's good to see you take such a strong stand about something."

My eyes narrow. "I take lots of things seriously."

"Let me rephrase that then," he starts, but movement from the garage draws my attention away from him.

"Is that ...?" I point behind him. My frown fades, and I forget all my angry thoughts.

"Are you two done arguing so you can give your big brother a hug?" Warren smiles at me from the doorway.

"Well, hell. When did you get here?" I rush past Liam and give my brother a hug. He so rarely comes home for a visit. Seeing him here now is such a surprise.

"Just this morning. Drove through the night." He pats my back before we release from the hug. All signs of the smile from moments ago are gone. "It was time to come home."

The way he says that causes me to pause. "Wait. Do you mean ...?"

He chuckles, but there's no humor in it. "Yeah. I'm moving home to stay." He glances past me at Liam. "That is, if it's okay with everyone."

Liam gives him a slight nod but doesn't smile. Maybe with Warren moving home, those two can finally settle whatever difference they had that drove them apart. Neither will talk about it when we ask. We all speculate that whatever falling out they had is the reason Warren moved away. Maybe now we'll finally learn the truth.

"Well I think it's fucking fantastic," I say. "It's about time you came home. Lord knows the racing team could use your expertise."

He nods but doesn't exactly look too pleased about that idea. "Yeah, maybe. I think I'll be taking some time off before I jump right into work."

"A break?" I raise my brow. "Since when does Dr. Mutter take a break from work? I thought work was your life."

He shrugs. "It was, and now it's not."

He turns and disappears through the door before I can ask him what that means. I look at Liam and frown. "Does that have anything to do with the fight you two have been in for more years than I care to count?"

He shakes his head. "I have nothing to do with that. But whatever it is, it has him messed up. I've caught him staring at the void like his mind is trapped multiple times and he's only been home for a few hours. Something is weighing heavily on him."

"Did anyone bother to ask him what it is?"

Liam sighs and starts for the door. "You know that's pointless. None of us talk until we want to, no matter how much we bug the shit out of each other. He'll talk when he's ready and not a moment sooner."

He's not wrong about that. Their silence on why Warren left in the first place is proof that no one can make them talk. But that doesn't mean I won't keep asking.

For now, I'll try to be content with the fact that all my brothers are finally home. That's something we've all wanted for a long time.

"Hey, Liam," I rush after him. He stops and turns to face me.

"For the record, Lina and I are serious. Not sure where this will go, but if I have a say in it, she's going to be around for a very long time."

He gives me a smile and nods. "Good. I like you two together. Sorry I didn't take it more seriously when she came by. I won't make that mistake again."

"Thanks."

Without another word, he heads deeper into the garage to check on the progress of a car Sophia is working on. I glance around, suddenly missing coming into the garage every day after I finish up on the farm. This is the first summer I've not worked alongside my brothers every day and it feels weird. I needed the break in my schedule, but that doesn't mean I don't miss it.

With a heavy sigh, I head for the side door and make my way back to the stables. I've got a long list of work to get done before I can call it quits.

Lina works tonight, so I won't see her until later. That should give me plenty of time to pay Edge a visit at Posey's after I finish up.

George gave me the rundown on all the ways Edge and the MC have tried to help them over the years, and that Lina has refused him every single time. I get why, but the MC is not the same as it was when George was a member or when Smoke tried to force her into an arranged marriage. Edge is different. He's a good man. I trust he'll do what's right without any expectations. Especially since the club owes me a debt too.

It's past time someone takes him up on his offer to help Lina and her father out. I just hope it doesn't land me in the doghouse when that someone is me.

Posey's Lounge is busy when I arrive. Every seat at the bar is taken and most of the tables are full. The dance floor is crowded with scantily dressed women with big hair and way too much make-up. They're swaying back and forth to bad eighties metal like they've got talent. It's not a good look.

Sally gives me a chin lift when he sees me approach. A few moments later, he's sliding a bottle of Bud in my direction.

"What brings you in on a weeknight?" he asks.

"Came to see Edge. He around?" I glance at the crowd. He's not in the main bar area that I can see.

Sally points toward the game room. "Poker game. Last I heard, he was winning. Should be in a good mood."

"Perfect." I flash him a wide grin before tossing enough cash down to cover my beer plus a tip. "Thanks."

I tip my beer before heading around the corner. The game room is more packed than the main bar area. It's busier than I've ever seen Posey's on a Friday or Saturday. Makes me wonder what I've been missing out on during the week.

I spot Edge on the opposite side of the poker table. He's staring at me like he knew I was coming, but I know that can't be true. I didn't know I was coming until this morning.

He whispers something to the man next to him before he tosses his cards down and pushes to his feet. The man next to him doesn't even look my way. He takes Edge's cards and continues the game as if there wasn't an interruption.

After taking a quick scan of the players, I don't recognize anyone. It's not our regular poker crowd. These men look rough and are all wearing cuts. And not cuts from the Unholy Ghosts.

"Hey, man." Edge takes my hand for a firm shake and pats my forearm. "Glad you came by."

I chuckle, and I hate that it sounds like a nervous chuckle. Not gonna lie—not even to myself—this crowd makes me uneasy. I feel like I walked into something I shouldn't have.

"Oh, yeah? Didn't know you wanted to see me." I glance around the room again before meeting Edge's playful gaze. "Should I, um ... come back another time? You seem kinda busy."

"No, man. Now is as good a time as any." He squeezes my shoulder and points toward a tall two top table against the wall. It's the only empty table here. It's as if everyone knew to leave it open for him.

Per his urging, I take the seat facing the room. He flags down a server and barely gets seated when the server appears with two beers. One for each of us.

"So." I clear my throat. I hate how nervous I sound. Edge and the MC have never made me nervous. They may be a little rough around the edges, but they're all good guys. "It sounded like you were expecting to see me. Or at least hoping to. Mind telling me why?"

He nods, looks around the room, and then back at me. "You're dating Lina."

It's not a question. He's letting me know he knows what goes on around this town, even if we've not made it public. "Yeah. Have been for a couple of months now. Sorta."

He raises his brow. "Sorta?"

I give him one of my charming grins that usually lets the receiver know I'm full of shit. "Well, she resisted me for the first month, but I can be persuasive. So I like to count that time."

He snorts and slowly drops his head. If I'm not mistaken, he rolled his damn eyes at me. "Anyway. Lina Lange. I need you to convince her to accept my help."

"Well, you're in luck." I take a pull from my beer before leaning forward on my elbows. "It so happens that I came here to convince you to help her and George. They can't live in that shit hole like it is, and I can't fix it all myself."

He gives me a pointed stare. "Does Lina know you're here?"

"Nope." I pop the P. "But I did tell her I was helping and not giving her a choice in the matter. I figure I've already pissed her off enough this summer with the things I keep doing for her. I pretty much wore her down. Now it's your turn to help."

He gives me an uncharacteristic grin that tells me I made the right choice in coming to him. He knows Lina the same as I do. Which means he knows she's gonna be pissed but will get over it once it's all said and done.

"I can get out there tomorrow with a crew. Have that place in tiptop shape before the sun goes down. That work for you?"

"Do I wanna know how you're gonna make that happen?"

"Nope." He pops his P the same as I did, and it makes me laugh.

"Alright. She'll be staying with me tonight and leaving for work from there. I told her I'd check on her dad. She doesn't get off work until six, but I think I can keep her there later if it'll help."

"Oh, it'll help." He tosses back the rest of his beer before pushing to his feet. Then he holds his hand out for a shake. I take it. "Gotta say, it was nice doing business with you. No bullshit, and straight to business."

"I see no reason for bullshit when the questions and answers are simple. Besides, you're paying the club's debt to me with this one. Just to be clear."

He stares at me for a moment like he's trying to figure out if I'm legit or full of shit. Because of my jovial personality, most assume I'm full of shit. Thankfully, Edge is the kind of man that can see past that and right to the heart of the matter.

"That's a hell of a debt, Chase." His voice is impersonal, but it's not directed toward me. He knows the score, and the club loses by a long shot.

The club's past actions are the reason my mom is an addict. They're the reason Christian is a recovering addict. When Edge took over as president, he promised me retribution. All I had to do was name the price.

"It is." I lean forward, resting my elbows on the table. "And I'm cashing it in. For her."

He takes a long pull from his beer before he speaks again. "In that case, we'll double up our efforts. She won't recognize the place by the time we're done."

"Thanks. I appreciate that."

"Lina's a good girl. I hate what my predecessor put her and her family through. I also hate what they did to your family. I've been waiting a long time to right that wrong. Thanks for making it happen."

I nod. "She means a lot to me. I only want the best for her. As much as she and George need a better place to live, she needs this closure with the MC more. I hope this act will give her that."

"Me too." He narrows his eyes and studies me. "What about you? Will this ease your mind? Give you the closure you're looking for?"

I shrug. "Don't know. But I hope this will get me one step closer."

With a heavy sigh, he pushes to his feet. Pausing next to me, he squeezes my shoulder. "You're a good man Chase. Lina is lucky to have you."

Then he heads back to the poker table. I finish my beer and head for the exit.

I came here tonight prepared to convince Edge to help. Thankfully, he made it easy on me.

Let's just hope Lina thinks this is a good thing. Otherwise I'm fucked.

Chapter 27

I'm so mad at you

Lina

Without my permission, my eyes wander over to the clock on the wall. I'm finishing up the details on my last client of the day, and instead of focusing on my work, I'm watching the damn clock.

Chase insisted on driving me to work today. He said he had a surprise for me when I got off. No one has ever given me a surprise before him, and he's already surprised me on more than one occasion.

If his teasing grin this morning was meant to evoke anticipation, it worked. I haven't been able to stop thinking about him and this surprise all day.

I shake my head and assess my work. Today is the last session for a regular of mine, Jazz. Every tattoo on her body is a custom design of yours truly. She came in for her first tattoo four years ago and was instantly hooked. After this large shoulder and back tattoo is complete, she won't have much skin left to ink.

"Almost done," I say as I grab the black ink. "Just need to add a hint of shadow in a few places to give this depth."

"Sounds great," her raspy voice replies.

Jazz is about ten years older than me and has probably had a much harder life than me too. She smokes a pack a day and drinks like a fish out of water. Her hair is a different color every time she comes in, and her clothes barely cover her body—even in the dead of winter.

But she's got a heart of gold and is one of the kindest people I've ever met.

She owns a small dive bar in Chillicothe that I've visited a few times. It doesn't look like much, and the drinks are cheap, but it's successful. She's got a regular crowd that is enough to keep in her business but still manages to pack the place on weekends.

She's got a sad story of her own that also happens to be connected to another MC in the area. Her story ended in heart-break, where mine ended in years of fear, followed by resentment and disdain.

Being a tattoo artist is sometimes like therapy sessions. People come in and sit in my chair and then dump their life stories on me. Sometimes I take in every detail, and other times I wish they'd just shut up. I am not therapist material. Lord knows I don't have good advice to give anyone. Look at how much I fuck up my life on a daily basis. I don't need to spread that to others.

But Jazz is different. And over the years, she became my friend.

Where I ran from the MC from my childhood, she ran to one as an adult. One random night at a dive bar named Crackers—the dive bar she now owns—and her life changed forever. I often wonder if that change was for the better, considering the outcome.

She was in her early twenties, took one look at Jimmy, and that was it. It was love at first sight. I'm not sure if I believe in such things, but she holds strong to her feelings.

She didn't care that he was in an MC. She didn't care that they did dangerous and illegal things. She loved him, and he loved her. That was all that mattered to them.

They never married, but from what she tells, they lived like they did. Losing him nearly destroyed her. A rival MC killed him, ending their romance far too soon. He left everything to her, including the bar.

Crackers is still an MC hangout, but they're not as prevalent as they were when Jimmy was still alive. She runs an honest business and doesn't take anyone's shit.

The love she shared with Jimmy scares me. To be that connected and beholden to another person can't be easy. Love makes people stupid. When you're stupid, you lose control. And losing control isn't something I can afford to lose.

"You're thinking awfully hard over there," Jazz says. "Mind telling me what's got you twisted up in a bunch?"

"I'm not all twisted up." I insist.

She scoffs. "And I'm Princess Diana. Spill."

"It's nothing. I swear. Just focused on this last bit of shading."

"Mm-hmm."

Before she can push further, the front door opens and the air in the room shifts. It's heavier, sending a rush of awareness through my veins. I don't have to look to know who just walked in. I feel it all the way to my bones.

Apparently, Jazz senses the shift too. She lifts her head and lets out a low whistle. "Is that tall drink of water that just walked in the reason for your distraction?"

I don't look. I can't. If I do, her tattoo is not getting finished. "I'm not distracted."

"Anyone ever tell you that you're a shit liar?" She chuckles.

"Anyone ever tell you not to piss off the person holding a needle to your skin?" I retort. This only makes her laugh harder. I shake my head and pull the needle away before I mess up. "If you don't stop shaking, you're going to make me fuck this up."

"Hey, baby," Chase's smooth, deep voice washes over me like a calming wave. I keep my eyes on Jazz's tattoo, but my focus is shit. Chase leans down and kisses the top of my head. "Damn that's good."

His words of admiration do the trick, and I can't stop myself from looking at him. He's staring at Jazz's tattoo like it's a Picasso.

"Thanks," I whisper. "I'm almost done. Then we can go."

"Take your time. We're in no hurry." He runs his hand down my hair and then squeezes the back of my neck. "Can I watch you finish up, or will that be too distracting?"

"Oh, she's distracted," Jazz cuts in. "Been that way all evening."

Chase lets out a deep rumbling chuckle that makes my belly feel light. "Is that right?"

"Yep, now get that sexy ass of yours over here, where I can see you better. Can't be looking over my shoulder to check you out."

Chase kisses my cheek before he moves around to the front of the chair where Jazz can see him. She studies him for a moment before she speaks. "You're a pretty boy. A good-looking one, but a pretty boy nonetheless."

"Is that a bad thing?" Chase asks.

"No, just not what I expected Lina to fall for." She looks him up and down. She's not wrong. Chase is very pretty and always well put together. "What do you do for a living?"

"I'm a farmer and a mechanic," he replies.

"A farmer and a mechanic?" She questions him with a heavy dose of disbelief in her tone. "You're too ... *clean* for either of those professions."

Chase tosses his head back and laughs. "You're not the first person to make that observation, but I am indeed both of those things."

"Hot damn." I can hear the smile in Jazz's words. "If you look this good all cleaned up, I don't think I could handle the dirty version of you."

Chase's grin turns positively smoldering as his eyes find mine. Then he winks, causing my belly to feel light again. "I save the dirty looks for those I hold special."

"Oh my!" Jazz fans off her face like she's burning up. Then she calls over her shoulder to me. "This one may not look like your type, but damn, he's cute."

"Thanks." He smirks. "Just remember, looks can be deceiving."

The laugh that bellows out of Jazz forces me to pause work on her tattoo again. "Will you two stop so I can finish this up?" I scold, but the humor is evident in my tone.

Chase tosses his hands up in surrender. "Sure thing, babe. Just don't put everything away when you're done."

I lift my eyes to meet his. "What do you mean?"

"You'll see." He winks, and I hate that it makes my insides melt. He's up to something, and I know I should be cautious, but that's becoming increasingly impossible with him.

For the first time in my life, a man has my heart. If he breaks it, I might not recover.

He leans against the wall next to my chair like he doesn't have a care in the world. Meanwhile, my heart won't stop fluttering and my belly is tied up in knots. By some miracle, I steady my hands long enough to finish up Jazz's tattoo.

Once she's set and out the door, I turn to face Chase, only to find him sitting in my chair with his feet kicked up.

"What are you doing?" I ask.

He shoots me a smoldering grin that breaks through all my defenses. "Waiting for you to get your sexy ass over here and give me a tattoo."

My eyes widen and a slow smile lifts my lips. "Are you serious?"

"Yep." He holds his arms out to his sides. "Your choice. I want a Lina original on my body."

I raise my brow. "Anything I want?"

"Anything."

"Can I put it wherever I want?"

He studies me for a moment with that playful gleam in his eyes that used to make me uncomfortable. Now, it turns me on. I pinch my lips together to keep from rushing toward him and kissing him senseless. What has this man turned me into?

"I think so," he says with a hint of hesitation. "But I get veto power if you choose some crazy spot that's going to cause me severe pain."

"Aw." My smile widens as I walk toward him. "Is my man scared of a needle?"

His eyes darken, never once breaking from mine as I step up next to the chair. "Fuck, I like the sound of that."

I narrow my eyes. "Sound of what?"

"Your man." His hand reaches around my neck and squeezes before he pulls my lips to his. His tongue parts my lips and tangles with mine. I melt into him, feeling my body fall. But then he breaks the kiss and pulls back.

I open my eyes and meet his hooded stare. Then I cup his cheeks and say, "Well, you are *my* man, aren't you?"

"Yes, and don't you forget it." He gives me one more quick kiss before he leans back in the chair. "Now, where are you going to give me this thing, and what will it be?"

"Hmm." I tap my chin, and then scan his body like I'm looking at him for the first time. Then I run my finger along his hip bone, from his outer hip to his groin. "Right here, and it's a surprise."

His gaze shifts to where my finger lingers close to his cock. He instantly grows hard. I can't help but chuckle at the sight of his erection pressing against his jeans.

"A surprise?" he asks.

"Yes." I grin. "Now strip off your jeans and get comfortable. I've got work to do."

"ALL DONE." I DAB AT THE EXCESS INK, AND THEN SIT UP TO admire my work. It turned out better than I envisioned.

"Can I look now?" Chase asks.

I refused to let him look at it until it was complete. It is, after all, a surprise. "Just a second. Let me clean it."

It's about fifteen minutes past closing time and we're the last two in the shop. Rob was off today. Felix came in to finish up on a client tattoo and had planned on sticking around to close up for Rob. I offered to do it, so he didn't have to sit around and wait for me to finish.

I study the lines of my art, now permanently inked on Chase's body, and a wave of nervousness washes over me. If he hates it or thinks is stupid, I'll be crushed.

He must see my hesitation because he reaches out and places his fingers under my chin. He gently forces my eyes to meet his. "Whatever it is, I know I'll love it."

"I hope so." I take a deep breath. When this idea first came to me, I thought it would be perfect. Now I'm second guessing myself. "Okay. Look."

The words rush out of me, but he doesn't move his eyes from mine. Instead, he slides his hand around my neck and pulls me to him. His grip tightens, causing his fingers to dig into my skin in the most delicious way. When he holds my neck like this, it screams *mine*.

I never thought I'd enjoy the idea of belonging to someone— not after how the MC treated me like property. But I want to belong to Chase. Dare I say, I need it.

He presses his lips to mine. I prepare myself for a deep, passionate kiss, but that's not what I get. It's way too quick, and I miss his lips the second he pulls away.

When he shifts his eyes to his tattoo, my heart rate kicks up and not in excitement. I've never been so nervous about a design before in my life. Probably because nothing I've done has ever been this personal for both people.

Chase's expression falls serious as he runs his finger along the edge of the cornstalk, and then down the long leaf that leads from his hip toward his groin. Sitting at the end are two ladybugs.

They're close—the way two lovers would huddle together. On the other side, running along the remaining edge of the leaf is a single word in a script font. *Protector*.

I study him while he studies it. His expression shifts from surprise to curiosity to something really close to awe. When he turns his gaze to mine, the look in his eyes steals my breath. Every ounce of doubt or worry I had over whether or not he would like it vanishes.

Before I can ask him what he thinks of it, his mouth crashes to mine. "It's fucking perfect," he mumbles against my lips.

I can't hold back my smile. "You like it?"

"I love it." He pulls me down until my body is spread over him like a blanket. I push against him, trying to avoid pressure on his tattoo. "Chase! You're going to hurt your hip."

"Pain is not what I'm feeling right now, baby." His arms tighten around me, and his growing erection presses into my lower stomach. "We're alone, right?"

"Yeah." I raise a brow.

"Good." He grips the back of my neck. "Because I need to be inside you right the fuck now."

"We can't!" The objection comes out of me louder than I intended. "Someone outside might see us."

He looks around and takes in the bright overhead lights and the large wall of windows with a perfect view of the parking lot and busy road. His eyes travel around the shop. He must see something he likes because he smiles and slaps my ass.

Before I can register what he's doing, he's on his feet with me wrapped up in his arms. "What are you doing?" I chuckle.

"Felix locked the door when he left, right?" He nods toward the entrance.

"Yeah, why?"

"Because I'm taking you around this corner where I can fuck you in private." As soon as we're out of sight, he sets me down. "Pants off."

He spins around and heads back into the main room, leaving me panting against the wall. "Where are you going?"

"Condom, babe. Strip." He demands.

I do as he says, and by the time he returns, all that remains on is my T-shirt. He pushes his boxers down and kicks them to the side, then slides the condom down his length.

"Are you ready for me?" he asks as his hand slides between my legs. His fingers dip into my wetness and he groans. "Fuck yes you are."

As if our thoughts are linked, I jump into his arms just as he slides an arm under my ass. His tip finds my entrance without guidance, and he slowly sinks into me. It's a slow, torturous intrusion. One that has tingling flickers of heat covering my entire body. I tighten my legs around him, sucking him deeper into me until he hits that sacred spot so few have ever found.

He pulls out just as slowly as he entered me as his other hand slides up my body and around my neck. I push my hips into him, needing more friction, but he doesn't give it to me. He tightens his hold on my neck and slowly fucks me. The way he moves inside me is fierce and reverent and promises so much more.

Between the strength of his grip on my neck and the way his hips thrust into me as he sinks in deep, I'm securely pinned against the wall.

He runs his thumb along the ridge of my throat with just enough pressure that it causes me to gasp for air. There's a dangerous undertone to the way he holds me, but not one that suggests he'll hurt me. It screams he wants to own me.

His mouth sucks on the skin right where my neck meets my shoulder. Then he slowly places open-mouthed kisses up my neck as he moves inside me. The way he's gripping my neck and fucking me are in complete contrast. His movements are slow, almost exploratory like he's discovering my body for the first time, but his hold on me suggests he knows me very well.

When his mouth reaches the sensitive spot just below my ear, he bites down. I cry out at the pain and pleasure it ensues.

My head spins as he moves faster—fucking me harder. I'm so close to my release that I can barely hold my head up any longer.

"So close." The words barely make it out before his teeth dig deeper and he sucks on my neck. That's definitely going to leave a mark, but I can't bring myself to care.

Everything this man does to me feels too good. Even the way his hand tightens around my neck in a choke hold. His palm presses against my throat as his thumb digs in under my chin, forcing my head back.

"Fuck, baby," he whispers, and then licks the spot he just bit and sucked. "I love your neck almost as much as I love you. Long, slender, and gorgeously decorated."

My mouth falls open, and my body goes rigid from the intensity of the orgasm that consumes me. It happens so fast my brain doesn't have time to fixate on what he said.

Instead of moving faster and joining me in his own release, he slows his thrusts, denying himself the pleasure of coming with me.

When he completely stills, confusion washes over me. "What are you doing?"

"Not yet," he rasps. "I want to make you come again."

"Chase. I'm not sure …" He cuts my words off when he pulls me into him and carries me into the break room. He sets me on the armrest on one side of the sofa and slowly pushes me down until my back is flat against the cushion and my hips are elevated.

He spreads my legs and stares at my center like he was just handed the best prize ever.

"So fucking pretty," he says as he lines his cock up with my entrance and slowly pushes in. "You look so good taking me in. I could watch my cock enter you all fucking day long."

He licks his thumb and then presses it against my clit. The pressure on the already sensitive bundle of nerves has my body lighting up again. He swirls it around, bringing some of my wetness over it.

He doesn't take his eyes off where we're joined. The look of pure satisfaction and pleasure in his eyes, combined with the way he's touching me, causes a second release to build.

"That's it, baby. I feel your body tightening around me."

He moves faster, fucking me harder, all the while never once taking his thumb off my clit. This man knows how to make my body sing for him. My back arches as my orgasm surfaces. I'm so close to coming undone again that nothing but the way he feels inside me registers.

This time, he doesn't hold back. His cock thickens inside me as his release overpowers his control. His thrust became erratic and his thumb presses harder into my sensitive flesh.

"Baby, please." He begs as the first wave of pleasure consumes him. The desperate tone of his words and the pulsing of his cock are enough to send me spiraling with him.

I don't know how it's possible, but I come harder than I did the first time. Maybe it's because we're coming together or that my first release never completely subsided. Regardless, I'm boneless and completely spent.

He thrusts one more time, filling me so completely, I can't tell where he ends, and I begin. He collapses over the edge, covering my body with his.

As he plants light kisses on my neck and down my chest, his words from earlier return. *I love your neck almost as much as I love you.*

Did he really say that? Did he mean it, or were they said in a moment of heated passion?

I shake my head. He couldn't have. He was just caught up in the moment. I don't care what my dad says, it's too soon for love. In a flash, my conversation with my dad runs through my mind.

Is this what he meant by the right kind of love? I shake my head, not able to think clearly with Chase's cock still inside me.

Besides, I don't think I'm ready for emotions and feelings that deep.

But still ...

I debate on asking him about it, but I can't seem to get my mouth to work. Instead, I focus on something else entirely.

"What made you decide to get a tattoo tonight?" He lifts his head, and when his eyes meet mine, my heart sinks. There's guilt behind that look. "What did you do?"

"Nothing I didn't already tell you I would do."

"And what was that, exactly?"

"Take care of you." He presses a quick kiss to my lips.

I narrow my eyes, not liking where this is going. "Did you let me give you a tattoo in the hopes it would lessen the blow back from whatever it is you did?"

"No." He rears his head back. "I'd already decided I'd let you do that at some point. I chose tonight to keep you distracted and away while Edge and his guys finished up the trailer."

"What?" I yell, and try to push him off me, but he won't budge. "Oh, I am so mad at you. I can't accept the MC's help. There's no way in hell I am ever owing them shit."

"You didn't accept their help. I did."

"Bullshit. Do you think that matters to people like them? They're bad people, and I don't want anything from them."

"They're not bad. Edge really cleaned up the club." His voice is softer and somewhat pained. "Besides, they *owe me*. This is a payment to me, which means you're free and clear of any obligation. Not that there would have been one without my involvement."

I furrow my brow and search his eyes. There's something hidden behind his gaze. A pain I don't yet understand. "What does that mean?"

He sighs and presses his lips to mine. "One day, I'll show you. Just not tonight."

He pushes to his feet, and I miss his warmth and closeness as he pulls out of me. He disappears down the hallway and slips into the bathroom while I gather my clothes. By the time he returns, I've got my jeans on and am slipping on my shoes.

He grabs his boxers before he heads back out front to get the rest of his clothes from my station. When he returns, he's fully dressed.

I look up at him as he leans against the doorway, a distant look on his face. I don't know what it means or how to handle this shift in his mood.

Is it because he knows I'm not happy about the MC? He has to understand why I'm upset about their involvement. Being indebted to the MC is a dangerous position no matter how *clean* they are now. They're still an MC.

My eyes shift to his hip, and I shake my head. "I need to cover your tattoo so it can properly heal. Pull those back down."

He does as I ask, and I quickly cover it and go over care instructions for the next several days. Once I'm done, he fixes his clothes and heads toward the front door.

"I'm still mad at you," I call out as I push to my feet.

He shrugs. "That's fine. You can be as mad as you want. Just don't run from me."

Our eyes lock, neither of us moving. A hint of worry pushes past his pain, and it causes the tension to leave my body.

"I won't," I say as I grab my things so we can leave.

I lock up in silence, and neither of us says a word as he drives me to his apartment. I want to argue with him to take me home. Not only do I want to see what the MC did, but I want some space. I need time to process his declaration of love. Hell, I don't even know if he meant it.

But I don't.

I let him lead me upstairs.

I let him help me clean up and slip one of his oversized T-shirts over me.

And then I let him curl up next to me in bed and hold me tight.

It's clear he needs this closeness more than I need to hang onto my anger or freak out over the fact that he might love me.

I'll give him this tonight and deal with my own emotional drama tomorrow.

A FEW DAYS LATER, I WALK INTO POSEY'S LOUNGE A LITTLE after noon with a serious chip on my shoulder. The bar opened about ten minutes ago and I hope to catch Edge before they get busy.

Edge and I need to have words, because Chase didn't just recruit the MC's help to fix up my dad's trailer. They replaced the whole damn thing.

I just about lost it when Chase drove me home the next morning. Right where our nearly condemned home once sat was one that looked twice as long and wider than what was there when I left the previous morning.

The outside is a bright white with charcoal gray trim, where the old one was a dingy white with various shades of brown covering it in a mottled design from years of weathering. The inside is fresh and clean and looks like it's never been lived in. The carpet is dark tan. The walls are crisp off-white, and the kitchen has granite countertops, stainless steel appliances, and dark wood cabinets.

Even the furniture is new. I didn't think anything would ever convince my dad to get a new recliner. He's refused to replace his old one for years. But he seems to love the new, soft leather recliner that came with this new home.

Whereas the old trailer only had two bedrooms and one bathroom, this one has three bedrooms and two bathrooms. Dad and I no longer have to share. He refused to take the bedroom with the en suite, saving that one for me. If I'd been here at the time, that wouldn't have happened. Hell, if I'd been there, that trailer wouldn't have happened.

The whole damn thing is a luxury that Dad and I have never experienced before. And there's no way in hell it comes with no strings attached.

I march up to the bar, and as soon as Sally sees me, he holds his hands up in surrender. "I had nothing to do with it. Edge is in the game room."

"Thanks, Sally." I keep on walking, not bothering to stop and dig for more information. Sally's quick deflection to Edge tells me all I need to know. Edge has been expecting my visit.

When I round the corner, Edge is sitting at the high-top table next to the wall that's always left open for him. He's leaning back in his chair with his arm propped up on the back. He's watching the door like he's been expecting me to pass through it.

"Lina," he says my name with too much enthusiasm for my comfort. He makes it sound like we're old friends when we're anything but. "I've been waiting for you. Glad you finally decided to stop by."

"Cut the shit. You had no right to swap our trailer. I told you I didn't want anything from you."

"Sit," he says. His voice is commanding and leaves no room for debate. He expects me to listen to him.

I cross my arms over my chest and hold my position. "I'm just fine right where I'm at."

His eyes narrow. "Suit yourself.

"I can't be indebted to the club. Take it back. All of it."

"Not happening. And you owe us nothing. There is no debt." He takes a long pull from his beer before he calls the server over. "I'll take another and go ahead and bring one for Lina too."

"I don't want a beer." I hiss.

"Bring her a beer," Edge's voice booms. The server scurries off like a scared little kitten. I don't flinch. All his behavior manages to do to me is piss me off more.

"I'm not scared of you," I say.

"Good. 'Cause I'm not trying to scare you."

"Then what are you trying to do?" Some of my anger dissipates, and much to my dismay, I take the seat opposite him. I am so tired of fighting everything and everyone. But I can't let him do this for my family. "You have to understand why I can't accept this from you."

"I do," he says without hesitation. His reaction surprises me.

"Then why did you do it?"

He shrugs. "I didn't do it for you. I did it for Chase. The club owed him a debt."

"What kind of debt?"

He shakes his head. "That's between Chase and the club. If he wants you to know, he'll tell you."

"But ..." My mind races with reasons why this could be the case. As far as I know, Chase never had any association with the MC. His mom did, but even that was on the periphery. She was never connected intimately to a club member that I'm aware of.

The server returns and sets a beer in front of each of us. I stare at it, but don't bother picking it up.

Edge picks up his and then pushes to his feet. "I think we're done here. Enjoy your new home and be sure to thank Chase for it. He made this happen for you."

He nods at someone behind me, but I don't look to see who. For once, I don't know what to say. If this is truly the club paying a debt owed to Chase, there isn't anything I can do about it. That's how it works.

My shoulders slump as feelings of defeat and helplessness run rampant through my mind. I don't like feeling like this. I'm used to being in control and taking care of everything myself.

Leaning forward, I rest my elbows on the table and bury my face in my hands. This is what Chase has reduced me to—a woman who lets someone else take care of her.

Is that really such a bad thing? I've taken care of myself for so long, I forgot what it's like to have someone around to help. Maybe I've never really experienced this kind of care before.

My heart beats faster and my lungs tighten. I feel like I'm losing too much control, and if I don't regain some of it, I'll lose myself in this downward spiral.

I squeeze my eyes closed and force my lungs to take slow, deliberate breaths. Once my breathing regulates, my heart rate slows to a normal pace. When I look up, I'm no longer alone at my table.

"Chase! I didn't hear you sit down." More like I didn't feel his presence. I usually sense when he's nearby. My body is tuned in to him, but this time he snuck up on me.

His eyes narrow and his frown doesn't look quite right.

"You okay?" I ask. "You seem upset."

I study him for a moment. His hair is neatly combed to one side, like usual. He's clean shaven, but I kind of wished he still had that little bit of scruff that he gets when he goes a few days without shaving. He's wearing a crisp blue button-down shirt and a pair of dark jeans.

He looks damn good, but something isn't right.

"You gonna answer me, or just stare?" That slow, devilish grin that he gets when he's about to tease me lifts his lips.

I hold his gaze. He may be grinning, but his eyes are missing that little extra something I see every time he looks at me. The man across from me is not looking at me like he wants me. My eyes fall closed, and I sigh.

"Why are *you* here?" I ask. "I'm in no mood for games."

He sits up straighter and looks around him like I'm talking to someone other than him. When his gaze settles back on me, he lifts a brow in question. "Games? What Games?"

I cross my arms over my chest and glare at him. "Give it up. I know you're Christian. Care to tell me why you're here dressed like Chase?"

The smile that spreads across Christian's face is one I've never seen before. This is not the forced grin he gave me when he walked in or the pretend smile of a man who doesn't really want to be smiling. He's smiling for real, and it causes me to shift back in my seat.

"Why are you so happy?" I point my finger at his face and wave it in a circular motion. "This smile is confusing as hell."

His smile instantly vanishes. He reaches across the table and snags the beer I have yet to touch. He takes a long pull before he answers me. "You really do care for my brother."

"I'm pissed at your brother," I say way too fast.

He shrugs. "Maybe so, but you still care about him. A lot."

I lean back in my chair and cross my arms over my chest. "You don't know anything about me."

"Maybe not, but you knew the moment you looked at me that I wasn't Chase. Not many can figure that out with just a look. You felt it, which means you care."

I look away, unable to hold his knowing gaze. I've been trying like hell to pretend I didn't hear Chase tell me he loves me during sex. I've also been pretending that I don't think I might actually love him back. It's too much to process along with the new trailer.

"I'm still pissed at him," I mumble under my breath, almost hoping he doesn't hear me.

"Why? Because he fucking cares about you? Come on, Lina. When is the last time someone did something nice for you just because they care? What has Chase asked for in return?"

He holds my stare. Once several beats pass without me responding, he answers for me. "Nothing. He's asked you for nothing. Why do you think that is?"

I shrug. I know he's right, but I can't seem to drop my stubborn streak and accept what he's saying.

"Fuck, you're dense."

"Hey. No need to be mean." I wave down the server and ask her for another beer. She nods and rushes to the bar. With the way this conversation is going, I need a few beers to make it through it in one piece.

"Mean? Honey, you ain't seen mean." His tone gets more

growly and rougher with every word he speaks. Either his true self is coming out or I'm pissing him off.

"Do you have a point?" I ask. "If so, I'd really appreciate it if you'd get to it so I can leave."

He grumbles, drops his head, and then runs his hands through his hair. Once it's all messed up, it's so much easier to see he is not Chase. "The idiot loves you. Can't you see that?"

I snort. "Doubt that," I say because I still prefer to pretend those words didn't already slip past his lips. "No one loves me."

Christian ignores me and keeps talking like I didn't just argue otherwise. "I'd bet money you love him too. You're just too damn stubborn to admit it."

"You don't know what you're talking about." The server sets two beers on the table, one in front of each of us. I pick up mine and toss it back.

"Don't I?" Christian challenges. "You knew I wasn't Chase before I even spoke a single word. I'd bet a hundred dollars no one else in this bar could've done that. Why do you think *you* were able to tell so quickly?"

"I don't know." I shout. "I just did."

"Well. I suggest you figure it out because here he comes."

Chapter 28

Three days of hell

Chase

When Christian messaged me asking me to meet him at Posey's, I rushed over assuming something was wrong. His message was cryptic and had me worried. I didn't expect to find him dressed like me and sitting with my girl.

Assuming she's still my girl. She's hardly spoken to me since the MC set up her new home, and it's been torture. I knew it would make her mad, and I thought I prepared myself for this reaction, but I was wrong.

It's only been three days, and I miss the fuck out of her.

I step up next to the table and run my hand down my short beard. I haven't bothered to shave in days. I glance between Lina and my brother. Lina looks pissed, but Christian is oddly happy. It's confusing as hell.

"What's going on here? Is this the emergency you messaged me about?" I ask.

"Just havin' a little chat with your girlfriend." Christian stands and pulls his wallet out of his pocket. He tosses enough cash to cover a few beers plus tip. Then he slaps me on the back. "She's all yours."

My eyes furrow as he walks away. I rush after him and grab his arm, pulling him to a stop. "What the fuck, man? Mind telling me what this is all about?"

He shrugs like he doesn't have a care in the world. It makes me want to punch him. "Ask her."

I step closer until I'm right in his face. "I'm asking you."

"Calm down, Chase." He rests his hand on my shoulder and gives me a slight shove back. "We just settled our differences. As far as I'm concerned, Lina's good."

I relax at his words. He's been against our relationship since the beginning. If he's finally come around, that'd make me happy. "You serious? You're no longer going to give me shit about dating her?"

He shakes his head. "Never again. Like I said, she's good."

Christian spins around and heads for the door, not bothering to acknowledge all the eyes on him. The bar isn't busy, but the patrons that are here are regulars. No doubt Christian's appearance is confusing the hell out of everyone.

I turn back to Lina and she's staring at me with a worried look in her eyes. I don't know why she's worried. I'm not the one who's doing the avoiding.

I march over to the table with a determination in my step that's on the verge of anger. I know Lina is pissed at me, but I'm pissed at her too.

"Mind telling me what that was about?" I ask as I plop down in the chair Christian vacated.

"Didn't he tell you?"

I shake my head. "He told me to ask you. So I'm asking. Talk."

Her eyes narrow, and she pinches her lips into a thin line. "Why are you mad?"

"Seriously?" My eyes widen and my nostrils flare. "You said you wouldn't run."

"I'm not running. I'm—"

I slam my hand on the table. "The hell you aren't. You've barely talked to me in three days. You've ignored my calls. Your text messages are limited to short answers, and you've refused to see me. If that's not running, then what the hell is it?"

"I'm processing." She yells. "You're a lot to take, Chase."

Her words are like a punch in the gut, and I instantly deflate. "Well then. Sorry to be such a burden to you. I'll never help you again."

I push to my feet and head for the door, but she grabs my arm before I make it past the table. "Chase." Her voice is soft and apologetic. "I didn't mean it like that."

I keep my eyes trained on the floor. I can't look at her right now. If I do, I'll break. "Then how did you mean it?"

"It's not you or the help. Sure, I'm pissed you asked the MC to help, but that's not what's wrong. It's these feelings." Her voice cracks, and when I look over at her, there are tears in her eyes. "I don't know how to process what you said."

"And what exactly did I say?"

She looks away and clenches her hands together on the table. She's nervous and unsure of herself, which is so unlike Lina. "At the parlor. When we were ... you know ... and you said you loved me."

I nod and glance around the game room. Thankfully, there aren't many people here and no one seems to be paying attention to us, but still. This is a private matter. "This isn't a conversation I'd like to have in public."

"Chase, please." This time her tears break free.

I want to pull her into my arms and comfort her, but if I do that, I'm screwed. I'm not exactly sure what those tears represent.

I hadn't meant for those words to come out. Telling her I loved her for the first time in the heat of the moment was not my plan. Clearly, it freaked her out. The problem is, I don't know what she's most freaked out about. The words? That I said them and she doesn't believe me? Or that she doesn't return the sentiment?

At least I can address one of those concerns easily enough. Not much I can do about the others.

I run my hands through my hair and take a deep breath. "I meant them. I love you, Lina. Very much. Those aren't words I meant to say until I thought you were ready to hear them. I don't expect you to tell me the same. Hell, I don't expect anything from you except to not run. That's what you promised me. But I guess this is too much for you."

"No!" She cries out and grabs my arm, tugging me closer. "It's not, but yet somehow it is." She sags in her chair and drops her head. With her free hand, she wipes her cheeks dry. "Fuck ... I sound like a crazy person. You're not too much for me, and neither are your words. To be honest, I didn't know if you meant them."

Knowing this is a mistake, I reach out and cup her cheek. The minute her eyes meet mine, I pull her into my chest. "Like I said, I meant them. Never doubt my feelings for you. My heart is yours."

When she looks up at me, her eyes widen and more tears well up in the corners. I sigh and drop my forehead to hers. "Take all the time you need, Lina. I'll be here when you're ready."

She fists her hands in my shirt and whimpers. I don't know if I should hold her tighter or walk away. "You say that like you think we're over."

"Not for me, we're not. What happens next is up to you." Then I do the last thing I want to do. I let her go and head for the door. If she needs time, I'll give it to her. I just hope it leads her back to my arms. Before I exit the game room, she calls out.

"Chase." I look over my shoulder and nearly break into a million pieces when I see the tears running down her face. "It's not over. I just ..." She looks away and takes a deep breath before her eyes meet mine again. Then she presses her hand to her heart. "I just need time to figure this out. This is new to me, and I don't want to hurt you."

I nod, dragging my eyes from hers. Because I already hurt. Watching the woman I love cry when I can't comfort her like I want to is one of the most painful moments of my life. Walking away only makes it hurt worse.

But I can't fix this for her. She has to figure this one out on her own. I just hope when she does, I end up owning her heart the same way she owns mine.

———

It's been less than ten minutes since I left Lina alone, crying at the bar. I've second guessed my decision to walk away at least a million times.

Seeing her cry nearly broke me. *My* Lina doesn't cry. She's strong and fierce. Those tears meant she was hurting just as much as me.

But if I stayed, and she decided I wasn't enough for her, then where would that leave me? I'd be hurting far worse than I already am.

I want her to return my love, but if she's not ready for love, I have no choice but to accept that. But before we can move forward, I need to know if she even sees the possibility of loving me.

If that answer is no, then I'll be the one crying.

But that's a problem for later, because I'm late for the Euchre tournament. If I've messed up our position and forced a forfeit in the first round, Grams is going to kill me.

After tossing my truck into park, I rush toward the side entrance to the community center. It's really an old elementary school that the town converted after they built the new school complex a few years back.

Frank, the owner of Frank's Frosty Kreme, the only restaurant in town, is sitting at a registration table next to the back entrance to the old auditorium. He gives me a smile and pushes to his feet.

"Just made it, boy," he says as he hands me my number and name tag. "Everyone just sat down, but the cards haven't been dealt. Better hurry it up and get in there. Mila is about to blow a gasket."

"Thanks, Frank." I slap him on the shoulder and rush past him.

As soon as I enter the door, the room falls silent. The Mutter team is always tough to beat, and I'm sure everyone was secretly hoping I wouldn't show. I scan the room, searching for Grams.

"Get your ass over here," she yells, making her position known. "I was about to hunt you down and skin you alive."

I sprint across the room and lean down to kiss the top of her head. She swats at me and tries to spank my ass like I'm a child. I jump out of the way and quickly sit opposite her before she embarrasses me.

"Where the hell have you been?" She narrows her eyes at me.

"Sorry." I hold my hands up in surrender. "Had to take care of something and it took longer than expected."

She eyes me for several beats before she lets out a breath. "You fucked things up, didn't you?"

I furrow my brows. "Why would you say that?"

She points a finger at my face and frowns. "You're not happy. I can only assume it's because you've messed things up with Lina."

I glance to my right to see Mrs. Engle staring at me with rapt attention. Of course the town gossip and her husband would be our first opponents. No matter what I say—or don't say—to Grams right now, rumors about Lina and me will be flying far and wide before the sun sets.

I glare at Grams, something I rarely ever do. "Can we talk about this later?"

"No! We're talking now. Tell me what happened so I can help you fix it."

"You can't, Grams." I yell, dragging even more eyes in our direction. I drop my head and rub the back of my neck, but it does nothing to relieve the tension knotted up inside me. I look up at Grams and whisper, "Unless you have some magical way to make Lina love me, you can't do a damn thing. Now drop it. Please."

She opens her mouth to speak, but the moderator walks up to deliver our cards.

"Game cards," he says as he lays the playing cards in front of

Mr. Engle. "I understand you drew the dealer's straw." Mr. Engle nods. "And here are the score cards." He hands the ten and six of hearts to me and the ten and six of diamonds to Mr. Engle. "The game cards are shuffled. Do not deal until we ring the bell. Good luck."

He leaves to pass out the cards to more tables. I look around the room, taking in how many teams are playing this year. I count at least fifteen tables which means at least thirty couples entered.

I let out a heavy breath and meet Grams's worried stare. She pinches her lips into a thin line and shakes her head. "Chase, talk to me."

I shake my head and look anywhere but at her. If she doesn't let this go, I'm going to lose it. Between her poking and the number of couples playing, this is going to be a long fucking day.

Chapter 29

Losing control isn't such a bad thing

Lina

By the time I pull into my driveway, I feel like a zombie. My eyes are puffy and red and my throat hurts. I've cried more in the past hour than I have in my entire life. Because I don't cry. Life in the MC taught me to never show weakness, and tears are definitely weakness.

But after Chase left and I made it to my car, I couldn't stop the tears from flowing. The image of a broken and hurt Chase is burned into my retina. I don't think I'll ever be able to forget that look.

He loves me, and I'm not sure if I can say it back. I'm not even sure I know how to love a man like Chase. He's good and kind and funny and will stop everything just to help me. He doesn't do it out of a sense of obligation. I get that now. He does it because he loves me.

Somehow that makes it so much worse.

I'd almost rather he does it because he wants something from me. Which just might be the stupidest thing I've ever thought, considering how much I've fought against that. But I know how to handle that scenario. My life trained me to deal with people who want things from me. No one ever showed me how to love and accept love.

Wiping my face dry yet again, I grab my purse and head inside. As soon as I step through the door, I startle at the sound of my best friend's voice.

"It's about time." Jayla yells. "Where the hell have you been?"

I meet her gaze and deflate even more. She's standing in the middle of my new living room with her hands on her hips and fire in her eyes. She scans my face and then her shoulders sag.

"Well shit. It's worse than I feared." She rushes toward me and pulls me into an embrace. As soon as her arms are tight around me, I sob again.

I don't know how long we stand there before I feel Dad's hand pat me on the back. It's a tentative pat like he doesn't know how to respond to seeing me like this. In all my thirty years, I don't think he's ever seen me cry. Not even when Mom left. He's probably just as confused by a crying Lina as I am.

"Shouldn't you be at work?" I mumble into Jayla's shoulder.

"Called in a personal leave day. Family emergency," she says like this is the most normal thing she's ever done.

I pull back to meet her gaze. "Is your mom okay? Lucy?"

She chuckles. "Yeah, they're fine. The family emergency is you, dummy."

"Me?" I feel my face wrinkle in confusion. "But I'm okay."

She lifts a single brow, calling my bullshit with one look. "Tears, Lina. There are lots and lots of tears running down your face. That is *not* okay."

"But—"

She lifts a hand before I can make up an excuse for why I'm fine. Jayla knows me better than that anyway.

"What happened with Chase?" she asks. Her tone is softer now. Almost like she's afraid to ask because hearing his name will upset me more.

I tilt my head to the side and study her. "How did you know? It only just happened."

She shrugs. "Small town gossip runs fast. Someone called Mom and then Mom called me. Now talk so we can fix this." She waves her hand around my face like it's broken. "I can't handle seeing you cry. Do I have to bury him? Please tell me no because I always liked Chase. The world is a better place with his smile in it."

I can't help but chuckle at her declaration, which I'm sure is what she intended. "No. Chase didn't do anything wrong."

"Then why are you crying?"

I sigh. Normally I'm quick to tell my best friend everything, but I don't want to talk about this. Not yet. Maybe I'd be able to hold off on this conversation if I wasn't crying like a hurt little girl, but there's not a chance in hell that she'll let this go now.

I drop my head and rub my hands over my face. I blurt the reason out so fast I almost hope she doesn't hear me. "Chase told me he loves me."

All I hear is silence. Even the sound of their breathing stops. When I look up, both Jayla and Dad are staring at me in confusion.

"Um, okay," Jayla says. "I don't understand. Then why do you look like someone died?"

"Because I don't know how to process this." I yell. "People don't love me. I'm the damaged daughter of an ex-MC member whose mom abandoned her, and the former president of the club tried to force into an arranged marriage. And not because he *liked me—the person*—he only wanted to marry me because I have a pretty face. That's all anyone sees. And that made me hard. I'm not a lovable person."

"Doll, that's not true." Dad steps up to me and takes me by the shoulders. "You are not a hard person. Guarded, sure, but not hard. You're trapped in the past, and it's time to let that go. How can you say you're unlovable? You are so easy to love, and you love just as hard in return. You're just scared, and that's okay."

"I'm terrified." Even though I try to fight them, more tears run down my face. I quickly wipe them away. "I don't know what to do. What if he decides I'm too much? I haven't made this easy on him so far."

"Lina, doll. Let go." Dad's voice is firm and forceful in a tone he's never used with me before. My eyes widen, and when I meet his gaze, he's looking at me like a father who's about to ground his child.

"What?" I ask, the word coming out in a timid squeak.

"Let go of this control you so desperately hang onto and let yourself feel for a change. If you don't, you're going to grow old alone and be miserable."

The look in my dad's eyes breaks something deep inside me. I reach for him and hug him close.

"Don't be like me," he whispers. "Please, doll. Be anything except like me."

"Oh, Dad." I cry. "You're not alone. You'll always have me."

"I know, and I love you for that. But you know that's not the same as having a partner, a person to love, to call your own. You love him. He's your person."

I nod. "I'm so scared, Dad. He has the power to really hurt me."

"Yeah, he does." He cups my cheek and forces me to look him in the eye. "That means you have the power to hurt him too. It goes both ways. You're both gonna have to trust that the other won't do that. That's love, doll. The *real* kind."

My eyes fall closed as I absorb his words. *The real kind of love.* Is that what Chase and I have? Not something fleeting or temporary that will be gone in a week or a month or even a year. The thought of not having him in my life makes me sick to my stomach.

"Okay, that's it." Jayla's voice cuts into my thoughts. "Let's go so you can tell him how you feel."

"What? But I—"

"That look your face just made says it all. You and I both know that losing him is a worse fate than the risk of letting yourself love him." Jayla declares as she heads toward the door and opens it. "So let's go so you can tell him."

"But ..." I take a deep breath and scrub my hands down my face. "I don't know where he is."

It's a lame excuse, and I know how dumb it sounds before the words are even out.

"Good thing I do, so move it."

"Are you sure about this?" I ask as Jayla drags me toward the entrance to the community center.

"Yep, positive. This moment calls for a grand gesture." She opens the door and waves me in.

I hesitate, staring at her like she's lost her mind. She raises a brow as if to say move it or I'm gonna kick your ass. I walk inside without a word.

She rushes past me and straight for the registration table down the hall where Frank Haas is sitting. He smiles up at us.

"Hello, ladies. Did you come to watch the last round? The tournament is almost over."

"Actually," Jayla says before I can answer him. "Are the Mutters still in it? We're looking for Chase."

Frank raises his brow at Jayla before he looks at me. I'm fiddling with the hem of my T-shirt and can't seem to stand still.

I immediately drop my head, attempting to hide my face. I'm sure my eyes are puffy and red. When I look at him through my lashes, he gives me a knowing smile and nods. "He's still in it. He and Mila are close to winning. Beat out the Kochs in the last round. That caused quite the stir. Now it's just them against the Baylors."

I sag at the mention of Vicki's in-laws. They've never outwardly treated me poorly, but I'm sure Vicki has said plenty to them to make sure they don't like me.

I don't want to do whatever Jayla thinks I need to do in front of a crowd, let alone one that includes someone connected to my life-long enemy. This is going to be hard enough as it is. I don't need an audience making it worse.

"Thank you." Jayla smiles and points toward the door. "Is it okay if we slip in and watch?"

"Of course." Frank returns her smile. He's always been such a sweet man and one of the few people I've never thought secretly judged me. He's older. All his kids are grown, and his wife passed some time ago. He's also a bit nosy and contributes his fair share to the gossip, but his kindness makes up for those flaws. "You ladies go right on in. Just keep it quiet so as not to disturb the players."

"We can wait until it's over." I take a few steps back.

Jayla turns to face me and grabs my arm. "Oh no you don't. You're marching your butt in that room and telling that man you love him."

"I can't. Not in front of everyone." I protest.

"Yes, you can." She insists while waving her hands in the air in a sweeping motion. "Grand, remember?"

"Um." Frank clears his throat. "I'm afraid I'm gonna have to side with Lina on this one. As much as I support those two declaring their love for one another, I can't let you interrupt the game."

Jayla glares at Frank, and for a second, I think she's going to object. But then she lets out a heavy sigh. "Fine. We'll wait until he's done playing and then I'll make her tell him."

Franks smiles. "That, I can let you do."

Jayla takes my hand and leads me into the auditorium. A few heads turn our way, but for the most part, no one notices that we enter.

We find a spot near the front of the bleachers and take a seat. There's only one table occupied with players, and it's about twenty feet away from where we're sitting.

Chase is sitting opposite me. All he has to do is look up and he'll see me.

"How long have they been playing this round?" Jayla whispers to the man sitting next to us.

"Just started. This is the first hand." He answers her.

That knowledge allows me to relax some. I've not played Euchre much, but I know the basics. If no one has scored yet, this could take at least ten rounds until they're done. That would give me plenty of time to figure out what I'm going to say to him.

But then Chase looks up and meets my gaze. Our eyes lock and so many emotions pass between us in a matter of seconds. Mila must see the shift in his expression because she turns around. A broad smile covers her face when she sees me.

"Well, thank the heavens," she says before she turns back to Chase. "Don't you get any dumb ideas until this game is over. You got that?"

Chase tosses his hands up in surrender. "I'm not going anywhere." Then he picks his cards up and tosses one in the center.

They play four rounds before Grams loses her temper. The Baylors take the winning tricks and score five points. In the last round, they won all five tricks, earning them two points instead of just one like in the previous three rounds.

Grams is pissed because Chase is distracted.

"Will you get your head out of your ass and back into this game?" she says loud enough for everyone in the auditorium to hear.

"My head isn't in my ass. Those were some shit hands. Can't win with shit cards."

I can't see Grams's expression, but I know her looks. She's probably glaring a hole right through Chase. "Bullshit. We haven't done this poorly all day. Lina walks in and suddenly you forget how to play Euchre. Get it together."

The crowd chuckles and someone pats me on the back. I don't

bother looking because my eyes are locked onto Chase. I give him a smile, and something shifts in his eyes. The worry that was there slips and is replaced with something I am all too familiar with. *Need.*

The game continues and the Mutters make a comeback, scoring six points while the Baylors rack up three more points. The score is eight to six.

Mr. Baylor deals and flips up the Queen of hearts. Chase passes on calling suit as do the rest of the players. When it comes back to Chase, he now has the chance to call suit based on the cards in his hand.

"Spades, and I'm going it alone," he says without hesitation. He doesn't even make eye contact with anyone at the table. His gaze is locked on me.

"The hell you are," Grams says. "If you don't win all five tricks, they win the tournament."

Chase looks at Mila. "I know how the game is played, and I'm going alone."

Mila huffs and tosses her cards down. "You're just as stubborn as she is. If we lose, no baked goods for you for at least a year."

A smoldering grin covers his face and winks at me. "Then I guess I better not lose."

Chase tosses down the king of spades. Mrs. Baylor follows that with the ten of spades and Mr. Baylor tosses down the nine of diamonds, showing he doesn't have any spades.

Chase's grin turns cocky. The next three rounds move fast, Chase taking each trick with little effort. When he tosses down the jack of spades, the highest-ranking card, in the last round, the game ends.

Without a glance at the other players, he pushes to his feet and charges toward me. He grabs my hand and pulls me to my feet. Neither of us speak as he leads me out of the auditorium and down the long hallway, away from the low rumble of voices.

Once we're alone and out of earshot, he stops and presses me against the wall.

"Please tell me you're done processing?" he whispers against my neck.

I slide my hands up his chest and fist them into his shirt. "Yes."

He drops light kisses just below my ear before he rests his forehead on my shoulder. "And?"

I rotate my head until my lips are right at his ear and then I whisper, "I love you too."

He lifts his head and cups my cheek. He searches my eyes like he's looking for a hidden meaning or trying to decipher if I really mean the words. "Do you mean it?"

I nod. "Not gonna lie. I'm terrified about what this means. You could really hurt me, Chase."

"You could hurt me too." He admits. "But I still love you and I still want to do this with you."

"Okay." I lean up and press my lips to his. "Then let's do this. Together."

"Yeah, baby." He sighs and pulls me closer. "Always together."

We stand there wrapped in each other's arms with my back pressed against the wall. His lips explore my neck, causing goosebumps to pebble my skin. Being in his arms feels so good after several days without him. There's comfort in his embrace and something else I never picked up on before. *Safety.*

I may be terrified that this could crash and burn on us, but Chase makes me feel safe. Safer than I've ever felt in all my life.

"Well, that wasn't quite as *grand* as I was hoping for," Jayla sighs. "But it gets the job done."

Chase lifts his head and looks at Jayla in confusion. Her response makes me laugh. My laughter causes Chase to furrow his brow. "Am I missing something?"

"Nope," Jayla says. "Nothing at all."

Then she spins on her heel and disappears down the hallway. Chase turns his gaze at me with raised brows.

"What was that all about?" he asks.

I shrug. "Just Jayla being Jayla."

He cups my cheek and drops his forehead to mine. "I'll take your word for it as long as you tell me again."

I smile and press my lips to his. "I love you."

"Sweetest words I've ever heard."

Then he kisses me long and hard and doesn't stop until we turn this declaration of love into something far too indecent for a small-town community center.

Chapter 30

Showing all my cards

Chase

Lina stares at me in confusion when I park outside the small apartment complex in Beaver and toss my truck into park.

"What are we doing here?" she asks, glancing around us like she's looking for the big reveal.

That's partly my fault since I made a big deal of wanting to share something with her today. I didn't give her any clues as to what, just that it was really important to me that she sees this.

Even though it's common knowledge who my mom is and that she has a drug addiction, introducing Mom to those I care about is a different story. She's not a pleasant woman. Not to me or anyone for that matter.

But Lina has shown me all her cards. Now it's time I do the same.

I rotate in my seat so I'm facing her, and then I take her hand in mine. I nod toward the apartment door I parked in front of and say, "This is where my mom lives."

"Oh." The surprise in her voice drags a small smile out of me. Her eyes shift to the door, and she stares at it like she's waiting for it to do something. When she looks back at me, all I see is love reflecting back. "Should we go in?"

I squeeze her hand and shift my gaze to the apartment. I know what's behind that door, and it's not pretty. Once she sees just how bad it is, there's no unseeing it. Ever.

I take a deep breath before I answer her. "I have to warn you first. What's behind that door is bad. My mom is a mess. There will be garbage and rotting food and probably drugs."

"Chase." She reaches across the cab and cups my cheek. "We don't have to do this if it's too much."

"No, we do. I *need* you to see this. My mom is a big reason why I am the way I am. Always needing to take care of you. She's also the reason for the debt the MC owed me."

"The drugs," she whispers. I don't need to tell her who's responsible for getting my mom hooked all those years ago. Before Edge cleaned up the MC, they were the only drug supplier in the county. Lina knows this better than most.

"Yeah, and then she got Christian addicted. The club played a vicious role in Christian's addiction. Smoke and some of the old members treated it like a game. I could have lost him. Almost did, twice. Thankfully, we were able to save Christian, but Mom ... she's a lost cause."

"I'm so sorry." There's not a hint of pity in her words. Just compassion and understanding. It makes me smile.

"Come on. We've got a lot of cleaning to do before Christian gets here." I open my truck door to step out, but her hand reaches for my arm to stop me.

"Wait. Christian is coming today too?"

I nod. "We visit with her on the first Sunday of every month. I come a couple of hours before him to clean up and make sure all the drugs are gone. He does the grocery shopping, and then we cook her dinner. It's not pleasant, but if you're up for it, I'd like you to see this part of me."

She squeezes her eyes closed and nods several times in quick succession. If I'm not mistaken, she's trying hard not to cry. When she opens them, they're glassy. "I'm honored that you want to introduce me, and I'm prepared for whatever is behind that door."

I huff out a laugh. "You say that, but you haven't seen it yet. What's behind that door is not pretty."

"Chase, you're talking to a former daughter of the MC that made your mom that way. I promise you I can handle it."

I give her a single nod before I take her hand and lift it to my lips. I kiss the palm and breathe in her sweet scent. "Okay, let's get this over with. The first fifteen minutes are always the worst."

Releasing her hand, we both climb out of my truck. I grab the new box of trash bags I bought since I used them all last time, and then meet her around the front. She slips her arm around my waist, presses into me, and gives me a kiss on the lips. That small action is enough to give me the strength I need to lead her inside.

As soon as I open the door, the stench of stale beer, cigarettes, and rotten food makes me gag. Lina coughs beside me, lifting her hand to cover her mouth and nose.

"I told you it would be bad."

"You were spot on," she says while doing her best to take in as little oxygen as possible. "Alright, what do we do first?"

"Find all the drugs and flush them. Then we take out the garbage." I hold up the new box of trash bags I brought.

"Let's do this." She takes the box from my hand. "I'll start on the garbage. You find the drugs."

She slips from my side and gets to work like she's done this with me countless times. I can't help but smile. My woman is the picture of strength and loyalty, and I'm damn lucky to call her mine.

We work in silence for a good twenty minutes before I find all the drugs—which surprisingly isn't as much as normal today—and Lina clears all of the trash out of the living room and moves on to the kitchen. She doesn't flinch or complain once.

"Where's your mom?" she asks when I come down the hallway with my arms piled high with dirty laundry.

"Passed out in her room." I dump the clothes on the floor beside the washer and start sorting. "Once I get a load started, I'll carry her to the shower. You thought this was fun? Just wait until you hear her mouth. Adds a whole new dimension to the day."

Lina snorts. "Can't wait."

I toss the load in the washer and head back down the hallway. The weight of dread pushing down on me has me causing me to drag my feet. Mom never has anything nice to say to me. Letting Lina see this part of our relationship makes me nervous.

Mom is still passed out on her bed, completely unaware that we're here. I take as deep a breath as I can stand considering the smell and slide my arms under her back and legs. She's limp and sags against me. If her chest wasn't rising and falling, I'd question whether or not she was still alive.

I place her in the tub, same as I do most months, and turn on the shower head. Cold water hits her in the stomach and she shoots up screaming. She blinks several times and tries to slide back to escape the spray but ends up sliding under the water further.

It only takes a few seconds for the water to turn warm. I adjust the temperature until it's a comfortable heat level. When I look down at her, she's glaring up at me with a murderous look in her eyes.

"Hey, Mom." I force a smile.

"Don't hey Mom me. What the fuck are you doing here? It's not time for you to visit again."

The laugh that escapes me is a tad on the sinister side. I typically try to keep my anger in check with Mom, but with Lina here, it's a struggle.

After all of these years, Mom has never once caught onto our schedule. For some reason, her acting like she has a clue what it is only feeds that anger more. "Don't know what to tell you, Mom.

We're right on schedule. I'll be back in a moment with some clean clothes."

I head to her room and grab some clothes. At least on this visit, she has some clean clothes in her drawers. That doesn't happen often.

By the time I make it back to the bathroom, she's stripped out of the clothes she was wearing and tossed them on the floor without care. Water puddles around them. She glances over her shoulder at me, still glaring, before she turns back to her shower. She doesn't bother pulling the shower curtain closed. Probably because she knows that pisses me off.

I step around her wet clothes and yank the curtain closed. Then I place her clean clothes and a towel on the counter. I gather up her wet clothes and toss them in the pile of dirty ones on the floor by the washer. Grabbing another towel from the linen closet, I spread it out on the bathroom floor to soak up the water from her wet clothes.

Lina and I work together for several minutes in the kitchen before Mom walks out. She's dressed, but her hair is dripping wet like she didn't even bother using the towel I left for her.

"Who the fuck is this?" Mom barks. When we look at her, she's frowning with her hands on her hips.

"This is Lina, my girlfriend," I say and then turn back to the pile of dishes in the sink.

"Girlfriend?" Mom questions. "How the fuck did you manage that?"

Lina frowns, and I chuckle. I pull her closer and give her a chaste kiss. "Persistence. I refused to let her ignore me."

Lina rolls her eyes and my mom scoffs. "So you forced her to date you? Sounds like something you'd do."

Lina raises her brows and stares at my mom like she just said the dumbest thing she's ever heard. "No one forces me to do anything. I do what I want."

"Then why are you dating this idiot? If you want a man, date my Christian. Now he's a good boy."

I stiffen at her words. Normally, Mom's comparisons between Christian and me never bother me. But considering how Lina and I got together, it stings to hear Mom say that to her.

"I'm sure Christian is a great man, but no one is better than Chase in my eyes. He's it for me." Lina shrugs with a grin on her face that begs to be challenged. Then she turns back to help me load the dishwasher.

When our eyes meet, I mouth, "I love you."

Her blue eyes light up with nothing but happiness staring back at me. She leans forward and cups my cheeks before she plants a kiss on my lips. "I love you too."

Mom grumbles something but I don't make out the words. She leaves us alone before I can ask her to repeat herself. That's probably for the best anyway.

Once Christian gets here, I'm sure I'll hear worse.

With Lina by my side, I can't bring myself to give a shit.

SUMMER IS COMING TO AN END AND THE DAY WE'VE BEEN working so hard toward for a couple months is finally here.

The county School Bus Derby starts any minute now. Five buses—one representing each of the county school districts—are lined up on one end of an open field. The first to make it to the other end wins.

Eastern Local—that's our bus—is by far the most menacing. Lina and her team did a kick ass job with the bald eagle on the sides. Waverly took a cute approach with their design.

Whoever led that effort must love My Little Pony. With as many ponies as I see, all the characters must be painted on the bus. It's a mix of bright blues and purples with soft pastels over a solid white bus. I'm glad that's not our bus.

The other three districts went with the same theme as us— school mascot—but their design is tame compared to ours. Lina really outdid herself. If we don't win from speed and power, at least we win on design.

Lina steps up beside me with a huge smile on her face. "You did good, babe. Our bus looks fucking fantastic."

"It does, doesn't it?" She beams as she takes in the other designs. None of them come close to hers.

"So how do we do this thing?" Mac asks as he steps up beside us. "Is it just me in that thing or do you all have to ride with me?"

"Just you, thank gawd," Lina says. "I wouldn't be here if I had to get in that thing."

Mac gives her a devilish grin. "What's wrong? Don't trust your boy to build a safe racing machine?"

"Considering he didn't build the entire bus? No. Not a chance in hell."

"Good thing I'm driving then," Mac says as he positions his helmet over his head. "Chase may not have built this body, but there isn't anyone else I'd trust to build my engines. My brother is the best. Even if he does prefer farming over racing."

Mac makes his way to the bus and climbs in. The other district drivers do the same. I take Lina's hand and drag her back to where the rest of our team is watching. My entire family came out for the event. Even Dad is here, and he rarely comes to events like this.

Clara steps up next to me with her arms crossed over her chest. She stares at the line of buses with such a fierce intensity that, if I didn't know better, I'd think she's trying to burn a hole right through them.

"You okay?" I ask.

She looks over her shoulder and sighs. "Yeah, I'm fine."

I follow her gaze and immediately spot the source of her tension. I furrow my brows as I watch Ash kissing his girlfriend like they're the only two here. "I thought that asshole was too busy this summer to be here?"

Clara shrugs. "That's what he said. I get that he couldn't help with the engine, but he also refused to drive. Guess we all know the real reason now."

"You okay?"

She nods but her expression says the opposite. "Just sucks. Regardless of my feelings, he's always been my best friend. I hate that it feels like I'm losing that too. He's never ditched me before. Not for anything or anyone. Guess she's special."

Her voice cracks. I wrap my arm around her and tug her close. Lina leans around me and whispers. "We need to find you a man. Let me know when you want to go out."

"Really?" Clara sounds hopeful.

"I don't know if that's such a good idea," I say, not liking the thought of Lina out in a bar without me.

Lina pats my chest and chuckles. "It's a great idea. Let's see how Ash likes it when Clara starts dating. He deserves to squirm and regret his actions."

I kiss the top of her head and groan. "Remind me to never get on your bad side."

"With the mistakes you've already made, I wouldn't think I'd need to remind you what that's like."

I growl, and both women laugh.

"This role reversal thing you two have going on is cute," Clara says.

Before I can say anything else, a horn blows, signaling the race is about to begin. An announcer comes over a loudspeaker and introduces each of the teams. He tells the drivers to start their engines, and a loud rumbling fills the air. The buses inch their way to the starting line.

Once everyone is in position, the announcer counts down. Rather than shouting go, the horn blows again.

The buses take off, and the crowd cheers.

Well, not quite.

Mac takes off. Pike CTC crawls behind him. Piketon and

Western move at a snail's pace. And Waverly doesn't make it past the starting line. Clearly their team put all their time and resources into their My Little Pony paint job and neglected the engine.

The crowd quiets as the excitement that has been building all summer for this race dies down as Mac nears the finish line. Pike CTC still hasn't crossed the hallway point.

"Ah, honey." Lina tugs on my arm. "I think maybe you did too good of a job on the engine. This isn't a fair race."

I shrug. "What was I supposed to do? Purposefully do a piss poor job?"

"No, but you could've at least given the other teams a fighting chance. This made for a very boring race."

I shake my head. "No way. When I see something I want, I give it my all. And I wanted to win."

Lina turns her gorgeous smile on me and it lights up my insides. "Yeah, I guess you do, don't you?"

I give her one of my smoldering grins that always makes her hot for me. "If you're the prize, I'll give it my all every single time."

She cups my cheeks and kisses me like she can't get enough of me. And I love every single minute of it.

Chapter 31

This is my life

Lina

A few weeks later ...

I'd be lying if I said everything has been perfect since the day I told Chase that I loved him. Far from it, in fact.

Mostly because I've consistently been a pain in his ass and have fought him on everything he insists on doing for me.

It's his own damn fault. I wouldn't have to fight with him if he'd listen to me. He hasn't let me pay for anything in weeks.

I thought he was going to have a coronary when I admitted that part of the reason my migraines got so bad was because I didn't eat enough. I haven't gone hungry since. He cooks for me on the evenings I don't work and makes sure my kitchen is stocked with enough food for both Dad and me.

My car never has less than a half a tank of gas. I still haven't figured out when or how he fills it up for me. I suspect he sneaks out in the middle of the night after I fall asleep and fills it up from one of the many gas cans they keep in the garage. When I ask him about it, he plays dumb.

The electric bill is on autopay to one of his credit cards. He bought my dad a new TV and upgraded his cable so he'd have the sports channels. He and Dad talk football all the time, and when Chase found out he couldn't watch the games, he took care of it.

Last week I caught him trying to make a payment to one of Dad's many medical bills. While I appreciate all his help, I can't let him do that. I snatched the bills away and hid them from him. He's still pissed at me about that.

With everything he's done for Dad and me, I have a lot of free cash that I didn't have before. I can take care of my dad without help. While I give Chase shit about how much he pays for—let's be honest, the makeup sex is amazing—I'm also eternally grateful for it.

Dad is getting better care because I can pay for the bills.

It also helps that the Village of Beaver was awarded the grant to fund the arts center. Mrs. Engle and Mrs. Hoffman could barely contain themselves when they got the news. They hunted me down until they found me at Chase's house. That was an embarrassing moment of my life. They caught us in the stables partially undressed.

That didn't stop them from telling me all about the grant and the job they hoped I'd accept. There's nothing quite like getting a job offer while topless and pressed against the wall with your half naked boyfriend as a shield. Thank God I hadn't gotten his pants undone yet.

Despite the challenges we've faced, things with Chase are damn good.

Mornings like this one have become my favorite. I don't stay the night with Chase every night but watching him care for his goats from his balcony makes me want to.

I've gotten used to his early morning routine, and I don't always wake when he gets up. Sometimes—like this morning—I'll wake when I hear the click of the door closing behind him. Other times, I wake when he comes back to bed once he's finished his chores.

As much as I love waking up to his warm body wrapped around me, I prefer to watch him like this from the single seat on his balcony that overlooks the farm. I only get this moment if I wake before he returns.

He doesn't like to sing with an audience other than his goats, and damn can my man sing. Anytime I ask him to sing for me, he refuses. It's the only time I've seen him get embarrassed.

So I treasure these mornings when I get them.

I grab my sketchbook and pencils and flip to a blank page. Since I started spending so much time here with Chase, I always keep a sketchbook with me. His farm is full of inspiration, but this morning it's him that's inspired me to draw.

He's too far away for me to see the details of his sculpted arms and washboard abs, but I've seen them up close enough that his body is burned in my memory. With hardly a thought, my pencil glides over the blank page.

I start with a rough form. Chase sitting on the stump with his guitar in his hands and his four goats jumping around him. His body takes shape first. I capture every curve and ridge of his roped muscles and defined chest.

His sexy legs are hidden behind the folds of his jeans as is his lap. I want to capture him exactly how I found him after the first morning we spent together.

I focus on the details of his hands next. One grips the neck of the guitar with his fingers splayed across the frets while his other pinches a pick between his fingers while he strums away. I pay close attention to his hands. How they bend. How they move. And how I imagine they'd feel holding that guitar.

His hand has been around my neck so many times over the past few months that his hold is not something I'll ever forget. There's passion and ownership behind the way he squeezes around me when we're intimate. There's also reverence and love.

I never thought I'd meet a man I'd ever give up control to. I don't make it easy on Chase—where's the fun in that?—but he owns me. Heart, body, and soul.

Once I'm done drawing his hands, I move to his face. I decide to draw him looking up—like he's watching me the same way I watch him—with a huge smile on his face. His smiles always make me a little weak in the knees, and that's saying something because he smiles a lot.

I can remember a time, long before we got together, when his smiles annoyed the piss out of me. I had no reason to be happy, and I was jealous of anyone who showed the slightest hint of it. Chase always looked happy. I wanted to be that happy but had no clue how to find it.

Then I mistook him for his twin, and my life changed forever. I've never smiled so much before in my life.

"Damn, babe," Chase says from right over my shoulder. I jump in surprise. "That's really good."

I press my hand to my chest and take a deep breath. "You scared me. I thought ..."

I look back down at the stump in the middle of the field where he was sitting to find the spot vacant. I'd been so lost in my drawing that I hadn't even noticed him leave.

"Sorry." He leans down and kisses the top of my head. "Didn't mean to. I assumed you heard me come in."

I shake my head. "Guess I was lost in my thoughts."

He places his fingers under my chin and lifts my lips to his. The kiss is quick but still causes my belly to flutter in excitement. Does this feeling ever dull? God, I hope not.

"I'll make us some breakfast." He turns to head back inside but then stops just inside the doorway. "How about going horseback riding later? You still interested in giving it a try?"

"Yeah, I'd love to."

His smile widens. "Good. There's somewhere I'd like to show you."

Before I can ask him where, he disappears around the corner

and into the kitchen. While he gets started on breakfast, I look out over the farm from my spot on the balcony.

I love this place, and I love this man.

Whoever thought that this would become my life? I sure as hell didn't, but I'm happy to claim it as mine.

Chapter 32

Just for her. Only her

Chase

"You doin' alright back there?" I glance over my shoulder at Lina. She's trailing behind me on Sunny while I ride Amber.

"Yeah, I'm fine," she says but her voice suggests she's struggling.

This is her first time horseback riding and I'm trying to go easy on her. The trail is an easy one, but kind of long for a first timer. I probably should have started her out with something shorter, but I really want to show her this spot and the only way to get here is by horseback. For now, at least.

That will change in the future if she loves this spot as much as I do. I hope she does, because I've got my heart set on these plans.

"We're almost there. Just a few more minutes." I call out. I can already see the break in the trees where the sun is shining bright.

We're on a forested trail that cuts through our property and leads to one of my favorite places in all of southern Ohio. We've got lots of trails that we ride through these woods. Sometimes on horseback, like today, but typically we take out our ATVs.

Racing through these woods on ATVs used to be one of our favorite things to do. Now that we're all older and busier with our jobs, we don't get out as much. We haven't taken them out for a ride all summer, which isn't like us.

Maybe I should suggest a ride the next time all of my brothers are together. I wonder if Warren still likes to ride.

He's been quiet and secluded since his return. All his belongings arrived a couple of days after him. Rather than storing it in one of our many garages, he opted to put it all in a storage unit. It was a lot of stuff. Enough to fill an entire house.

We never visited Warren in North Carolina, and I regret that decision. He always came to us. On the few times we suggested a visit, he always gave us an excuse to why it wasn't a good time. We should have ignored him and came anyway.

We don't know anything about his life while he was gone. Anytime we ask him questions, he immediately shoots us down and leaves the room.

I thought Garret was a grumpy recluse. He's got nothing on Warren. He didn't used to be like that. Growing up Warren was always smiling and joking around like me. He's a different man today, and I hope one day he'll open up to us about why.

"Oh my God. It's a lake!" Lina calls out from behind me. The trail opens up to a grassy meadow overgrown with wildflowers. Just beyond that is one of the most beautiful lakes in this county.

"Not just any lake babe." I smile over my shoulder at her.

She glances around, and then her eyes go wide as recognition hits. "It's Pee Pee Lake. My home is over there."

She points across the lake to where her trailer sits on the opposite shore. The lake isn't huge, maybe about ten acres, but it's pristine and there's not much development along the shores.

"Are we still on your property?" she asks.

I nod. "We own about four aces along this side. I'm the only one who comes out here and even then, it's not often."

"I had no idea your land extended this far."

"Not many do," I say as I stop next to a shade tree and hop off Amber. I tie her up before I head over to help Lina.

"This stretch wasn't a part of the original homestead that my ancestors won off the Kochs. Grandpops bought this as a wedding present for Grams. We used to come out here to fish and play in the water as kids, but after he passed, we stopped. The memories were too hard on Grams. But I'm still drawn to it."

"I can see why. It's gorgeous. The view is better than mine, and mine is pretty damn good."

"I'm glad you like it." I grab the blanket I packed from the saddle bag and place it on the ground under a neighboring tree. Then I retrieve the lunch I packed.

"What's all this?" Lina asks.

"Lunch." I sit and then pat the blanket next to me. "Join me."

She drops down beside me and leans into my side, resting her head on my shoulder. "It's so pretty out here. I love the wildflowers. Kinda makes me wish I'd brought my painting supplies."

"I'll bring you back whenever you want." I kiss the top of her head before I unpack our lunch. I hand her a turkey and swiss sandwich just the way she likes it, and then set out a platter of fresh fruit. I made myself a roast beef sandwich with cheddar and horseradish and brought us each a root beer. Something I recently learned is her favorite drink.

We eat our sandwiches in silence, enjoying the peaceful serenity the lake provides. Summer is coming to an end, but I can still hear kids playing in the distance. Giggles and shrills fill the air every few minutes.

I close my eyes and let my mind imagine a future with Lina right here on this lake. We're laughing and splashing in the water with our own kids. Maybe a couple girls with her deep blue eyes and long dark hair. Or a little boy with my troublemaker grin and jovial personality.

It would be one hell of a life, and one I desperately want.

I glance over at Lina. She has her head tipped back, her eyes closed, and a smile on her beautiful face. A breeze blows over us, brushing her hair over her shoulders. I wonder if she's imagining a similar future.

"Lina." I reach for her hand and give it a gentle squeeze.

"Hmm?" She opens one eye and peers at me from the side.

I take a deep breath and look back out over the lake. I don't know why I'm so nervous right now. She loves me—this I believe with all my heart. But that doesn't mean she sees a future with me. A life beyond the here and now.

"I want to build a home in this spot," I say quickly. "I want my bedroom to face the lake, with a wall of glass so I can watch the sunset behind those hills. I want to build an outside kitchen on a large deck so I can grill my family dinner and enjoy the warm summer evenings while drinking a cold beer. I want to be surrounded by laughter like what we can hear in the distance. I want the dream."

When I dare a glance at Lina, she's staring at me with wetness in her eyes. "I can see that future for you. You deserve that life, and I hope you get it."

I nod and swallow back the nerves threatening to stop me from asking what I really came here to ask. "I know it's early in our relationship, and we're still working through growing pains, but I need to know if you can see yourself here with me. One day."

"I can," she says without hesitation. My heart soars.

"Really?"

The soft smile on her face grows and lights up her eyes. Rather than answering me, she slides her leg over me and straddles my lap. Her hands slide around my neck into my hair. "I'm all in, Chase. For once in my life, I'm willing to risk it all to see where this goes. With you."

Her lips come to mine in a slow, exploratory kiss. Her tongue swipes across my bottom lip and I open, sucking it into my mouth. She tastes like root beer with a hint of mustard.

As the kiss deepens, her hands roam down my back and tugs at my T-shirt. She breaks the kiss to pull it over my head.

"You tryin' to get me naked?" I tease.

"Yes." She presses her hand against my chest and pushes me down onto my back. "Tell me you have a condom."

"Back pocket." We've talked about other forms of birth control, and she has an appointment to see her doctor soon. I can't wait until she's on the pill so I can feel her bare. It's something we both want to share with each other.

We frantically work to rid each other of our clothes. I retrieve the condom and start to rip it open, but she snatches it from my hand. She repositions her naked body over mine and fists my cock. I let out a loud, guttural groan at the feel of her soft hand around my erection.

My hands dip into her hips as I pull her closer to me. I'm desperate to feel her heat slide down my cock and ride me. Thankfully she has the same idea.

She rolls the condom down my length and then lifts up on her knees. With my cock at her entrance, she slowly slides down at an agonizingly painful pace. Her body sliding down on mine—squeezing me—just might be the best feeling in the world.

Once she's fully seated on top of me, and I'm buried deep, she lifts her hands and pulls her hair back to the base of her neck. The motion causes her back to arch and her chest to lean toward me. Her neck is elongated and every inch of her glorious body is on display for my eyes to feast.

My mouth waters to suck her pebbled nipples between my teeth, and my hand aches to wrap around that pretty neck. But I resist. She's in charge right now, and I'm not going to take this moment away from her.

Fuck the lake view. This one of her and only her, is so much better. I'll take watching Lina chase her pleasure over any view in the world.

If I play my cards right, I'll get to enjoy this view for the rest of my life.

Epilogue

She surprises me every day.

Chase

A few months later ...

Knock, knock, knock.

Even though I'm expecting it, the knock on my door causes me to jump and I drop the colander of pasta I just drained. I quickly grab it before I lose it all to the floor.

"Come in!" I call out before I turn back to the stove.

Lina is coming over for one of our stay-in date nights. It's become our thing. Rather than going out to the bar or hitting up a restaurant out of town, I cook, and we hang out on my bed and watch movies. It's simple and not all that exciting, but it's us.

"Hey," Lina says as she comes up behind me. I lean toward her and give her a quick kiss. "Smells delicious."

"Thanks. Chicken carbonara. Never made it before, so I hope it's good." I glance down at the box in her hand. "What's that?"

Her smile widens. "I stopped at that bakery close to work and got some of those eclairs you love."

My head falls back and I press my hand to my heart. "Babe, how did you know I've been craving those?"

She chuckles. "Maybe because you're always craving them."

"Not as much as I crave you." I toss her a wink and the smoldering grin that I know will earn me an eye roll. Same as always, she doesn't disappoint.

"You know," she places her hands on her hips like she's about to lecture me, "you're not as cute as you think you are."

I dump the pasta into the sauce and give it a quick turn before I take it off the heat and spin to face her. I pull her into my arms and plant an indecent kiss on her lips. She's caught off guard and lets out a yelp before I swallow down the sound.

Pressing her hips into the counter, I grind my growing erection against her stomach. But it isn't until I slide my hand up her body and around her glorious neck that she whimpers and melts into me.

I don't know what it is about her neck, but I can't get enough of it and she loves it when I'm a little rough with my hold on her. I give it a gentle squeeze and her leg lifts and wraps around my waist.

She tilts her hips and rotates, trying to gain some friction against her core. But I deny her and pull away. I keep my hand on her neck and hold her in place. We're both panting and ready for so much more than a quick make out session in my kitchen.

"Dammit, Chase." She groans. "You know I hate it when you do this to me."

I step closer, tightening my grip on her neck. My body is almost flush against hers, but I purposely leave a hair's breadth of space between us.

"And what exactly is it that I'm doing to you?"

"Denying me."

"Hmm." I smile against her lips. "I guess you should have thought about that before you insulted my looks."

I release her and turn my attention back to dinner before I ruin it. I've spent too much time on it to let it go to waste.

With a grumble, and I'm sure daggers at my back, Lina sets the table. I let my smile take over my expression while I finish assembling the food. I love getting Lina all worked up and dragging out her pleasure.

I pour the pasta in a large bowl and sprinkle it with freshly made bacon bits. Then I pull the garlic bread out of the oven. It's a little browner than I would have liked, but it's still edible. That's what I get for allowing Lina's arrival to distract me.

Once the garlic bread is in a bowl, I pick up both dishes and head to the table. I stumble and almost drop dinner when my eyes land on Lina.

She's sitting at one end of the table with her legs propped up on a neighboring chair in nothing but her sexy black underwear. Her bra is a thin, see-through material and her hardened nipples are on full display.

"Fuck, babe." I groan. "Are you trying to kill me?"

"What's the matter? See something you like?" She twirls a strand of her long dark hair around a finger and nibbles on her bottom lip.

I growl and my nostrils flare. I set the food on the table and stare down at her. This is a new move for her and I'm not quite sure how to proceed. It's usually me that does all the teasing.

I reach for her hand to pull her up and into my arms but she refuses me. "You denying me now?"

The grin that covers her face is seductive and teasing and it makes me even harder. "Turnabout is fair play. You can look but not touch."

I narrow my gaze and fight back a grin. "Alright. Let's do this then."

I reach behind me, grab the back of my T-shirt, and pull it over my head. I undo my jeans next and shove them down. Unlike her, I don't stop there. I strip off my boxers too and toss them aside.

Her eyes flare with desire as I stroke my cock before heading back to the kitchen to get us both a beer. I stop at the sink long enough to wash my hands and return a moment later.

I take my seat next to her and serve up our plates as if tonight is just like any other night we've spent together.

"New rule," she says. I look over at her and catch her staring at my erection. She reaches behind her and unfastens her bra, slipping it off her shoulders. My mouth waters to suck her nipples into my mouth. "We always eat dinner naked."

I shrug, doing my best to act unaffected by her exposed chest. "Fine by me. It'll make it that much faster to get to dessert."

By some miracle, we make it through dinner without falling into each other's arms and fucking next to our plates.

Once her plate is cleared of all her food, she sits back and moans. "That was so good. Might be your best meal yet."

"Thanks." I stand to take her plate. My erection bobs right in front of her face and her eyes shift to mine. "Hope you saved room for dessert."

She shakes her head, fighting back a smile. "I'm stuffed. Couldn't eat another bite if my life depended on it."

I run my finger along her jaw and then lift her chin so I can plant a kiss on her lips. "We'll see about that."

Turning back to my task, I take the dirty dishes to the kitchen. A few moments later, she joins me and together we load the dishwasher. Cleaning up the kitchen naked with my girlfriend is by far the strangest thing I've ever done in my life.

"Any suggestions on what you wanna watch tonight?" I ask as I shut the dishwater.

She shrugs. "Nothing too long. I've got to be at the parlor early for a custom job tomorrow."

I frown because that usually means she plans on heading home tonight. Any time she works early she prefers to sleep in her own bed. It drives me fucking nuts to be without her.

"If you would just move in with me, all of your shit would be here. Then you wouldn't need to go home. You'd already *be* home."

She lets out a heavy sigh before she looks up at me. There's a hint of nervousness in her gaze that sends a wave of worry through me. "Tell you what. I'll move in with you when you marry me."

"Done." I don't hesitate to answer. Relief washes over me.

"Chase. I'm being serious. Marry me. Then I'll move in with you."

"I'm being serious too." I place my hands on her hips and tug her to me. "Tell me when and where, and it's done."

She huffs and narrows her gaze. "That's not what I expected you to say."

I grin and kiss the end of her nose. "What did you expect?"

"I don't know. That you'd freak out and backpedal."

"Babe. Threatening me with marriage is not the way to do that. I'd marry you right now if it were possible."

Her eyes well up with tears. "Really?"

"Yeah, really."

She smiles up at me and a tear escapes from her eye. "We're getting married?"

I nod. "We're getting married."

She squeals and jumps into my arms. I wrap my arms under her ass and carry her to bed.

We don't watch a movie, and she sure as hell doesn't go home. Instead, we stay up half the night exploring each other's bodies like it's the first time.

WANT MORE **CHASE AND LINA**? CLICK HERE (HTTPS:// ariabliss.com/bonus-content-sign-up/) to get your **FREE** *Truck Off* bonus scene for a sneak peek into their future.

THE MUTTER BROTHER'S FAMILY SAGA CONTINUES IN *TRUCK Up*: An Enemies Sister, Forbidden Love Small Town Romance with **Christian and Amelia**. COMING SOON!!!

———

OR DIVE INTO THE A DRUNK LOVE CONTEMPORARY Romance Series! In this sweeping family saga, you'll meet the four siblings, a few of their closest friends, and their sexy, irresistible counterparts. Start at the beginning with Aria's reader favorite.

Heath and Alicia fight for love in *Not for Me*: A Fake Dating Romance

A Drunk Love Contemporary Romance, Book 1.

CLICK HERE (My Book) to grab your copy.

Books by Aria Bliss

The Mutter Brothers

Truck You: A Hate to Love Small Town Romance

Truck Me: A Grumpy-Sunshine Small Town Romance

Truck Off: An Enemies to Lovers, Mistaken Identity Small Town Romance

A Drunk Love Contemporary Romance

Not for Me: A Fake Dating Romance

Let Me Stay: A Friends to Lovers, Best Friend's Sister Romance

Lead Me Here: A Grumpy-Sunshine Romance

Aside From Me: A Roommate to Lovers Romance

Make Me Go: An Age Gap Romance

Hearts of Watercress Falls

Healing Hearts: A Second Chance at Love Small Town Romance

Trusting Hearts: A Single Dad Small Town Romance

Falling Hearts: A Secret Marriage Small Town Romance

Laughing Hearts: A Best Friend's Sister Small Town Romance

Forgiving Hearts: A Hate to Love Small Town Romance

Standalone

Good Wine & Bad Decisions: A Sexy Romance

An After-Hours Affair

In Charge: Book 1

Connect with Me

Website: http://ariabliss.com
Subscribe to my Newsletter: https://ariabliss.com/sign-up/
Follow me on Amazon Author Central: http://www.amazon.com/
author/ariabliss.author
Follow me on Instagram: http://www.instagram.com/ariabliss.
author
Follow me on goodreads: http://www.goodreads.com/
ariablissauthor
Follow me on Bookbub: https://www.bookbub.com/authors/aria-
bliss
Join my Facebook Street Team: https://www.facebook.com/
groups/SassySuperFans/
Follow me on Facebook: http://www.facebook.com/ariabliss.
author/
Follow me on Twitter: http://www.twitter.com/ariablissauthor

Author Bio

Steamy Emotional Contemporary Romance

Aria Bliss writes steamy, emotionally charged contemporary romance with humor, drama, and big feels. She has a soft spot for single dads, second chances, forbidden romance, and grumpy bad boys with sweet centers that are impossible not to love.

Made in the USA
Middletown, DE
02 August 2023